Titles by Robin Cook

ROBIN COOK
FATAL CURE

BERKLEY BOOKS, NEW YORK

FATAL CURE

A Berkley Book / published by arrangement with
the author

PRINTING HISTORY
G. P. Putnam's Sons hardcover edition / January 1994
Berkley mass-market edition / February 1995

Visit our website at
www.penguinputnam.com

ISBN: 0-425-14563-8

BERKLEY®
Berkley Books are published by The Berkley Publishing Group,
a division of Penguin Putnam Inc.,
375 Hudson Street, New York, New York 10014.
BERKLEY and the "B" design
are trademarks belonging to Penguin Putnam Inc.

PRINTED IN THE UNITED STATES OF AMERICA

30   29   28   27   26   25   24   23   22

*This book is dedicated to the spirit of health-care reform
and the sanctity of the doctor-patient relationship.
It is my fervent hope that they need not
be mutually exclusive.*

FATAL CURE

PROLOGUE

FEBRUARY SEVENTEENTH WAS A FATEFUL DAY FOR SAM Flemming.

Sam considered himself an extremely lucky person. As a broker for one of the major Wall Street firms, he'd become wealthy by the age of forty-six. Then, like a gambler who knew when to quit, Sam had taken his earnings and fled north from the concrete canyons of New York to idyllic Bartlet, Vermont. There he'd begun to do what he'd always wanted to do: paint.

Part of Sam's good fortune had always been his health, yet at half past four on February seventeenth, something strange began to happen. Numerous water molecules within many of his cells began to split apart into two fragments: a relatively inoffensive hydrogen atom and a highly reactive, viciously destructive hydroxyl free radical.

As these molecular events transpired, Sam's cellular defenses were activated. But on this particular day those defenses against free radicals were quickly exhausted; even the antioxidant vitamins E, C, and beta carotene which he diligently took each day could not stem the sudden, overwhelming tide.

The hydroxyl free radicals began to nibble away at the core of Sam Flemming's body. Before long, the cell membranes of the affected cells began to leak fluid and electrolytes. At the same time some of the cells' protein enzymes were cleaved and inactivated. Even many DNA molecules were assaulted, and specific genes were damaged.

In his bed at Bartlet Community Hospital, Sam remained unaware of the high-stakes molecular battle within his cells. What he did notice was some of its sequelae: an elevation of his temperature, some digestive rumblings, and the beginnings of chest congestion.

Later that afternoon when Sam's surgeon, Dr. Portland, came in to see him, the doctor noted Sam's fever with disappointment and alarm. After listening to Sam's chest, Dr. Portland tried to tell Sam that a complication had apparently set in. Dr. Portland said that a touch of pneumonia was interfering with Sam's otherwise smooth recovery from the operation to repair his broken hip. But by then Sam had become apathetic and mildly disoriented. He didn't understand Dr. Portland's report on his status. The doctor's prescription for antibiotics and his assurances of a rapid recovery failed to register with him.

Worse still, the doctor's prognosis proved wrong. The prescribed antibiotic failed to stop the developing infection. Sam never recovered enough to appreciate the irony that he'd survived two muggings in New York City, a commuter plane crash in Westchester County, and a bad four-vehicle accident on the New Jersey Turnpike, only to die from complications arising from a fall on a patch of ice in front of Staley's Hardware Store on Main Street, Bartlet, Vermont.

THURSDAY, MARCH 18

Standing before Bartlet Community Hospital's most important employees, Harold Traynor paused long enough to relish the moment. He'd just called the meeting to order. The group assembled—all heads of departments—had obediently fallen silent. All eyes were riveted on him. Traynor's dedication to his office as chairman of the hospital board was a point of pride. He savored moments such as this when it became clear his very presence inspired awe.

"Thank you all for coming out on this snowy evening. I've called this meeting to impress upon you how seriously the hospital board is taking the unfortunate assault on Nurse Prudence Huntington in the lower parking lot last week. The fact that the rape was thwarted by the serendipitous arrival of a member of the hospital security staff does not in any way lessen the seriousness of the offense."

Traynor paused, his eyes falling significantly on Patrick Swegler. The head of hospital security averted his gaze to avoid Traynor's accusatory glance. The attack on Miss Huntington had been the third such episode in the last year, and Swegler felt understandably responsible.

"These attacks must be stopped!" Traynor looked to Nancy Widner, the director of nursing. All three victims had been nurses under her supervision.

"The safety of our staff is a prime concern," Traynor said as his eyes jumped from Geraldine Polcari, head of dietary, to Gloria Suarez, head of housekeeping. "Consequently, the executive board has proposed the construction of a multi-storied parking facility to be built in the area of the lower parking lot. It will be directly attached to the main hospital building and will contain appropriate lighting and surveillance cameras."

Traynor gave Helen Beaton, president of the hospital, a nod. On his cue, Beaton lifted a cloth from the conference table to reveal a detailed architectural model of the existing hospital complex as well as the proposed addition: a massive, three-story structure protruding from the rear of the main building.

Amid exclamations of approval, Traynor stepped around the table to position himself next to the model. The hospital conference table was often a repository for medical paraphernalia under consideration for purchase. Traynor reached over to remove a rack of funnel-shaped test tubes so that the model could be better seen. Then he scanned his audience. All eyes were glued to the model; everyone except Werner Van Slyke had gotten to his feet.

Parking had always been a problem at Bartlet Community Hospital, especially in inclement weather. So Traynor knew that his proposed addition would be popular even before the recent string of attacks in the lower lot. He was pleased to see that his unveiling was progressing as successfully as he'd anticipated. The room was aglow with enthusiasm. Only sullen Van Slyke, the head of engineering and maintenance, remained impassive.

"What's the matter?" Traynor asked. "Doesn't this proposal meet with your approval?"

Van Slyke looked at Traynor, his expression still vacant.

"Well?" Traynor felt himself tense. Van Slyke had a way of irritating him. Traynor had never liked the man's laconic, unemotional nature.

"It's okay," Van Slyke said dully.

Before Traynor could respond the door to the conference room burst open and slammed against its stop on the floor. Everyone jumped, especially Traynor.

Standing in the doorway was Dennis Hodges, a vigorous, stocky seventy-year-old with rough-hewn features and weathered skin. His nose was rosy and bulbous, his beady eyes rheumy. He was dressed in a dark green boiled wool coat over creaseless corduroy trousers. On top of his head was a red plaid hunter's cap dusted with snow. In his raised left hand he was clutching a sheaf of papers.

There was no doubt Hodges was angry. He also smelled strongly of alcohol. His dark, gun-barrel-like eyes strafed the gathering, then trained in on Traynor.

"I want to talk to you about a few of my former patients, Traynor. You too, Beaton," Hodges said, throwing her a quick, disgusted look. "I don't know what kind of hospital you think you've been running here, but I can tell you I don't like it one bit!"

"Oh, no," Traynor muttered as soon as he'd recovered from Hodges' unexpected arrival. Irritation quickly overtook his shock. A rapid glance around the room assured him that the others were about as happy to see Hodges as he was.

"Dr. Hodges," Traynor began, forcing himself to be civil. "I think it is quite apparent that we are having a meeting here. If you will excuse us . . ."

"I don't care what the hell you people are doing," Hodges snapped. "Whatever it is, it pales in respect to what you and the board have been up to with my patients." He stalked toward Traynor. Instinctively, Traynor leaned back. The smell of whiskey was intense.

"Dr. Hodges," Traynor said with obvious anger. "This is not the time for one of your interruptions. I'll be happy to meet with you tomorrow to talk about your grievances. Now if you will kindly leave and let us get on with our business . . ."

"I want to talk now!" Hodges shouted. "I don't like what you and your board are doing."

"Listen, you old fool," Traynor snapped. "Lower your voice! I have no earthly idea what is on your mind. But I'll tell you what I and the board have been doing: we've been breaking our necks in the struggle to keep the doors of this hospital open, and that's no easy task for any hospital in this day and age. So I resent any implication to the contrary. Now be reasonable and leave us to our work."

"I ain't waiting," Hodges insisted. "I'm talking to you and Beaton right now. Nursing, dietary, and housekeeping nonsense can wait. This is important."

"Ha!" Nancy Widner said. "It's just like you, Dr. Hodges, bursting in here and suggesting that nursing concerns aren't important. I'll have you know . . ."

"Hold on!" Traynor said, extending his hands in a conciliatory gesture. "Let's not get into a free-for-all. The fact of the matter is, Dr. Hodges, we are here talking about the rape attempt that occurred last week. I'm sure you are not suggesting that one rape and two attempted rapes by a man in a ski mask are not important."

"It's important," Hodges agreed, "but not as important as what's on my mind. Besides, the rape problem is obviously an in-house affair."

"Just one second!" Traynor demanded. "Are you implying that you know the identity of the rapist?"

"Let's put it this way," Hodges said. "I have my suspicions. But right now I'm not interested in discussing them. I'm interested in these patients." For emphasis he slammed the papers he'd been holding onto the table.

Helen Beaton winced and said: "How dare you come charging in here as if you own the place, telling us what is important and what isn't. As administrator emeritus that's hardly your role."

"Thank you for your uninvited advice," Hodges said.

"All right, all right," Traynor sighed with frustration. His meeting had dissolved into a verbal melee. He picked up Hodges' papers, thrust them into the man's hand, then escorted the doctor from the room. Hodges resisted initially, but ultimately let himself be ushered out.

"We've got to talk, Harold," Hodges said once they were in the hall. "This is serious stuff."

"I'm sure it is," Traynor said, trying to sound sincere. Traynor knew that at some point he'd have to hear Hodges' grievances. Hodges had been the hospital administrator back when Traynor was still in grammar school. Hodges had taken the position when most doctors hadn't been interested in the responsibility. In his thirty years at the helm, Hodges had built Bartlet Community Hospital from a small rural hospital to a true tertiary care center. It was this sprawling institution he'd passed on to Traynor when he'd stepped down from his position three years before.

"Look," Traynor said, "whatever is on your mind, it can surely wait until tomorrow. We'll talk at lunch. In fact, I'll arrange for Barton Sherwood and Dr. Delbert Cantor to join us. If what you want to discuss concerns policy, which I assume it does, then it would be best to have the vice chairman and the chief of the professional staff there as well. Don't you agree?"

"I suppose," Hodges admitted reluctantly.

"Then it's settled," Traynor said soothingly, eager to get back and salvage what he could of his meeting now that Hodges was placated for the time being. "I'll contact them tonight."

"I might not be administrator any longer," Hodges added, "but I still feel responsible for what goes on around here.

After all, if it hadn't been for me you wouldn't have been named to the board, much less elected chairman."

"I understand that," Traynor said. Then he joked: "But I don't know whether to thank you or curse you for this dubious honor."

"I'm worried you've let the power go to your head," Hodges said.

"Oh, come on!" Traynor said. "What do you mean, 'power'? This job is nothing but one headache after another."

"You're essentially running a hundred-million-dollar entity," Hodges said. "And it's the largest employer in this whole part of the state. That means power."

Traynor laughed nervously. "It's still a pain in the neck. And we're lucky to be in business. I don't have to remind you that our two competitors no longer are. Valley Hospital closed, and the Mary Sackler has been turned into a nursing home."

"We might still be open, but I'm afraid you money men are forgetting the hospital's mission."

"Oh, bullcrap!" Traynor snapped, losing a bit of control. "You old docs have to wake up to a new reality. It's not easy running a hospital in the current environment of cost-cutting, managed care, and government intervention. It isn't cost-plus anymore like you had it. Times have changed, demanding new adaptations and new strategies for survival. Washington is mandating it."

Hodges laughed derisively: "Washington sure isn't mandating what you and your cohorts are doing."

"The hell they aren't," Traynor argued. "It's called competition, Dennis. Survival of the fittest and the leanest. No more sleight-of-hand cost-shifting like you used to get away with."

Traynor paused, realizing that he was losing his composure. He wiped away the perspiration that had broken out on his forehead. He took a deep breath. "Listen, Dennis, I've got to get back into the conference room. You go home, calm down, relax, get some sleep. We'll get together tomorrow and go over whatever is on your mind, okay?"

"I am a bit tuckered," Hodges admitted.

"Sure you are," Traynor agreed.

"Tomorrow for lunch? Promise? No excuses?"

"Absolutely," Traynor said as he gave Hodges a prodding pat on the back. "At the inn at twelve sharp."

With relief Traynor watched his old mentor trudge toward the hospital lobby with his distinctive lumbering gait, rocking on his hips as if they were stiff. Turning back toward the conference room, Traynor marveled at the man's uncanny flair for causing turmoil. Unfortunately, Hodges was going beyond being a nuisance. He was becoming a virtual albatross.

"Can we have some order here," Traynor called out over the bedlam to which he returned. "I apologize for the interruption. Unfortunately, old Doc Hodges has a particular knack for showing up at the most inopportune times."

"That's an understatement," Beaton said. "He's forever barging into my office to complain that one of his former patients isn't getting what he considers VIP treatment. He acts as if he's still running this place."

"The food is never to his liking," Geraldine Polcari complained.

"Nor is the room cleaning," added Gloria Suarez.

"He comes into my office about once a week," Nancy Widner said. "It's always the same complaint. The nurses aren't responding quickly enough to his former patients' requests."

"He's their self-elected ombudsman," Beaton said.

"They're the only people in the town that can stand him," Nancy said. "Just about everyone else thinks he's a crotchety old coot."

"Do you think he knows the identity of the rapist?" Patrick Swegler asked.

"Heavens, no," Nancy said. "The man's just a blowhard."

"What do you think, Mr. Traynor?" Patrick Swegler persisted.

Traynor shrugged. "I doubt he knows anything, but I'll certainly ask when I meet with him tomorrow."

"I don't envy you that lunch," Beaton said.

"I'm not looking forward to it," Traynor admitted. "I've always felt he deserved a certain amount of respect, but to be truthful my resolve is wearing a bit thin.

"Now, let's get back to the matter at hand." Traynor soon had the meeting back on track, but for him the joy of the evening had been lost.

Hodges trudged straight up Main Street in the middle of the road. For the moment there were no vehicles moving in either direction. The plows hadn't come through yet; two inches of powdery new snow blanketed the town as still more flakes fell.

Hodges cursed under his breath, giving partial vent to his unappeased anger. Now that he was on his way home he felt angry for having allowed Traynor to put him off.

Coming abreast of the town green with its deserted, snow-covered gazebo, Hodges could see north past the Methodist church. There, in the distance, directly up Front Street, he could just make out the hospital's main building. Hodges paused, gazing wistfully at the structure. A sense of foreboding descended over him with a shiver. He'd devoted his life to the hospital so that it would serve the people of the town. But now he feared that it was faltering in its mission.

Turning away, Hodges recommenced his trek up Main Street. He jammed the copy-machine papers he was holding into his coat pocket. His fingers had gone numb. Half a block farther he stopped again. This time he gazed at the mullioned windows of the Iron Horse Inn. A beckoning, incandescent glow spilled out onto the frigid, snow-covered lawn.

It only took a moment of rationalization for Hodges to decide he could use another drink. After all, now that his wife, Clara, spent more time with her family in Boston than she did with him in Bartlet, it wasn't as if she'd be waiting up for him. There were certainly some advantages to their virtual estrangement. Hodges knew he would be glad for the extra fortification for the twenty-five-minute walk he faced to get home.

In the outer room Hodges stomped the snow from his rubber-soled workboots and hung up his coat on a wooden peg. His hat went into a cubbyhole above. Passing an empty coat-check booth used for parties, Hodges went down a short hallway and paused at the entryway of the bar.

The room was constructed of unfinished pine that had an almost charred look from two centuries of use. A huge field-stone fireplace with a roaring fire dominated one wall.

Hodges scanned the chamber. From his point of view, the cast of characters assembled was unsavory, hardly reminiscent of NBC's "Cheers." He saw Barton Sherwood, the president of the Green Mountain National Bank, and now, thanks to Traynor, vice chairman of the hospital's board of directors. Sherwood was sitting in a booth with Ned Banks, the obnoxious owner of the New England Coat Hanger Company.

At another table, Dr. Delbert Cantor was sitting with Dr. Paul Darnell. The table was laden with beer bottles, baskets of potato chips, and platters of cheese. To Hodges they looked like a couple of pigs at the trough.

For a split second Hodges thought about pulling his papers from his coat and getting Sherwood and Cantor to sit down and talk with him. But he abandoned the idea immediately. He didn't have the energy and both Cantor and Darnell hated his guts. Cantor, a radiologist, and Darnell, a pathologist, had both suffered when Hodges had arranged for the hospital to take over those departments five years earlier. They weren't likely to be a receptive audience for his complaints.

At the bar stood John MacKenzie, another local Hodges would just as soon avoid. Hodges had had a long-standing disagreement with the man. John owned the Mobil station out near the interstate and had serviced Hodges' vehicles for many years. But the last time he'd worked on Hodges' car, the problem had not been fixed. Hodges had had to drive all the way to the dealership in Rutland to get it repaired. Consequently he'd never paid John.

A couple of stools beyond John MacKenzie, Hodges saw Pete Bergan, and he groaned inwardly. Pete had been a "blue baby" who'd never finished the sixth grade. At age eighteen he dropped out of school and supported himself by doing odd jobs. Hodges had arranged for his job helping the hospital grounds crew but had had to acquiesce to his firing when he proved too unreliable. Since then Pete had held a grudge.

Beyond Pete stretched a row of empty bar stools. Beyond the bar and down a step were two pool tables. Music thudded out of an old-fashioned fifties-style jukebox against the far wall. Grouped around the pool tables were a handful of students from Bartlet College, a small liberal arts institution that had recently gone coed.

For a moment Hodges teetered on the threshold, trying to decide if a drink was worth crossing paths with any of these people. In the end the memory of the cold and the anticipation of the taste of the scotch propelled him into the room.

Ignoring everyone Hodges went to the far end of the bar and climbed up on an empty stool. The radiant heat from the fire warmed his back. A tumbler appeared in front of him, and Carleton Harris, the overweight bartender, poured him a glass of Dewar's without ice. Carleton and Hodges had known each other for a long time.

"I think you'll want to find another seat," Carleton advised.

"Why's that?" Hodges asked. He'd been pleased that no one had noticed his entrance.

Carleton nodded at a half-empty highball glass on the bar two stools away. "I'm afraid our fearless chief of police, Mr. Wayne Robertson, has stopped in for a snort. He's in the men's room."

"Oh, damn!" Hodges said.

"Don't say I didn't warn you," Carleton added as he headed toward several students who'd approached the bar.

"Hell, it's six of one, half a dozen of the other," Hodges murmured to himself. If he moved to the other end, he'd have to face John MacKenzie. Hodges decided to stay where he was. He lifted his glass to his lips.

Before he could take a drink, Hodges felt a slap on his back. It was all he could do to keep his drink from clanking against his teeth and spilling.

"Well, if it isn't the Quack!"

Swinging around, Hodges glared into the inebriated face of Wayne Robertson. Robertson was forty-two and heavyset.

At one time he'd been all muscle. Now he was half muscle and half fat. The most prominent aspect of his profile was his abdomen, which practically draped his official belt buckle. Robertson was still in uniform, gun and all.

"Wayne, you're drunk," Hodges said. "So why don't you just go home and sleep it off." Hodges turned back to the bar and tried once more to take a sip of his drink.

"There's nothing to go home to, thanks to you."

Hodges slowly turned around again and looked at Robertson. Robertson's eyes were red, almost as red as his fat cheeks. His blond hair was clipped short in a fifties-style butch.

"Wayne," Hodges began, "we're not going over this again. Your wife, rest her soul, was not my patient. You're drunk. Go home."

"You were running the freakin' hospital," Robertson said.

"That doesn't mean I was responsible for every case, you lunkhead," Hodges said. "Besides, it was ten years ago." He again tried to turn away.

"You bastard!" Robertson snarled. Reaching out, he grabbed Hodges' shirt at the collar and tried to lift Hodges off the barstool.

Carleton Harris came around the bar with a swiftness that belied his bulk and insinuated himself between the two men. He opened Robertson's grip on Hodges' shirt one finger at a time. "Okay, you two," he said. "Off to your own corners. We don't allow sparring here at the Iron Horse."

Hodges straightened his shirt indignantly, snatched up his drink, and walked to the other end of the bar. As he passed behind John MacKenzie he heard the man mutter: "Deadbeat." Hodges refused to be provoked.

"Carleton, you shouldn't have interfered," Dr. Cantor called out to the bartender. "If Robertson had blown old Hodges away half the town would have cheered."

Dr. Cantor and Dr. Darnell laughed uproariously at Cantor's comment. Each one encouraged the other until they were slapping their knees and choking on their beers. Carleton ignored them as he stepped around the bar to help Barton Sherwood who'd approached for refills.

"Dr. Cantor's right," Sherwood said loud enough for everyone in the bar to hear. "Next time Hodges and Robertson face off, leave them be."

"Not you too," Carleton said as he deftly mixed Sherwood's drinks.

"Let me tell you about Dr. Hodges," Sherwood said, still loud enough for everyone to hear. "A good neighbor he isn't. By a historical accident he owns a little tongue of land that happens to separate my two lots. So what does he do? He builds this gigantic fence."

"Of course I fenced that land," Hodges called out, unable to hold his tongue. "It was the only way to keep your goddamn horses from dropping their shit all over my property."

"Then why not sell the strip of land?" Sherwood demanded, turning to face Hodges. "It's of no use to you."

"I can't sell it because it's in my wife's name," Hodges answered.

"Nonsense," Sherwood said. "The fact that your house and land are in your wife's name is merely a legacy of an old ruse to protect your assets from any malpractice judgment. You told me so yourself."

"Then perhaps you should know the truth," Hodges said. "I was trying to be diplomatic. I won't sell you the land because I despise you. Is that easier for your pea brain to comprehend?"

Sherwood turned to the room and addressed everyone present. "You're all witnesses. Dr. Hodges is admitting he's acting out of spite. No surprise, of course, and hardly a Christian attitude."

"Oh, shut up," Hodges retorted. "It's a bit hypocritical for a bank president to question someone else's Christian ethics with all the foreclosures on your conscience. You've put families out of their homes."

"That's different," Sherwood said. "That's business. I have my stockholders to consider."

"Oh, bull," Hodges said with a wave of dismissal.

A sudden commotion at the door caught Hodges' attention. He turned in time to see Traynor and the rest of the attendees of the hospital meeting troop into the bar. He could tell that Traynor was not at all pleased to see him. Hodges shrugged and turned back to his drink. But he couldn't dismiss the fortuitous fact that all three principals were there: Traynor, Sherwood, and Cantor.

Grabbing his whiskey, Hodges slipped off his stool and followed Traynor to Sherwood and Banks's table. Hodges tapped him on his shoulder.

"How about talking now?" Hodges suggested. "We're all here."

"Goddamn it, Hodges," Traynor blurted out. "How many times do I have to tell you? I don't want to talk tonight. We'll talk tomorrow!"

"What does he want to talk about?" Sherwood asked.

"Something about a few of his old patients," Traynor said. "I told him that we'd meet him for lunch tomorrow."

"What's going on?" Dr. Cantor asked, joining the fray. He'd sensed blood and had been drawn over to the table like a shark attracted to chum.

"Dr. Hodges isn't happy with the way we are running the hospital," Traynor said. "We're to hear about it tomorrow."

"No doubt the same old complaint," Sherwood interjected. "No VIP treatment for his old patients."

"Some gratitude!" Dr. Cantor said, interrupting Hodges who'd tried to respond. "Here we are donating our time pro bono to keep the hospital afloat and what do we get in return: nothing but criticism."

"Pro bono my ass," Hodges sneered. "None of you fool me. Your involvement isn't charity. Traynor, you've come to use the place to support your newly discovered grandiosity. Sherwood, your interest isn't even that sophisticated. It's purely financial, since the hospital is the bank's largest customer. And Cantor, yours is just as simple. All you're interested in is the Imaging Center, that joint venture I allowed in a moment of insanity. Of all the decisions I made as hospital administrator, that's the one I regret the most."

"You thought it was a good deal when you made it," Dr. Cantor said.

"Only because I thought it was the only way to update the hospital's CAT scanner," Hodges said. "But that was before I realized the machine would pay for itself in less than a year which, of course, made me realize you and the other private radiologist were robbing the hospital of money it should have been earning."

"I'm not interested in opening this old battle," Dr. Cantor said.

"Nor am I," Hodges agreed. "But the point is there's little or no charity involved with you people. Your concern is financial gain, not the good of your patients or the community."

"You're no one to talk," Traynor snapped. "You ran the hospital like a personal fiefdom. Tell us who's been taking care of that house of yours all these years?"

"What do you mean?" Hodges stammered, his eyes darting back and forth among the men in front of him.

"It's not a complicated question," Traynor said, his anger driving him on. He'd stuck Hodges with a knife and now he wanted to push it in to the hilt.

"I don't know what my house has to do with this," Hodges managed.

Traynor went up on his toes to survey the room. "Where's Van Slyke?" he asked. "He's here somewhere."

"He's by the fire," Sherwood said, pointing. He had to struggle to suppress a contented smile. This issue about Hodges' house had nettled him for some time. The only reason he'd never brought it up was because Traynor had forbidden it.

Traynor called to Van Slyke, but the man didn't seem to hear. Traynor called again, this time loud enough for everyone in the bar to hear. Conversation stopped. Except for the music emanating from the jukebox, the room was momentarily silent.

Van Slyke moved slowly across the room, uncomfortable in the spotlight. He was aware most of the people were watching him. But they soon lost interest and conversations recommenced where they had left off.

"Good grief, man," Traynor said to Van Slyke. "You look like you're moving through molasses. Sometimes you act eighty years old instead of thirty."

"Sorry," Van Slyke said, maintaining his bland facial expression.

"I want to ask you a question," Traynor continued. "Who has been taking care of Dr. Hodges' house and property?"

Van Slyke looked from Traynor to Hodges, a wry smile curling on his lips. Hodges looked away.

"Well?" Traynor questioned.

"We have been," Van Slyke said.

"Be a little more specific," Traynor said. "Who is 'we'?"

"The hospital grounds crew," Van Slyke said. He didn't take his eyes off Hodges. Nor did his smile change.

"How long has this been going on?" Traynor asked.

"Since way before I arrived," Van Slyke said.

"It's going to stop as of today," Traynor said. "Understand?"

"Sure," Van Slyke said.

"Thank you, Werner," Traynor said. "Why don't you go over to the bar and have a beer while we finish chatting with Dr. Hodges." Van Slyke returned to his place by the fire.

"You know that old expression," Traynor said, " 'People in glass houses ...' "

"Shut up!" Hodges snapped. He started to say something else but stopped himself. Instead he stalked from the room in a fit of frustrated anger, grabbed his coat and hat, and plunged out into the snowy night.

"You old fool," Hodges muttered as he headed south out of town. He was furious at himself for allowing a "perk" to derail momentarily his indignation about patient care. Yet it was true that hospital maintenance had been taking care of his grounds. It had started years ago. The crew had simply shown up one day. Hodges had never asked for the service, but he'd never done anything to stop it, either.

The long walk home in the frosty night helped dampen Hodges' guilt about the yard service. After all, it didn't have anything to do with patient care. As he turned into his unplowed driveway he resolved to offer to pay some reasonable figure for the services rendered. He wasn't about to allow this affair to stifle his protest about more serious matters.

When Hodges reached the midpoint of his long driveway he could see down into the lower meadow. Through
the blowing snow he could just make out the fence that
he'd erected to keep Sherwood's horses from crossing his
property. He'd never sell that strip of land to that bastard.
Sherwood had gotten the second piece of land on a fore-
closure of a family whose breadwinner had been one of
Hodges' patients. In fact, he was one of the patients whose
hospital admission summary Hodges had in his pocket.

Leaving the driveway, Hodges took a shortcut that skirted
the frog pond. He could tell some of the neighborhood kids
had been skating because the snow had been pushed off the
ice and a makeshift hockey goal had been erected. Beyond
the pond Hodges' empty house loomed out of the snowy
darkness.

Rounding the building, Hodges approached the side door
of the clapboard addition that connected the house with the
barn. He knocked the snow off his boots and entered. In the
mud room he removed his coat and hat and hung them up.
Fumbling in his coat pocket he pulled out the papers he'd
been carrying and took them into the kitchen.

After placing the papers on the kitchen table, Hodges
headed for the library to pour himself a drink in lieu of
the one he'd abandoned at the inn. Insistent knocking at
his door stopped him midway across the dining room.

Hodges looked at his watch in puzzlement. Who could
be calling at that hour and on such a night? Reversing
his direction, he went back through the kitchen and into
the mud room. Using his shirt sleeve he wiped away the
condensation on one of the door's panes of glass. He could
just make out the figure outside.

"What now?" Hodges muttered as he reached down and
unlatched the door. He pulled it wide open and said: "Considering everything it's a bit strange for you to come visiting, especially at this hour."

Hodges stared at his visitor, who said nothing. Snow
swirled in around Hodges' legs.

"Oh, hell," Hodges said with a shrug. "Whatever you
want, come in." He let go of the door and headed toward
the kitchen. "Just don't expect me to play the role of the

hospitable host. And close the door behind you!"

When Hodges reached the single step up to the kitchen level, he started to turn to make sure the door had been closed tight against the weather. Out of the corner of his eye he saw something speeding toward his head. By reflex, he ducked.

The sudden movement saved Hodges' life. A flat metal rod glanced off the side of his head, but not before cutting deeply into his scalp. The force of the blow carried the metal rod to the top of his shoulder where it fractured his collarbone. Its power also sent the stunned Hodges hurtling into the kitchen.

Hodges collided with the kitchen table. His hands clutched the edges, keeping him on his feet. Blood spurted in tiny pulsating jets from the open scalp wound onto his papers. Hodges turned in time to see his attacker closing in on him with arm raised. In a gloved hand he clutched a rod that looked like a short, flat crowbar.

As the weapon started down for a second blow, Hodges reached up and grabbed the exposed forearm, impeding the impact. Still, the metal cut into Hodges' scalp at the hairline. Fresh blood squirted from severed arteries.

Hodges desperately dug his fingernails into the assail-ant's forearm. He knew intuitively he could not let go; he had to keep from being struck again.

For a few moments the two figures struggled against each other. In a dance of death they pirouetted around the kitchen, smashing into the walls, upsetting chairs, and breaking dishes. Blood spattered indiscriminately.

The attacker cried in pain as he pulled his arm free from Hodges' grip. Once again the steel rod rose up to a fright-ening apogee before smashing down onto Hodges' raised forearm. Bones snapped like twigs under the impact.

Again the metal bar was lifted above the now hapless Hodges and brought down hard. This time its arc was unhindered, and the weapon impacted directly onto the top of Hodges' unprotected head, crushing in a sharply defined fragment of his skull and driving it deeply into his brain.

Hodges fell heavily to the floor, mercifully insensitive.

SATURDAY, APRIL 24

"WE'RE COMING TO A RIVER UP AHEAD," DAVID WIL-
son said to his daughter, Nikki, who was sitting in the
passenger seat next to him. "Do you know what its name
is?"

Nikki turned her mahogany eyes toward her father and
pushed a wisp of hair to the side. David hazarded a glance
in her direction, and with the help of the sunlight coming
through the windshield, he caught some of the subtle spokes
of yellow that radiated from her pupils through her irises.
They were matched with strands of honey in her hair.

"The only rivers I know," Nikki said, "are the Mississip-
pi, the Nile, and the Amazon. Since none of them are here
in New England, I'll have to say I don't know."

Neither David nor his wife, Angela, could suppress a
giggle.

"What's so funny?" Nikki demanded indignantly.

David looked into the rearview mirror and exchanged
knowing glances with Angela. Both were thinking the same

thought, and they had spoken of it often: Nikki frequently sounded more mature than expected for her chronological age of eight. They considered the trait an endearing one, indicative of her intelligence. At the same time, they realized their daughter was growing up faster than she might otherwise have because of her health problems.

"Why did you laugh?" Nikki persisted.

"Ask your mother," David said.

"No, I think your father should explain."

"Come on, you guys," Nikki protested. "That's not fair. But I don't care if you laugh or not because I can find the name of the river myself." She took a map from the glove compartment.

"We're on Highway 89," David said.

"I know!" Nikki said with annoyance. "I don't want any help."

"Excuse me," David said with a smile.

"Here it is," Nikki said triumphantly. She twisted the map on its side so she could read the lettering. "It's the Connecticut River. Just like the state."

"Right you are," David said. "And it forms the boundary between what and what?"

Nikki looked back at the map for a moment. "It separates Vermont from New Hampshire."

"Right again," David said. And then, gesturing ahead, he added: "And here it is."

They were all quiet as their blue, eleven-year-old Volvo station wagon sped over the span. Below the water roiled southward.

"I guess the snow is still melting in the mountains," David said.

"Are we going to see mountains?" Nikki asked.

"We sure are," David said. "The Green Mountains."

They reached the other side of the bridge where the highway gradually swung back toward the northwest.

"Are we in Vermont now?" Angela asked.

"Yes, Mom!" Nikki said with impatience.

"How much further to Bartlet?" Angela asked.

"I'm not quite sure," David said. "Maybe an hour."

An hour and fifteen minutes later the Wilsons' Volvo

passed the sign reading: "Welcome to Bartlet, Home of Bartlet College."

David let up on the accelerator and the car slowed. They were on a wide avenue aptly called Main Street. The street was lined with large oaks. Behind the trees were white clapboard homes. The architecture was a potpourri of colonial and Victorian.

"So far it looks story-bookish," Angela said.

"Some of these New England towns look like they belong in Disney World," David said.

Angela laughed. "Sometimes I think you feel a replica is better than an original."

After a short drive the homes gave way to commercial and civic buildings which were constructed mostly of brick with Victorian decorations. In the downtown area stood rows of three- and four-story brick structures. Engraved stone plaques announced the year each was constructed. Most of the dates were either late nineteenth century or early twentieth.

"Look!" Nikki said. "There's a movie theater." She pointed at a shabby marquee announcing a current movie in large block letters. Next to the movie theater was a post office with a tattered American flag snapping in the breeze.

"We're really lucky with this weather," Angela remarked. The sky was pale blue and dotted with small, puffy white clouds. The temperature was in the high sixties.

"What's that?" Nikki questioned. "It looks like a trolley with no wheels."

David laughed. "That's called a diner," he said. "They were popular back in the fifties."

Nikki was straining against her seat belt, excitedly leaning forward to peer out the front windshield.

As they approached the heart of the town they discovered a number of gray granite buildings that were significantly more imposing than the brick structures, especially the Green Mountain National Bank with its corbeled and crenellated clock tower.

"That building really looks like something out of Disney World," Nikki said.

"Like father, like daughter," Angela said.

They came to the town green whose grass had already achieved a luxurious, almost midsummer color. Crocuses, hyacinths, and daffodils dotted the park, especially around the gingerbread central gazebo. David pulled the car over to the side of the road and stopped.

"Compared with the section of Boston around Boston City Hospital," David said, "this looks like heaven."

At the north end of the park was a large white church whose exterior was rather plain except for its enormous steeple. The steeple was neo-Gothic, replete with elaborate tracery and spires. Its belfry was enclosed by columns supporting pointed arches.

"We've got several hours before our interviews. What do you think we should do?" David asked.

"Why don't we drive around a little more, then have lunch?" Angela said.

"Sounds good to me." David put the car in gear and continued along Main Street. On the west side of the town green they passed the library which, like the bank, was constructed of gray granite. But it looked more like an Italian villa than a castle.

Just beyond the library was the elementary school. David pulled over to the side of the road so Nikki could see it. It was an appealing turn-of-the-century three-story brick building connected to a nondescript wing of more recent vintage.

"What do you think?" David asked Nikki.

"Would that be where I'd go to school if we come here to live?" Nikki asked.

"Probably," David said. "I can't imagine they'd have more than one school in a town of this size."

"It's pretty," Nikki said noncommittally.

Driving on, they quickly passed through the commercial section. Then they found themselves in the middle of the Bartlet College campus. The buildings were mostly the same gray granite they'd seen in the town and had the same white trim. Many were covered with ivy.

"A lot different from Brown University," Angela said. "But charming."

"I often wonder what it would have been like if I'd gone to a small college like this," David said.

"You wouldn't have met Mommy," Nikki said. "And then I wouldn't be here."

David laughed. "You're so right and I'm so happy I went to Brown."

Looping through the college, they headed back toward the center of town. They crossed over the Roaring River and discovered two old mill buildings. David explained to Nikki how water power was used in the old days. One of the mills now housed a computer software company, but its water wheel was slowly turning. A sign advertised that the other mill was now the New England Coat Hanger Company.

Back in town David parked at the town green. This time they got out and strolled up Main Street.

"It's amazing, isn't it: no litter, no graffiti, and no home-less people," Angela said. "It's like a different country."

"What do you think of the people?" David asked. They had been passing pedestrians since they'd gotten out of the car.

"I'd say they look reserved," Angela said. "But not unfriendly."

David stopped outside of Staley's Hardware Store. "I'm going to run in and ask where we should eat."

Angela nodded. She and Nikki were looking into the window of the neighboring shoe store.

David was back in a flash. "The word is that the diner is best for a quick lunch, but the Iron Horse Inn has the best food. I vote for the diner."

"Me too," Nikki said.

"Well, that settles that," Angela said.

All three had hamburgers the old-fashioned way: with toasted buns, raw onion, and lots of ketchup. When they were through, Angela excused herself.

"There's no way I'm going to an interview until I brush my teeth," she said.

David took a handful of mints after paying the check.

On the way back to the car they approached a woman coming in their direction with a golden retriever puppy on a leash.

"Oh, how cute!" Nikki exclaimed.

The woman graciously stopped so Nikki could pet the dog.

"How old is she?" Angela asked.

"Twelve weeks," the woman said.

"Could you direct us to the Bartlet Community Hospital?" David asked.

"Certainly," the woman said. "Go up to the town green. The road on the right is Front Street. Take that right up to the hospital's front door."

They thanked the woman and moved on. Nikki walked sideways to keep the puppy in sight. "He was darling," she said. "If we come to live here, may I have a dog?"

David and Angela exchanged glances. Both were touched. Nikki's modest request after all the medical problems she'd been through melted their hearts.

"Of course you may have a dog," Angela said.

"You can even pick it out," David said.

"Well, then I want to come here," Nikki said with conviction. "Can we?"

Angela looked at David in hopes he would answer, but he gestured for her to field the question. Angela wrestled with her answer. She didn't know what to say. "Whether we come here or not is a difficult decision," she said finally. "There are many things we have to consider."

"Like what?" Nikki asked.

"Like whether they want me and your father," Angela said, relieved to have come up with a simple explanation, as the three got back in their car.

Bartlet Community Hospital was larger and more imposing than David or Angela had expected, even though they knew it was a referral center for a significant portion of the state.

Despite a sign that clearly said "Parking in the Rear," David pulled to the curb in the turnout before the front entrance. He put the car in park but left the engine running.

"This is truly beautiful," he said. "I never thought I would say that about a hospital."

"What a view," Angela said.

The hospital was midway up a hill just north of the town. It faced south and its facade was bathed in bright sunlight. Just below them at the base of the hill they could see the whole town. The Methodist church's steeple was especially prominent. In the distance the Green Mountains provided a scalloped border to the horizon.

Angela tapped David's arm. "We'd better get inside," she said. "My interview is in ten minutes."

David put the car in gear and drove around to the back of the hospital. There were two parking lots rising up in terraced tiers separated by a stand of trees. They found visitor slots next to the hospital's rear entrance in the lower lot.

Appropriately placed signs made finding the administrative offices easy, and a helpful secretary directed them to Michael Caldwell's office. Michael Caldwell was Bartlet's medical director.

Angela knocked on the jamb of the open door. Inside, Michael Caldwell looked up from his desk, then rose to greet her. He immediately reminded Angela of David with his olive coloring and trim, athletic build. He was also close to David's age of thirty, as well as his height of six feet. Like David's, his hair tended to form a natural center part. But there the similarities ended. Caldwell's features were harder than David's; his nose was hawk-like and narrower.

"Come in!" Caldwell said with enthusiasm. "Please! All of you." He quickly got more chairs.

David looked at Angela for guidance. Angela shrugged. If Caldwell wanted to interview the whole family, it was fine with her.

After brief introductions, Caldwell was back behind his desk with Angela's folder in front of him. "I've been over your application, and I have to tell you I am indeed impressed," he said.

"Thank you," Angela said.

"Frankly, I didn't expect a woman pathologist," Caldwell said. "Subsequently I've learned it's a field that is appealing to more and more women."

"The hours tend to be more predictable," Angela said. "It makes the practice of medicine and having a family more compatible." She studied the man. His comment made her slightly uncomfortable, but she was willing to withhold judgment.

"From your letters of recommendation I have the feeling that the department of pathology at the Boston City Hospital thinks you have been one of their brightest residents."

Angela smiled. "I've tried to do my best."

"And your transcript from Columbia's medical school is equally impressive," Caldwell said. "Consequently, we would like to have you here at Bartlet Community Hospital. It's as simple as that. But perhaps you have some questions for me."

"David has also applied for a job in Bartlet," Angela said. "It's with one of the major health maintenance organizations in the area: Comprehensive Medical Vermont."

"We call it CMV," Caldwell said. "And it's the only HMO in the area."

"I indicated in my letter that my availability is contingent on his acceptance," Angela said. "And vice versa."

"I'm well aware of that," Caldwell said. "In fact I took the liberty of contacting CMV and talking about David's application with the regional manager, Charles Kelley. CMV's regional office is right here in our professional building. Of course I cannot speak for them officially, but it is my understanding there is no problem whatsoever."

"I'm to meet with Mr. Kelley as soon as we're through here," David said.

"Perfect," Caldwell said. "So, Dr. Wilson, the hospital would like to offer you a position as associate pathologist. You'll join two other full-time pathologists. Your first year's compensation will be eighty-two thousand dollars."

When Caldwell looked down at the folder on his desk, Angela looked David's way. Eighty-two thousand dollars sounded like a fortune after so many years of burdensome debt and meager income. David flashed her a conspiratorial smile in return, obviously sharing her thoughts.

"I also have some information in response to your query letter," Caldwell said. He hesitated, then added: "Perhaps this is something we should talk about privately."

"It's not necessary," Angela said. "I assume you are

referring to Nikki's cystic fibrosis. She's an active participant in her care, so there are no secrets."

"Very well," Caldwell said. He smiled meekly at Nikki before continuing. "I found out that there is a patient with that condition here in Bartlet. Her name is Caroline Helmsford. She's nine years old. I've arranged for you to meet with her doctor, Dr. Bertrand Pilsner. He's one of CMV's pediatricians."

"Thank you for making such an effort," Angela said.

"No problem," Caldwell said. "Obviously we want you folks to come here to our delightful town. But I must confess that I didn't read up on the condition when I made the inquiries. Perhaps there is something I should know in order to be of more assistance."

Angela looked at Nikki. "Why don't you explain to Mr. Caldwell what cystic fibrosis is."

"Cystic fibrosis is an inherited problem," Nikki said in a serious and practiced tone. "When both parents are carriers there is a twenty-five percent chance a child will have the condition. About one in every two thousand babies is affected."

Caldwell nodded and tried to maintain his smile. There was something unnerving about getting a lecture from an eight-year-old.

"The main problem is with the respiratory system," Nikki continued. "The mucus in the lungs is thicker than in the lungs of normal people. The lungs have difficulty clearing the thicker mucus which leads to congestion and infection. Chronic bronchitis and pneumonia are the big worries. The condition is quite variable: some people are severely affected; others, like me, just have to be careful not to catch colds and do our respiratory therapy."

"Very interesting," Caldwell said. "You certainly sound professional. Maybe you should be a doctor when you grow up."

"I intend to," Nikki said. "I'm going to study respiratory medicine."

Caldwell got up and gestured toward the door. "How about you doctors and doctor-to-be going over to the medical office building to meet Dr. Pilsner."

It was only a short walk from the hospital's administrative area in the old central building to the newer professional building. In just a few minutes they passed through a fire door, and the corridor covering changed from vinyl tile to posh carpet.

Dr. Pilsner was in the middle of his afternoon office hours but graciously took time to meet the Wilsons. His thick white beard made him look a bit like Kris Kringle. Nikki took to him immediately when he bent down and shook her hand, treating her more like an adult than a child.

"We've got a great respiratory therapist here at the hospital," Dr. Pilsner said to the Wilsons. "And the hospital is well equipped for respiratory care. On top of that I took a fellowship in respiratory medicine at Children's in Boston. So I think we can take care of Nikki just fine."

"Wow!" Angela said, obviously impressed, and relieved. "This is certainly comforting. Ever since Nikki's diagnosis we take her special needs into consideration in all our decision-making."

"And indeed you should," Dr. Pilsner said. "Bartlet would be a good choice with its low pollution and clean, crisp air. Provided she has no tree or grass allergies, I think it would be a healthy environment for your daughter."

Caldwell escorted the Wilsons to CMV's regional headquarters. Before he left he made them promise to return to his office after David's interview.

The CMV receptionist directed the Wilsons to a small waiting area. The three of them barely had time to pick up magazines before Charles Kelley emerged from his private office.

Kelley was a big man who towered eight inches over David as they shook hands. His face was tanned and his sandy-colored hair had pure blond streaks running through it. He was dressed in a meticulously tailored suit. His manner was outgoing and ebullient, more like a high-powered super-salesman than a health care administrator.

Like Caldwell, Kelley invited the whole Wilson family into his office. He was also equally complimentary.

"Frankly, we want you, David," Kelley said, tapping a

closed fist on his desk. "We need you as part of our team. We're pleased that you've taken an internal medicine residency, especially at a place like the Boston City Hospital. As more of the city moves to the country, we're finding we need your kind of expertise. You'll be an enormous addition to our primary care/gatekeeper crew, no doubt about it."

"I'm pleased you're pleased," David said with an embarrassed shrug.

"CMV is expanding rapidly in this area of Vermont, especially in Bartlet itself," Kelley boasted. "We've signed up the coat-hanger mill, the college, and the computer software company, as well as all the state and municipal employees."

"Sounds like a monopoly," David joked.

"We'd rather think it has to do with our dedication to quality care and cost control," Kelley said.

"Of course," David agreed.

"Your compensation will be forty-one thousand the first year," Kelley said.

David nodded. He knew he'd be in for some teasing from Angela even though they'd known all along that her earnings would be significantly larger than his. On the other hand, they hadn't expected hers would be double his.

"Why don't I show you your prospective office," Kelley said eagerly. "It will give you a better feeling for our operation and what it will be like working here."

David looked at Angela. Kelley's approach was certainly a harder sell than was Caldwell's.

To David's mind the office was dream-like. The view south over the Green Mountains was so picture-perfect, it looked like a painting.

David noticed four patients sitting in the waiting area reading magazines. He looked to Kelley for an explanation.

"You'll be sharing this suite with Dr. Randall Portland," Kelley explained. "He's an orthopedic surgeon. A good guy, I might add. We've found that sharing receptionists and nurses is an efficient use of resources. Let me see if he's available to say hello."

Kelley walked over and tapped on what David thought was merely a mirror. It slid open. Behind it was a receptionist. Kelley spoke to her for a moment before the mirrored partition slid closed.

"He'll be out in a second," Kelley said, rejoining the Wilsons. He then explained the layout of the office. Opening a door on the west side of the waiting room, he gave them a tour of empty, newly redecorated examining rooms. He also took them into the room that would be David's private office. It had the same fabulous view to the south as the waiting room.

"Hello everybody," a voice called out. The Wilsons turned from gaping out the window to see a youthful but strained-appearing man stride into the room. It was Dr. Randall Portland. Kelley introduced them all, even Nikki, who shook hands like she'd done with Dr. Pilsner.

"Call me Randy," Dr. Portland said as he shook David's hand.

David sensed the man was sizing him up.

"You play basketball?" Randy asked.

"Occasionally," David said. "Lately I haven't had much time."

"I hope you come to Bartlet," Randy said. "We need some more players around here. At least someone to take my place."

David smiled.

"Well, it's nice to meet you folks. I'm afraid I have to get back to work."

"He's a busy man," Kelley explained after Dr. Portland left. "We currently only have two orthopedists. We need three."

David turned back to the mesmerizing view.

"Well, what do you say?" Kelley questioned.

"I'd say we're pretty impressed," David said. He looked at Angela.

"We'll have to give it all a lot of thought," Angela said.

After leaving Charles Kelley, the Wilsons returned to Caldwell's office. He insisted on taking David and Angela on a quick tour of the hospital. Nikki was left in the hospital day-care center, run by pink-frocked volunteers.

The first stop on the tour was the laboratory. Angela was not surprised to find that the lab was truly state-of-the-art. After he showed her the pathology section where she'd be doing most of her work, Caldwell took her in to meet the department chairman, Dr. Benjamin Wadley.

Dr. Wadley was a distinguished-looking, silver-haired gentleman in his fifties. Angela was immediately struck by how much he reminded her of her father.

After the introductions, Dr. Wadley said he understood that David and Angela had a little girl. Before they could respond, he raved about the local school system. "My kids really thrived. One is now at Wesleyan in Connecticut. The other is a senior in high school and has already gotten early acceptance into Smith College."

A few minutes later, after bidding Dr. Wadley goodbye, Angela pulled David aside as they followed Caldwell.

"Did you notice the similarity between Dr. Wadley and my father?" Angela whispered.

"Now that you say it, yes," David said. "He has that same kind of poise and confidence."

"I thought it was rather remarkable," Angela said.

"Let's not have any hysterical transference," David joked.

Next on the tour was the ER, followed by the Imaging Center. David was particularly impressed with the newly acquired MRI machine.

"This is a better machine than the one at Boston City Hospital," David remarked. "Where did the money come from for this?"

"The Imaging Center is a joint venture between the hospital and Dr. Cantor, one of the staff doctors," Caldwell explained. "They upgrade the equipment all the time."

After the Imaging Center, David and Angela toured the new radiotherapy building which boasted one of the newest linear accelerators. From there they returned to the main hospital and the new neonatal critical care unit.

"I don't know what to say," David admitted when the tour was over.

"We'd heard the hospital was well equipped," Angela

said, "but this is far better than we'd imagined."

"We're understandably proud of it," Caldwell said as he led them back into his office. "We had to significantly upgrade in order to land the CMV contract. We had to compete with the Valley Hospital and the Mary Sackler Hospital for survival. Luckily, we won."

"But all this equipment and upgrading had to cost a fortune," David said.

"That's an understatement," Caldwell agreed. "It's not easy these days running a hospital, especially in this era of government-mandated competition. Revenues are down, costs are going up. It's hard just to stay in business." Caldwell handed David a manila envelope. "Here's a packet of information about the hospital. Maybe it will help convince you to come up here and accept our job offers."

"What about housing?" Angela asked as an afterthought.

"I'm glad you asked," Caldwell said. "I was supposed to ask you to go down to the Green Mountain National Bank to see Barton Sherwood. Mr. Sherwood is the vice chairman of the hospital board. He's also president of the bank. He'll give you an idea how much the town supports the hospital."

After rescuing a reluctant Nikki from the day-care center where she'd been enjoying herself, the Wilsons drove back to the town green and walked to the bank. Typical of their reception in Bartlet, Barton Sherwood saw them immediately.

"Your applications were favorably discussed at the last executive board meeting," Barton Sherwood told them as he leaned back in his chair and hooked his thumbs in his vest pockets. He was a slight man, nearing sixty, with thinning hair and a pencil-line mustache. "We sincerely hope you'll be joining the Bartlet family. To encourage you to come to Bartlet, I want you to know that Green Mountain National Bank is prepared to offer both first and second mortgages so that you'll be able to buy a house."

David and Angela were stunned and their jaws dropped in unison. Never in their wildest imaginations had they thought they would have been able to buy a house the first year out of their residencies. They had very little cash, and a mountain of tuition debt: over a hundred and fifty thousand dollars.

Sherwood went on to give them the specifics, but neither David nor Angela could focus on the details. It wasn't until they were back in their car that they dared to speak.

"I can't believe this," David said.

"It's almost too good to be true," Angela agreed.

"Does this mean we're coming to Bartlet?" Nikki asked.

"We'll see," Angela said.

Since David had driven up from Boston, Angela offered to drive home. As she drove, David perused the information packet Caldwell had given them.

"This is interesting," David said. "There's a clip from the local paper about the signing of the contract between Bartlet Community Hospital and CMV. It says that the deal was consummated when the hospital board, under the leadership of Harold Traynor, finally agreed to CMV's demand to provide hospitalization for an unspecified monthly capitation fee, a method of cost control encouraged by the government and favored by HMO organizations."

"That's a good example of how providers like hospitals and doctors are being forced to make concessions," Angela said.

"Right you are," David agreed. "By accepting capitation the hospital has been forced to act like an insurance organization. They are assuming some of the health risk of the CMV subscribers."

"What's capitation?" Nikki asked.

David swung around. "Capitation is when an organization is paid a certain amount of money per person," he explained. "With health plans it's usually by the month."

Nikki still looked puzzled.

David tried again. "Let's be specific. Say that CMV pays Bartlet Hospital a thousand dollars each month for each person in the plan. Then if anybody has to be hospitalized during the month for whatever reason, CMV doesn't have to pay any more. So if no one gets sick for the month, the hospital makes out like a bandit. But what if everybody gets sick and has to go to the hospital? What do you think will happen then?"

"I think you still might be over her head," Angela said.

"I understand," Nikki said. "If everybody got sick the hospital would go broke."

David smiled with satisfaction and gave Angela a playful poke in the ribs. "Hear that?" he said triumphantly. "That's my daughter."

A few hours later, they were back home near their Southend apartment. Angela was lucky enough to find a spot only half a block from their door. David gently woke Nikki, who'd drifted off to sleep. Together the three walked to their building and mounted the stairs to their fourth-floor walk-up.

"Uh oh!" Angela said. She was the first to reach their apartment.

"What's the matter?" David asked. He looked over her shoulder.

Angela pointed at the door. The trim was split from the point where a crowbar had been inserted. David reached out and pushed the door. It opened with no resistance. All three locks had been broken.

David reached in and turned on the light. The apartment had been ransacked: furniture upended and the contents of cabinets and drawers scattered about the floor.

"Oh, no!" Angela cried as tears welled in her eyes.

"Easy!" David said. "What's been done is done. Let's not get hysterical."

"What do you mean, 'Let's not get hysterical'?" Angela demanded. "Our home's been ruined. The TV's gone."

"We can get another TV," David said calmly.

Nikki came back from her room and reported that it hadn't been touched.

"At least we can be thankful for that," David said.

Angela disappeared into their bedroom while David surveyed the kitchen. Except for a partially empty container of ice cream melted on the counter, the kitchen was fine.

David picked up the phone and dialed 911. While he was waiting for the call to go through, Angela appeared with tears streaming down her face, holding a small, empty jewelry box.

After David gave the details to the 911 operator, he

turned to Angela. She was struggling to maintain control.

"Just don't say anything super-rational," Angela managed through her tears. "Don't say we can get more jewelry."

"Okay, okay," David said agreeably.

Angela dried her face on her sleeve. "Coming home to this rape of our apartment makes Bartlet seem that much more appealing," she said. "At this point I'm more than ready to leave urban ills behind."

"I don't have anything against him personally," Dr. Randall Portland told his wife, Arlene, as they got up from the dinner table. She motioned their two sons, Mark and Allen, to help clear the table. "I just don't want to share my office with an internist."

"Why not?" Arlene asked, taking the dishes from her sons and scraping food scraps into the disposal.

"Because I don't want my post-ops sharing a waiting room with a bunch of sick people," Randy snapped. He recorked the unfinished bottle of white wine and put it into the refrigerator.

"Okay," Arlene said. "That I can understand. I was afraid it was some juvenile surgeon-internist squabble."

"Don't be ridiculous," Randy said.

"Well, you remember all the jokes you used to have about internists when you were a resident," Arlene reminded him.

"That was healthy verbal sparring," Randy said. "But this is different. I don't want infectious people around my patients. Call it superstitious, I don't care. But I've been having more than my share of complications with my patients and it has me depressed."

"Can we watch TV?" Mark asked. Allen, with his angelically huge eyes, was standing behind him. They were seven and six years old respectively.

"We already agreed that . . ." Arlene began, but then she stopped. It was hard to resist her sons' pleading expressions. Besides, she wanted a moment alone with Randy. "Okay, a half hour."

"Yippie!" Mark exclaimed. Allen echoed him before they dashed off to the family room.

Arlene took Randy by the arm and led him into the living

room. She had him sit on the couch, and she took the chair opposite. "I don't like the way you are sounding," she said. "Are you still upset about Sam Flemming?"

"Of course I'm still upset about Sam Flemming," Randy said irritably. "I didn't lose a patient all through my residency. Now I've lost three."

"There are some things you cannot control," Arlene said.

"None of them should have died," Randy said. "Especially under my care. I'm just a bone doctor screwing around with their extremities."

"I thought you were over your depression," Arlene said.

"I'm having trouble sleeping again," Randy admitted.

"Maybe you should call Dr. Fletcher," Arlene suggested.

Before Randy could respond the phone rang. Arlene jumped. She'd been learning to hate its sound, especially when Randy had post-ops in the hospital. She answered on the second ring, hoping that it was a social call. Unfortunately it wasn't. It was one of the floor nurses at Bartlet Community Hospital wanting to speak with Dr. Portland.

Arlene handed the phone to her husband. He took it reluctantly and put it to his ear. After he'd listened for a moment, his face blanched. He replaced the receiver slowly and raised his eyes to Arlene's.

"It's the knee I did this morning," Randy said. "William Shapiro. He's not doing well. I can't believe it. It sounds the same. He's spiked a fever and he's disoriented. Probably pneumonia."

Arlene stepped up to her husband and put her arms around him and gave him a squeeze. "I'm sorry," she said, not knowing what else to say.

Randy didn't respond. Nor did he try to move for a few minutes. When he did, he silently disengaged Arlene's arms, and went out the back door without speaking. Arlene watched from the kitchen window as his car descended the driveway and pulled out into the street. She straightened up and shook her head. She was worried about her husband, but she didn't know what to do.

2

MONDAY, MAY 3

HAROLD TRAYNOR FINGERED THE MAHOGANY AND inlaid gold gavel he'd bought for himself at Shreve Crump & Low in Boston. He was standing at the head of the library table in the Bartlet Community Hospital. In front of him was the lectern that he had had built for the hospital conference room. Scattered on its surface were his extensive notes which he'd had his secretary type up early that morning. Stretching out from the lectern and scattered down the center of the table was the usual collection of medical paraphernalia in various stages of evaluation by the hospital board. Dominating the confusion was the model of the proposed parking garage.

Traynor checked his watch. It was exactly six P.M. Taking the gavel in his right hand, he struck it sharply against its base. Attentiveness to detail and punctuality were two characteristics Traynor particularly prized.

"I would like herewith to call to order the Executive Committee of the Bartlet Community Hospital," Traynor called out with as much pompousness as he could muster. He was dressed in his best pin-striped suit. On his feet were freshly polished elevator shoes. He was only five foot seven and felt cheated as far as stature was concerned. His dark, receding hair was neatly trimmed and carefully combed over his apical bald spot.

Traynor spent a great deal of time and effort preparing for hospital board meetings, both in terms of content and his appearance. That day he'd gone directly home to shower and change clothes after a day trip to Montpelier. With no time to spare, he did not stop at his office. Harold Traynor was an attorney in Bartlet specializing in estate planning and tax work. He was also a businessman with interests in a number of commercial ventures in the town.

Seated before him were Barton Sherwood, vice chairman; Helen Beaton, president and CEO of the hospital; Michael Caldwell, vice president and medical director of the hospital; Richard Arnsworth, treasurer; Clyde Robeson, secretary; and Dr. Delbert Cantor, current chief of staff.

Strictly following parliamentary procedure as specified in *Robert's Rules of Order,* which he'd purchased after being elected to the chairmanship, Traynor called on Clyde Robeson to read the minutes of the last meeting.

As soon as the minutes had been read and approved, Traynor cleared his throat in preparation for his monthly chairman's report. He looked at each member of his executive committee in turn, making sure they were all attentive. They were, except for Dr. Cantor who was, typically, bored and busily cleaning under his fingernails.

"We face significant challenges here at the Bartlet Community Hospital," Traynor began. "As a referral center we have been spared some of the financial problems of smaller rural hospitals, but not all of them. We're going to have to work even harder than we have in the past if the hospital is to survive these difficult days.

"However, even in these dark times there is occasional light. As some of you have undoubtedly heard, an esteemed client of mine, William Shapiro, passed away last week of pneumonia coming on after knee surgery. While I very much regret Mr. Shapiro's untimely passing, I am pleased to announce officially that Mr. Shapiro had generously designated the hospital as the sole beneficiary of a three-million-dollar insurance policy."

A murmur of approval spread through the people present.

Traynor lifted his hand for silence. "This charitable gesture couldn't have come at a better time. It will pull us out of the red and push us into the black, although not for long. The bad news for the month is the recent discovery that our sinking fund for our major bond issues is considerably short of its projected goals."

Traynor looked directly at Sherwood, whose mustache twitched nervously.

"The fund will need to be bolstered," Traynor said. "A good portion of the three-million-dollar bequest will have to go to that end."

"It wasn't all my fault," Sherwood blurted out. "I was urged to maximize return on the fund. That necessitated risk."

"The chair does not recognize Barton Sherwood," Traynor snapped.

For a moment, Sherwood looked as if he might respond, but instead he remained silent.

Traynor studied his notes in an effort to compose himself after Sherwood's outburst. Traynor hated disorder.

"Thanks to Mr. Shapiro's bequest," Traynor went on, "the sinking fund debacle will not be lethal. The problem is to keep any outside examiners from getting wind of the shortfall. We can't afford to have our bond rating change. Consequently, we will be forced to put off floating a bond issue for the parking garage until the sinking fund is restored.

"As a temporary measure to forestall assaults on our nurses I have instructed our CEO, Helen Beaton, to have lighting installed in the parking lot."

Traynor glanced around the room. According to the *Rules of Order,* the matter should have been presented as a motion, debated, and voted on, but no one moved to be recognized.

"The last item concerns Dr. Dennis Hodges," Traynor said. "As you all know, Dr. Hodges disappeared last March. During this past week I met with our chief of police,

Wayne Robertson, to discuss the case. No clues as to his whereabouts have surfaced. If Dr. Hodges did meet with foul play, there has been no evidence of it, although Chief Robertson allowed that the longer Dr. Hodges is missing, the more likely it is that he is no longer living."

"My guess is he's still around," Dr. Cantor said. "Knowing that bastard, he's probably sitting down in Florida, laughing himself silly every time he thinks of us wrestling with all this bureaucratic bullshit."

Traynor used his gavel. "Please!" he called out. "Let's maintain some order here."

Cantor's bored expression changed to disdain, but he remained silent.

Traynor glared at Dr. Cantor before resuming: "Whatever personal feelings we may have about Dr. Hodges, the fact remains that he played a crucial role in the history of this hospital. If it hadn't been for him this institution would be merely another tiny, rural hospital. His welfare merits our concern.

"I wanted the executive committee to know that Dr. Hodges' estranged wife, Mrs. Hodges, has decided to sell her home. She relocated to her native Boston some years ago. She had held out some hope that her husband might resurface, but based on her conversations with Chief Robertson, she has decided to sever her connections with Bartlet. I only raise this matter now because I think that sometime in the near future the board might wish to erect a memorial befitting Dr. Hodges' considerable contributions to Bartlet Community Hospital."

Having finished, Traynor gathered up his notes and formally turned the meeting over to Helen Beaton so that she could give her monthly president's report. Beaton stood up in her place, pushing her chair back from the table. She was in her mid-thirties with reddish-brown hair cut short. Her face was wide, not unlike Traynor's. She wore a businesslike blue suit accented with a silk scarf.

"I've spoken to several civic groups this month," she said. "My topic on each occasion was the financial plight of the hospital. It was interesting for me to ascertain that most people were generally unaware of our problems even though health-care issues have been almost constantly in the news. What I emphasized in my talks was the economic importance of the hospital to the town and the immediate area. I made it very clear that if the hospital were to close, every business and every merchant would be hurt. After all, the hospital is the largest employer in this part of the state. I also reminded everyone that there is no tax base for the hospital and that fundraising has been and will remain key to keeping the doors open."

Beaton paused as she turned over the first page of her notes. "Now for the bad news," she said, referring to several large graphs illustrating the information she was about to relay. She held the graphs at chest height as she spoke. "Admissions for April were twelve percent over forecast. Our daily census was up eight percent over March, and our average length of stay was up six percent. Obviously these are serious trends as I'm sure our treasurer, Richard Arnsworth, will report."

Beaton held up the last graph. "And finally I have to report that there has been a drop in utilization of the emergency room which, as you know, is not part of our capitation agreement with CMV. And to make matters worse, CMV has refused to pay a number of our ER claims, saying the subscribers violated CMV rules."

"Hell, that's not the hospital's fault," Dr. Cantor said.

"CMV doesn't care about such technicalities," Beaton said. "Consequently, we've been forced to bill the patients directly and they are understandably upset. Most have refused to pay, telling us to go to CMV."

"Health care is becoming a nightmare," Sherwood said.

"Tell that to your representative in Washington," Beaton said.

"Let's not digress," Traynor said.

Beaton looked back at her notes, then continued: "Quality indicators for April were within normal expectations. Incident reports were actually fewer than in March and no new malpractice actions have been initiated."

"Will wonders never cease," Dr. Cantor commented.

"Other disturbing news for April involved union agitation," Beaton continued. "It was reported to us that both dietary and housekeeping have been targeted. Needless to say, unionization would significantly add to our financial problems."

"It's one crisis after another," Sherwood said.

"Two areas of under-utilization," Beaton continued, "are the neonatal intensive care unit and the linear accelerator. During April, I discussed this situation with CMV since our fixed costs for maintaining these units are so high. I emphasized it had been they who demanded these services. CMV promised me that they would look into ferrying patients from areas without these facilities to Bartlet and reimbursing us accordingly."

"That reminds me," Traynor said. As chairman, he felt he had the right to interrupt. "What is the status of the old cobalt-60 machine that the linear accelerator replaced? Have there been any inquiries from the state licensing division or the nuclear regulatory commission?"

"Not a word," Beaton answered. "We informed them the machine is in the process of being sold to a government hospital in Paraguay and that we are waiting for the funds."

"I don't want to get involved in any bureaucratic snafu with that machine," Traynor warned.

Beaton nodded and turned to the last page of her notes. "And finally, I'm afraid I have some additional bad news. Last night just before midnight there was another attempted assault in the parking lot."

"What?" Traynor cried. "Why wasn't I informed about this?"

"I didn't hear about it until this morning," Beaton explained. "I tried to call you as soon as I heard, but you weren't in. I left a message for you to call back but you never did."

"I was in Montpelier all day," Traynor explained. He shook his head in dismay. "Damn, this has to stop. It's a PR nightmare. I hate to imagine what CMV thinks."

"We need that garage," Beaton said.

"The garage has to wait until we can float a bond issue," Traynor said. "I want that lighting done quickly, understand?"

"I've already talked to Werner Van Slyke," Beaton said. "And he's already gotten back to me that he's been in touch with the electrical contractor. I'll follow up on it so that it's done ASAP."

Traynor sat down heavily and blew through pursed lips. "It's almost mind-boggling what running a hospital today entails. Why did I get myself into this?" He picked up the current meeting's agenda, glanced at it, then called Richard Arnsworth, the treasurer, to give his report.

Arnsworth got to his feet. He was a bespectacled, precise, accountant type whose voice was so soft everyone had to strain to hear him. He started by referring everyone to the balance sheet each had received in his information packet that morning.

"What's immediately obvious," Arnsworth said, "is that the monthly expenses still significantly outstrip the monthly capitation payments from CMV. In fact, the gap has expanded relative to the increase in admissions and lengths of stay. We're also losing money on all Medicare patients not enrolled in CMV as well as all indigents who are not enrolled in any plan. The percentage of paying patients or those with standard indemnity insurance is so tiny we cannot cost-shift enough to cover our losses.

"As a result of this continued loss, the hospital's cash position has deteriorated. Consequently, I recommend switching from one hundred and eighty days investing to thirty days."

"It's already been taken care of," Sherwood announced.

When Arnsworth took his seat, Traynor asked for a motion to approve the treasurer's report. It was immediately seconded and carried with no opposition. Traynor then turned to Dr. Cantor to give the medical staff report.

Dr. Cantor got to his feet slowly and leaned his knuckles on the table. He was a big, heavyset man with a pasty complexion. Unlike other presenters he didn't refer to notes.

"Just a couple of things this month," he said casually. Traynor glanced over at Beaton and caught her eye, then shook his head in disgust. He hated Cantor's jaded behavior at their meetings.

"The anesthesiologists are all up in arms," Dr. Cantor said. "But of course it's expected now that they have been officially informed that the hospital is taking over the department, and they're to be on straight salary. I know how they feel since I experienced the same situation during Hodges' tenure."

"Do you think they'll sue?" Beaton asked.

"Of course they'll sue," Dr. Cantor said.

"Let them," Traynor said. "The precedent's been well established with pathology and radiology. I cannot believe they'd think they could continue with private billing while we're under capitation. It doesn't make sense."

"A new utilization manager has been chosen," Dr. Cantor said, changing the subject. "His name is Dr. Peter Chou."

"Will Dr. Chou cause any problems for us?" Traynor asked.

"I doubt it," Dr. Cantor said. "He didn't even want the position."

"I'll meet with him," Beaton said.

Traynor nodded.

"And the last item concerning the medical staff," Dr. Cantor said, "involves M.D. 91. I've been told he's not been drunk all month."

"Leave him on probation just the same," Traynor said. "Let's not take any chances. He's relapsed before."

Dr. Cantor sat down.

Traynor asked if there was any new business. When no one moved, he asked for a motion to adjourn. Dr. Cantor eagerly "so moved." After a resounding chorus of "yeas," Traynor struck the gavel and ended the meeting.

Traynor and Beaton slowly gathered up their papers. Everyone else trooped out of the conference room, heading for the Iron Horse Inn. When the sound of the outer door closing behind the departing group drifted back to the room, Traynor's eyes met Beaton's. Leaving his briefcase, Traynor stepped around the table and passionately embraced her.

Hand in hand they hurriedly left the conference room and retreated across the hall to a couch in Beaton's office as they had so many times before. There in the semi-darkness they made frenzied love just as they had after each executive committee meeting for almost a year. It was a familiar scenario and didn't take long. They didn't bother to remove their clothes.

"I thought it was a good meeting," Traynor said as they rearranged their apparel after they were through.

"I agree," Beaton said. She turned on a light and went over to a wall mirror. "I liked the way you handled the lighting issue for the parking lot. It avoided needless debate."

"Thank you," Traynor said, pleased with himself.

"But I'm worried about the financial situation," Beaton admitted as she reapplied her makeup. "The hospital has to break even at the very least."

"You're right," Traynor admitted with a sigh. "I'm worried too. I'd love to wring some of those CMV people's necks. It's ironic that this 'managed competition' nonsense could very well force us into bankruptcy. That whole year of negotiations with CMV was a lose-lose situation. If we hadn't agreed to capitate, we wouldn't have gotten the contract and we would have had to close like the Valley Hospital. Now that we did agree to capitate, we still might have to close."

"Every hospital is having trouble," Beaton said. "We should keep that in mind, although it's hardly consolation."

"Do you think there is any chance we could renegotiate the contract with CMV?" Traynor asked.

Beaton laughed scornfully. "Not a chance," she said.

"I don't know what else to do," Traynor said. "We're losing money despite our DUM plan that Dr. Cantor proposed."

Beaton laughed with true mirth. "We have to alter that acronym. It sounds ridiculous. How about changing from Drastic Utilization Measures to Drastic Utilization Control. DUC sounds a lot better than DUM."

"I kind of like DUM," Traynor said. "It reminds me that it was dumb to set our capitation rate so low."

"Caldwell and I have come up with an idea that might help significantly," she said. She pulled a chair over and sat down in front of Traynor.

"Shouldn't we be getting down to the Iron Horse?" Traynor said. "We don't want anybody getting suspicious. This is a small town."

"This will only take a moment," Beaton promised. "What Caldwell and I did was brainstorm about how the consultants we hired came up with a capitation rate that has proved to be too low. What we realized was that we'd provided them with hospitalization statistics that CMV had given us. What no one remembered was that those statistics were based on experience CMV had with its own hospital in Rutland."

"You think CMV gave us fraudulent numbers?" Traynor asked.

"No," Beaton said. "But like all HMOs when they are dealing with their own hospitals, CMV has an economic incentive for their doctors to limit hospitalization, something the public has no idea about."

"You mean like actual payments to the doctors?" Traynor asked.

"Exactly," Beaton said. "It's a bonus bribe. The more each doctor cuts his hospitalization rates the bigger the bonus. It's very effective. Caldwell and I believe we can fashion a similar economic incentive here at Bartlet Community Hospital. The only problem is that we will have to fund it with some start-up capital. Once it's operational, it will pay for itself by reducing hospitalization."

"Sounds great," Traynor said with enthusiasm. "Let's pursue it. Maybe this kind of program, combined with DUM, will eliminate the red ink."

"I'll arrange a meeting with Charles Kelley to discuss it," Beaton said as she got her coat.

"While we're on the topic of utilization," Beaton said as they started down the long hall toward the exit, "I hope to heaven that we're not going to get the Certificate of Need for open-heart surgery. It's crucial we don't. We have to keep CMV sending their bypass patients to Boston."

"I agree wholeheartedly," Traynor said as he held the door open for Beaton. They passed out of the hospital into the lower parking area. "That was one of the reasons I was in Montpelier today. I've started some behind-the-scenes negative lobbying."

"If we get that CON we'll be looking at a lot more red ink," Beaton warned.

They arrived at their respective cars which were parked side by side. Before he climbed behind the wheel, Traynor glanced around the dark parking area, particularly up toward the copse of trees that separated the lower lot from the upper.

"It's darker out here than I remembered," he called over to Beaton. "It's like asking for trouble. We need those lights."

"I'll get right on it," she promised.

"What a pain!" Traynor said. "With everything else we have to worry about, we've got to worry about a damn rapist. What are the details about last night's episode?"

"It occurred about midnight," Beaton said. "And this time it wasn't a nurse. It was one of the volunteers, Marjorie Kleber."

"The teacher?" Traynor asked.

"That's right," Beaton said. "Ever since she got sick herself she's been doing a lot of volunteering on weekends."

"How about the rapist?" Traynor asked.

"Same description: about six feet, wearing a ski mask. Ms. Kleber said he had handcuffs."

"That's a nice touch," Traynor said. "How'd she get away?"

"It was just lucky," Beaton said. "The night watchman just happened along while making his rounds."

"Maybe we should beef up security," Traynor suggested.

"That's money we don't have," Beaton reminded him.

"Maybe I should talk to Wayne Robertson and see if the police can do any more," Traynor said.

"I've already done that," Beaton said. "But Robertson doesn't have the manpower to have someone up here every night."

"I wonder if Hodges really did know the rapist's identity?"

"Do you think his disappearance could have had anything to do with his suspicions?" Beaton asked.

Traynor shrugged. "I hadn't thought of that. I suppose it's possible. He wasn't one to keep his opinion to himself."

"It's a scary thought," Beaton said.

"Indeed," Traynor said. "Regardless, I want to be informed about any such assaults immediately. They can have disastrous consequences for the hospital. I especially don't want any surprises at an executive board meeting. It makes me look bad."

"I apologize," Beaton said, "but I did try to call. From now on I'll make sure you are informed."

"See you down at the Iron Horse," Traynor said as he got into his car and started the engine.

3

THURSDAY, MAY 20

"I'VE GOT TO LEAVE TO PICK UP MY CHILD FROM HER after-school program," Angela said to one of her fellow residents, Mark Danforth.

"What are you going to do about all these slides?" Mark asked.

"What can I do?" Angela snapped. "I've got to get my daughter."

"Okay," Mark said. "Don't jump on me. I was only asking. I thought maybe I could help."

"I'm sorry," Angela said. "I'm just strung out. If you could just see these few I'd be forever in your debt." She picked five slides from the rack.

"No problem," Mark said. He added Angela's to his own stack.

Angela covered her microscope, grabbed her things, and ran out of the hospital. No sooner had she pulled out of the lot than she was bogged down in rush-hour Boston traffic.

When Angela finally pulled up to the school, Nikki was sitting forlornly on the front steps. It was not a pretty area. The school was awash with graffiti and surrounded by a sea of concrete. Except for a group of sixth- and seventh-graders shooting baskets beyond a high chain-link fence, there were no grammar-school-aged children in sight. A group of listless teenagers in ridiculously oversized clothing loitered alongside the building. Directly across the street was the cardboard shanty of a homeless person.

"I'm sorry I was late," Angela said as Nikki climbed into the car and plugged in her seat belt.

"It's all right," Nikki said, "but I was a little scared. There was a big problem in school today. The police were here and everything."

"What happened?"

"One of the sixth-grade boys had a gun in the playground," Nikki said calmly. "He shot it and got arrested."

"Was anybody hurt?"

"Nope," Nikki said with a shake of her head.

"Why did he have a gun?" Angela asked.

"He's been selling drugs," Nikki replied.

"I see," Angela said, trying to maintain her composure as well as her daughter could. "How did you hear about this? From the other kids?"

"No, I was there," Nikki said, suppressing a yawn.

Angela's grip on the steering wheel involuntarily tightened. Public school had been David's idea. The two of them had gone to considerable effort in choosing the one that Nikki attended. Up until this episode, Angela had been reasonably satisfied. But now she was appalled, partly because Nikki was able to talk about the incident so matter-of-factly. It was frightening to realize that Nikki viewed this as an ordinary event.

"We had a substitute again today," Nikki said. "And she wouldn't let me do my postural lung drainage after lunch."

"I'm sorry, dear," Angela said. "Do you feel congested?"

"Some," Nikki said. "I was wheezing a little after being outside, but it went away."

"We'll do it as soon as we get home," Angela said. "And

I'll call the school office again, too. I don't know what their problem is."

Angela did know what the problem was: too many kids and not enough staff, and what staff they had was always changing. Every few months Angela had to call to tell them about Nikki's need for respiratory therapy.

While Nikki waited in the car, Angela double-parked and dashed into the local grocery store for something to make for dinner. When she came out there was a parking ticket under the windshield wiper.

"I told the lady you'd be right out," Nikki explained, "but she said 'Tough' and gave it to us anyway."

Angela cursed under her breath.

For the next half hour they cruised around their immediate neighborhood looking for a parking space. Just when Angela was about ready to give up they found a spot.

After putting cold groceries in the refrigerator, Angela and Nikki attended to Nikki's respiratory physiotherapy. Usually they only did it in the morning. But on certain days, usually those with heavy pollution, they had to do it more often.

The routine they had established started with Angela listening with her stethoscope to make sure Nikki didn't need a bronchodilating drug. Then, by using a large beanbag chair that they'd bought at a garage sale, Nikki would assume nine different positions that utilized gravity to help drain specific areas of her lungs. While Nikki held each position, Angela percussed over the lung area with a cupped hand. Each position took two or three minutes. In twenty minutes they were finished.

With the respiratory therapy done, Nikki turned to her homework while Angela went into the galley-like kitchen to start dinner. A half hour later David came home. He was exhausted, having been up the entire previous night attending a number of sick patients.

"What a night!" he said. He tried to give Nikki a kiss on the cheek, but she pulled away, concentrating on her book. She was sitting at the dining-room table. Her bedroom wasn't large enough for a desk.

David stepped into the kitchen and was similarly rebuffed

by Angela, who was busy with the dinner preparations. Twice spurned, David turned to the refrigerator. After having some difficulty getting the door open with both him and Angela in the same small area, he pulled out a beer.

"We had two AIDS patients come in through the ER with just about every disease known to man," he said. "On top of that, there were two cardiac arrests. I never even got to see the inside of the on-call room, much less get any sleep."

"If you're looking for sympathy you're talking to the wrong person," Angela said as she put some pasta on to boil. "You are also in my way."

"You're in a great mood," David said. He moved out of the tiny kitchen and draped himself over one of the stools at the counter that separated the kitchen from the living and dining area.

"My day has been stressful too," she said. "I had to leave unfinished work in order to pick Nikki up from school. I don't think it's fair that I have to do it every day."

"So this is what you're hysterical about?" David said. "Picking Nikki up? I thought that had been discussed and decided. Hell, you're the one who offered, saying your schedule was so much more predictable than mine."

"Can't you two be more quiet?" Nikki said. "I'm trying to read."

"I'm not hysterical!" Angela snapped sotto voce. "I'm just stressed out. I don't like depending on others to do my work. And on top of that, Nikki had some disturbing news today."

"Like what?" David asked.

"Ask her," Angela said.

David slipped off the barstool and squeezed into one of the dining-room chairs. Nikki told him about her day. Angela came into the room and began setting the table around Nikki's books.

"Are you still as supportive of public school when you hear about guns and drugs in the sixth grade?" Angela asked.

"Public schools have to be supported," David said. "I went to public school."

"Times have changed," Angela said.

"If people like us run away," David said, "the schools don't have a chance."

"I'm not willing to be idealistic when it comes to my daughter's safety," Angela snapped.

Once dinner was ready, they ate their spaghetti marinara and salads in strained silence. Nikki continued to read, ignoring her parents. Angela sighed loudly several times and ran her fingers through her hair. She was on the verge of tears. David fumed. After working as hard as he had for the previous thirty-six hours he did not think he deserved this kind of treatment.

Angela suddenly scraped back her chair, picked up her dish, and dropped it into the sink. It broke and both David and Nikki jumped.

"Angela," David said, struggling to keep his voice under control. "You're being overly emotional. Let's talk about picking Nikki up. There has to be another solution."

Angela wiped a few wayward tears from the corners of her eyes. She resisted the temptation to lash back at David and tell him that his conception of himself as the rational, agreeable partner was hardly reality.

Angela turned around from facing the sink. "You know," she said, "the real problem is that we have been avoiding making a decision about what to do come July first."

"I hardly think this is the opportune time to discuss what we are going to do with the rest of our lives," David said. "We're exhausted."

"Oh, beans," Angela said. She returned to the table and took her seat. "You never think it's the right time. The problem is time is running out, and no decision is a decision of sorts. July first is less than a month and a half away."

"Okay," David said with resignation. "Let me get my lists." He started to get up. Angela restrained him.

"We hardly need your lists," Angela said. "We have three choices. We've been waiting for New York to respond and they did three days ago. Here are our choices in a nutshell: we can go to New York and I'll start a fellowship in forensics and you in respiratory medicine; we can stay here in

Boston where I'll do forensics and you'll go to the Harvard School of Public Health; or we can go to Bartlet and start to work."

David ran his tongue around the inside of his mouth. He tried to think. He was numb from fatigue. He wanted his lists, but Angela still had a hold on his arm.

"It's a little scary leaving academia," David said finally.

"I couldn't agree more," Angela said. "We've been students for so long it's hard to think of any other life."

"It's true we've had little personal time over these last four years," he said.

"Quality of life has to become an issue at some point," Angela agreed. "The reality is that if we stay here in Boston we'll probably have to stay in this apartment. We have too much debt to do anything else."

"It would be about the same if we went to New York," David said.

"Unless we accepted help from my parents," Angela said.

"We've avoided that in the past," David reminded her. "There have always been too many strings attached to their help."

"I agree," Angela said. "Another thing that we have to consider is Nikki's condition."

"I want a dog," Nikki said.

"Nikki's been doing okay," David said.

"But there's a lot of pollution here and in New York," Angela said. "That's bound to take its toll. And I'm getting pretty tired of all the crime here in the city."

"Are you saying you want to go to Bartlet?" David asked.

"No," Angela said, "I'm just trying to think of all the issues. But I have to admit, when I hear about guns and drugs in the sixth grade, Bartlet starts to sound better and better."

"I wonder if it is as heavenly as we remember," David questioned. "Since we go so few places maybe we've idealized it too much."

"There's one way to find out," Angela said.

"Let's go back!" Nikki cried.

"All right," David said. "Today's Thursday. How about Saturday?"

"Sounds good to me," Angela said.

"Yippee!" Nikki said.

4

FRIDAY, MAY 21

TRAYNOR SIGNED ALL THE LETTERS HE'D DICTATED that morning and piled them neatly on the corner of his desk. Eagerly he got up and pulled on his coat. He was on his way through the outer office en route to the Iron Horse for lunch when his secretary, Collette, called him back to take a call from Tom Baringer.

Muttering under his breath, Traynor returned to his desk. Tom was too important a client to miss his call.

"You'll never guess where I am," Tom said. "I'm in the emergency room waiting for Dr. Portland to come in to put me back together."

"My God, what happened?" Traynor asked.

"Something stupid," Tom admitted. "I was cleaning some leaves out of my gutters when the ladder I was on fell over. I broke my damn hip. At least that's what the doctor tells me here in the emergency room."

"I'm sorry," Traynor said.

"Oh, it could be worse," Tom said. "But obviously I

won't be able to make the meeting we had scheduled for this afternoon."

"Of course," Traynor said. "Was there something important you wanted to discuss?"

"It can wait," Tom said. "But listen, as long as I have you on the phone, how about giving the powers that be here at the hospital a call. I figure I deserve some VIP attention."

"You got it," Traynor said. "I'll see to it personally. I'm just on my way out to have lunch with the hospital's CEO."

"Good timing," Tom said. "Put in the good word."

After hanging up, Traynor told his secretary to cancel Tom's appointment and leave the slot open. The break would give him a chance to catch up on dictation.

Traynor was first to arrive for his luncheon meeting. After ordering a dry martini, he scanned the beam-ceilinged room. As usual of late, he'd been given the best table in the house, one in a cozy bay with a particularly dramatic view of the Roaring River which raced past the rear of the inn. Traynor's pleasure was enhanced when he saw Jeb Wiggins, his old rival and a scion of one of the few old moneyed families of Bartlet, sitting at a far less conspicuous table. Jeb had always treated Traynor with condescension. Traynor's father had worked in the coat-hanger factory, which at that time had been one of the Wigginses' holdings. Traynor relished the role reversal: now he was running the biggest business in town.

Helen Beaton and Barton Sherwood arrived together. "Sorry we're late," Sherwood said, holding back Beaton's chair.

Beaton and Sherwood were served their usual drinks and they all ordered their meals. As soon as the waiter left them, Beaton spoke: "I have some good news. I met with Charles Kelley this morning, and he has no problem with our idea of instituting a bonus program for the CMV doctors. His only concern is whether it would cost CMV anything, which it won't. He promised to run the idea past his bosses, but I don't anticipate any problem."

"Wonderful," Traynor said.

"We'll be meeting again on Monday," Beaton added. "I'd like you to attend if you have the time."

"By all means," Traynor said.

"Now all we need is the start-up capital," Beaton said. "So I met with Barton and I think we have it solved." Beaton gave Sherwood's arm a squeeze.

Sherwood leaned forward and spoke in hushed tones: "Remember that small slush fund we'd created with the kickbacks from the construction on the radiotherapy building? I'd deposited it in the Bahamas. What I'll do is bring it back in small increments as needed. Also we can use some of it for vacations in the Bahamas. That's the easiest. We can even pay for the air tickets in the Bahamas."

The food arrived and no one spoke until the waitress had departed.

"We thought a vacation in the Bahamas could function as a grand prize," Beaton explained. "It could be awarded to the doctor with the lowest hospitalization percentage for the year."

"That's perfect," Traynor said. "This whole idea is sounding better and better."

"We'd better get it up and running ASAP," Beaton said. "So far the May figures are worse than those for April. Admissions are higher and the money loss correspondingly greater."

"I have some good news," Sherwood said. "The hospital sinking fund is back to its projected level with the infusion of the cash from the insurance bequest. It was done in a way that none of the bond examiners will ever detect."

"It's just one crisis after another," Traynor complained. He wasn't about to give Sherwood credit for fixing a problem he'd created.

"Do you want me to go ahead with the bond issue for the parking garage?" Sherwood asked.

"No," Traynor answered. "Unfortunately, we can't. We have to go back to the Board of Selectmen for another vote. Their approval had been contingent on starting the project immediately." With a scornful expression Traynor gestured with his head toward a neighboring table. "The Selectmen's chairman, Jeb Wiggins, thinks the tourist season might get screwed up if we build during the summer."

"How unfortunate," Sherwood said.

"I've got a bit of good news myself," Traynor added. "I just heard this morning that our CON for open-heart surgery has been turned down for this year. Isn't that terrible?"

"Oh, what a tragedy," Beaton said with a laugh. "Thank God!"

After the coffee had been served, Traynor remembered the call from Tom Baringer. He relayed the information on to Beaton.

"I'm already aware of Mr. Baringer's admission," Beaton said. "Some time ago I programmed a tickler file into the computer to alert me when such a patient is hospitalized. I've already spoken to Caldwell and he'll be taking care to be sure Mr. Baringer gets proper VIP treatment. What's the value of the fund?"

"One million," Traynor said. "It's not huge, but nothing to scoff at."

After they had finished their lunch, they walked out into the bright late spring sunshine.

"What's the status on the lighting of the parking lots?" Traynor asked.

"It's all done," Beaton said. "It's been done for over a week. But we decided to restrict the lighting to the lower lot. The upper is used only during the day, and by doing only the lower, we saved a considerable amount of money."

"Sounds reasonable," Traynor said.

Close to the Green Mountain National Bank they ran into Wayne Robertson. His wide-brimmed, trooper style hat was low on his forehead to shield his eyes from the sun. As added protection he was wearing highly reflective sunglasses.

"Afternoon," Traynor said amicably.

Robertson touched the brim of his hat in a form of salute.

"Any startling developments in the Hodges case?" Traynor asked.

"Hardly," Robertson said. "In fact, we're thinking about dropping it."

"I wouldn't be too premature," Traynor warned. "Remember, that old geezer had a penchant for appearing when least expected."

"And unwanted," Beaton added.

"Dr. Cantor thinks he's in Florida," Robertson said. "I'm starting to believe it myself. I think that little scandal about the hospital taking care of his house embarrassed him enough to leave town."

"I would have thought he'd have thicker skin than that," Traynor said. "But who am I to guess."

After exchanging farewells and good wishes for the weekend, the four returned to their respective jobs.

As Beaton drove up the hill toward the hospital, she thought about Traynor and her relationship with him. She wasn't happy; she wanted more. Trysts once or twice a month were hardly what she'd expected.

Beaton had met Traynor several years previously when he'd come to Boston to take a refresher course in tax law. She'd been working in the city as an assistant administrator in one of the Harvard hospitals. The attraction was instantaneous and mutual. They spent a torrid week together, then rendezvoused intermittently until he'd recruited her to come to Bartlet to run the hospital. She'd been led to believe that they would eventually live together, but so far it hadn't happened. Traynor had not gotten the divorce he'd promised was imminent. Beaton felt she had to do something to rectify the situation; she just didn't know what.

Back at the hospital, Beaton went directly to room 204, where she expected to find Tom Baringer. She intended to make sure he was comfortable. He wasn't there. Instead Beaton was surprised to discover another patient: a woman by the name of Alice Nottingham. Beaton set her jaw, descended to the first floor, and marched into Caldwell's office.

"Where's Baringer?" she asked curtly.

"Room 204," Caldwell said.

"Unless Mr. Baringer has had a sex change operation and is going by the name of Alice, he's not in 204."

Caldwell quickly got to his feet. "Something's gone wrong." He pushed past Beaton and hurried across the hall to admissions. There he sought out Janice Sperling and asked her what had happened to Tom Baringer.

"I put him in 209," Janice said.

"I told you to put him in 204," Caldwell said.

"I know," Janice admitted. "But since we talked, 209 came available. It's a larger room. You said Mr. Baringer was a special patient. I thought he'd like 209 better."

"204 has a better view, plus it has the new orthopedic bed," Caldwell said. "The man has a broken hip. Either change rooms or change beds."

"Okay," Janice said, rolling her eyes. Some people could never be pleased.

Caldwell went to Beaton's office and stuck his head through the door. "I'm sorry for not having followed up on that situation," he said. "But it will be rectified within the hour. I promise."

Beaton nodded and went back to her work.

5

SATURDAY, MAY 22

DAVID HAD SET THE ALARM FOR FIVE FORTY-FIVE AS if it were a normal workday. By six-fifteen he was on his way to the hospital. The temperature had already climbed into the low seventies and the skies were clear. Before nine he was finished with his rounds and on his way home.

"Okay, you guys," he called as he entered the apartment. "I don't want to spend this whole day waiting. Let's get this show on the road."

Nikki appeared in her doorway. "That's not fair, Daddy. We've been waiting for you."

"Just kidding," David said with a laugh as he gave Nikki a playful tickle.

Soon they were off. Before long, urban sprawl gave way to tree-dotted suburbia followed by long stretches of forest. The farther north they went, the prettier the surroundings became, especially now that leaves were on the trees.

When they reached Bartlet, David slowed to a crawl. Like eager tourists they drank in the sights.

"This is even more picturesque than I remembered," Angela said.

"There's that same puppy!" Nikki cried. She pointed across the street. "Can we stop?"

David pulled into an empty diagonal parking slot. "You're right," he said. "I recognize the lady."

"I recognize the dog," Nikki said. She opened the car door and got out.

"Just a second," Angela called. She jumped out of the car and took Nikki's hand to cross the street. David followed.

"Hello again," the woman said when Nikki approached. The puppy caught sight of Nikki and strained at its leash. As Nikki bent down, the dog licked her face. Nikki laughed with surprise.

"I don't know if you'd be interested, but Mr. Staley's retriever just had puppies a few weeks ago," the woman said. "They're right over in the hardware store across the street."

"Can we go see them?" Nikki pleaded.

"Why not," David said. He thanked the woman.

Recrossing the street the Wilsons entered the hardware store. Near the front in a makeshift playpen was Mr. Staley's dog, Molly, suckling five floppy puppies.

"They're adorable," Nikki cried. "Can I pet them?"

"I don't know," David said. He turned to look for a store attendant and practically bumped into Mr. Staley, who was standing directly behind them.

"Sure, she can pet them," Mr. Staley said after introducing himself. "In fact, they're for sale. No way I need six golden retrievers."

Nikki collapsed on her knees and, reaching into the pen, gently stroked one of the puppies. He responded by attaching himself to Nikki's finger as if it were a teat. Nikki squealed with delight.

"Pick him up if you like," Mr. Staley said. "He's the brute of the litter."

Nikki scooped the puppy up in her arms. The tiny dog snuggled against her cheek and licked her nose.

"I love him," Nikki said. "I wish we could get him. Can we? I'll take care of him."

David felt an unexpected surge of tears that he had to forcibly suppress. He took his eyes off Nikki and looked at Angela. Angela dabbed a tissue into the corners of her eyes and glanced up at her husband. Their eyes met in a moment of complete understanding. Nikki's modest request affected them even more than it had on their first visit to Bartlet. Considering all that she'd been through with her cystic fibrosis, it wasn't much to ask for.

"Are you thinking what I'm thinking?" David asked.

"I think so," Angela said. Her tears gave way to a smile. "It would mean we could buy a house."

"Goodbye, crime and pollution," he said. He looked down at Nikki. "Okay," he said. "You can have the dog. We're moving to Bartlet!"

Nikki's face lit up. She hugged the puppy to her chest as it licked her face.

David turned to Mr. Staley and settled on a price.

"I figure they will be ready to leave the mother in four weeks or so," Mr. Staley said.

"That will be perfect," David said. "We'll be coming up here at the end of the month."

With some difficulty, Nikki was separated from her puppy, and the Wilsons went back outside.

"What will we do now?" Angela asked with excitement.

"Let's celebrate," David said. "Let's have lunch at the inn."

A few minutes later they were sitting at a cloth-covered table with a view of the river. David and Angela each ordered a glass of white wine. Nikki had a cranberry juice. They touched their glasses.

"I'd like to toast our arrival in the Garden of Eden," David said.

"And I'd like to toast the beginning of paying back our debt," Angela said.

"Hear, hear!" David said, and they drank.

"Can you believe it?" Angela asked. "Our combined income will be over one hundred and twenty thousand dollars."

David sang a few bars of the song "We're in the Money."

"I think I'll call my dog Rusty," Nikki said.

"That's a wonderful name," David said.

"What do you think about me earning twice what you do?" Angela teased.

David had known the barb would come at some point so he was prepared. "You'll be earning it in your dark, dreary lab," he teased back. "At least I'll be seeing real, live, appreciative people."

"Won't it challenge your delicate masculinity?" Angela continued.

"Not in the slightest," David said. "Also it's nice to know that if we ever get divorced I'll get alimony."

Angela lunged across the table to give David a poke in the ribs.

David parried Angela's playful gesture. "Besides," he said, "that kind of differential won't last much longer. It's a legacy of a past era. Pathologists, like surgeons and other overpaid specialists, will soon be brought down to earth."

"Says who?" Angela demanded.

"Says me," David said.

After lunch, they decided to go straight to the hospital to let Caldwell know their decision. Once they presented themselves to his secretary, they were ushered in right away.

"That's fantastic!" Caldwell said when they informed him of their decision. "Does CMV know yet?" he asked.

"Not yet," David said.

"Come on," Caldwell said. "Let's go give them the good news."

Charles Kelley was equally pleased with the news. After a congratulatory handshake he asked David when he thought he'd be ready to start seeing patients.

"Just about immediately," David said without hesitation. "July first."

"Your residency isn't over until the thirtieth," Kelley said. "Don't you want some time to get settled?"

"With our debt," David said, "the sooner we start working the better we'll feel."

"Same for you?" Caldwell asked Angela.

"Absolutely," Angela answered.

David asked if they could go back to the office he'd be assigned. Kelley was happy to oblige.

David paused outside the waiting room door, fantasizing how his name would look in the empty slot under Dr. Randall Portland's name. It had been a long, hard road, starting from the moment in the eighth grade when he'd decided to become a doctor, but he'd finally made it.

David opened the door and stepped over the threshold. His reverie was broken when a figure dressed in surgical scrubs leaped off the waiting room couch.

"What is the meaning of this?" the man angrily demanded.

It took David a moment to recognize Dr. Portland. It was partly due to the unexpectedness of the encounter, but it was also because Dr. Portland had changed in the month since David had last seen him. He'd lost considerable weight; his eyes seemed sunken, even haunted, and his cheeks were gaunt.

Kelley pushed his way to the front of the group, reintroduced David and Randall, and then explained to Randall why they were there. Dr. Portland's anger waned. Like a balloon losing its air, he collapsed back onto the couch. David noticed that not only had Randall lost weight but he was pale.

"Sorry to have bothered you," David said.

"I was just getting a bit of sleep," Dr. Portland explained. His voice was flat. He sounded as exhausted as he looked. "I did a case this morning, and I felt tired."

"Tom Baringer?" Caldwell asked.

Dr. Portland nodded.

"I hope it went okay," Caldwell said.

"The operation went fine," Dr. Portland said. "Now we have to keep our fingers crossed for the post-op course."

David apologized again, then herded everyone, including himself, out of the office.

"Sorry about that," Kelley said.

"What's wrong with him?" David asked.

"Nothing that I know of," Kelley said.

"He doesn't look well," David said.

"I thought he looked depressed," Angela said.

"He's busy," Kelley admitted. "I'm sure he's just over-worked."

The group stopped outside Kelley's office. "Now that we know you are coming," Kelley said, "is there anything that we can do to help?"

"We'll have to go look at a few houses," Angela said. "Who do you suggest we call?"

"Dorothy Weymouth," Caldwell said.

"He's right," Kelley said.

"She's far and away the best realtor in town," Caldwell added. "Come back to my office and use my phone."

A half hour later, the whole family was in Dorothy Weymouth's office on the second floor of the building across the street from the diner. She was a huge, pleasant woman attired in a shapeless, tent-like dress.

"I have to tell you, I'm impressed," Dorothy said. Her voice was surprisingly high-pitched for such a large woman. "While you were on your way over here from the hospital, Barton Sherwood called to tell me the bank is eager to help you. Now it doesn't happen often that the president of the bank calls before I've even met the client.

"I'm not sure exactly what your tastes are," Dorothy said as she began putting photos of properties currently on the market out on her desk. "So you'll have to help me. Do you think you'd like a white clapboard house in town or an isolated stone farmhouse? What about size? Is that an important consideration? Are you planning any more children?"

Both David and Angela tensed at the question of whether they would have more children. Until Nikki's birth, neither had suspected they were carriers of the cystic fibrosis gene. It was a reality they could not ignore.

Unaware she'd hit a nerve, Dorothy continued laying out photos of homes, while she maintained a steady monologue.

"Here's a particularly charming property that's just come on the market. It's a beauty."

Angela caught her breath. She picked up the photo. Nikki tried to look over her shoulder.

"I do like this one," Angela said. She handed the picture to David. It was a brick, late Georgian or early Federal

style home with double bow windows on either side of a
central, paneled front door. Fluted white columns held up a
pedimented portico over the door. Above the pediment was
a large Palladian window.

"That's one of the oldest brick homes in the area," Dorothy
said. "It was built around 1820."

"What's this in the back?" David asked, pointing to the
photo.

Dorothy looked. "That's the old silo," she said. "Behind
the house and connected to it is a barn. You can't see the
barn in that photo because the picture was taken directly in
front of the house, down the hill. The property used to be
a dairy farm, quite a profitable one, I understand."

"It's gorgeous," Angela said wistfully. "But I'm sure we
could never afford it."

"You could according to what Barton Sherwood told
me," Dorothy said. "Besides, I know that the owner, Clara
Hodges, is very eager to sell. I'm sure we could get you a
good deal. Anyway, it's worth a look. Let's pick four or
five others and go see them."

Cleverly orchestrating the order of the visits, Dorothy left
the Hodges house for last. It was located about two and a
half miles south of the town center on the crest of a small
hill. The nearest house was an eighth of a mile down the
road. When they pulled into the driveway, Nikki noticed
the frog pond and was immediately sold.

"The pond is not only picturesque," Dorothy said, "it's
also great for skating in the wintertime."

Dorothy pulled to a halt between the house and the
frog pond and slightly to the side. From there they had
a view of the structure with its connected barn. Neither
Angela nor David said a word. They were both awed by
the home's noble and imposing character. They now realized that the house was three stories instead of two. They
could see four dormers on each side of the pitched slate
roof.

"Are you sure Mr. Sherwood thinks we can afford this?"
David asked.

"Absolutely," Dorothy said. "Come on, let's see the interior."

In a state of near hypnosis, David and Angela followed
Dorothy around the inside of the house. Dorothy continued
her steady stream of realtor chatter, saying things like "This
room has so much promise" and "With just a little creativity
and work, this room would be so cozy." Any problems
such as peeling wallpaper or dry-rotted window sashes she
minimized. The good points, like the sizes of the many
fireplaces and the beautiful cornice work, she lauded with
an uninterrupted flow of superlatives.

David insisted on seeing everything. They even descended
the gray granite steps into the basement, which seemed
exceptionally damp and musty.

"There seems to be a strange smell," he said. "Is there a
water problem down here?"

"Not that I've heard of," Dorothy said. "But it is a nice
big basement. There's room enough for a shop if you're the
handy type."

Angela suppressed a giggle as well as a disparaging
comment. She'd been about to say that David had trouble
changing light bulbs, but she held her tongue.

"There's no floor," David said. He bent down and pried
up a bit of dirt with his fingernail.

"It's a packed earth floor," Dorothy explained. "It's common in older homes like this. And this basement has other features typical of a nineteenth-century dwelling." She
pulled open a heavy wooden door. "Here's the old root
cellar."

There was shelving for preserves and bins for potatoes
and apples. The room was poorly lit with one small bulb.

"It's scary," Nikki said. "It's like a dungeon."

"This will be handy if your parents ever come to visit,"
David said. "We can put them up down here."

Angela rolled her eyes.

After showing them the root cellar, Dorothy took them
over to the other corner of the basement and proudly pointed
out a large freezer chest. "This house has both the old and
the new methods of food storage," she said.

Before they left the basement Dorothy opened a second
door. Behind it was a second flight of granite steps which
led up to a hatch-like door. "These stairs lead out to the

back yard," Dorothy explained. "That's why the firewood is here." She pointed to several cords of firewood neatly stacked against the wall.

The last thing of note in the basement was the huge furnace. It looked almost like an old-fashioned steam locomotive. "This used to burn coal," Dorothy explained, "but it was converted to oil." She pointed out a large fuel tank perched on cinder blocks in the corner opposite the freezer chest.

David nodded, though he didn't know much about furnaces no matter what they burned.

On the way back up the steps to the kitchen, David smelled the musty smell again and asked about the septic system.

"The septic system is fine," Dorothy said. "We had it inspected. It's to the west of the house. I can point out the leach field if you like."

"As long as it's been inspected, I'm sure it's okay," David said. He had no idea what a leach field was or what it should look like.

David and Angela had Dorothy drop them off at the Green Mountain National Bank. They were nervous and excited at the same time. Barton Sherwood saw them almost immediately.

"We found a house that we like," David said.

"I'm not surprised," Sherwood said. "There are lots of wonderful houses in Bartlet."

"It's a house owned by Clara Hodges," David continued. He handed over the real estate summary sheet. "The asking price is two hundred and fifty thousand dollars. What does the bank think about the property and the price?"

"It's a great old house," Sherwood said. "I know it well." He scanned the summary sheet. "And the location is fabulous. In fact it borders my own property. As far as the price is concerned, I think it's a steal."

"So the bank would be willing to underwrite our purchase at that price?" Angela questioned. She wanted to be sure. It seemed too good to be true.

"Of course, you'll offer less," Sherwood said. "I'd suggest an initial offer of one hundred and ninety thousand.

But the bank will be willing to back the purchase up to the asking price."

Fifteen minutes later David, Angela, and Nikki stepped back out into the warm Vermont sunshine. They had never bought a house before. It was a monumental decision. Yet having decided to come to Bartlet they were in a decisive frame of mind.

"Well?" David asked.

"I can't imagine finding something we'd like better," Angela said.

"I can even have a desk in my room," Nikki said.

David reached out and tousled Nikki's hair. "With as many rooms as that house has, you can have your own study."

"Let's do it," Angela said.

Back in Dorothy's office they told the pleased realtor their decision. A few minutes later Dorothy had Clara Hodges on the phone, and although it was a bit unconventional, a deal was concluded orally at a price of two hundred and ten thousand dollars.

As Dorothy drew up the formal documents, David and Angela exchanged glances. They were stunned to realize they were the new owners of a home more gracious than they could have ever hoped to have owned for years to come. Yet there was some anxiety as well. Their debt had more than doubled, to over three hundred and fifty thousand dollars.

By the end of the day, after a bit of shuttling back and forth between Dorothy's office and the bank, all the appropriate papers were filled out and a closing date was set.

"I have some names for you," Dorothy said when they were through with the paperwork. "Pete Bergan does odd jobs around the town. He's not the world's smartest fellow, but he does good work. And for painting, I use John Murray."

David wrote the names down with their phone numbers.

"And if you need a sitter for Nikki, my older sister, Alice Doherty, would be delighted to help out. She lost her husband a few years ago. Besides, she lives out your way."

"That's a wonderful tip," Angela said. "With both of us working we'll need someone just about every day."

Later that same afternoon David and Angela met the handyman and the painter out at their new home. They arranged to have a general cleaning as well as a minimum of painting and repairing to make the house weatherproof.

After one more visit to the hardware store so Nikki could pet Rusty one last time and say goodbye, the Wilsons got on the road for the drive back to Boston. Angela drove. Neither David nor Nikki dozed. They were all keyed up from what they'd accomplished and full of dreams about their new life that was imminently to begin.

"What did you think about Dr. Portland?" David asked after a period of silence.

"What do you mean?" said Angela.

"The man was hardly friendly," David said.

"I think we woke him up."

"Still, most people wouldn't act that irritable. Besides, he looked like death warmed over. He's changed so drastically in a month."

"I thought he sounded and looked depressed."

David shrugged. "He wasn't even that friendly the first time we met him, now that I think of it. All he wanted to know was whether I played basketball. Something about him makes me feel uncomfortable. I hope sharing an office with him doesn't become a sore spot."

It was dark by the time they returned to Boston; they'd stopped for dinner on the way. When they got back to their apartment, they looked around in wonderment, amazed that they'd been able to live for four years in such a tiny, claustrophobic space.

"This entire apartment would fit into the library of the new house," Angela commented.

David and Angela decided to call their parents to share the excitement. David's were delighted. Having retired to Amherst, New Hampshire, they felt like Bartlet was next door. "We'll get to see a lot more of you guys," they said.

Angela's parents had a different response.

"It's easy to drop out of the academic big leagues," Dr. Walter Christopher said. "But it's hard getting back in. I think you could have asked my opinion before you made such a foolish move. Here's your mother."

Angela's mother came on the line and expressed her disappointment that Angela and David hadn't come to New York. "Your father spent a lot of time talking to all sorts of people to make sure you had good positions here," she said. "I think it was inconsiderate of you not to take advantage of his effort."

After Angela hung up she turned to David. "They've never been particularly supportive," she said. "So I suppose I shouldn't have expected them to change now."

6

MONDAY, MAY 24

TRAYNOR ARRIVED AT THE HOSPITAL WITH TIME TO spare for his afternoon meeting. Instead of going directly to Helen Beaton's office, he went to the patient area on the second floor and walked down to room 209. After taking a breath to fortify himself, he pushed the door open. Being chairman of the board of directors of the hospital had not changed Traynor's aversion to medical situations, particularly bad medical situations.

Conscious of breathing shallowly in the presence of the seriously ill, Traynor moved across the darkened room and approached the large orthopedic bed. Bending over and scrupulously avoiding touching anything, he peered at his client, Tom Baringer. Tom didn't look good, and Traynor didn't want to get too close lest he catch some awful illness. Tom's face was gray and his breathing was labored. A plastic tube snaked from behind his head, feeding oxygen into his nose. His eyes were closed with tape, and ointment oozed out between his eyelids.

"Tom," Traynor called softly. When there was no response, he called louder. But Tom did not move.

"He's beyond responding."

Traynor jumped and the blood drained from his own face. Except for Tom, he'd thought he was alone.

"His pneumonia is not responding to treatment," the stranger said angrily. He'd been sitting in a corner of the room. He was cloaked in shadows; Traynor could not see his face.

"He's dying like the others," the man said.

"Who are you?" Traynor asked. He wiped his forehead where perspiration had instantly appeared.

The man got to his feet. Only then could Traynor see that he was dressed in surgical scrubs, covered with a white jacket.

"I'm Mr. Baringer's doctor, Randy Portland." He advanced to the opposite side of the bed and gazed down at his comatose patient. "The operation was a success but the patient is about to die. I suppose you've heard a variation of that quip before."

"I suppose I have," Traynor said nervously. Shock at Dr. Portland's presence was changing to anxious concern. There was something decidedly strange about the man's manner. Traynor wasn't sure what he would do next.

"The hip has been repaired," Dr. Portland said. He lifted the edge of the sheet so Traynor could see the tightly sutured wound. "No problem whatsoever. But unfortunately it's been a fatal cure. There's no way Mr. Baringer will walk out of here." Portland dropped the sheet and defiantly raised his eyes to Traynor's. "There's something wrong with this hospital," he said. "I'm not going to take all the blame."

"Dr. Portland," Traynor said hesitantly. "You don't look well to me. Maybe you should see a doctor yourself."

Dr. Portland threw back his head and laughed. But it was a hollow, mirthless laugh which ended as suddenly as it had begun. "Maybe you're right," he said. "Maybe I'll do that." He then turned and left the room.

Traynor felt stunned. He looked down at Tom as if he expected him to wake up and explain Dr. Portland's behavior. Traynor could understand how doctors might become emotionally involved in their patients' conditions, but Portland seemed unhinged.

Traynor tried one last time to communicate with Tom. Recognizing the futility, he backed away from the bed and slipped out of the room. Warily he looked for Dr. Portland. When he didn't see him, Traynor quickly walked to Beaton's office. Caldwell and Kelley were already there.

"Do you all know Dr. Portland?" Traynor asked as he took a chair.

Everyone nodded. Kelley spoke: "He's one of ours. He's an orthopedic surgeon."

"I just had a very peculiar and unnerving encounter with him," Traynor said. "On my way here I popped in to see my client, Tom Baringer, who's very sick. Dr. Portland was sitting in the corner of Tom's darkened room. I didn't even see him when I first went in. When he spoke, he acted strangely, even belligerently. I imagine he's distraught over Tom's condition, but he said something about not taking all the blame and that there was something wrong with the hospital."

"I think he's been under strain from overwork," Kelley said. "We're short at least one orthopedic surgeon. Unfortunately our recruiting efforts have been unsuccessful so far."

"He looked ill to me," Traynor said. "I advised him to see a doctor, but he only laughed."

"I'll have a talk with him," Kelley promised. "Maybe he needs a little time off. We can always get a locum tenens for a few weeks."

"Well, so much for that," Traynor said, trying to compose himself more in keeping with his role as chairman of the board. "Let's get our meeting underway."

"Before we do that," Kelley said, flashing one of his winning smiles, "there's something I have to say. My superiors are very upset about the negative ruling on the CON for open-heart surgery."

"We were disappointed about that as well," Traynor said nervously. He didn't like beginning on a negative note. "Unfortunately it's out of our hands. Montpelier turned us down even though we thought we'd made a good case."

"CMV had expected the open-heart program to be up and running by now," Kelley said. "It was part of the contract."

"It was part of the contract provided we got the CON," Traynor corrected. "But we didn't. So let's look at what has been done. We've updated the MRI, built the neonatal ICU, and replaced the old cobalt-60 machine with a new state-of-the-art linear accelerator. I think we have been showing remarkably good faith, and we've been doing all this while the hospital has been losing money."

"Whether the hospital loses money or not is not CMV's concern," Kelley said. "Especially since it's probably due to minor management inefficiencies."

"I think you are wrong," Traynor said, swallowing his anger at Kelley's insulting insinuation. He hated being put on the defensive, especially by this young, brazen bureaucrat. "I think CMV has to be concerned if we are losing money. If things get much worse we could be forced to close our doors. That would be bad for everyone. We have to work together. There's no other choice."

"If Bartlet Community Hospital goes under," Kelley said, "CMV would take its business elsewhere."

"That's not so easy anymore," Traynor said. "The two other hospitals in the area are no longer functioning as acute care facilities."

"No problem," Kelley said casually. "If need be, we would ferry our patients to the CMV hospital in Rutland."

Traynor's heart skipped a beat. The possibility of CMV ferrying its patients had never occurred to him. He'd hoped that the lack of nearby hospitals would give him some bargaining power. Apparently it didn't.

"I don't mean to imply that I'm not willing to work together with you people," Kelley said. "This should be a dynamic relationship. After all, we have the same goal: the health of the community." He smiled again as if to show off his perfectly straight white teeth.

"The problem is the current capitation rate is too low," Traynor said bluntly. "Hospitalization from CMV is running more than ten percent above projections. We can't support such an overrun for long. We need to renegotiate the capitation rate. It's that simple."

"The capitation rate doesn't get renegotiated until the contract term is over," Kelley said amicably. "What do you take us for? You offered the present rate in a competitive bidding process. And you signed the contract. So it stands. What I can do is start negotiations on a capitation rate for ER services, which was left out of the initial agreement."

"Capitating the ER is not something we can do at the moment," Traynor said, feeling perspiration run down the insides of his arms. "We have to stem our red ink first."

"Which is the reason for our meeting this afternoon," Beaton said, speaking up for the first time. She then presented the final version of the proposed bonus program for CMV physicians.

"Each gatekeeper CMV physician will be allocated a bonus payment provided his number of monthly hospital days per assigned subscriber stays at a given level. As the level goes down, the payment goes up and vice versa."

Kelley laughed. "Sounds like clever bribery to me. As sensitive as doctors are to economic incentives, it certainly should reduce hospitalization and surgery."

"It's essentially the same plan CMV has in effect at the CMV hospital in Rutland."

"If it works there then it should work here," Kelley said. "I have no trouble with it, provided it doesn't cost CMV anything."

"It will be totally funded by the hospital," Beaton said.

"I'll present it to my superiors," Kelley said. "Is that it for this meeting?"

"That's it," Beaton said.

Kelley got to his feet.

"We'd appreciate all the speed you can muster," Traynor said. "I'm afraid we're looking at a lot of red ink on our balance sheet."

"I'll do it today," Kelley promised. "I'll try to have a definitive answer by tomorrow." With that, he shook hands with everyone and left the room.

"I'd say that went as well as could be expected," Beaton said once he was gone.

"I'm encouraged," Caldwell said.

"I didn't appreciate his impudent suggestion of incompetent management," Traynor said. "I don't like his cocky attitude. It's unfortunate we have to deal with him."

"What I didn't like hearing was the threat to ferry patients to Rutland," Beaton said. "That worries me. It means our bargaining position is even weaker than I thought."

"Something just occurred to me," Traynor said. "Here we've had this high-level meeting that could possibly determine the fate of the hospital and there were no doctors present."

"It's a sign of the times," Beaton said. "The burden of dealing with the health-care crisis has fallen on us administrators."

"I think it's the medical world's equivalent of the expression, 'War is too important to leave up to the generals,' " Traynor said.

They all laughed. It was a good break from the tension of the meeting.

"What about Dr. Portland?" Caldwell asked. "Should I do anything?"

"I don't think there's anything to be done," Beaton said. "I haven't heard anything but good things about his surgical abilities. He certainly hasn't violated any rules or regulations. I think we'll have to wait and see what CMV does."

"He didn't look good to me," Traynor reiterated. "I'm no psychiatrist and I don't know what someone looks like when they're about to have a nervous breakdown, but if I had to guess, I'd guess they'd look the way he does."

The buzz of the intercom surprised them all, especially Beaton who'd left explicit instructions there were to be no interruptions.

"Some bad news," she said once she hung up. "Tom Baringer has died."

The three fell silent. Traynor was the first to speak: "Nothing like a death to remind us that for all the red and black ink, a hospital really is a very different kind of business."

"It's true," Beaton said. "The burden of the work is that

the whole town, even the whole region, becomes like an extended family. And as in any large family, someone is always dying."

"What is our death rate here at Bartlet Community Hospital?" Traynor asked. "It's never occurred to me to ask."

"We're just about in the middle of the road," Beaton said. "Plus or minus a percentage point. In fact, our rate is better than most of the inner-city teaching hospitals."

"That's a relief," Traynor said. "For a moment I was afraid there was something else I had to worry about."

"Enough of this morbid talk," Caldwell said. "I have some good news. The husband-and-wife team that we and CMV have been recruiting so actively has decided to come to Bartlet. So we'll be getting a superbly trained pathologist."

"I'm glad to hear it," Traynor said. "That brings pathology up to speed."

"They've even purchased the old Hodges house," Caldwell added.

"No kidding!" Traynor said. "I like that. There's something wonderfully ironic about it."

Charles Kelley slipped into his Ferrari coupe, started the engine, and gave it some gas. It responded like the engineering marvel it was, pressing him against the seat as he accelerated out of the hospital parking lot. He loved to drive the car, especially in the mountains. The way it hugged the road and cornered was a true delight.

After the meeting with the Bartlet Hospital people Kelley had phoned Duncan Mitchell directly, thinking it was a good opportunity to make his presence known to the man at the pinnacle of power. Duncan Mitchell was the CEO of CMV, as well as of several other HMOs and hospital management companies in the South. Conveniently the home office was in Vermont where Mr. Mitchell had a farm.

Kelley had not known what to expect and had been nervous when he called, but the CEO turned out to be gracious. Although Kelley had caught the man preparing to go to Washington, he had generously agreed to meet with Kelley outside the Burlington Airport general aviation building.

With CMV's Learjet in its final stages of fueling, Mitchell invited Kelley into the back of his limousine. He offered Kelley a drink from the limo's bar. Kelley politely refused.

Duncan Mitchell was an impressive man. He wasn't as tall as Kelley, yet he emanated a sense of power. He was meticulously dressed in a conservative business suit with a silk tie and gold cufflinks. His Italian loafers were dark brown crocodile.

Kelley introduced himself and gave a brief history of his association with CMV, mentioning that he was the regional director for the area centered around Bartlet Community Hospital, just in case Mitchell didn't know. But Mitchell seemed acquainted with Kelley's position.

"We eventually want to buy that facility," he said.

"I assumed as much," Kelley said. "And that's why I wanted to come to talk with you directly."

Mr. Mitchell slipped a gold cigarette case from his vest pocket and took out a cigarette. He tapped it thoughtfully against the case's flat front surface. "There's a lot of profit to be squeezed out of these rural hospitals," Mitchell said. "But it takes careful management."

"I couldn't agree more," Kelley said.

"What is it you wanted to talk about?" Mr. Mitchell asked.

"Two issues," Kelley said. "The first involves a bonus program the hospital wants to initiate similar to our own with our hospitals. They want to cut down on hospitalization."

"And what's the other?" Mitchell asked. He blew smoke up toward the ceiling of the car.

"One of our CMV physicians has begun acting bizarrely in response to post-operative complications in his patients," Kelley said. "He's saying things like he's not to blame and there's something wrong with the hospital."

"Does he have a psychiatric history?" Mr. Mitchell asked.

"Not that we can determine," Kelley said.

"Regarding the first issue, let them have their bonus program. At this point it doesn't matter about their balance sheet."

"What about the doctor?" Kelley asked.

"Obviously you'll have to do something," Mitchell said. "We can't let that type of behavior go on."

"Any suggestions?" Kelley asked.

"Do what you need to do," Mitchell said. "I'll leave the details up to you. Part of the skill of running a large organization like ours is knowing when to delegate responsibility. This is one of those times."

"Thank you, Mr. Mitchell," Kelley said. He was pleased. It was obvious to him that he was being given a vote of confidence.

Elated, Kelley climbed out of the limousine and got back into his Ferrari. As he was pulling out of the airport he caught a glimpse of Mitchell walking from his car to the CMV jet.

"Someday," Kelley vowed, "it'll be me using that plane."

7

WEDNESDAY, JUNE 30

BOTH THE INTERNAL MEDICINE DEPARTMENT AND the pathology department had small, informal ceremonies for that year's group of graduates, marking the end of their residencies. After collecting their diplomas, David and Angela passed up the parties scheduled for that afternoon and hurried home. This was the day they would leave Boston for their new home and careers in Bartlet, Vermont.

"Are you excited?" David asked Nikki.

"I'm excited to see Rusty," Nikki announced.

They'd rented a U-Haul truck to help make the move. It took quite a few trips up and down the stairs to get their possessions in the two vehicles. Once they were finally packed, Angela got in their station wagon and David got in the U-Haul. For the first half of the trip, Nikki elected to ride with her dad.

David used the time to talk with Nikki about starting at a new school and ask her if she'd miss her friends.

"Some of them I'll miss," Nikki said, "but others I won't. Anyway, I think I'll cope."

David smiled, promising himself that he would remember to tell Angela about Nikki's precocious comment.

Just south of the New Hampshire border, they stopped for lunch. Eager to arrive at their new home, they ate quickly.

"I feel wonderful about leaving the frantic, crime-filled city behind," Angela said as they left the restaurant and approached their vehicles. "At this point I don't care if I ever go back."

"I don't know," David joked. "I'm going to miss hearing sirens, gunshots, breaking glass, and cries for help. Country life is going to be so boring."

Both Nikki and Angela pummeled him in mock anger.

For the rest of the trip Nikki joined Angela in the station wagon.

As they drove north the weather improved. In Boston it had been hot, muggy, and hazy. By the time they crossed into Vermont it was still warm but clear and much less humid.

Bartlet appeared serene in the early summer heat. Flower-filled window boxes adorned almost every sill. Slowing down, the Wilsons' two-vehicle caravan crept through the lazy town. Few people were on the streets. It was as if everyone were napping.

"Can we stop and get Rusty?" Nikki asked as they neared Staley's Hardware Store.

"Let's get a bit settled first," Angela said. "We'll have to build something to keep him in until he gets housebroken."

David and Angela pulled into their driveway and parked side by side. Now that the house was officially theirs they felt even more awed than they had on their initial visit.

David climbed out of the truck, his eyes glued to the house. "The place is lovely," he said. "But it looks like it needs more attention than I realized."

Angela walked over to David and followed his line of sight. Some of the decorative dentil work had fallen from the cornice. "I'm not worried," she said. "That's why I married someone who is handy around the house."

David laughed. "I can see it'll take some effort to make a believer out of you."

"I'll try to keep an open mind," she teased.

With a key they had been sent in the mail, they opened the front door and stepped inside. It looked very different without furniture. When they'd seen it before it had been filled with the Hodgeses' belongings.

"It has a dance hall feel," David said.

"There's even an ècho," Nikki said. She yelled "Hello" and the word reverberated.

"That's when you know you've arrived at your proper station in life," David said, affecting an English accent. "When your house has an echo."

The Wilsons slowly passed through the foyer. Now that there were no rugs, their heels clicked on the wide wooden flooring. They had forgotten their new home's enormity, especially in contrast to their Boston apartment. Aside from a few pieces of furniture they'd agreed Clara would leave behind—a stool, a kitchen table—the place was bare.

In the center hall just before the grand staircase an imposing chandelier hung. There was a library and dining room to the left and a huge living room to the right. A central hall led to a spacious country kitchen which stretched across the back of the house. Beyond the kitchen was the two-story clapboard addition that connected the house to the barn. It had a mud room, several storerooms, and a back staircase leading up to the second level.

Returning to the grand staircase, the Wilsons climbed up to the second story. There were two bedrooms with connecting baths on each side and a master suite over the kitchen area.

Opening a door off the central hallway next to the master suite, they climbed a narrow staircase up to the third level where there were four unheated rooms.

"Plenty of storage," David quipped.

"Which room will be my bedroom?" Nikki asked.

"Whatever room you want," Angela said.

"I want the room facing the frog pond," she said.

They went down to the second level and walked into the room Nikki wanted. They discussed where her furniture would go, including the desk she did not yet own.

"Okay, you guys," Angela commanded. "Enough procrastination. Time to unload."

David gave her a military salute.

Returning to the vehicles, they began to bring their belongings into the house and put them into the appropriate rooms. The couch, the bedding, and the heavy boxes of books made it quite a struggle. When they were finished David and Angela stood beneath the archway leading into the living room.

"It would be funny if it wasn't so pathetic," Angela said. The rug that had been almost wall to wall in their apartment seemed little better than a doormat in the middle of the expansive room. Their threadbare couch, two armchairs, and coffee table looked like they had been rescued from a garage sale.

"Understated elegance," David said. "Minimalist decor. If it were in *Architectural Digest,* everyone would be trying to imitate it."

"What about Rusty?" Nikki asked.

"Let's go get him," David said. "You've been a good sport and a big help. You want to come, Angela?"

"No thanks," Angela said. "I'll stay and get more organized, especially in the kitchen."

"I assumed we'd eat down at the inn tonight," David said.

"No, I want to eat here in our new home," Angela answered.

While David and Nikki went to town, Angela unpacked a few of the boxes in the kitchen including their pots, pans, dishes, and flatware. She also figured out how to work the stove and got the refrigerator running.

Nikki returned carrying the adorable puppy with its wrinkled face and floppy ears. She had the dog pressed against her chest. He'd grown considerably since they'd seen him last. His feet were the size of Nikki's fists.

"He's going to be a big dog," David said.

While Nikki and David fashioned a pen for Rusty in the mud room, Angela made dinner for Nikki. Nikki wasn't happy about eating before her parents, but she was too tired to complain. After she'd eaten and done some postural drainage, she and Rusty, both exhausted, were put to bed.

"Now I have a little surprise for you," Angela said as she and David descended from Nikki's room. She took him by the hand and led him into the kitchen. Opening the refrigerator, she pulled out a bottle of Chardonnay.

"Wow," David exclaimed, inspecting the label. "This isn't our usual cheap stuff."

"Hardly," Angela said. Reaching back into the refrigerator, she took out a dish covered with a paper towel. Lifting the towel she exposed two thick veal chops.

"I have the feeling we're in for a feast," David said.

"You'd better believe it," Angela said. "Salad, artichokes, wild rice, and veal chops. Plus the best Chardonnay I could buy."

David cooked the meat on an outdoor barbecue built into the side of the terrace off the library. By the time he came in Angela had the rest of the food on the table in the dining room.

Night had descended softly, filling the house with shadow. In the darkness the glow from the two candles that formed the centerpiece on the table only illuminated the immediate area. The disarray of the rest of the house was hidden.

They sat at opposite ends of the table. They didn't speak. Instead they merely gazed at each other as they ate. Both of them were moved by the romantic atmosphere, realizing that romance had been missing from their lives over the last years; the demands of their respective residencies and Nikki's ongoing health problems had taken precedence.

Long after they'd finished eating they continued to sit and stare at each other while a symphony of sounds of a Vermont summer night drifted in through the open windows. The candle flames flickered sensuously as the clean, cool air wafted across the room and caressed their faces. It was a magical moment they both wanted to savor.

Mutual desire drove them from the dining room into the dark living room. They fell onto the couch, their lips meeting as they enveloped each other in a warm embrace. They removed their clothing, each eagerly aiding the other.

With a chorus of crickets in the background, they made love in their new home.

Morning brought mass confusion. With the dog barking to be fed and Nikki whining that she couldn't find her favorite jeans, Angela felt her patience was at an end. David was no help. He couldn't find the list he'd made of what was in each of the dozens of boxes left to be unpacked.

"All right, that's enough," Angela shouted. "I don't want to hear any more whining or barking."

For the moment, even Rusty quieted down.

"Calm down, dear," David said. "Getting upset isn't going to solve anything."

"And don't you tell me not to get upset," Angela cried.

"All right," David said calmly. "I'll go get the babysitter."

"I'm not a baby," Nikki whined.

"Oh, save me," Angela said with her face raised to the ceiling.

While David was off fetching Alice Doherty, Dorothy Weymouth's older sister, Angela was able to regain control of herself. She realized that it had been a mistake to tell their respective employers that they would be willing to start on July first. They should have given themselves a few days to get settled.

Alice turned out to be a godsend. She looked quite grand-motherly with her warm caring face, a twinkle in her eye, and snow-white hair. She had an engaging manner and surprising energy for a woman of seventy-nine. She also had the compassion and patience a chronically ill, willful child like Nikki required. Best of all, she loved Rusty which immediately endeared her to Nikki.

The first thing Angela did was show her how to do Nikki's respiratory therapy. It was important for Alice to learn the procedure, and she proved to be a quick study.

"Don't you two worry about a thing," Alice called to David and Angela as they went out the back door. Nikki was holding Rusty, and she waved the dog's paw to say goodbye.

"I want to ride my bike," David announced once he and Angela got outside.

"Are you serious?" Angela asked.

"Absolutely," David said.

"Suit yourself," Angela said as she climbed into the Volvo and started the engine. She waved once to David as she descended the long drive and turned right toward town.

Although Angela was confident about her professional capabilities, she still felt nervous about starting her first real job.

Mustering her courage and reminding herself that first-day jitters were natural, she reported to Michael Caldwell's office. Caldwell immediately took her to meet Helen Beaton, the president of the hospital. Beaton happened to be in conference with Dr. Delbert Cantor, the chief of the professional staff, but she interrupted the meeting to welcome Angela. She invited Angela into her office and introduced her to Dr. Cantor as well.

While shaking her hand, Dr. Cantor unabashedly looked Angela up and down. She had chosen to wear one of her best silk dresses for her first day. "My, my," he said. "You certainly don't look like the few girls in my medical school class. They were all dogs." He laughed heartily.

Angela smiled. She felt like saying her class was just the opposite—the few men were all dogs—but she held her tongue. She found Dr. Cantor instantly offensive. He was clearly part of the old-school minority that still wasn't comfortable with women in the medical profession.

"We are so glad to have you join the Bartlet Community Hospital family," Beaton said as she escorted Angela to the door. "I'm confident you'll find the experience both challenging and rewarding."

Leaving the administration area, Caldwell took Angela to the clinical lab. As soon as Dr. Wadley saw her he leaped up from his desk and even gave her a hug as if they were old friends.

"Welcome to the team," Dr. Wadley said with a warm smile, his hands still gripping Angela's arms. "I've been anticipating this day for weeks."

"I'll be off," Caldwell said to Angela. "I can see you're in good hands here."

"Great job recruiting this talented pathologist," Wadley told Caldwell. "You're to be commended."

Caldwell beamed.

"A good man," Wadley said, watching him leave.

Angela nodded, but she was thinking about Wadley. Although she was again aware of how much the man reminded her of her father, now she was equally aware of their differences. Wadley's enthusiastic fervor was a welcome change from her father's aloof reserve. Angela was even charmed by Wadley's demonstrative welcome. It was reassuring to feel so wanted on her first day.

"First things first," Wadley said, rubbing his hands together. His green eyes shone with child-like excitement. "Let me show you your office."

He pushed open a connecting door from his own office into another that looked as though it had been recently decorated. The room was entirely white: the walls, the desk, everything.

"Like it?" Wadley asked.

"It's wonderful," Angela said.

Wadley pointed back toward the connecting door. "That will always be open," he said. "Literally and figuratively."

"Wonderful," Angela repeated.

"Now let's tour the lab again," Wadley said. "I know you saw it once, but I want to introduce you to the staff." He took a long, crisp, professional white coat from a hook and put it on.

For the next fifteen minutes Angela met more people than she could hope to remember. After circling the lab, they stopped at a windowless office next to the microbiology section. The office belonged to Dr. Paul Darnell, Angela's fellow pathologist.

In contrast to Wadley, Darnell was a short man whose clothing was rumpled and whose white coat was spotted haphazardly with stains used in preparing pathological slides. He seemed agreeable but plain and retiring, almost the antithesis of the affable and flamboyant Wadley.

After the tour was over, Wadley escorted Angela back to

his office where he explained her duties and responsibilities. "I'm going to try to make you one of the best pathologists in the country," he said with a true mentor's enthusiasm.

David had enjoyed his three-and-a-half-mile bicycle ride immensely. The clean, crisp morning air had been delicious, and the bird life even more abundant than he'd imagined. He'd spotted several hummingbirds along the way. To top it off, he caught a fleeting glimpse of several deer across a dew-laden field just after crossing the Roaring River.

Arriving at the professional building, David discovered he was too early. Charles Kelley didn't show up until almost nine.

"My word, you are eager!" Kelley said when he spotted David perusing magazines in the CMV waiting area. "Come on in."

David followed Kelley into his office where Kelley had him fill out a few routine forms. "You're joining a cracker-jack team," Kelley said while David worked. "You're going to love it here: great facilities, superbly trained colleagues. What else could you want?"

"I can't think of anything," David admitted.

When the paperwork was completed and after Kelley explained some of the ground rules, he accompanied David to his new office. As Kelley opened the office suite door and entered, David stopped to admire his nameplate that had already been installed in the slot on the outside of the door. He was surprised to see the name "Dr. Kevin Yansen" above his.

"Is this the same suite?" David asked in a lowered voice after catching up with Kelley. There were six patients in the waiting room.

"Same one," Kelley said. He knocked on the mirror, and after it had slid open, he introduced David to the receptionist he would be sharing with Dr. Yansen.

"Glad to meet you," Anne Withington said in a heavy South Boston accent. She cracked her gum, and David winced.

"Come in to see your private office," Kelley said. Over his shoulder he told Anne to send Dr. Yansen in to meet

Dr. Wilson when he appeared between patients.

David was confused. He followed Kelley into what had been Dr. Portland's office. The walls had been repainted a light gray, and new gray-green carpet had been installed.

"What do you think?" Kelley asked, beaming.

"I think it's fine," David said. "Where did Dr. Portland go?"

Before Kelley could respond, Dr. Yansen appeared at the doorway and whisked into the room with his hand outstretched. Ignoring Kelley, he introduced himself to David, telling David to call him Kevin. He then slapped David on the back. "Welcome! Good to have you join the squad," he said. "You play basketball or tennis?"

"A little of both," David said, "but none recently."

"We'll have to get you back in the swing," Kevin said.

"Are you an orthopedist?" David asked as he looked at his new suitemate. He was a squarely built man with an aggressive-looking face. A mildly hooked nose supported thick glasses. He was four inches shorter than David, and standing next to Kelley, he appeared diminutive.

"Orthopedist?" Kevin laughed scornfully. "Hardly! I'm at the opposite end of the operative spectrum. I'm an ophthalmologist."

"Where's Dr. Portland?" David asked again.

Kevin looked at Kelley. "You haven't told him yet?"

"Haven't had a chance," Kelley said, spreading his hands, palms up. "He just got here."

"I'm afraid Dr. Portland is no longer with us," Kevin said.

"He's left the group?" David asked.

"In a manner of speaking," Kevin said with a wry smile.

"I'm afraid Dr. Portland committed suicide back in May," Kelley said.

"Right here in this room," Kevin said. "Sitting there at that desk." He pointed at the desk. Then Kevin formed his hand into a pistol with his index finger serving as the barrel, and pointed it at his forehead. "Bam!" he said. "Shot himself right through the forehead out the back. That's why the walls had to be painted and the carpet changed."

David's mouth went bone-dry. He gazed at the blank wall behind the desk and tried not to imagine what it had looked like after the incident. "How awful," David said. "Was he married?"

"Unfortunately," Dr. Yansen said with a nod. "Wife and two young boys. A real tragedy. I knew something was wrong. All of a sudden he stopped playing basketball on Saturday mornings."

"He didn't look good the last time I saw him," David said. "Was he ill? He'd looked as if he'd lost a lot of weight."

"Depressed," Kelley said.

David sighed. "Boy, you never know!"

"Let's move on to a happier subject," Kelley said after he'd cleared his throat. "I took you at your word, Dr. Wilson. We've scheduled patients for you this morning. Are you up to it?"

"Absolutely," David said.

Kevin wished David well and headed back to one of the examining rooms. Kelley introduced David to Susan Beardslee, the nurse he'd be working with. Susan was an attractive woman in her mid-twenties, with dark hair cut short to frame her face. What David immediately liked about her was her lively, enthusiastic personality.

"Your first patient is already in the examining room," Susan said cheerfully. She handed him the chart. "When you need me, just buzz. I'll be getting the next patient ready." She disappeared into the second examining room.

"I think this is where I leave," Kelley said. "Good luck, David. If there are any questions or problems, just holler."

David flipped open the cover of the chart and read the name: Marjorie Kleber, aged thirty-nine. The complaint was chest pain. He was about to knock on the examining room door when he read the diagnostic summary: breast cancer treated with surgery, chemotherapy, and radiation. The cancer had been diagnosed four years previously at age thirty-five. At the time of the discovery, the cancer had spread to the lymph nodes.

David quickly scanned the rest of the chart. He was mildly unnerved and needed a moment to prepare himself.

A patient with breast cancer that had metastasized, or spread from the breast to other areas of the body, was a serious case with which to begin his medical career. Happily Marjorie had been doing well.

David knocked on the door and entered. Marjorie Kleber was sitting patiently on the examining table dressed in an examining gown. She looked up at David with large, sad, intelligent eyes. Her smile was the kind of smile that warmed his heart.

David introduced himself and was about to ask about her current complaint when she reached out and took one of his hands in hers. She squeezed it and held it to her chest at the base of her neck.

"Thank you for coming to Bartlet," she said. "You'll never know how much I have prayed for someone like you to come here. I'm truly overjoyed."

"I'm happy to be here," David stammered.

"Prior to your coming, I've had to wait up to four weeks to be seen," she said as she finally released David's hand. "That's the way it's been since the school's health-care coverage was switched to CMV. And every time it's been a different doctor. Now I've been told that you will be my doctor. It's so reassuring."

"I'm honored to be your doctor," David said.

"Waiting four weeks to be seen was so scary," Marjorie continued. "Last winter I had the flu so bad that I thought it was pneumonia. Luckily, by the time I was seen I was over the worst of it."

"Maybe you should have gone to the emergency room," David suggested.

"I wish I could have," Marjorie said. "But we're not allowed. I did go once the winter before last, but CMV refused to pay because it turned out to be the flu. Unless my problem is life-threatening, I have to come here to the office. I can't go to the emergency room without prior approval from a CMV physician. If I do, they won't pay."

"But that's absurd," David said. "How can you know in advance if your problem is life-threatening?"

Marjorie shrugged. "That's the same question I asked, but they didn't have an answer. They just reiterated the rule. Anyway, I'm glad you're here. If I have a problem I'll call you."

"Please do," David said. "Now let's start talking about your health. Who is following you in regard to your cancer?"

"You are," Marjorie said.

"You don't have an oncologist?" David asked.

"CMV doesn't have an oncologist," Marjorie said. "I'm to see you routinely and Dr. Mieslich, the oncologist, when you think it is necessary. Dr. Mieslich is not a CMV physician. I can't see him unless you order it."

David nodded, recognizing that there were realities about his new practice that would take time to learn. He also knew he'd have to spend considerable time going over Marjorie's chart in detail.

For the next fifteen minutes, David applied himself to the process of "working up" Marjorie's chest pain. While listening to her chest and in between her deep breathing, he asked her what she did at the school.

"I'm a teacher," Marjorie said.

"What grade?" he asked. He took his stethoscope from his ears and began preparations to run an EKG.

"Third grade," she said proudly. "I taught second grade for a number of years, but I much prefer third. The children are really blossoming then."

"My daughter is to start the third grade in the fall," David said.

"How wonderful," Marjorie said. "Then she'll be in my class."

"Do you have a family?" David asked.

"My word, yes!" Marjorie said. "My husband, Lloyd, works at the computer software company. He's a programmer. We have two children: a boy in high school and a girl in the sixth grade."

Half an hour later David felt confident enough to reassure Marjorie that her chest pain was not at all serious and that it had nothing to do with either her heart or her cancer, Marjorie's two chief concerns. She thanked him profusely once again for coming to Bartlet before he stepped out of the room.

David ducked into his private office with a sense of exuberance. If all his patients were as warm and appreciative as Marjorie, he could count on a rewarding career in Bartlet. He put her chart on his desk for further study.

Taking the file from its holder on the second examining room door, David perused his next patient's chart. The diagnostic summary read: leukemia treated with massive chemotherapy. David inwardly groaned; it was another difficult case that would require more "homework." The patient's name was John Tarlow. He was a forty-eight-year-old man who'd been under treatment for three and a half years.

Stepping into the room, David introduced himself. John Tarlow was a handsome, friendly man whose face reflected intelligence and warmth equal to Marjorie's. Despite his complicated history, John's complaint of insomnia was both easier and quicker to deal with than Marjorie's chest pain. After a short conversation it was clear to David that the problem was an understandable psychological reaction to a death in the family. David gave him a prescription for some sleeping medication that he was certain would help John get back to his usual routine.

After he was through with John, David added his chart to Marjorie's for further review. Then he searched for Susan. He found her in the tiny lab used for simple, routine tests.

"Are there a lot of oncology patients in the practice?" David asked hesitantly.

David very much admired the sort of people who chose to go into oncology. He knew himself well enough to know that he was not suited for the specialty. So it was with some trepidation that he discovered his first two CMV patients were both dealing with cancer.

Susan assured him that there were only a few such patients. David wanted to believe her. When he went back to get the chart out of the box on examining room one, he felt reassured. It wasn't an oncological problem; the case concerned diabetes.

David's morning passed quickly and happily. The patients had been a delight. They'd all been affable, attentive to what David had to say, and, in contrast to the non-compliant patients he'd dealt with during his residency, eager to follow his recommendations. All of them had also expressed appreciation for David's arrival, not as fervently as Marjorie, but enough to make David feel good about his reception.

For lunch, David met Angela at the coffee shop run by the volunteers. Over sandwiches, they discussed their morning.

"Dr. Wadley is terrific," Angela said. "He's very helpful and interested in teaching. The more I see him, the less he reminds me of my father. He's far more demonstrative than my father ever would be—far more enthusiastic and affectionate. He even gave me a hug when I arrived this morning. My father would die before he'd do that."

David told Angela about the patients he'd seen. She was particularly touched to hear about Marjorie Kleber's reaction to David's arrival.

"She's a teacher," David added. "In fact she teaches the third grade so she'll be Nikki's teacher."

"What a coincidence," Angela said. "What's she like?"

"She seems warm, giving, and intelligent," David said. "I'd guess she's a marvelous teacher. The problem is she's had metastatic breast cancer."

"Oh, dear," Angela said.

"But she's been doing fine," David said. "I don't think she's had any recurrence yet, but I haven't gone over her chart in detail."

"It's a bad disease," Angela said, thinking how many times she'd worried about it herself.

"The only complaint I have so far about the practice is that I've seen too many oncology patients," David said.

"I know that's not your cup of tea," Angela said.

"The nurse says it was just a coincidence that I started with two in a row," David said. "I'll have to keep my fingers crossed."

"Now don't get depressed," Angela said. "I'm sure your nurse was right." Angela remembered all too well David's response to the deaths of several oncology patients when he'd been a junior resident.

"Talk about depression," David said. He leaned closer and whispered. "Did you hear about Dr. Portland?"

Angela shook her head.

"He committed suicide," David said. "He shot himself in the office that I'm now using."

"That's terrible," Angela said. "Do you have to stay there? Maybe you can move to a different suite."

"Don't be ridiculous," David said. "What am I going to say to Kelley? I'm superstitious about death and suicide? I can't do that. Besides, they repainted the walls and recarpeted the floor." David shrugged. "It'll be okay."

"Why did he do it?" Angela asked.

"Depression," David said.

"I knew it," Angela said. "I knew he was depressed. I even said it. Remember?"

"I didn't say he wasn't depressed," David said. "I said he looked ill. Anyway, he must have killed himself soon after we met him because Charles Kelley said he'd done it in May."

"The poor man," Angela said. "Did he have a family?"

"A wife and two young boys."

Angela shook her head. Suicide among doctors was an issue of which she was well aware. One of her resident colleagues had killed herself.

"On a lighter note," David said, "Charles Kelley told me that there's a bonus plan to reward me for keeping hospitalization at a minimum. The less I hospitalize the more I get paid. I can even win a trip to the Bahamas. Can you believe it?"

"I've heard of that kind of incentive plan," Angela said. "It's a ploy health maintenance organizations use to reduce costs."

David shook his head in disbelief. "Some of the realities of this 'managed care' and 'managed competition' stuff are really mind-boggling. I personally find it insulting."

"Well, on a lighter note of my own, Dr. Wadley's invited us to his home for dinner tonight. I told him I'd have to ask you. What do you think?"

"Do you want to go?" David asked.

"I know we have a lot to do at home, but I think we should go. He's being so thoughtful and generous. I don't want to appear ungrateful."

"What about Nikki?" David asked.

"That's another piece of good news," Angela said. "I found out from one of the lab technicians that Barton Sherwood has a daughter in high school who does a lot of sitting. They are our closest neighbors. I called and she's eager to come over."

"Think Nikki will mind?" David asked.

"I already asked her," Angela said. "She said she didn't care and that she's looking forward to meeting Karen Sherwood. She's one of the cheerleaders."

"Then let's go," David said.

Just before seven Karen Sherwood arrived. David let her in. He wouldn't have guessed she was a cheerleader. She was a thin, quiet young woman who unfortunately looked a lot like her father. Yet she was pleasant and intuitive. When she was introduced to Nikki she was smart enough to say she loved dogs, especially puppies.

While David drove, Angela finished putting on her makeup. David could tell she was tense, and he tried to reassure her that everything would be fine and that she looked terrific. When they pulled up to the Wadley home, both were impressed. The house wasn't as grand as theirs, but it was in far better condition and the grounds were immaculate.

"Welcome," Wadley said as he threw open his front door to greet the Wilsons.

The inside of the house was even more impressive than the outside. Every detail had been attended to. Antique furniture stood on thick oriental carpets. Pastoral nineteenth-century paintings adorned the walls.

Gertrude Wadley and her courtly husband were significantly different people, lending credence to the saying "opposites attract." She was a retiring, mousy woman who had little to say. It was as if she'd been submerged by her husband's personality.

Their teenage daughter, Cassandra, seemed more like her mother initially, but as the evening progressed, she became more like her outgoing father.

But it was Wadley who dominated the evening. He pontificated on a number of subjects. And he clearly doted on

Angela. At one point he looked skyward and thanked the fates that he had been rewarded with such a competent team now that Angela had arrived.

"One thing is for sure," David said as they drove home, "Dr. Wadley is thrilled with you. Of course, I can't blame him."

Angela snuggled up to her husband.

Arriving home, David accompanied Karen across the fields to her home, even though she insisted she'd be fine. When David got back, Angela met him at the door in lingerie she hadn't worn since their honeymoon.

"It looks better now when I'm not pregnant," Angela said. "Don't you agree?"

"It looked great then and it looks great now."

Stealing into the semi-dark living room, they lowered themselves onto the couch. Slowly and tenderly they made love again. Without the frenzy of the previous evening, it was even more satisfying and fulfilling.

Once they were through, they held each other and listened to the symphony of chirping crickets and croaking frogs.

"We've made love more here in the last two days than in the previous two months in Boston," Angela said with a sigh.

"We've been under a lot of stress."

"It makes me wonder about another child," Angela said.

David moved so that he could make out Angela's profile in the darkness. "Really?" he asked.

"With a house this size, we could have a litter," Angela said with a little laugh.

"We'd want to know if the child had cystic fibrosis. I suppose we could always rely on amniocentesis."

"I suppose," Angela said without enthusiasm. "But what would we do if it were positive?"

"I don't know," David said. "It's scary. It's hard to know what the right thing to do is."

"Well, like Scarlett O'Hara said, let's think about it tomorrow."

SUMMER IN VERMONT

DAYS MELTED INTO WEEKS AND WEEKS INTO MONTHS as summer advanced. The sweet white corn grew chest-high across the road from the Wilsons' house and could be heard rustling in the evening breeze from the front porch. Plump tomatoes ripened to a deep red in the garden by the terrace. Crab apples the size of golf balls began to drop from the tree next to the barn. Cicadas buzzed incessantly in the midmorning August heat.

David and Angela's work continued to be stimulating and rewarding as they settled into their jobs. Each day brought some new experience that they enthusiastically shared with each other as they lingered over quiet suppers.

Rusty's appetite remained undiminished and a source of wonder as he grew quickly and with great exuberance, catching up to the size of his feet. Yet despite his growth he maintained the same adorable quality he'd had as a tiny puppy. Everyone found it impossible to pass him without offering a pat on the head or a scratch behind a golden ear.

Nikki flourished in the new environment. Her respiratory status remained normal and her lungs stayed clear. She also made new friends. She was closest to Caroline Helmsford by far; Caroline was a petite child a year older than Nikki who also suffered from cystic fibrosis. Having had so many unique experiences in common, the girls formed a particularly strong bond.

They had met quite by accident. Although the Wilsons had been told about Caroline on their first visit to Bartlet, they'd made no attempt to contact her. The two girls had bumped into each other in the local grocery store which Caroline's parents owned and ran.

Nikki also befriended the Yansen boy, Arni, who happened to be exactly Nikki's age. Their birthdays were only a week apart. Arni was like his father: short, squarely built, and aggressive. He and Nikki hit it off and spent hours in and out of the barn, never at a loss for things to do.

As much as they loved their work, the Wilsons delighted in their weekends. Saturday mornings David rose with the sun to make hospital rounds, then played three-on-three basketball in the high school gym with a group of physicians.

Saturday and Sunday afternoons David and Angela devoted to work on the house. While Angela worked on the interior, busying herself with curtains and stripping old furniture, David tackled outdoor projects like fixing the porch or replacing the drainpipes. David proved even less handy than Angela had feared. He was forever running off to Staley's Hardware Store for more advice. Fortunately, Mr. Staley took pity on David and gave him many lectures on fixing broken screens, leaky faucets, and burned-out electrical switches.

On Saturday, the twenty-first of August, David got up early as usual, made himself coffee, and left for the hospital. Rounds went quickly since he only had to see one patient, John Tarlow, the leukemia victim. Like David's other oncology patients, John had to be hospitalized frequently for a variety of problems. This latest hospitalization resulted from an abscess on his neck. Fortunately, he was doing fine. David anticipated discharging him in the next few days.

After completing his rounds, David biked over to the high school for basketball. Entering the gym he discovered that there were more people than usual waiting to play. When David finally got into the game he noticed that the competition was fiercer than usual. The reason was that no one wanted to lose because the losers had to sit out.

David responded to the heightened competition by playing more vigorously himself. Coming down from a rebound, his elbow collided solidly with Kevin Yansen's nose.

David stopped mid-stride, turning in time to see Kevin cradling his nose in both hands. Blood was dripping between his fingers.

"Kevin," David called in alarm. "Are you all right?"

"Chrissake," Kevin snarled through his cupped hands. "You ass!"

"I'm sorry," David said. He felt embarrassed at his own aggressiveness. "Let me see." David reached out and tried to ease Kevin's hands away from his face.

"Don't touch me," Kevin snapped.

"Come on, Mr. Aggressive," Trent Yarborough called from across the floor. Trent was a surgeon and one of the better ballplayers. He'd played at Yale. "Let's see the old schnozzola. Frankly, I'm glad to see you get a little of your own medicine."

"Screw you, Yarborough," Kevin said. He lowered his hands. His right nostril dripped blood. The bridge of his nose bent to the right.

Trent came over for a better look. "Looks like your beak's been broken."

"Shit!" Kevin said.

"Want me to straighten it?" Trent asked. "I won't charge much."

"Let's just hope your malpractice insurance is paid up," Kevin said. He tilted his head back and closed his eyes.

Trent grabbed Kevin's nose between his thumb and the knuckle of his index finger and snapped it back into position. The cracking sound that resulted made everyone—even the surgeon—wince.

Trent stepped back to admire his handiwork. "Looks better than the original," he said.

David asked if he could give Kevin a ride home, but Kevin told him he'd drive himself, still sounding angry.

A sub stepped into the game, taking Kevin's place. For a moment David stood and gazed at the door where Kevin had exited. Then he winced as someone slapped him on the back. David turned and looked into Trent's face.

"Don't let Kevin bother you," Trent said. "He's broken two other people's noses here that I know of. Kevin is not a particularly good sport, but otherwise he's okay."

Reluctantly, David resumed the game.

When David returned home, Nikki and Angela were ready for the day's outing. There were to be no projects that Saturday because they had been invited to a nearby lake for an overnight stay. An afternoon of swimming was to be followed by a cookout. The Yansens, the Yarboroughs, and the Youngs, the "three Y's" as they called themselves, had rented a lakeside cottage for the month. Steve Young was an obstetrician/gynecologist as well as one of the basketball regulars.

"Come on, Daddy," Nikki said impatiently. "We're already late."

David looked at the time. He'd played basketball longer than usual. Running upstairs, he jumped into the shower. A half hour later they were in the car and on their way.

The lake was an emerald green jewel nestled into a lushly wooded valley between two mountains. One of the mountains boasted a ski resort that David and Angela were told was one of the best in the area.

The cottage was charming. It was a rambling, multi-bedroomed structure built around a massive fieldstone fireplace. A spacious screened porch fronted the entire house and faced the lake. Extending out from the porch was a large deck. A flight of wooden steps connected the deck to a T-shaped dock that ran out fifty feet into the water.

Nikki immediately teamed up with Arni Yansen, and they ran off into the forest where Arni was eager to show her a treehouse. Angela went into the kitchen where Nancy

Yansen, Claire Young, and Gayle Yarborough were happily involved in the food preparation. David joined the men who were nursing beers while casually watching a Red Sox game on a portable TV.

The afternoon passed languidly, interrupted only by the minor tragedies associated with eight active children who had the usual proclivities of tripping over rocks, skinning knees, and hurting each other's feelings. The Yansens had two children, the Youngs had one, and the Yarboroughs had three.

The only blip in the otherwise flawless day was Kevin's mood. He'd developed mildly black eyes from his broken nose. On more than one occasion he yelled at David for being clumsy and fouling him continuously. David finally took him aside, amazed that Kevin was making such an issue of the affair.

"I apologized," David said. "And I'll apologize again. I'm sorry. It was an accident. I certainly didn't mean it."

Kevin irritably eyed David, giving David the impression that Kevin was not going to forgive him. But then Kevin sighed. "All right," he said. "Let's have another beer."

After dinner the adults sat around the huge table while the children went out onto the dock to fish. The sky was still red in the west and the color reflected off the water. The tree frogs and crickets and other insects had long since started their incessant nightly chorus. Fireflies dotted the deep shadows under the trees.

At first the conversation dealt with the beauty of the surroundings and the inherent benefits of living in Vermont where most people only got to visit for short vacations. But then the conversation turned to medicine, to the chagrin of the other three wives.

"I'd almost rather hear sports trivia," Gayle Yarborough complained. Nancy Yansen and Claire Young heartily agreed.

"It's hard not to talk about medicine with all this so-called 'reform' going on," Trent said. Neither Trent nor Steve were CMV physicians. Although they had been trying to form a preferred provider organization with a large insurance company and Blue Shield, they were not having much luck. They were a little late. Most of the patient base had been snapped up by CMV because of the plan's aggressive, competitive marketing.

"The whole business has got me depressed," Steve said. "If I could think of some way of supporting myself and my family, I'd leave medicine in the blink of an eye."

"That would be a terrible waste of your skill," Angela said.

"I suppose," Steve said. "But it would be a hell of a lot better than blowing my brains out like you-know-who."

The reference to Dr. Portland intimidated everyone for a few moments. It was Angela who broke the silence. "We've never heard the story about Dr. Portland," she said. "I've been curious, I have to admit. I've seen his poor wife. She's obviously having enormous trouble dealing with his death."

"She blames herself," Gayle Yarborough said.

"All we heard was that he was depressed," David said. "Was it about something specific?"

"The last time he played basketball he was all uptight about one of his hip fracture patients dying," Trent said. "It was Sam Flemming, the artist. Then I think he lost a couple of others."

David felt a shiver pass down his spine. The memory of his own reaction as a junior resident to the deaths of several of his patients passed through him like an unwelcome chill.

"I'm not even sure he killed himself," Kevin said suddenly, shocking everyone. Other than complaining about David's clumsiness, Kevin had said very little that day. Even his wife Nancy looked at him as if he'd blasphemed.

"I think you'd better explain yourself," Trent said.

"Not much to explain except Randy didn't have a gun," Kevin said. "It's one of those nagging details that no one has been able to explain. Where'd he get it? No one has stepped forward to say that he'd borrowed it from him. He didn't go out of town. What did he do, find it along the road?" Kevin laughed hollowly. "Think about it."

"Come on," Steve said. "He must have had it, just no one knew."

"Arlene said she didn't know anything about it," Kevin persisted. "Plus he was shot directly through the front of the head and angled downward. That's why it was his cerebellum that was splattered against the wall. I've personally never heard of anyone shooting himself like that. People usually put the barrel in their mouths if they want to be sure not to mess it up. Other people shoot themselves in the side of the head. It's hard to shoot yourself from the front, especially with a long-barreled magnum." Kevin made a pistol with his hand as he'd done on David's first day of work. This time when he tried to point the gun straight into his forehead, he made the gesture look particularly awkward.

Gayle shivered through fleeting nausea. Even though she was married to a doctor, talk of blood and guts made her ill.

"Are you trying to suggest he was murdered?" Steve said.

"All I'm saying is I'm personally not sure he killed himself," Kevin repeated. "Beyond that, everybody can make his own assessment."

The sounds of crickets and tree frogs dominated the night as everyone pondered Kevin's disturbing comments. "Well, I think it's all poppycock," Gayle Yarborough said finally. "I think it was cowardly suicide, and my heart goes out to Arlene and her two boys."

"I agree," Claire Young said.

Another uncomfortable silence followed until Steve broke it: "What about you two?" he asked, looking across the table at Angela and David. "How are you finding Bartlet? Are you enjoying yourselves?"

David and Angela exchanged glances. David spoke first: "I'm enjoying it immensely," he said. "I love the town, and since I'm already part of CMV I don't have to worry about medical politics. I walked into a big practice, maybe a little too big. I've got more oncology patients than I'd anticipated and more than I'd like."

"What's oncology?" Nancy Yansen asked.

Kevin gave his wife an irritated look of disbelief. "Cancer," he said disdainfully. "Jesus, Nance, you know that."

"Sorry," Nancy said with equal irritation.

"How many oncology patients do you have?" Steve asked.

David closed his eyes and thought for a moment. "Let's see," he said. "I've got John Tarlow with leukemia. He's in the hospital right now. I've got Mary Ann Schiller with ovarian cancer. I've got Jonathan Eakins with prostatic cancer. I've got Donald Anderson who they thought had pancreatic cancer but who ended up with a benign adenoma."

"I recognize that name," Trent said. "That patient had a Whipple procedure."

"Thanks for telling us," Gayle said sarcastically.

"That's only four patients," Steve said.

"There's more," David said. "I've also got Sandra Hascher with melanoma and Marjorie Kleber with breast cancer."

"I'm impressed you've committed them all to memory," Claire Young said.

"It's easy," David said. "I remember them because I've befriended them all. I see them on a regular basis because they have a lot of medical problems, which is hardly surprising considering the amount of treatment they've undergone."

"Well, what's the problem?" Claire asked.

"The problem is that now that I've befriended them and accepted responsibility for their care, I'm worried they'll die of their illness and I'll feel responsible."

"I know exactly what he means," Steve said. "I don't understand how anybody can go into oncology. God bless them. Half the reason I went into OB was because it's generally a happy specialty."

"Ditto for ophthalmology," Kevin said.

"I disagree," Angela said. "I can understand very well why people go into oncology. It has to be rewarding because people with potentially terminal illnesses have great needs. With a lot of other specialties you never truly know if you have helped your patients or not. There's never a question with oncology."

"I know Marjorie Kleber quite well," Gayle Yarborough said. "Both TJ and my middle, Chandler, had her as their teacher. She's a marvelous woman. She had this creative way to get the kids interested in spelling with tiny plastic airplanes moving across a wall chart."

"I enjoy seeing her every time she comes in for an appointment," David admitted.

"How's your job?" Nancy Yansen asked Angela.

"Couldn't be better," Angela said. "Dr. Wadley, the chief of the department, has become a true mentor. The equipment is state-of-the-art. We're busy but not buried. We're doing between five hundred and a thousand biopsies a month, which is respectable. We see interesting pathology because Bartlet Hospital is acting as a tertiary care center. We even have a viral lab which I didn't expect. So all in all it's quite challenging."

"Have you had any run-ins with Charles Kelley yet?" Kevin asked David.

"Not at all," David said with surprise. "We've gotten along fine. In fact just this week I met with Kelley and the CMV quality management director from Burlington. They were both complimentary about the responses patients had given on forms asking them to evaluate care and satisfaction."

"Ha!" Kevin laughed scornfully. "Quality management is a piece of cake. Wait until you have your utilization review. It usually takes two or three months. Let me know what you think of Charles Kelley then."

"I'm not concerned," David said. "I'm practicing good, careful medicine. I don't give a hoot about the bonus program concerning hospitalization and I'm certainly not in the running for one of the grand prize trips to the Bahamas."

"I wouldn't mind," Kevin said. "I think it's a good program. Why not think twice before hospitalizing someone? Patients around here follow your orders. People are better off home than in the hospital. If the hospital wants to send Nance and me to the Bahamas, I'm not going to complain."

"It's a bit different for ophthalmology than for internal medicine," David said.

"Enough of this medical talk," Gayle Yarborough said. "I was just thinking we should have brought the movie *The Big Chill*. It's a great movie to watch with a group like this."

"Now that would stimulate some discussion," Nancy Yansen said. "And it would be a lot more stimulating than this medical drivel."

"I don't need the movie to think about whether I would be willing to let my husband make love to one of my friends so she could have a baby," Claire Young said. "No way, period!"

"Oh, come on," Steve said, sitting up from his slouch. "I wouldn't mind, especially if it were Gayle." He reached over and gave Gayle a hug. Gayle was sitting next to him. She giggled and pretended to squirm in his arms.

Trent poured a bit of beer over the top of Steve's head. Steve tried to catch it with his tongue.

"It would have to be a desperate situation," Nancy Yansen said. "Besides, there's always the turkey baster."

For the next several minutes everyone except David and Angela doubled up with laughter. Then followed a series of off-color jokes and sexual innuendoes. David and Angela maintained half smiles and nodded at punch lines, but they didn't participate.

"Wait a minute, everybody," Nancy Yansen said amid laughter after a particularly salacious doctor's joke. She struggled to contain herself. "I think we should get the kids off to bed so we can have ourselves a skinny dip. What do you say?"

"I say let's do it," Trent said as he clicked beer bottles with Steve.

David and Angela eyed each other, wondering if the suggestion was another joke. Everyone else stood up and started calling for their children who were still down on the dock fishing in the darkness.

Later in their room as Angela washed her face at the wall sink she complained to David that she thought the group had suddenly regressed to some early, adolescent stage. As she spoke they both could hear the rest of the adults leaping from the dock amid giggles, shouts, and splashing.

"It does smack of college fraternity behavior," David agreed. "But I don't think there's any harm. We shouldn't be judgmental."

"I'm not so sure," Angela said. "What worries me is feeling that we're in a John Updike novel about suburbia. All that loose sexual talk and now this acting out makes me uncomfortable. I think it could be a reflection of boredom. Maybe Bartlet isn't the Eden we think it is."

"Oh, please!" David said with amazement. "I think you're being overly critical and cynical. I think they just have an exuberant, fun-loving, youthful attitude toward life. Maybe we're the ones with hang-ups."

Angela turned from the sink to face David. Her expression was one of surprise, as if David were a stranger. "You're entirely welcome to go out there naked and join the bacchanalia if you so desire," she said. "Don't let me stop you!"

"Don't get all bent out of shape," David said. "I don't want to participate. But at the same time I don't see it in such black and white terms as you apparently do. Maybe it's some of your Catholic baggage."

"I refuse to be provoked," Angela said, turning back to the sink. "And I specifically refuse to be baited into one of our pointless religious discussions."

"Fine by me," David said agreeably.

Later when they had gotten into bed and turned out the light the sounds of merriment from the dock had been replaced by the frogs and insects. It was so quiet they could hear the water lapping against the shore.

"Do you think they're still out there?" Angela whispered.

"I haven't the faintest idea," David said. "Moreover I don't care."

"What did you think of Kevin's comments about Dr. Portland?" Angela asked.

"I don't know what to think," David said. "To be truthful, Kevin has become somewhat of a mystery to me. He's a weird duck. I've never seen anyone carry on so much about getting bumped in the nose in a pickup basketball game."

"I found his comments unsettling to say the least," Angela said. "Thinking about murder in Bartlet even for a second leaves me strangely cold. I'm beginning to have this uncomfortable nagging feeling that something bad is going to happen, maybe because we're too happy."

"It's that hysterical personality of yours," David said, half in jest. "You're always looking for the dramatic. It makes you pessimistic. I think we're happy because we made the right decision."

"I hope you are right," Angela said as she snuggled into the crook of David's arm.

9

Monday, September 6

TRAYNOR PULLED HIS MERCEDES OFF THE ROAD AND bumped across the field toward the line of cars parked near a split-rail fence. During the summer months, the fairgrounds beyond the fence were used most often for crafts fairs, but today Traynor and his wife, Jacqueline, were headed there for the eighth annual Bartlet Community Hospital Labor Day picnic. Festivities had begun at nine starting with field day races for the children.

"What a way to ruin a perfectly good holiday," Traynor said to his wife. "I hate these picnics."

"Fiddlesticks!" Jacqueline snorted. "You don't fool me for a second." She was a petite woman, mildly overweight, who dressed inordinately conservatively. She was wearing a white hat, white gloves, and heels even though the outing was a cookout with corn, steamed clams, and Maine lobster.

"What are you talking about?" Traynor asked as he pulled to a stop and turned off the ignition.

"I know how much you love these hospital affairs, so don't play martyr with me. You love basking in the limelight. You play your part of Mr. Chairman of the Board to the hilt."

Traynor eyed his wife indignantly. Their marriage was filled with antagonism, and it was his routine to lash back, but he held his tongue. Jacqueline was right about the picnic, and it irritated him that over their twenty-one years of marriage, she'd come to know him so well.

"What's the story?" Jacqueline asked. "Are we going to the affair or not?"

Traynor grunted and got out of the car.

As they trudged back along the line of parked cars, Traynor saw Beaton who waved and started to come to meet them. She was with Wayne Robertson, the chief of police, and Traynor immediately suspected something was wrong.

"How convenient," Jacqueline said, seeing Beaton approach. "Here comes one of your biggest sycophants."

"Shut up, Jacqueline!" Traynor snarled under his breath.

"I've got some bad news," Beaton said without preamble.

"Why don't you head over to the tent and get some refreshments," Traynor told Jacqueline. He gave her a nudge. After she tossed Beaton a disparaging look, she left.

"She seems less than happy to be here this morning," Beaton commented.

Traynor gave a short laugh of dismissal. "What's the bad news?"

"I'm afraid there was another assault on a nurse last night," Beaton said. "Or rather, this morning. The woman was raped."

"Damn it all!" Traynor snarled. "Was it the same guy?"

"We believe so," Robertson said. "Same description. Also the same ski mask. This time the weapon was a gun rather than a knife, but he still had the handcuffs. He also forced her into the trees which is what he's done in the past."

"I'd hoped the lighting would have prevented it," Traynor said.

"It might have," Beaton said hesitantly.

"What do you mean?" Traynor demanded.

"The assault occurred in the upper lot, where there are no lights. As you remember, we illuminated only the lower lot to save money."

"Who knows about this rape?" Traynor asked.

"Not very many people," Beaton said. "I took it upon myself to contact George O'Donald at the *Bartlet Sun,* and he's agreed to keep it out of the paper. So we might get a break. I know the victim's not about to tell many people."

"I'd like to keep it away from CMV if it's at all possible," Traynor said.

"I think this underlines how much we need that new garage," Beaton said.

"We need it, but we might not get it," Traynor said. "That's my bad news for tonight's executive meeting. My old nemesis, Jeb Wiggins, has changed his mind. Worse still, he's convinced the Board of Selectmen that the new garage is a bad idea. He's got them all convinced it would be an eyesore."

"Is that the end of the project?" Beaton asked.

"It's not the end, but it's a blow," Traynor admitted. "I'll be able to get it on the ballot again, but once something like this gets turned down, it's hard to resurrect it. Maybe this rape, as bad as it is, could be the catalyst we need to get it to pass."

Traynor turned to Robertson. Traynor could see two bloated images of himself in Robertson's mirrored sunglasses. "Can't the police do anything?" he asked.

"Short of putting a deputy up there on a nightly basis," Robertson said, "there's not much we can do. I already have my men sweep the lots with their lights whenever they're in the area."

"Where's the hospital security man, Patrick Swegler?" Traynor asked.

"I'll get him," Robertson said. He jogged off toward the pond.

"Are you ready for tonight?" Traynor asked once Robertson was out of earshot.

"You mean for the meeting?" Beaton asked.

"The meeting and after the meeting," Traynor said with a lascivious smile.

"I'm not sure about after," Beaton said. "We need to talk."

"Talk about what?" Traynor asked. This was not what he wanted to hear.

"Now isn't a good time," Beaton said. She could already see Patrick Swegler and Wayne Robertson on their way over.

Traynor leaned against the fence. He felt a little weak. The one thing he counted on was Beaton's affection. He wondered if she were cheating on him, seeing someone like that ass Charles Kelley. Traynor sighed; there was always something wrong.

Patrick Swegler approached Traynor and looked him squarely in the eye. Traynor thought of him as a tough kid. He'd played football for Bartlet High School during the brief era that Bartlet dominated their interscholastic league.

"There wasn't much we could have done," Swegler said, refusing to be intimidated about the incident. "The nurse had done a double shift and she did not call security before she left as we'd repeatedly instructed nurses to do whenever they leave late. To make matters worse, she'd parked in the upper lot when she'd come to work for the day shift. As you know, the upper lot is not illuminated."

"Jesus H. Christ!" Traynor muttered. "I'm supposed to be supervising the running of a multimillion-dollar operation, and I've got to worry about the most mundane details. Why didn't she call security?"

"I wasn't told, sir," Swegler said.

"If we get the new garage, the problem will be over," Beaton said.

"Where's Werner Van Slyke of engineering?" Traynor said. "Get him over here."

"You of all people know Mr. Van Slyke doesn't attend any of the hospital's social functions," Beaton said.

"Dammit, you're right!" Traynor said. "But I want you to tell him for me that I want that upper parking lot lit just like the lower. In fact, tell him to light it up like a ballfield."

Traynor then turned back to Robertson. "And why haven't you been able to find out who this goddamn rapist is, anyway? Considering the size of the town and the number of rapes all presumably by the same person, I'd think you'd have at least one suspect."

"We're working on it," Robertson said.

"Would you like to head over to the tent?" Beaton asked.

"Why not?" Traynor fumed. "At least I'd like to get a few clams out of this." Traynor took Beaton by the arm and headed for the food.

Traynor was about to get back to the subject of their proposed rendezvous when Caldwell and Cantor spotted them and approached. Caldwell was in a particularly cheerful mood.

"I guess you've already heard how well the bonus program is working," he said to Traynor. "The August figures are encouraging."

"No, I haven't heard," Traynor said, turning to Beaton.

"It's true," Beaton said. "I'll be presenting the stats tonight. The balance sheet is okay. August CMV admissions are down four percent over last August. That's not a lot, but it's in the right direction."

"It's warming to hear some good news once in a while," Traynor said. "But we can't relax. I was talking with Arnsworth on Friday, and he warned me that the red ink will reappear with a vengeance when the tourists leave. In July and August a good portion of the hospital census has been paying patients, not CMV subscribers. Now that it's past Labor Day, the tourists will be going home. So we cannot afford to relax."

"I think we should reactivate our strict utilization control," Beaton said. "It's our only hope of holding out until the current capitation contract runs out."

"Of course we have to recommence," Traynor said. "We don't have any choice. By the way, for everyone's information, we have officially changed the name from DUM to DUC. It's now 'Drastic Utilization Control.' "

Everyone chuckled.

"I have to say I'm disappointed," Cantor said, still chuckling. "As the architect for the plan I was partial to DUM."

Despite the long, sunny summer his facial pallor had changed very little. The skin on his surprisingly slender legs was paler still. He was wearing bermuda shorts and black socks.

"I have a policy question," Caldwell said. "Under DUC, what's the status of a chronic disease like cystic fibrosis?"

"Don't ask me," Traynor said. "I'm no doctor. What the hell is cystic fibrosis? I mean, I've heard the term but that's about all."

"It's a chronic inherited illness," Cantor explained. "It causes a lot of respiratory and GI problems."

"GI stands for gastro-intestinal," Caldwell explained. "The digestive system."

"Thank you," Traynor said sarcastically. "I know what GI means. What about the illness; is it lethal?"

"Usually," Cantor said. "But with intensive respiratory care, some of the patients can live productive lives into their fifties."

"What's the actuarial cost per year?" Traynor asked.

"Once the chronic respiratory problems set in it can run twenty thousand plus per year," Cantor said.

"Good Lord!" Traynor said. "With that kind of cost, it has to be included in utilization considerations. Is it a common affliction?"

"One in every two thousand births," Cantor said.

"Oh, hell!" Traynor said with a wave. "Then it's too rare to get excited over."

After promises to be prompt for the executive board meeting that night, Caldwell and Cantor went their separate ways. Caldwell headed over to a volleyball game in the process of forming on the tiny beach at the edge of the pond. Cantor made a beeline for the tub of iced beer.

"Let's get to the food," Traynor said.

Once again they set out toward the tent that covered the rows of charcoal grills. Everyone Traynor passed either nodded or called out a greeting. Traynor's wife was right: he did love this kind of public occasion. It made him feel like a king. He'd dressed casually but with decorum; tailored slacks, his elevator loafers without socks, and an open-necked short-sleeved shirt. He'd never wear shorts to such an occasion and was amazed that Cantor cared so little about his appearance.

His happiness was dampened by the approach of his wife. "Enjoying yourself, dear?" she asked sarcastically. "It certainly appears that way."

"What am I supposed to do?" he asked rhetorically. "Walk around with a scowl?"

"I don't see why not," Jacqueline said. "That's the way you are most of the time at home."

"Maybe I should leave," Beaton said, starting to step away.

Traynor grabbed her arm, holding her back. "No, I want to hear more about August statistics for tonight's meeting."

"In that case, I'll leave," Jacqueline said. "In fact, I think I'll head home, Harold, dear. I've had a bite and spoken to the two people I care about. I'm sure one of your many colleagues will be more than happy to give you a lift."

Traynor and Beaton watched Jacqueline totter away through the deep grass in her pumps.

"Suddenly I'm not hungry," Traynor said after Jacqueline had disappeared from sight. "Let's circulate some more."

They walked down by the lake and watched the volleyball game for a while. Then they strolled toward the softball diamond.

"What is it you want to talk about?" Traynor asked, marshaling his courage.

"Us, our relationship, me," Beaton said. "My job is fine. I'm enjoying it. It's stimulating. But when you recruited me, you implied that our relationship would go somewhere. You told me you were about to get a divorce. It hasn't happened. I don't want to spend the rest of my life sneaking around. These trysts aren't enough. I need more."

Traynor felt a cold sweat break out on his forehead. With everything else going on at the hospital, he couldn't handle this. He didn't want to stop his affair with Helen, but there was no way he could face Jacqueline.

"You think about it," Beaton said. "But until something changes, our little rendezvous in my office will have to stop."

Traynor nodded. For the moment it was the best he could hope for. They reached the softball field and absently watched. A game was in the process of being organized.

"There's Dr. Wadley," Beaton said. She waved and Wadley waved back. Next to him was a young, attractive woman with dark brown hair, dressed in shorts. She was wearing a baseball cap turned jauntily to the side.

"Who is that woman with him?" Traynor asked, eager to change the subject.

"She's our newest pathologist," Beaton said. "Angela Wilson. Want to meet her?"

"I think that would be appropriate," Traynor said.

They walked over and Wadley did the honors. During his lengthy introduction, he extolled Traynor as the best chairman of the board the hospital had ever had and Angela as the newest and brightest pathologist.

"I'm delighted to meet you," Angela said.

A yell from the other players took Wadley and Angela away. The game was ready to start.

Beaton watched as Wadley shepherded Angela to her position at second base. He was playing shortstop.

"There's been quite a change in old Doc Wadley," Beaton commented. "Angela Wilson has evoked the suppressed teacher in the man. She's given him a new lease on life. He's been on cloud nine ever since she got here."

Traynor watched Angela Wilson field practice ground balls and lithely throw them to first base. He could well understand Wadley's interest, only unlike Beaton, he didn't attribute it purely to a mentor's enthusiasm. Angela Wilson didn't look like a doctor, at least not any doctor Traynor had ever met.

10

FALL IN VERMONT

EVEN THOUGH DAVID AND ANGELA HAD SPENT FOUR years in Boston during their residencies, they hadn't truly experienced the full glory of a New England fall. In Bartlet it was breathtaking. Each day the splendiferous color of the leaves became more intense, as if trying to surpass the previous day's efforts.

Besides the visual treats, fall brought more subtle pleasures associated with a sense of well-being. The air turned crisp and crystal clear and more pure to breathe. There was a feeling of invigoration in the atmosphere that made waking up in the morning a pleasure. Each day was filled with energy and excitement; each evening offered cozy contentment, with the sound of a crackling fire to keep the nighttime chill at bay.

Nikki loved her school. Marjorie Kleber became her teacher and, as David had surmised, she was superb. Although Nikki had always been a good student, she now became an excellent one. She looked forward to Mondays when a new schoolweek would commence. At night she was full of stories about all she had learned that day in class.

Nikki's friendship with Caroline Helmsford blossomed and the two became inseparable during after-school activities. Nikki's friendship with Arni also grew. After much discussion of the pros and cons Nikki won the right to ride her bike to school provided she stayed off main roads. It was an entirely new type of freedom for Nikki, and one that she loved. The route took her past the Yansen house, and every morning Arni waited for her. The last mile they rode together.

Nikki's health continued to be good. The cool, dry, clean air seemed therapeutic for her respiratory system. Except for her daily morning therapy in her beanbag chair, it was almost as if she were not afflicted by a chronic disease. The fact that she was doing so well was a source of great comfort to David and Angela.

One of the big events of the fall was the arrival of Angela's parents in the latter part of September. Angela had felt a great amount of ambivalence about whether to invite them. David's support had tipped the balance.

Dr. Walter Christopher, Angela's father, was reservedly complimentary about the house and the town but condescending about what he called "rural medicine." He stubbornly refused to visit Angela's lab with the excuse that he spent too much of his life inside hospitals.

Bernice Christopher, Angela's mother, found nothing to be complimentary about. She thought the house was too large and much too drafty, especially for Nikki. It was also her opinion that the color of the leaves was just as good in Central Park as in Bartlet, and that no one needed to drive six hours to look at trees.

The only truly uncomfortable episode occurred at the dinner table Saturday night. Bernice insisted on drinking more than her share of wine, and, as usual, became tipsy. She then accused David and his family of being the source of Nikki's illness.

"There's never been cystic fibrosis on our side," she said.

"Bernice!" Dr. Christopher said sharply. "Displays of ignorance are unbecoming."

Strained silence ensued until Angela managed to contain her anger. She then changed the subject to her and David's quest for furniture in the neighboring antique and used furniture shops.

Everyone was relieved when the time of the Christophers' departure arrived midday on Sunday. David, Angela, and Nikki dutifully stood alongside the house and waved until the Christophers' car disappeared down the road. "Kick me next time I talk about them coming up here," Angela said. David laughed and assured her it hadn't been that bad.

The magnificent fall weather continued well into October. Although there had been some cool days in late September, Indian summer arrived and brought days as warm as those of summer itself. An auspicious combination of temperature and moisture preserved the peak foliage long after what the Bartlet natives said was usual.

In mid-October during a break in Saturday morning basketball, Steve, Kevin, and Trent cornered David.

"How about you and your family coming with us this weekend?" Trent said. "We're all going over to Waterville Valley in New Hampshire. We'd love to have you guys come along."

"Tell him the real reason we want them to come," Kevin said.

"Shut up!" Trent said, playfully rapping Kevin on the top of his head.

"The real reason is that we've rented a condo with four bedrooms," Kevin persisted, ducking away from Trent. "These tightwads will do anything to reduce the cost."

"Bull," Steve said. "The more people the more fun."

"Why are you going to New Hampshire?" David asked.

"It'll be the last weekend for foliage for sure," Trent said. "It's different over in New Hampshire. More rugged scenery. Some people think the foliage is even more spectacular there."

"I can't imagine it could be any prettier than it is right here in Bartlet," David said.

"Waterville's fun," Kevin said. "Most people know it only for winter skiing. But it's got tennis, golf, hiking, even a basketball court. The kids love it."

"Come on, David," Steve said. "Winter will be here soon enough. You've got to get out and take advantage of fall as long as possible. Trust us."

"It sounds okay to me," David said. "I'll run it by Angela tonight, and I'll give one of you guys a call."

With that decided, the group joined the others to finish their basketball game.

That night Angela was not enthused when David mentioned the invitation. After the experience of the weekend at the lake combined with being busy around the house, David and Angela had not socialized much. Angela did not want to participate in another weekend of off-color jokes and sexual innuendo. Despite David's feelings to the contrary, Angela continued to wonder if their friends were bored, especially the women, and the idea of being together in such close quarters sounded a little too claustrophobic for her.

"Come on," David said. "It will be fun. We should see more of New England. As Steve said, winter will be here all too soon, and for the most part we'll be imprisoned indoors."

"It'll be expensive," Angela said, trying to think up reasons not to go.

"Come on, Mom," Nikki said. "Arni told me Waterville was neat."

"How can it be expensive?" David questioned. "We'll be splitting the condo four ways. Besides, consider our income."

"Consider our debt," Angela countered. "We've got two mortgages on the house, one of which is a balloon, and we've started paying off our student loans. And I don't know if the car will make it through a Vermont winter."

"You're being silly," David said. "I'm keeping close tabs on our finances, and we are doing perfectly well. It's not as if this is some extravagant cruise. With four families in a condo it will be no more expensive than a camping trip."

"Come on, Mom!" Nikki cried.

"All right," Angela said at last. "I can tell when I'm outnumbered."

As the week progressed excitement about the trip grew. David got one of the other CMV doctors, Dudley Markham, to cover his practice. Thursday night they packed to leave the following afternoon.

The initial plan was to leave at three P.M., but the difficulties of getting five doctors away from the hospital in the middle of the afternoon proved impossible to overcome. It wasn't until after six that they actually departed.

They took three vehicles. The Yarboroughs took their own van with their three children; the Yansens and Youngs doubled up in the Yansens' van; David, Angela, and Nikki took the Volvo. They could have squeezed in with the Yarboroughs, but Angela liked the independence of having their own vehicle.

The condo was enormous. Besides the four bedrooms, there was an upper loft where the kids could sleep in sleeping bags. After the trip everyone was tired. They headed straight for bed.

The next morning, Gayle Yarborough took it upon herself to wake everyone early. She marched through the house drumming a wooden spoon on the bottom of a saucepan, calling out that they were to leave for breakfast in half an hour.

Half an hour turned out to be an optimistic estimate of the time of departure. Although there were four bedrooms and a sleeping loft, there were only three and a half baths. Showers, hair drying, and shaving were a traffic control nightmare. On top of that, Nikki had to do her postural drainage. It was almost an hour and a half before the group was ready to go.

Climbing into the vehicles in the same order as the night before, they motored out of the valley with its circle of mountains and headed up Interstate 93. Driving through Franconia Notch both David and Angela were taken by the riotous beauty of the fall foliage silhouetted against stark, sheer walls of gray granite.

"I'm starved," Nikki said after a half hour of driving.

"Me too," Angela said. "Where are we going?"

"A place called Polly's Pancake Parlor," David said. "Trent told me it's an institution up here in northern New Hampshire."

Arriving at the restaurant, they were informed there would be a forty-minute wait for a table. Fortunately, as soon as they finally started eating, everybody said the wait had been worth it. The pancakes, smothered in pure New Hampshire maple syrup, were delicious, as were the smoked bacon and sausage.

After breakfast they toured around New Hampshire looking at the leaves and the mountain scenery. There were arguments about whether the fall foliage was better in Vermont or New Hampshire. No one won. As Angela said, it was like comparing superlatives.

As they drove back toward Waterville Valley on a particularly scenic stretch of road called the Kancamagus Highway, David noticed that high cirrus clouds had drifted over the vast dome of the sky. By the time they got back to Waterville the clouds were thicker, effectively blocking out the sun and causing the temperature to plummet into the mid-fifties.

Once they were back at the condo, Kevin was eager for a game of tennis. No one was interested, but he managed to talk David into playing. After driving most of the day, David thought that some exercise would do him good.

Kevin was an accomplished player, and he usually beat David with relative ease. But on this particular occasion, he wasn't up to his usual game. To Kevin's chagrin, David began winning.

With his keen competitive nature, Kevin tried harder, but his intensity only caused him to make more mistakes. He began getting angry at himself, then at David. When David called a shot out, Kevin dropped his racket in a show of disbelief.

"That was not out," Kevin yelled.

"It was," David answered. David circled the mark in the clay with his racket. Kevin walked all the way around the net to look.

"That wasn't the mark," Kevin said angrily.

David looked at his officemate. He could see the man was angry. "Okay," David said, hoping to defuse the tension. "Why don't we play the point over?"

When they replayed the point David won again, and in an attempt to lighten the atmosphere, he called out: "Cheating shows."

"Screw you," Kevin called back. "Serve the ball!"

Any enjoyment that David derived from the game was destroyed by Kevin's poor attitude. Kevin got more and more angry, contesting almost all of David's calls. David suggested they stop. Kevin insisted they play to the bitter end. They did and David won.

Walking back to the condo Kevin refused to talk, and David gave up trying to make conversation. A few sprinkles urged them on. When they arrived Kevin went into one of the bathrooms and slammed the door. Everyone looked at David. David shrugged. "I won," he said and felt strangely guilty.

Despite a cheerful fire, plenty of good food, and lots of beer and wine, the evening was overshadowed by Kevin's gloom. Even his wife, Nancy, told him he was acting childish. The comment sparked a nasty exchange between husband and wife that left everyone feeling uncomfortable.

Eventually Kevin's despondency spread. Trent and Steve began to lament that their practices had fallen to a point where they had to think seriously of leaving Bartlet. CMV had already hired people in their specialties.

"A lot of my former patients have told me they'd like to come back to me," Steve said, "but they can't. Their employers have negotiated with CMV for health coverage. If these patients see me they have to pay out of their pockets. It's a bad scene."

"Maybe you're better off getting the hell out while you can," Kevin said, speaking up for the first time without having been specifically spoken to.

"Now that's a sufficiently cryptic comment to beg an explanation," Trent said. "Does Dr. Doom and Gloom have some privileged information that we mortals are unaware of?"

"You wouldn't believe me if I told you," Kevin said while staring into the fire. The glow of the embers reflected off the surface of his thick glasses, giving him an eerie, eyeless appearance.

"Try us," Steve encouraged.

David glanced at Angela to see how she was faring amid this depressing evening. As far as David was concerned he found the experience much more disturbing than the one at the lake in August. He could handle sexual innuendo and crude jokes, but he had a lot of trouble with hostility and despondency, especially when it was openly expressed.

"I've learned a little more about Randy Portland," Kevin said without taking his eyes away from the fire. "But you people wouldn't believe any of it. Not after the way you responded to my suggestion that maybe his death wasn't suicide."

"Come on, Kevin," Trent said. "Stop making such a damn production out of this. Tell us what you heard."

"I had lunch with Michael Caldwell," Kevin said. "He wants me to serve on one of his innumerable committees. He told me that the chairman of the hospital board, Harold Traynor, had had a weird conversation with Portland the day he died. And Traynor related what was said to Charles Kelley."

"Yansen, get to the point," Trent said.

"Portland said there was something wrong with the hospital."

Trent's mouth dropped open in mock horror. "Something is wrong with the hospital? I'm shocked, just shocked." Trent shook his head. "Good gravy, man, there's plenty wrong with the hospital. If that's the payoff to this story, I'm not exactly impressed."

"There was more," Kevin said. "Portland told Traynor that he wouldn't take the blame."

Trent looked at Steve. "Am I missing something here?"

"Was Portland referring to a patient when he was making these claims?" Steve asked.

"Obviously," Kevin said. "But that's too subtle for a surgeon like Trent to pick up. What's clear to me is that Portland thought that something weird was going on with one of his patients. I think he should have kept his mouth shut. If he had, he'd probably still be around today."

"Sounds like Portland was just getting paranoid," Trent said. "He was already depressed. I don't buy it. You're trying to make a conspiracy out of nothing. What did Portland's patient die of, anyway?"

"Pneumonia and endotoxin shock," Steve said. "That's how it was presented in death conference."

"There you go," Trent said. "There's not a lot of mystery about a death when there's a bunch of gram-negative bacteria running around in the corpse's bloodstream. Sorry, Kev, you haven't convinced me."

Kevin stood up suddenly. "Why do I bother?" he said, throwing up his hands. "You're all blind as bats. But you know something? I don't give a rat's ass."

Stepping over Gayle, who'd sprawled on the floor in front of the fire, Kevin stomped up the half flight of stairs to the bedroom he and Nancy were occupying. He slammed the door behind him hard enough to rattle the bric-a-brac on the wooden mantel.

Everyone stared into the fire. No one spoke. Rain could be heard hitting the skylight like so many grains of rice. Finally Nancy stood up and said she'd be turning in.

"Sorry about Kevin," Trent said. "I didn't mean to provoke him."

"It's not your fault," Nancy said. "He's been a bear lately. There's something he didn't tell you. He recently lost a patient himself—which isn't exactly a common occurrence for an ophthalmologist."

The next day they woke to gusty wind, a heavy mist, and a cold, driving rain. When Angela looked out the window, she cried out for David. Fearing some catastrophe, David leaped from the bed. With heavily lidded eyes he looked out. He saw the car. He saw the rain.

"What am I supposed to be seeing?" he asked sleepily.

"The trees," Angela said. "They're bare. There are no leaves. All the foliage has vanished in one night!"

"It must have been the wind," David said. "It rattled the storm windows all night." He dropped onto the bed and burrowed back under the comforter.

Angela stayed at the window, captivated by the skeletal remains of the trees. "They all look dead," she said. "I can't believe what a difference it makes. It's hard not to see it as an omen. It adds to that feeling I've had that something bad is going to happen."

"It's melancholia left over from last night's conversational requiem," David said. "Don't get morbidly dramatic on me. It's too early. Come on back to bed for a few minutes."

The next shock was the temperature. Even by nine in the morning it was still in the thirties. Winter was on its way.

The gloomy weather did not improve the general moodiness of the adults, who'd awakened with the same sullenness they'd taken to bed. The children were initially happy, although even they started to be affected by their parents' ill humor. David and Angela were relieved to get away. As they drove down the mountain David asked Angela to remind him never to play tennis with Kevin again.

"You men can be such children with your sports," Angela said.

"Hey!" David snapped. "I wasn't the problem. He was the problem. He's so competitive. I didn't even want to play."

"Don't get so riled up," Angela said.

"I resent you implying I was at fault," David said.

"I wasn't implying anything of the kind," Angela said. "I was merely making a comment about men and their sports."

"All right, I'm sorry," David said. "I suppose I'm a bit out of sorts. It drives me crazy to be around morose people. This wasn't the most fun weekend."

"It's a strange group of people," Angela said. "They seem normal on the surface, yet underneath I'm not so sure. But at least they didn't get into any sexual discussions or start acting out like at the lake. On the other hand they did manage to dredge up the Portland tragedy again. It's like an obsession with Kevin."

"Kevin's weird," David said. "That's what I've been trying to tell you. I hate to be reminded of Portland's suicide. It makes going into my office an ordeal. Whenever he brings it up, I can't help but picture what the wall must have looked like behind my desk, splattered with blood and brains."

"David," Angela said sharply. "Please! If you don't have any concern for my sensibilities, think about Nikki's."

David glanced into the rearview mirror at Nikki. She was staring ahead without moving.

"You all right, Nikki?" David asked.

"My throat hurts," Nikki said. "I don't feel good."

"Oh, no!" Angela said. She turned around and looked at her daughter. She reached out and put the back of her hand to Nikki's forehead.

"And you insisted on going on this stupid trip," Angela muttered.

David started to defend himself, but changed his mind. He didn't want to get into an argument. He already felt irritable enough.

11

Monday, October 18

Nikki did not have a good night, nor did her parents. Angela was particularly distressed. By the wee hours of morning it was clear that Nikki was becoming progressively more congested. Well before dawn Angela tried the usual postural drainage combined with percussion. When they were through, she listened to Nikki's chest with her stethoscope. She heard rales and rhonchi, sounds that meant Nikki's breathing tubes were becoming clogged with mucus.

Before 8:00 A.M., David and Angela called their respective offices to explain that they would be late. Bundling Nikki in multiple layers of clothing, they took her to see Dr. Pilsner. Initially their reception was not encouraging. The receptionist informed them that Dr. Pilsner had a full schedule. Nikki would have to return the following day.

Angela was not to be denied. She told the receptionist that she was Dr. Wilson from pathology and that she wanted to talk with Dr. Pilsner. The receptionist disappeared into the interior of the office. Dr. Pilsner himself appeared a moment later and apologized.

"My girl thought you folks were just the usual CMV subscriber," Dr. Pilsner explained. "What's the problem?"

Angela told the doctor how a sore throat had led to congestion overnight and that the congestion did not respond to the usual postural drainage. Dr. Pilsner took Nikki into one of the examining rooms and listened to her chest.

"Definitely clogged up," he said, removing the stethoscope from his ears. Then, giving Nikki's cheek a playful pinch, he asked her how she felt.

"I don't feel good," Nikki said. Her breathing was labored.

"She's been doing so well," Angela said.

"We'll have her back to normal in a wink," Dr. Pilsner said, stroking his white beard. "But I think we'd better admit her. I want to start intravenous antibiotics and some intensive respiratory therapy."

"Whatever it takes," David said. He stroked Nikki's hair. He felt guilty for having insisted on the New Hampshire weekend.

Janice Sperling in admissions recognized both David and Angela. She commiserated with them about their daughter.

"We've got a nice room for you," she said to Nikki. "It has a beautiful view of the mountains."

Nikki nodded and allowed Janice to slip on a plastic identification bracelet. David checked it. The room was 204, one that indeed had a particularly pleasant view.

Thanks to Janice, the admitting procedure went smoothly. In only a few minutes they were on their way upstairs. Janice led them to room 204 and opened the door.

"Excuse me," Janice said with confusion. Room 204 was already occupied; there was a patient in the bed.

"Mrs. Kleber," Nikki said with surprise.

"Marjorie?" David questioned. "What on earth are you doing in here?"

"Just my luck," Marjorie said. "The one weekend you go away, I have trouble. But Dr. Markham was very kind."

"I'm so sorry to bother you," Janice said to Marjorie.

"I can't understand why the computer gave me room 204 when it was already occupied."

"No trouble," Marjorie said. "I like the company."

David told Marjorie he'd be back shortly. The Wilsons followed Janice to the nurses' station where she phoned admitting.

"I want to apologize for the mix-up," Janice said after the call. "We'll put Nikki in room 212."

Within minutes of their arrival in room 212, a team of nurses and technicians appeared and attended to Nikki. Antibiotics were started, and the respiratory therapist was paged.

When everything was under control, David told Nikki he'd be back to check on her periodically throughout the day. He also told her to do everything the nurses and the technicians asked her to do. He gave Angela a peck on the cheek, Nikki one on the forehead, and was on his way.

David returned directly to Marjorie's room and gazed down at his patient. She'd become one of his favorites over the months. She appeared tiny in the large orthopedic bed. David thought that Nikki would have been dwarfed.

"Okay," David said, feigning anger, "what's the story here?"

"It started on Friday afternoon," Marjorie said. "Problems always start on Friday when you are reluctant to call the doctor. I didn't feel well at all. By Saturday morning my right leg started to hurt. When I called your office they switched me to Dr. Markham. He saw me right away. He said I had phlebitis and that I had to go into the hospital to get antibiotics."

David examined Marjorie and confirmed the diagnosis.

"You think it was necessary for me to come into the hospital?" Marjorie asked.

"Absolutely," David assured her. "We don't like to take chances with phlebitis. Inflammation of veins goes hand in hand with blood clots. But it's looking good. I'd guess it's already improved."

"There's no doubt it's improved," Marjorie said. "It feels twenty times better than it did when I came in on Saturday."

Although he was already late getting to the office, David spent another ten minutes talking with Marjorie about her phlebitis to be sure she understood the problem. When he was finished he went to the nurses' station and read her chart. All was in order.

Next he called Dudley Markham to thank him for covering for him over the weekend and for seeing Marjorie.

"No problem," Dudley said. "I enjoyed Marjorie. We got to reminisce. She had my oldest in the second grade."

Before leaving the nurses' station David asked the head nurse, Janet Colburn, why Marjorie was in an orthopedic bed.

"No reason," Janet said. "It just happened to be in there. At the moment, it's not needed elsewhere. She's better off in that one, believe me. The electronic controls to raise and lower the head and feet never break down, something I can't say about our regular beds."

David wrote a short note in Marjorie's chart to make it official that he was assuming responsibility for her care; then he checked in on Nikki. She was already doing much better, even though the respiratory therapist had yet to arrive. Her improvement was probably due to hydration from her IV.

Finally, David headed over to the professional building to start seeing his patients. He was almost an hour late.

Susan was upset when David arrived. She had tried to juggle the patients' appointments and cancel those that she could, but there were still a number waiting. David calmed her as he slipped into his office to put on his white coat. She followed him like a hound, ticking off phone messages and consult requests.

With his white jacket half on, David abruptly stopped moving. Susan halted in mid-sentence, seeing David's face go pale.

"What's the matter?" Susan asked with alarm.

David didn't move or speak. He was staring at the wall behind his desk. To his tired, sleep-deprived eyes, the wall was covered with blood.

"Dr. Wilson!" Susan called. "What is it?"

David blinked and the disturbing image disappeared.

Stepping over to the wall, he ran his hand over its smooth surface to reassure himself it had been a fleeting visual hallucination.

David sighed, marveling at how suggestible he'd become. He turned from the wall and apologized to Susan. "I think maybe I watched too many horror pictures when I was a kid," he said. "My imagination is working overtime."

"I think we better start seeing patients," Susan said.

"I agree."

Launching into work with gusto, David made up for lost time. By midmorning he was caught up. He took a brief time-out from seeing patients in order to return some of the phone calls. The first person he tried was Charles Kelley.

"I was wondering when you would call," Kelley said. His voice was unusually businesslike. "I have a visitor in my office. His name is Neal Harper. He's from CMV utilization in Burlington. I'm afraid there's something we have to go over with you."

"In the middle of my office hours?"

"This won't take long," Kelley said. "I'm afraid I must insist. Could you please come over?"

David slowly put the receiver down. Although he didn't know why, he felt immediately anxious, as if he were a teenager being asked to come to the principal's office.

After telling Susan where he was going, David left. As he arrived at the CMV offices, the receptionist told him to go right in.

Kelley got up from behind his desk, appearing tall and tan as usual. But his manner was different. He was serious, almost dour, a far cry from his usual ebullient self. He introduced Neal Harper, a thin, precise man with pale skin and a small amount of acne. To David he appeared the apotheosis of the bureaucrat who'd been forever locked in his office, filling out his forms.

They all sat down. Kelley picked up a pencil and played with it with both hands.

"The statistics are in for your first quarter," Kelley said in a somber tone. "And they are not good."

David looked back and forth between the two men, feeling increasingly anxious.

"Your productivity is not satisfactory," Kelley continued. "You are in the lowest percentile in the whole CMV organization according to the number of patient visits per hour. Obviously you are spending entirely too much time with each patient. To make matters worse, you are in the highest percentile in ordering laboratory tests per patient from the CMV lab. As far as ordering consults from outside the CMV community, you're completely off the graph."

"I didn't know these statistics were gathered," David said lamely.

"And that's not all," Kelley said. "Too many of your patients have been seen in the Bartlet Community Hospital emergency room rather than in your office."

"That's understandable," David said. "I'm fully booked out for two weeks plus. When someone calls with an obviously acute problem needing immediate attention, I send them to the ER."

"Wrong!" Kelley snapped. "You don't send patients to the ER. You see them in your office provided they're not about to croak."

"But such disruptions throw my schedule into a turmoil," David said. "If I take time out to deal with emergencies, I can't see my scheduled patients."

"Then so be it," Kelley said. "Or make the so-called emergency patients wait until you've seen the people with appointments. It's your call, but whatever you decide, don't use the ER."

"Then what's the ER for?" David asked.

"Don't try to be a wiseass with me, Dr. Wilson," Kelley said. "You know damn well what the ER is for. It's for life-and-death emergencies. And that reminds me. Don't suggest that your patients call an ambulance. CMV will not pay for an ambulance unless there is pre-approval and pre-approval is only granted in cases that are truly life-threatening."

"Some of my patients live alone," David said. "If they're ill . . ."

"Let's not make this more difficult than it need be," Kelley interrupted. "CMV doesn't operate a bus service. All this is pretty simple. Let me spell it out for you. You must seriously increase your productivity, you must lower your use of laboratory tests drastically, you must reduce, or better yet stop, using consults outside the CMV family, and you must keep your patients out of the ER. That's all there is to it. Understand?"

David stumbled out of the CMV office. He was flabbergasted. He'd never considered himself extravagant in the use of medical resources. He'd prided himself on always keeping the patient's needs to the fore. Kelley's tirade was unnerving to say the least.

Reaching his office suite, David limped inside. He caught sight of Kevin disappearing behind a closed door with a patient and remembered his prophecy about the utilization evaluation. Kevin had been right on target; it had been devastating. What also bothered David was that Kelley had not made a single reference to quality or patient approval.

"You'd better get hopping," Susan said the instant she saw him. "You're getting behind again."

Midmorning Angela ducked out of the lab and went to check on Nikki. She was pleased to find her doing as well as she was. The fact that she wasn't running a fever was particularly encouraging. There was also a definite subjective decrease in Nikki's congestion following a prolonged visit by the respiratory therapist. Angela used a nurse's stethoscope to listen to Nikki's chest. There were still sounds of excessive mucus, but not nearly as much as there had been that morning.

"When can I go home?" Nikki asked.

"You just got here," Angela said, giving Nikki's hair a tousle. "But if you continue to improve the way you've been going, I'm sure Dr. Pilsner won't want to keep you long."

Returning to the lab, Angela went to the microbiology section to check on Nikki's sputum swab; she wanted to make certain it had been plated. It was crucial to determine the mix of bacteria in Nikki's respiratory tract. The technician assured her it had been done.

Returning to her office, Angela hung up her white coat in preparation to read a series of hematology slides. Just before she sat down she noticed the connecting door between her office and Wadley's was ajar.

Angela went over to the door and peeked in. Wadley was sitting at a double-headed teaching microscope. He caught sight of her and waved for her to come over.

"This is something I want you to see," Wadley said.

Angela stepped over to the 'scope and sat opposite her mentor. Their knees almost touched beneath the table. She put her eyes to the eyepiece and peered in. Immediately she recognized the specimen as a sample of breast tissue.

"This is a tricky case," Wadley said. "The patient is only twenty-two years old. We have to make a diagnosis, and we have to be right. So take your time." To make his point, he reached under the table and grasped Angela's thigh just above the knee. "Don't be too impulsive about your impression. Look carefully at all the ducts."

Angela's trained eye began to scan the slide in an orderly fashion, but her concentration faltered. Wadley's hand had remained on her thigh. He continued talking, explaining what he thought were the key points for making the diagnosis. Angela had trouble listening. The weight of his hand made her feel acutely uncomfortable.

Wadley had touched her often in the past, and she had had occasion to touch him as well. But it had always been within acceptable social bounds, such as contact on an arm, or a pat on the back, or an exuberant hug. They had even done several "high fives" during the softball game at the Labor Day picnic. There had never been any implication of intimacy until now, when his hand remained rooted to her leg with his thumb on the inside of her thigh.

Angela wanted to move away or remove his hand, but she did neither. She kept hoping that Wadley would suddenly realize how uncomfortable she felt and withdraw. But it didn't happen. His hand stayed on her thigh throughout a long explanation about why the biopsy had to be considered positive for cancer.

Finally Angela got up. She knew she was trembling. She bit her tongue and turned back toward her office.

"I'll be ready to review those hematology slides as soon as you are through with them," Wadley called after her.

Closing the connecting door between the offices, Angela went over to her desk and sank into her chair. Near tears, she cradled her face in her hands as a flood of thoughts cascaded through her mind. Going over the course of events of the previous months, she recalled all the episodes when Wadley offered to stay late to go over slides, and all the times he appeared when she had a few free moments. If she ever went to the coffee shop he appeared and always took the seat next to her. And as far as touching was concerned, now that she thought about it, he never passed up an opportunity.

All at once the mentor-like effort and demonstrative affection Wadley had been expending had a different, less generous, more unpleasant connotation. Even the recent talk of attending a pathology meeting in Miami during the next month made her feel uneasy.

Lowering her hands Angela stared ahead. She wondered if she was overreacting. Maybe she was blowing this episode way out of proportion, getting herself all worked up. After all, David was forever accusing her of being overly dramatic. Maybe Wadley hadn't been aware. Maybe he'd been so engrossed in his didactic role, he didn't realize what he was doing.

She angrily shook her head. Deep down she knew she wasn't overreacting. She was still grateful for Wadley's time and effort, but she could not forget how it felt to have his hand on her thigh. It was so inappropriate. He had to have known. It had to have been deliberate. The question was what she could do to put an end to his unwanted familiarity. After all, he was her boss.

At the end of his office hours, David walked over to the central hospital building to check on Marjorie Kleber and a few other patients. Once he determined that all were doing well, he stopped by to see Nikki.

His daughter was feeling fine thanks to a judicious combination of antibiotics, mucolytic agents, bronchodilators, hydration, and physical therapy. She was leaning back against a pile of pillows with a TV remote in her hand.

She was watching a game show, a pastime frowned upon at home.

"Well, well," David said. "If it isn't a true woman of leisure."

"Come on, Dad," Nikki said. "I haven't watched much TV. Mrs. Kleber came to my room, and I even had to do some schoolwork."

"That's terrible," David said with improvised dismay. "How's the breathing?"

After so many sojourns in the hospital, Nikki was truly experienced at assessing her condition. Pediatricians had learned to listen to her evaluations.

"Good," Nikki said. "It's still a little tight, but it's definitely better."

Angela appeared at the doorway. "Looks like I'm just in time for a family reunion," she said. She came in and gave both Nikki and David a hug. With Angela sitting on one side of the bed and David on the other, they talked with Nikki for half an hour.

"I want to go home," Nikki whined when David and Angela got up to go.

"I'm sure you do," Angela said. "And we want you home, but we have to follow Dr. Pilsner's orders. We'll talk to him in the morning."

After waving goodbye and watching her parents disappear down the hall, Nikki wiped a tear from the corner of her eye and reached for the TV remote. She was accustomed to being in the hospital, but she still didn't like it. The only good thing about it was that she could watch as much TV as she wanted and any type of programming—something she definitely couldn't get away with at home.

David and Angela didn't talk until they were outside under the awning covering the hospital's rear entrance. Even then the conversation was minimal. David merely said that it was silly for both of them to get wet and then ran to get the car.

On the way home there was no conversation. The only noise was the repetitive and lugubrious sound of the windshield wipers. David and Angela both thought the other was responding to a combination of Nikki's hospitalization, the disappointing weekend, and the incessant rain.

As if to confirm David's suspicions Angela broke the silence as they pulled into their driveway by telling David that a preliminary look at Nikki's sputum culture suggested pseudomonas aeruginosa. "That's not a good sign," Angela continued. "When that type of bacteria gets established in someone with cystic fibrosis it usually stays."

"You don't have to tell me," David said.

Dinner was a stifled affair without Nikki's presence. They ate at the kitchen table as the rain pelted the windows. Finally, after they'd finished eating, Angela found the emotional strength and the words to describe what had happened between herself and Wadley.

David's mouth had slowly opened as the story unfolded. By the time Angela was finished his mouth was gaping in astonishment. "That bastard!" David said. He slammed his palm down onto the table and angrily shook his head. "There were a couple of times it passed through my mind he was acting a bit too enamored, like the day at the hospital picnic. But then I convinced myself I was being ridiculously jealous. But it sounds like my intuition was right."

"I don't know for sure," Angela said. "Which is partly why I hesitated to tell you. I don't want us to jump to conclusions. It's confusing as much as it is aggravating. It's so unfair that we women have to deal with this kind of problem."

"It's an old problem," David said. "Sexual harassment has been around forever, especially since women joined the work force. It's been part of medicine for a long time, especially back when all doctors were men and all nurses were women."

"And it's still around despite the rapid increase in the number of women physicians," Angela said. "You remember some of the bullcrap I had to put up with from some of the medical school instructors."

David nodded. "I'm sorry this has happened," he said. "I know how pleased you'd been with Dr. Wadley. If you'd like I'll get in the car, drive over to his house, and punch him in the nose."

Angela smiled. "Thanks for the support."

"I thought you were being quiet tonight because you were worried about Nikki," David said. "Either that or angry about the weekend."

"The weekend is history," Angela said. "And Nikki is doing fine."

"I had a bad day too," David finally admitted. He got himself a beer from the refrigerator, took a long drink, and then told Angela about his utilization review with Kelley and the CMV man from Burlington.

"That's outrageous!" Angela said when David was finished. "What nerve to talk to you like that. Especially with the kind of positive response you've been getting from your patients."

"Apparently that's not a high priority," David said despondently.

"Are you serious? Everyone knows that doctor-patient relationships are the cornerstone of good medical care."

"Maybe that's passé," David said. "The current reality is determined by people like Charles Kelley. He's part of a new army of medical bureaucrats being created by government intervention. All of a sudden economics and politics have reached the ascendancy in the medical arena. I'm afraid the major concern is the bottom line on the balance sheet, not patient care."

Angela shook her head.

"The problem is Washington," David said. "Every time the government gets seriously involved in medical care they seem to screw things up. They try to please everybody and end up pleasing no one. Look at Medicare and Medicaid; they're both a mess and both have had a disastrous effect on medicine in general."

"What are you going to do?" Angela asked.

"I don't know," David said. "I'll try to compromise somehow. I guess I'll just take it a day at a time and see what happens. What about you?"

"I don't know either," Angela said. "I keep hoping that

I was wrong, that I'm overreacting."

"It's possible, I suppose," David said gently. "After all, this is the first time you've felt this way. And all along Wadley's been a touchy-feely kind of guy. Since you never said anything up to this point, maybe he doesn't think you mind being touched."

"What exactly are you implying?" Angela demanded sharply.

"Nothing really," David said quickly. "I was just responding to what you said."

"Are you saying I brought this on myself?"

David reached across the table and grasped Angela's arm. "Hold on!" he said. "Calm down! I'm on your side. I don't think for a second that you are to blame."

Angela's sudden anger abated. She realized that she was overreacting, reflecting her own uncertainties. There was the possibility that she had been unknowingly encouraging Wadley. After all, she'd wanted to please the man as any student might, especially since she felt a debt to him for all the time and effort he'd expended on her behalf.

"I'm sorry," Angela said. "I'm just stressed out."

"Me too," David said. "Let's go to bed."

12

TO DAVID'S AND ANGELA'S DISAPPOINTMENT, IT WAS still raining in the morning. In contrast to the gloomy weather, however, Nikki was in high spirits and doing marvelously. Even her color had returned. The sore throat, presaging an extended illness, had disappeared with the antibiotics, indicating that if it had been infectious, it had been bacterial rather than viral in origin. Thankfully there was still no fever.

"I want to go home," Nikki repeated.

"We haven't talked with Dr. Pilsner," David reminded her. "But we will, sometime this morning. Be patient."

After the visit with Nikki, Angela left for the lab while David went to the nurses' station to pick up Marjorie's chart. He'd been considering discharging her until he walked into her room. Her response to his greeting told him something was wrong.

"Marjorie, what's the matter?" David asked as he felt his own pulse quicken. She was lethargic. He touched the back of his hand to her forehead and her arms. Her skin was warm to the touch. He guessed she had a fever.

Marjorie responded to David's persistent questioning with barely intelligible mumbling. She acted drugged although not in any apparent pain.

Noticing Marjorie's breathing was mildly labored, David listened carefully to her chest. He heard faint sounds of congestion. Next he checked the area of phlebitis and found it was all but resolved. With mounting anxiety David examined the rest of his patient. Finding nothing he hurried back to the nurses' station and ordered a barrage of stat laboratory tests.

The first thing to come back from the lab was her blood count, but it only added to David's puzzlement. Her white cell level, which had been appropriately falling with the resolution of the phlebitis, had continued to fall and was now in the lower percentile of normal.

David scratched his head. The low white count seemed contradictory to her clinical state, which suggested developing pneumonia. Getting up from the desk, David went back to Marjorie's room and listened to her chest again. The incipient congestion was real.

Returning to the nurses' station, David debated what to do. More lab tests came back, but they were all normal, even the portable chest X ray, and hence no help. David thought about calling in some consults, but after his poor utilization review the day before, he was reluctant. The problem was that the consults who might have been helpful were not part of the CMV organization.

Instead of requesting any consults, David took the *Physicians' Desk Reference* off the bookshelf. Since his main concern was that a gram-negative bacteria might have appeared as a superinfection, he looked up an antibiotic that was specific for such an eventuality. When he found one he felt confident it would take care of the problem.

After the appropriate orders were written, including a request to be called immediately if there was any change in Marjorie's status, David headed over to his office.

It was Angela's turn to handle the day's surgical frozen sections. She always found the task nerve-wracking since she knew that while she worked, the patient remained under anesthesia awaiting her verdict whether the biopsy was cancerous or benign.

The frozen sections were done in a small lab within the operating suite. The room was tucked off to the side and visited infrequently by the operating room staff. Angela worked with intense concentration, studying the patterns of cells in the specimen under the microscope.

She did not hear the door silently open behind her. She was unaware that anyone was in the room until he spoke.

"Well, honey, how's it going?"

Startled, Angela's head shot up as a bolus of adrenaline coursed through her body. With her pulse pounding in her temples, she found herself looking into Wadley's smiling face. She hated to be called "honey" by anyone, except maybe David. And she didn't appreciate being snuck up on.

"Any problems?" Wadley asked.

"No," Angela said sharply.

"Let me take a look," Wadley said, motioning toward the microscope. "What's the case?"

Angela gave Wadley her seat. Succinctly she gave the history. He glanced at the slide, then stood up.

For a moment they talked about the slide in pathological jargon. It was apparent they agreed the growth was benign, happy news for the anesthetized patient.

"I want to see you later in my office," Wadley said. He winked.

Angela nodded, ignoring the wink. She turned away and was about to sit down again when she felt Wadley's hand brush across her buttocks.

"Don't work too hard, honey!" he called out. And with that, he slipped out the door.

The episode had happened so fast that Angela had not been able to respond. But she knew it had not been inadvertent, and now she knew for certain that the thigh-touching the day before had not been an innocent oversight.

For a few minutes Angela sat in the tiny lab and trembled with indignation and confusion. She wondered what was encouraging this sudden boldness. She certainly had not changed her behavior over the last few days. And what should she do? She couldn't just idly sit by and allow it to go on. That would be an open invitation.

Angela decided she had two possibilities. She could confront Wadley directly or she could go to the medical director, Michael Caldwell. But then she thought about Dr. Cantor, the current chief of staff. Maybe she should go to him.

Angela sighed. Neither Caldwell nor Cantor struck her as ideal authorities to turn to in a case of sexual harassment. Both were macho types, and Angela remembered their responses when she'd first met them. Caldwell had seemed shocked that women were actually pathologists while Cantor had offered that ignorant remark about the few women in his medical school class being "dogs."

She thought again about confronting Wadley herself, but she didn't like that alternative any better.

The raucous buzz of static coming over the intercom shocked Angela back to reality. The static preceded the voice of the head nurse. "Dr. Wilson," she said. "They are waiting on the biopsy results down in OR three."

David found concentrating on his patients' problems harder that morning than the previous afternoon. Not only was he still upset about his review with Kelley, now he had Marjorie Kleber's worsening condition to worry about.

Midmorning, David saw another of his frequent visitors, John Tarlow, the leukemia patient. John didn't have an appointment; David had Susan squeeze him in as a semi-emergency after he'd called that morning. Only the day before David would have directed John to the ER, but feeling chastened by Kelley's lecture, he felt obliged to see the man himself.

John was feeling poorly. Following a meal of raw shellfish the night before, he'd developed severe GI problems with both vomiting and diarrhea. He was dehydrated and in acute discomfort with colicky abdominal pain.

Seeing how bad John was and remembering his leukemic history, David hospitalized him immediately. He ordered a number of tests to try to determine the cause of John's symptoms. He also started intravenous fluid to rehydrate him. For the moment he held off on antibiotics, preferring to wait until he had some idea of what he was dealing with. It could have been a bacterial infection or it could have been merely a response to toxins: food poisoning, in the vernacular.

Just before eleven in the morning Traynor was told the bad news by his secretary, Collette. She'd just been informed by phone that Jeb Wiggins had again carried the Board of Selectmen. The final vote on the hospital parking garage, which Traynor had managed once more to get on the agenda, had been thumbs down. Now there probably wasn't even a way to get it on the ballot again before spring.

"Goddamn it," Traynor raged. He pummeled the surface of his desk with both hands. Collette didn't flinch. She was accustomed to Traynor's outbursts. "I'd love to grab Wiggins around that fat neck of his and choke him until he turns blue."

Collette discreetly left the room. Traynor paced the area in front of his desk. The lack of support he had to deal with when it came to running the hospital galled him. He could not understand how the Board of Selectmen could be so shortsighted. It was obvious that the hospital was the most important enterprise in the entire town. It was equally obvious that the hospital needed the parking garage.

Unable to work, Traynor grabbed his raincoat, hat, and umbrella and stormed out of his office. Climbing into his car he drove up to the hospital. If there was to be no parking garage, he would at least personally inspect the lighting. He didn't want to risk any more rapes in the hospital parking lot.

Traynor found Werner Van Slyke in his windowless cubbyhole that served as the engineering/maintenance department's office. Traynor had never been particularly comfortable around Van Slyke. Van Slyke was too quiet, too much of a loner, and mildly unkempt. Traynor also found Van Slyke physically intimidating; he was several

inches taller than Traynor and significantly huskier, with
the kind of bulky muscles that suggested weightlifting was
a hobby.

"I want to see the lights in the parking lots," Traynor
said.

"Now?" Van Slyke asked, without the usual rise in the
pitch of his voice that normal people use when asking
questions. Every word he said was flat and it grated on
Traynor's ears.

"I had a little free time," Traynor explained. "I want to
make sure it's adequate."

Van Slyke pulled on a yellow slicker and walked out
of the office. Outside the hospital he pointed to each of
the lights in the lower lot, walking from one to the next
without comment.

Traynor tagged along beneath his umbrella, nodding at
each fixture. As he followed Van Slyke through the copse of
evergreen trees and climbed the wooden steps that separated
the two lots, Traynor wondered what Van Slyke did when
he wasn't working. He realized he never saw Van Slyke
walking around the town or shopping in the shops. And
the man was notorious for not attending hospital functions.

Uncomfortable with the continued silence, Traynor
cleared his throat: "Everything okay at home?" he asked.

"Fine," Van Slyke said.

"House okay, no problems?"

"Nope," Van Slyke said.

Traynor started feeling challenged to get Van Slyke to
respond with more than monosyllables. "Do you like civilian life better than the navy?"

Van Slyke shrugged and began pointing out the lights in
the upper lot. Traynor continued to nod at each one. There
seemed to be plenty. Traynor made a mental note to swing
up there with his car some evening to see how light it was
after dark.

"Looks good," Traynor said.

They started back toward the hospital.

"You being careful with your money?" Traynor asked.

"Yeah," Van Slyke said.

"I think you are doing a great job here at the hospital," Traynor said. "I'm proud of you."

Van Slyke didn't respond. Traynor looked over at Van Slyke's wet profile with its heavy five o'clock shadow. He wondered how Van Slyke could be so unemotional, but then again he realized that he'd never understood the boy ever since he'd been little. Sometimes Traynor found it hard to believe they were related, yet they were. Van Slyke was Traynor's only nephew, the son of his deceased sister.

When they reached the stand of trees separating the two lots, Traynor stopped. He looked among the branches. "How come there are no lights on this path?"

"No one said anything about lights on the path," Van Slyke said. It was the first full sentence he had uttered. Traynor was almost pleased.

"I think one or two would be nice," Traynor said.

Van Slyke barely nodded.

"Thanks for the tour," Traynor said in parting. He was relieved to make his escape. He had always felt guilty for feeling so estranged from his own kin, but Van Slyke was such an enigma. Traynor had to admit that his sister hadn't exactly been a paragon of normality. Her name had been Sunny, but her disposition had been anything but. She'd always been quiet, retiring, and had suffered from depression for most of her life.

Traynor still had a hard time understanding why Sunny had married Dr. Werner Van Slyke, knowing the man was a drunk. Her suicide was the final blow. If she'd only come to him, he would have tried to help.

In any case, given Werner Van Slyke's parentage, it was hardly a surprise that he was as strange as he was. Yet with his naval machinist's training he'd been both helpful and reliable. Traynor was glad he'd suggested that the hospital hire him.

Traynor roused himself from this reflection and headed for Beaton's office.

"I've got some bad news," Traynor said as soon as Beaton's secretary admitted him. He told her about the Board of Selectmen's vote on the parking garage.

"I hope we don't have any more assaults," Beaton said. She was clearly disappointed.

"Me too," Traynor said. "Hopefully the lights will be a deterrent. I just walked around the parking lots and took a look at them. They seem adequate enough, except on the path between the two lots. I asked Van Slyke to add a couple there."

"I'm sorry I didn't do both lots from the start," Beaton said.

"How are the finances looking for this month?" Traynor questioned.

"I was afraid you'd ask," Beaton said. "Arnsworth gave me the mid-month figures just yesterday and they are not good. October will definitely be worse than September if the second half of the month is anything like the first. The bonus program is helping, but admissions for CMV are still over the projected level. To make matters worse, we seem to be getting sicker patients."

"I suppose that means we have to put more pressure on utilization," Traynor said. "DUC has to save the day. Other than the bonus program, we're on our own. I don't antici-pate any more insurance bequests in the near future."

"There are a few other nuisances of which you should be aware," Beaton said. "M.D. 91 has relapsed. Robertson picked him up on a DUI. He was driving his car on the sidewalk."

"Pull his privileges," Traynor said without hesitation. "Alcoholic physicians have already caused enough heart-ache in my life." He recalled once again his sister's good-for-nothing husband.

"The other problem," Beaton said, "is that Sophie Stephangelos, the head nurse in the OR, has discovered significant theft of surgical instruments over the last year. She thinks one of the surgeons is taking them."

"What next?" Traynor said with a sigh. "Sometimes I think running a hospital is an impossible task."

"She has a plan to catch the culprit," Beaton said. "She wants an okay to go ahead with it."

"By all means," Traynor said. "And if she catches him let's make an example out of him."

• • •

Coming out of one of his examining rooms, David was surprised to find that the basket on the other room's door was empty.

"No charts?" he asked.

"You're ahead of yourself," Susan explained. "Take a break."

David took advantage of the opportunity to dash over to the hospital. The first stop was Nikki's room. When he walked in he was surprised to find both Caroline and Arni sitting on Nikki's bed. Somehow the two kids had managed to get into the hospital without being challenged. They were supposed to be accompanied by an adult.

"You won't get us into trouble, will you, Dr. Wilson?" Caroline asked. She looked much younger than nine. Her illness had stunted her growth much more than it had Nikki's. She looked more like a child of seven or eight.

"No, I won't get you in trouble," David assured them. "But how did you get out of school so early?"

"It was easy for me," Arni said proudly. "The substitute teacher doesn't know what's going on. She's a mess."

David turned his attention to his daughter. "I spoke with Dr. Pilsner, and he said it's okay for you to go home this afternoon."

"Cool," Nikki said excitedly. "Can I go to school tomorrow?"

"I don't know about that," David said. "We'll have to discuss it with your mother."

After leaving Nikki's room, David looked in on John Tarlow to make sure that he was settled, his IV was started, and the tests David had ordered were in progress. John said he didn't feel any better. David told him to be patient and assured him there'd be improvement after he'd been hydrated.

Finally David stopped in to see Marjorie. He hoped that the added antibiotic would have already improved her condition, but it hadn't. In fact, David was shocked to see how much she had deteriorated; she was practically comatose.

Panic-stricken, David listened to Marjorie's chest. There was more congestion than earlier but still not enough to explain her clinical state. Rushing back to the nurses' station, David demanded to know why he hadn't been called.

"Called on what?" Janet Colburn asked. She was the head nurse.

"Marjorie Kleber," David yelled while he wrote orders for more stat bloodwork and another portable chest X ray.

Janet consulted with several of the other floor nurses, then told David that no one had noticed any change. She even said that one of the LPNs had just been in Marjorie's room less than half an hour previously and had reported no change.

"That's impossible," David snapped as he grabbed the phone and started making calls. Earlier, he'd been reluctant to call in consults. Now he was panicked to get them to come in as soon as possible. He called Marjorie's oncologist, Dr. Clark Mieslich, and an infectious disease specialist, Dr. Martin Hasselbaum. Neither of them were CMV doctors. David also called a neurologist named Alan Prichard, who was part of the CMV organization.

All three specialists were available for David's call. When they heard David's frantic appeal and his description of the case, they all agreed to come in immediately. David then called Susan to alert her to what was happening. He told her to advise the patients who came into the office that he would be delayed.

The oncologist was the first to arrive, followed in short order by the infectious disease specialist and the neurologist. They reviewed the chart and discussed the situation with David, before descending en masse on Marjorie. After examining her closely they withdrew to the nurses' station to confer. But hardly had they begun to discuss Marjorie's condition when disaster struck.

"She's stopped breathing," a nurse yelled from Marjorie's room. She'd stayed behind to clean up the debris left by the examining specialists.

While David and the consults raced back, Janet Colburn called the resuscitation team. They arrived in minutes and converged on room 204.

With so much manpower immediately available, Marjorie was quickly intubated and respired. It had been done with such dispatch that her heart rate did not change. Everyone was confident she'd experienced only a short period of decreased oxygen. The problem was they did not know why she'd stopped breathing.

As they began to discuss possible causes, her heart suddenly slowed and then stopped. The monitor displayed an eerie flat line. The resuscitation team shocked her in hopes of restarting her heart, but there was no response. They quickly shocked her again. When that didn't work, they began closed chest cardiac massage.

They worked frenetically for thirty minutes, trying every trick they could think of, but nothing worked. The heart would not even respond to external pacing. Gradually, discouragement set in, and finally, by general consensus, Marjorie Kleber was declared dead.

While the resuscitation team unhooked their wires and the nurses cleaned up, David walked back to the nurses' station with the consults. He was devastated. He could not imagine a worse scenario. Marjorie had come into the hospital with a relatively minor problem while he was off enjoying himself. Now she was dead.

"It's too bad," Dr. Mieslich said. "She was such a terrific person."

"I'd say she did pretty well considering the history in the chart," Dr. Prichard said. "But her disease was bound to catch up with her."

"Wait a second," David said. "Do you think she died of her cancer?"

"Obviously," Dr. Mieslich said. "She had disseminated cancer when I first saw her. Although she'd done better than I would have predicted, she was one sick lady."

"But there wasn't any clinical evidence of her tumor," David said. "Her problems leading up to this fatal episode seemed to suggest some sort of immune system malfunction. How can you relate that to her cancer?"

"The immune system doesn't control breathing or the heart," Dr. Prichard said.

"But her white count was falling," David said.

"Her tumor wasn't apparent, that's true," Dr. Mieslich said. "But if we were to open her up, my guess is that we would find cancer all over, including in her brain. Remember, she had extensive metastases when she was originally diagnosed."

David nodded. The others did the same. Dr. Prichard slapped David on the back. "Can't win them all," he said.

David thanked the consults for coming in. They all politely thanked him for the referral, then went their separate ways. David sat at the nurses' station desk. He felt weak and disconsolate. His sadness and sense of guilt at Marjorie's passing was even more acute than he'd feared. He'd come to know her too well. To make it even worse, she was Nikki's beloved teacher. How would he explain this to her?

"Excuse me," Janet Colburn said softly. "Lloyd Kleber, Marjorie's husband, is here. He'd like to talk to you."

David stood up. He felt numb. He didn't know how long he'd been sitting at the nurses' station. Janet directed him into the patients' lounge.

Lloyd Kleber was staring out the window at the rain. David guessed he was in his mid-forties. His eyes were red from crying. David's heart went out to the man. Not only had he lost a wife, but now he had the responsibility of two motherless children.

"I'm sorry," David said lamely.

"Thank you," Lloyd said, choking back tears. "And thank you for taking care of Marjorie. She really appreciated your concern for her."

David nodded. He tried to say things that reflected his compassion. He never felt adequate at moments like this, but he did the best he could.

Finally, David ventured to ask for permission to do an autopsy. He knew it was a lot to ask, but he was deeply troubled by Marjorie's swift deterioration. He wanted desperately to understand.

"If it could help others in some small way," Mr. Kleber said, "I'm sure Marjorie would want it done."

David stayed and talked with Lloyd Kleber until more members of the immediate family arrived. Then David, leaving them to their grief, walked over to the lab. He found Angela at the desk in her office. She was pleased to see him and told him so. Then she noticed his strained expression.

"What's wrong?" she asked anxiously. She stood up and took his hand.

David told her. He had to stop a few times to compose himself.

"I'm so sorry," Angela said. She put her arms around him and gave him a reassuring hug.

"Some doctor!" he chided himself, fighting tears. "You'd think I'd have adjusted better to this kind of thing by now."

"Your sensitivity is part of your charm," Angela assured him. "It's also what makes you a good doctor."

"Mr. Kleber agreed to an autopsy," David said. "I'm glad because I haven't the slightest idea why she died, especially so quickly. Her breathing stopped and then her heart. The consults all think it was her cancer. It probably was. But I'd like Bartlet to confirm it. Could you see that it gets done?"

"Sure," Angela said. "But please don't get too depressed over this. It wasn't your fault."

"Let's see what the autopsy shows," David said. "And what am I going to tell Nikki?"

"That's going to be hard," Angela admitted.

David returned to his office to try to see his patients in as short order as possible. For their sake, he hated being so backed up, but there had been no way to avoid it. He'd only managed to see four when Susan waylaid him between examining rooms.

"Sorry to bother you," she said, "but Charles Kelley is in your private office, and he demands to see you immediately."

Fearing Kelley's visit had something to do with Marjorie's death, David stepped across the hall into his office. Kelley was impatiently pacing. He stopped when David arrived. David closed the door behind himself.

Kelley's face was hard and angry. "I find your behavior particularly galling," he said, towering over David.

"What are you talking about?" David asked.

"Just yesterday I spoke with you about utilization," Kelley said. "I thought it was pretty clear and that you understood. Then today you irresponsibly ordered two non-CMV consults to see a hopelessly terminal patient. That kind of behavior suggests that you have no comprehension of the major problem facing medicine today: unnecessary and wasteful expense."

With his emotions raw, David struggled to keep himself under control. "Just a minute. I'd like you to tell me how you know the consults were unnecessary."

"Oh, brother!" Kelley said with a supercilious wave of his head. "It's obvious. The patient's course wasn't altered. She was dying and she proceeded to die. Everyone must die at some time or another. Money and other resources should not be thrown away for the sake of hopeless heroics."

David stared into Kelley's blue eyes. He didn't know what to say. He was dumbfounded.

Hoping to avoid Wadley, Angela sought out Dr. Paul Darnell in his windowless cubicle on the other side of the lab. His desk was piled high with bacterial culture dishes. Microbiology was his particular area of interest.

"Can I speak to you for a moment," Angela called from Paul's doorway.

He waved her in and leaned back in his swivel chair.

"What's the autopsy protocol around here?" she asked. "I haven't seen any done since I got here."

"That's an issue you'll have to discuss with Wadley," Paul said. "It's a policy problem. Sorry."

Reluctantly, Angela went to Wadley's office.

"What can I do for you, honey?" Wadley said. He smiled a kind of smile Angela had previously seen as paternal but now saw as lewd.

Wincing at being addressed as "honey," Angela swallowed her pride and asked about the procedure for arranging an autopsy.

"We don't do autopsies," Wadley said. "If it's a medical examiner case, the body goes to Burlington. It costs too much to do autopsies, and the contract with CMV doesn't include them."

"What if the family requests it?" Angela asked, knowing this wasn't precisely true in the Kleber case.

"If they want to shell out eighteen hundred and ninety dollars, then we'll accommodate them," Wadley said. "Otherwise, we don't do it."

Angela nodded, then left. Instead of getting back to her own work, she walked over to the professional building and went into David's office. She was appalled by the number of patients waiting to be seen. Every chair in the waiting room was occupied; a few people were even standing in the hall. She caught David as he shuttled between examining rooms. He was clearly frazzled.

"I can't do an autopsy on Marjorie Kleber."

"Why not?" David asked.

Angela told him what Wadley had said.

David shook his head with frustration and blew out between pursed lips. "My opinion of this place is going downhill fast," he said. He then told Angela about Kelley's opinion of his handling of the Kleber case.

"That's ridiculous," Angela said. She was incensed. "You mean he suggested that the consults were unnecessary because the patient died. That's crazy."

"What can I tell you?" David said with a shake of his head.

Angela didn't know what to say. Kelley was beginning to sound dangerously uninformed. Angela would have liked to talk more, but she knew David didn't have the time. She motioned over her shoulder. "You've got an office full of patients out there," she said. "When do you think you'll be done?"

"I haven't the slightest idea."

"How about I take Nikki home and you give me a call when you're ready to leave. I'll come back and pick you up."

"Sounds good," David said.

"Hang in there, dear," Angela said. "We'll talk later."

Angela went back to the lab, finishing up for the day, collected Nikki, and drove home. Nikki was ecstatic to get out of the hospital. She and Rusty had an exuberant reunion.

David called at seven-fifteen. With Nikki comfortably ensconced in front of the TV, Angela returned to the hospital. She drove slowly. It was raining so hard the wipers had to struggle to keep the windshield clear.

"What a night," David said as he jumped into the car.

"What a day," Angela said as she started down the hill toward town. "Especially for you. How are you holding up?"

"I'm managing," David said. "It was a help to be so busy. I was grateful for the diversion. But now I have to face reality; what am I going to tell Nikki?"

"You'll just have to tell her the truth," Angela said.

"That's easier said than done," David said. "What if she asks me why she died? The trouble is I don't know, neither physiologically nor metaphysically."

"I've thought more about what Kelley said," Angela said. "It seems to me he has a fundamental misunderstanding about the basics of patient care."

"That's an understatement," David said with a short, sarcastic laugh. "The scary part is that he's in a supervisory position. Bureaucrats like Kelley are intruding into the practice of medicine under the guise of health-care reform. Unfortunately the public has no idea."

"I had another minor run-in with Wadley today," Angela said.

"That bastard!" David said. "What did he do now?"

"He called me 'honey' a few times," Angela said. "And he brushed his hand across my backside."

"God! What an insensitive jerk," David said.

"I really have to do something. I just wish I knew what."

"I think you should talk to Cantor," David said. "I've given it some thought. At least Cantor is a physician, not just a health-care bureaucrat."

"His comment about 'the girls,' as he called them, in his medical school class was not inspiring," Angela said.

They pulled into their driveway. Angela came to a stop as close as possible to the door to the mud room. They both prepared to run for shelter.

"When is this rain going to stop?" David complained. "It's been raining for three days straight."

Once they were inside, David decided to make a fire to cheer up the house while Angela reheated the food she'd made earlier for herself and Nikki. Descending into the basement, David noticed that moisture was seeping through the grout between the granite foundation blocks. Along with the moisture was the damp, musty odor he'd occasionally smelled before. As he collected the wood, he comforted himself with the thought of the earthen floor. If a significant amount of water were to come into the basement, it would just soak in and eventually disappear.

After eating, David joined Nikki in front of the TV. Whenever she was ill they were lenient about how much time she was allowed to watch. David feigned interest in the show in progress, while he built up the courage to tell Nikki about Marjorie. Finally, during a commercial break, David put his arm around his daughter.

"I have to tell you something," he said gently.

"What?" Nikki asked. She was contentedly petting Rusty who was curled up on the couch next to her.

"Your teacher, Marjorie Kleber, died today," David said gently.

Nikki didn't say anything for a few moments. She looked down at Rusty, pretending to be concerned about a knot behind his ear.

"It makes me very sad," David continued, "especially since I was her doctor. I'm sure it upsets you, too."

"No, it doesn't," Nikki said quickly with a shake of her head. She brushed a strand of hair away from her eyes. Then she looked at the television as if she were interested in the commercial.

"It's okay to be sad," David said. He started to talk about missing people you cared about when Nikki suddenly threw herself at him, enveloping him in a flood of tears. She hugged him tighter than he could ever remember her having hugged him.

David patted her on the back and continued to reassure her.

Angela appeared at the doorway. Seeing David holding their sobbing child, she came over. Gently pushing Rusty aside, she sat down and put her arms around both David and Nikki. Together the three held onto each other, rocking gently as the rain beat against the windows.

13

WEDNESDAY, OCTOBER 20

DESPITE NIKKI'S SUSTAINED PROTESTS, DAVID AND Angela insisted that she stay home from school another day. Considering the weather and the fact that she was still on antibiotics there was no reason to take a chance.

Although Nikki was not as cooperative as usual, they carried out her morning respiratory therapy with great diligence. Both David and Angela listened to her chest afterward and both were satisfied.

Alice Doherty arrived exactly at the time she promised. David and Angela were thankful to have someone so reliable and so conveniently available.

As Angela and David climbed into their blue Volvo, David complained that he'd not been able to ride his bike all week. It wasn't raining as hard as it had been, but the clouds were low and ponderous, and a heavy mist rose out of the saturated earth.

They got to the hospital at seven-thirty. While Angela headed off for the lab, David went up to the patient floor.

When he entered John Tarlow's room he was surprised to find drop cloths, stepladders, and an empty bed. Continuing on to the nurses' station he inquired after his patient.

"Mr. Tarlow has been moved to 206," Janet Colburn said.

"How come?" David asked.

"They wanted to paint the room," Janet said. "Maintenance came up and informed us. We let admitting know, and they told us to transfer the patient to 206."

"I think that's inconsiderate," David complained.

"Well, don't blame us," Janet said. "Talk to maintenance."

Feeling irritated for his patient's sake, David took Janet's suggestion and marched down to maintenance. He knocked on the jamb of the maintenance/engineering office. Inside and bent over a desk was a man close to David's age. He was dressed in rumpled, medium-green cotton twill work shirt and pants. His face was textured with a two-day growth of whiskers.

"What?" Van Slyke asked as he looked up from his scheduling book. His voice was flat and his expression was emotionless.

"One of my patients was moved from his room," David said. "I want to know why."

"If you are talking about room 216, it's being painted," Van Slyke said in a monotone.

"It's obvious it's being painted," David said. "What isn't obvious is why it's being painted."

"We have a schedule," Van Slyke said.

"Schedule or no schedule," David said, "I hardly think patients should be inconvenienced, especially patients who are ill, and patients in the hospital are invariably ill."

"Talk to Beaton if you have a problem," Van Slyke said. He went back to his book.

Taken aback by Van Slyke's insolence, David stood stunned in the doorway for a moment. Van Slyke ignored him with ease. David shook his head, then turned to go. On his way back to the patient floor, he was seriously considering taking Van Slyke's advice to discuss the situation with the hospital administrator until he walked into John

Tarlow's new room. Suddenly David was presented with a more pressing problem: John Tarlow's condition was worse.

John's diarrhea and vomiting, which initially had been controlled, had returned with a vengeance. On top of that, John was obtunded, and when aroused, apathetic. David could not understand these symptoms since John had been on IVs since his admission and was clearly not dehydrated.

David examined his patient carefully but couldn't find an explanation for the marked change in his clinical state, particularly his depressed mental status. The only thing David could think of was the possibility John could have been overly sensitive to the sleeping medication that David had prescribed as a PRN order, meaning it was to be given if the patient requested it.

Hurrying back to the nurses' station, David pulled John's chart from the rack. He desperately pored over the data that had returned overnight from the lab in an attempt to understand what was going on and to try to decide what to do next. As a result of the run-in with Kelley the day before he was reluctant to request any consults since neither of the two he wanted—oncology and infectious disease—were CMV doctors.

David closed his eyes and rubbed his temples. He did not feel he was making much progress. Unfortunately, a key piece of information was lacking: the results of the stool cultures plated the day before were not yet available. Consequently David still didn't know if he was dealing with a bacteria or not, and if he was, what kind of bacteria it was. On the positive side was the fact that John was still afebrile.

Redirecting his attention to the chart, David ascertained that John had been given the PRN sleeping medication. Thinking that it might have contributed to John's lethargy, David canceled it. He also ordered another stool culture and another blood count. As a final request, he asked for John's temperature to be taken every hour along with the express order for David to be called if it rose above normal.

• • •

After completing the last scheduled biopsy, Angela tidied up the small pathology lab in the OR suite, and headed for her office. Her morning had been productive and pleasant; she'd managed to avoid Wadley entirely. Unfortunately, she knew she'd eventually have to see him, and she worried about his behavior. Although she considered herself an optimistic person, she was fearful that the problem with Wadley would not spontaneously resolve.

Entering the office, Angela immediately noticed the connecting door from her office into Wadley's was ajar. As silently as possible she moved over to the door and began to close it.

"Angela!" Wadley called out, making Angela flinch. She hadn't realized how tense she was. "Come in here. I want to show you something fascinating."

Angela sighed and reluctantly opened the door. Wadley was sitting at his desk in front of his regular microscope, not the teaching microscope.

"Come on," Wadley called again. He waved Angela over and tapped the top of his microscope. "Take a gander at this slide."

Warily Angela advanced into the room. Several feet away she hesitated. As if sensing her reluctance, Wadley gave himself a little push, and his chair rolled back from the desk. Angela stepped up to the microscope and leaned over to adjust the eyepieces.

Before she could look in Wadley lunged forward and grabbed her around the waist. He pulled her onto his lap and locked his arms around her.

"Gotcha!" Wadley cried.

Angela shrieked and struggled to get away. The unexpected forcefulness of the contact shocked her. She'd been concerned about him touching her subtly, not manhandling her.

"Let me go!" Angela demanded angrily, trying to unlock his fingers and break his grip.

"Not until you let me tell you something," Wadley said. He was chuckling.

Angela stopped struggling. She had her eyes closed. She was as humiliated as she was furious.

"That's better," Wadley said. "I've got good news. The trip is all set. I even got the tickets already. We're going to the pathology meeting in Miami in November."

Angela opened her eyes. "Wonderful," she said with as much sarcasm as she could muster. "Now let me go!"

Wadley released her and Angela sprang from his lap. But as she pulled away he managed to grab her wrist. "It's going to be fantastic," Wadley said. "The weather will be perfect. It's the best time of year in Miami. We'll be staying on the beach. I got us rooms in the Fontainbleau."

"Let go!" Angela demanded through clenched teeth.

"Hey," Wadley said. He leaned forward and looked at her closely. "Are you mad or something? I'm sorry if I scared you. I just wanted it to be a surprise." He let go of her hand.

Angela was beside herself with anger. Biting her tongue to keep herself from exploding, she dashed into her office. Mortified and demeaned, she slammed the connecting door.

Forcibly she rubbed her face with both hands, trying to regain a modicum of control. She was shaking from the adrenaline coursing through her body. It took her a few minutes to settle down and for her breathing to return to normal. Once it had, she grabbed her coat, and angrily stalked out of her office. At least Wadley's oafishly inappropriate advances had finally spurred her to action.

Avoiding the misty rain as much as possible, she dashed from the main hospital building to the Imaging Center. Once under the projecting eaves she slowed to a fast walk. Inside she went directly to Cantor's office.

Not having called beforehand, Angela had to wait almost a half hour before Dr. Delbert Cantor could see her. While she waited she calmed down considerably and even began once more to question if she were partly to blame for Wadley's behavior. She wondered if she should have anticipated it and not have been so naive.

"Come in, come in," Cantor said agreeably when he could finally see her. He'd gotten up from his disordered desk to escort Angela into the room. He had to move a stack of unopened radiology journals from a chair for her to sit down. He offered her some refreshment. She politely refused. He sat down, crossed his legs and arms, and asked what he could possibly do for her.

Now that she was face to face with the chief of the professional staff, Angela was not encouraged. All her misgivings about the man and his attitude toward women came back in a rush. His face had assumed a smirk as if he had already decided that whatever was on her female mind was of little consequence.

"This is not easy for me," Angela began. "So please bear with me. It was hard for me to come here, but I don't know what else to do."

Cantor encouraged her to continue.

"I'm here because I'm being sexually harassed by Dr. Wadley."

Cantor uncrossed his legs and leaned forward. Angela was encouraged that at least he was interested, but then she noticed that the smirk had remained.

"How long has this been going on?" Cantor asked.

"Probably the whole time I've been here," Angela said, intending to elaborate, but Cantor interrupted her.

"Probably?" he questioned with raised eyebrows. "You mean you're not sure?"

"It wasn't apparent initially," Angela explained. "At first I just thought he was acting like a particularly enthusiastic mentor, almost parental." She then went on to describe what had happened from the beginning; how it started as a problem of boundaries. "He always took advantage of opportunities to be close to me and touch me seemingly innocently," Angela explained. "He also insisted on confiding in me about personal family issues that I felt were inappropriate."

"This behavior you are describing can all be within the framework of friendship and the role of the mentor," Cantor said.

"I agree," Angela said. "That's why I allowed it to go on. The problem is that it has progressed."

"You mean it has changed?" Cantor asked.

"Most definitely," Angela said. "Quite recently." She then described the hand-on-the-thigh incident, feeling strangely embarrassed as she did so. She mentioned the hand brushing

her backside and Wadley's sudden use of the appellation
"honey."

"I personally don't see anything wrong with the word
'honey,'" Cantor said. "I use it all the time with my girls
here in the Imaging Center."

Angela could only stare at the man while she wondered
how the women in the Center felt about his behavior.
Clearly she was in the wrong place. She couldn't begin
to expect a fair hearing from a doctor whose views on
women were probably more archaic than Wadley's. Nonetheless, she figured she should finish what she started, so
she described the most recent incident: Wadley's pulling
her onto his lap to announce their trip to Miami.

"I don't know what to say about all this," Cantor said
once she finished. "Has Dr. Wadley ever implied that your
job depends on sexual favors?"

Inwardly Angela groaned, fearing that Cantor's comprehension of sexual harassment was limited to the most overt
circumstances. "No," she said. "Dr. Wadley has never intimated anything like that. But I find his unwanted familiarity
extremely upsetting. It goes way beyond the bounds of
friendship or a professional relationship, or even mutual
respect. It makes working very difficult."

"Maybe you're overreacting. Wadley is just an expres-
sive guy. You yourself said he's enthusiastic." When Cantor
saw the look on Angela's face he added, "Well, it's a
possibility."

Angela stood up. She forced herself to thank him for
his time.

"Not at all," Cantor said as he pushed himself upright.
"Keep me informed, young lady. Meanwhile, I promise I'll
talk with Dr. Wadley as soon as I have an opportunity."

Angela nodded at this final offer and walked out. As she
returned to her office, she couldn't help but feel that turning
to Cantor wasn't going to help matters any. If anything, it
was only going to make the situation worse.

Throughout the afternoon David had dashed over to check
on John Tarlow every chance he had. Unfortunately, John
hadn't improved. At the same time he hadn't deteriorated

since David had made sure his IV's had kept up with his fluid loss from his vomiting and diarrhea. As David entered his room late in the afternoon for his final visit of the day, he hoped he would at least find John's mental status improved. But it wasn't. John was as listless as he'd been that morning, perhaps even a degree more so. When pressed, John could still say his name, and he knew he was in the hospital, but as to the month or the year, he had no clue.

Back at the nurses' station David went over the laboratory and diagnostic results that he had available, most of which were normal. The blood count done that day showed some decrease in John's white count, but in light of John's leukemic history, David had no idea how to interpret the drop. The preliminary stool culture which was now available was negative for pathological bacteria.

"Please call me if Mr. Tarlow's temperature goes up or his GI symptoms get worse," he told the nurses before he left their station.

David and Angela met in the hospital lobby. Together they ran for their car. The weather was getting worse. Not only was it still raining, it had gotten much colder.

On their way home, Angela told David about the latest incident with Wadley and Cantor's reaction to her complaint.

David shook his head. "Wadley I give up on. He's an ass. But I'd expected more from Cantor, especially in his position as chief of the professional staff. Even if he's insensitive you'd think he'd be aware of the law—and the hospital's liability. Do you think he's slept through the last decade's worth of legal decisions on sexual harassment?"

Angela shrugged. "I don't want to think about it anymore. How was your day? Has Marjorie's death been on your mind?"

"I haven't had time to dwell on it," David said. "I've got John Tarlow in the hospital and he's scaring me."

"What's wrong?"

"That's just it: I don't know," David said. "That's what scares me. He's become apathetic, much the way Marjorie was. He has a lot of functional GI complaints. That's what brought him into the hospital, and they have gotten worse.

I don't know what's going on, but my sixth sense is setting off alarm bells. The trouble is I don't know what to do. At this point I'm just treating his symptoms."

"That's the kind of story that makes me glad I went into pathology," Angela said.

David then told Angela about his visit to Werner Van Slyke. "The man was more than rude," David complained. "He hardly gave me the time of day. It gives you an idea of the doctor's position in the new hospital environment. Now the doctor is just another employee, merely working in a different department."

"It makes it hard to be a patient advocate when even the maintenance department isn't responsive."

"My thoughts exactly," David said.

When David and Angela arrived home, Nikki was happy to see them. She'd been bored for most of the day until Arni stopped over to tell her about their new teacher.

"He's a man," Arni told David. "And real strict."

"I hope he's a good teacher," David said. He felt another stab of guilt about Marjorie's passing.

While Angela started dinner David drove Arni home. When David returned, Nikki met him at the door with a complaint. "It feels cold in the family room," she said.

David walked into the room and patted the radiator. It was blisteringly hot. He walked over to the French doors leading to the terrace and made sure they were closed. "Where did you feel cold?" David asked.

"Sitting on the couch," Nikki said. "Come over and try it."

David followed his daughter and sat down next to her. Immediately he could feel a cool draft on the back of his neck. "You're right," he said. He checked the windows behind the couch. "I think I've made the diagnosis," he said. "We need to put up the storm windows."

"What are storm windows?" Nikki asked.

David launched into an involved explanation of heat loss, convection currents, insulation, and Thermopane windows.

"You're confusing her," Angela called from the kitchen. She'd overheard a portion of the conversation. "All she asked was what a storm window was. Why don't you show her one?"

"Good idea," David said. "Come on. We'll get firewood at the same time."

"I don't like it down here," Nikki said as they descended the cellar stairs.

"Why not?" David asked.

"It's scary," Nikki protested.

"Now, don't be like your mother," David teased her. "One hysterical female in the house is enough."

Leaning against the back of the granite staircase was a stack of storm windows. David moved one away from the others so Nikki could see it.

"It looks like a regular window," Nikki said.

"But it doesn't open," David said. "It traps air between this glass and the glass of the existing window. That's what serves as insulation."

While Nikki inspected the window, David noticed something for the first time.

"What is it, Daddy?" Nikki asked, aware that her father had become distracted.

"Something I've never noticed before," David said. He reached over the stack of storm windows and ran his hand over the wall that formed the back of the stairs. "These are cinder blocks."

"What are cinder blocks?" Nikki asked.

Preoccupied with his discovery, David ignored Nikki's question.

"Let's move these storm windows," David said. He lifted the window he was holding and carried it over to the foundation wall. Nikki tipped the next one upright.

"This wall is different from the rest of the basement," David said after the last window had been moved away. "And it doesn't appear to be that old. I wonder why it's here."

"What are you talking about?" Nikki asked.

David showed her that the staircase was made of granite. Then he took her back beneath the stairs and showed her the cinder blocks. He explained that they must be covering some kind of triangular storage space.

"What's in it?" Nikki asked.

David shrugged. "I wonder." Then he said: "Why don't we take a peek. Maybe it's a treasure."

"Really?" Nikki asked.

David got the sledgehammer that was used along with a wedge to split the firewood and brought it over to the base of the stairs.

Just as David hefted the sledgehammer Angela called down the stairs to ask what mischief they were getting themselves into. David lowered the sledgehammer and put a finger to his lips. Then he shouted up to Angela that they'd be coming up with the firewood in a minute.

"I'll be upstairs taking a shower," Angela called down. "After that we'll eat."

"Okay," David called back. Then to Nikki he said: "She might take a dim view of our busting out part of the house."

Nikki giggled.

David waited long enough for Angela to get to the second floor before picking up the sledgehammer again. After telling Nikki to avert her eyes, David knocked out a portion of a cinder block near the top of the wall, creating a small hole.

"Run up and get a flashlight," David said. A musty odor wafted out of the walled-off space.

While Nikki was gone, David used the sledgehammer to enlarge the hole. With a final blow a whole cinder block came loose, and David lifted it out of the wall. By then Nikki was back with the flashlight. David took it and peered in.

David's heart jumped in his chest. He pulled his head out of the hole so quickly he skinned the back of his neck on the sharp edge of the cinder block.

"What did you see?" Nikki asked. She didn't like the look on her father's face.

"It's not a treasure," David said. "I think you'd better get your mother."

While Nikki was gone, David enlarged the hole even more. By the time Angela came down the stairs in her bathrobe David had a whole course of the cinder blocks dismantled.

"What's going on?" Angela demanded. "You've got Nikki upset."

"Take a look," David said. He handed Angela the flashlight and motioned for her to come see.

"This better not be a joke," Angela said.

"It's no joke," David assured her.

"My God!" Angela said. Her voice echoed in the small space.

"What is it?" Nikki asked. "I want to see too."

Angela pulled her head out and looked at David. "It's a body," she said. "And it's obviously been in there for some time."

"A person?" Nikki asked with disbelief. "Can I see?"

Angela and David both nearly shouted, "No."

Nikki started to protest, but her voice lacked conviction.

"Let's go upstairs and build that fire," David said. He took Nikki over to the woodpile and handed her a log. Then he picked up an armload himself.

While Angela phoned the town police David and Nikki worked on the fire. Nikki was full of questions that David couldn't answer.

Half an hour later a police cruiser turned into the Wilsons' driveway and pulled up to the house.

Two policemen had responded to Angela's call.

"My name's Wayne Robertson," the shorter of the pair said. He was dressed in mufti with a quilted cotton vest over a plaid flannel shirt. On his head was a Boston Red Sox baseball cap. "I'm chief of police and this is one of my deputies, Sherwin Morris."

Sherwin touched the brim of his hat. Tall and lanky, he was dressed in uniform. He was carrying a long flashlight: the kind that took four batteries.

"Officer Morris stopped by to pick me up after you called," Robertson explained. "I wasn't on duty, but this sounded important."

Angela nodded. "I appreciate your coming," she said.

Angela and David led the way. Only Nikki remained upstairs. Robertson took the flashlight from Morris and poked his head into the hole.

"I'll be damned!" he said. "It's the quack."

Robertson faced the Wilsons. "Sorry this has happened to you folks," he said. "But I recognize the victim despite the fact that he looks a little worse for wear. His name is Dr. Dennis Hodges. In fact, this was his house, as you probably are aware."

Angela's eyes met David's and she stifled a shiver. Gooseflesh had appeared on the back of her neck.

"What we have to do is knock the rest of this wall down so we can remove the body," Robertson continued. "Do you folks have any problem with that?"

David said that they didn't.

"What about calling the medical examiner?" Angela asked. Through her interest in forensics, she knew it was protocol to call the medical examiner on any suspicious death. This one certainly qualified.

Robertson regarded Angela for a few moments trying to think of something to say. He didn't like anyone telling him how to do his job, especially a woman. The only problem was that Angela was right. And now that he'd been reminded he couldn't ignore it.

"Where's the phone?" Robertson said.

"In the kitchen," Angela said.

Nikki had to be pried from the phone. She'd been back and forth between Caroline and Arni with the exciting news about finding a body in their basement.

Once the medical examiner had been called, Robertson and Morris set to work removing the cinder block wall.

David brought down an extension cord and a floor lamp to help them see what they were doing. The added light also gave them all a better look at the body. Although it was generally well preserved, there was some skeletonization of the lower half of the face. Some of the jawbones and most of the teeth were garishly exposed. The upper part of the face was surprisingly intact. The eyes were hideously open. In the center of the forehead at the hairline was a caved-in area covered with a green mold.

"That pile of stuff in the corner looks like empty cement bags," Robertson said. He was using the beam of the flashlight as a pointer. "And there's the trowel. Hell, he's got everything in there with him. Maybe it was a suicide."

David and Angela looked at each other with the same thought: Robertson was either the world's worst detective or a devotee of crude humor.

"I wonder what those papers are?" Robertson said, directing the light at a number of scattered sheets of paper in the depths of the makeshift tomb.

"Looks like copy machine paper," David said.

"Well, look at that," Robertson said as he directed the flashlight at a tool that was partially concealed under the body. It resembled a flat crowbar.

"What is it?" David asked.

"That's a pry bar," Robertson said. "It's an all-purpose tool, used mostly for demolition."

Nikki called down the stairs to say that the medical examiner had arrived. Angela went up to meet him.

Dr. Tracy Cornish was a thin man of medium height with wire-rimmed spectacles. He carried a large, old-fashioned black leather doctor's bag.

Angela introduced herself and explained that she was a pathologist at Bartlet Community Hospital. She asked Dr. Cornish if he'd had formal forensic training. He admitted he hadn't, and he explained that he filled in as a district medical examiner to supplement his practice. "But I've been doing it for quite a number of years," Dr. Cornish added.

"I was only asking because I have an interest in forensics myself," Angela said. She hadn't meant to embarrass the man.

Angela led Dr. Cornish down to the tomb. He stood and stared at the scene for a few minutes. "Interesting," he said finally. "The body is in a particularly good state of preservation. How long has he been missing?"

"About eight months," Robertson said.

"Shows what a cool, dry place will do," Dr. Cornish said. "This tomb has been like a root cellar. It's even dry after all this rain."

"Why is there some skeletonization around the jaws?" David asked.

"Rodents, probably," Dr. Cornish answered as he bent down and snapped open his bag.

David shuddered. His mouth had gone dry at the thought of rodents gnawing on the body. Glancing at Angela, he could tell that she had taken this information in stride and was fascinated by the proceedings.

The first thing Dr. Cornish did was take a number of photos, including extreme close-ups. Then he donned rubber gloves and began removing the objects from the tomb, placing them in plastic evidence bags. When he got to the papers, everyone crowded around to look at them. Dr. Cornish made certain that no one touched them.

"They're part of medical records from Bartlet Community Hospital," David said.

"I'll bet these stains are all blood," Dr. Cornish said, pointing to large brown areas on the papers. He put all the papers into a plastic bag which he then sealed and labeled.

When all the objects had been removed, Dr. Cornish turned his attention to the body. The first thing he did was search the pockets. He immediately found the wallet with bills still inside. There were also a number of credit cards in Dennis Hodges' name.

"Well, it wasn't a robbery," Robertson said.

Dr. Cornish then removed Hodges' watch, which was still running. The time was correct.

"One of the battery manufacturers should use this for one of their zany commercials," Robertson suggested. Morris laughed until he realized no one else was.

Dr. Cornish then pulled a body bag out of his satchel and asked Morris to give him a hand getting Hodges into it.

"What about bagging the hands?" Angela suggested.

Dr. Cornish thought for a moment, then nodded. "Good idea," he said. He got paper bags from his kit and secured them over Hodges' hands. That done, he and Morris got the body into the bag and zipped it closed.

Fifteen minutes later the Wilsons watched as the police cruiser and the medical examiner's van turned around, descended their driveway, and disappeared into the night.

"Anyone hungry?" Angela asked.

Both Nikki and David groaned.

"I'm not either," Angela admitted. "What a night."

They adjourned to the family room where David stoked the fire and added wood. Nikki turned on the television. Angela sat down to read.

By eight o'clock all three decided they might eat something after all. Angela reheated the dinner she had made while David and Nikki set the table.

"Every family has a skeleton in the closet," David said when they were midway through the meal. "Ours just happened to be in the cellar."

"I don't think that's very funny," Angela said.

Nikki said she didn't get it, and Angela had to explain the figurative meaning. Once Nikki understood, she didn't think it was funny either.

David was not pleased about the gruesome discovery in their basement. He was particularly concerned about the potential effect on Nikki. He'd hoped bringing a little humor to the situation might defuse the tension. But even he had to admit his joke fell flat.

After Nikki's respiratory treatment, they all went to bed. Though not an antidote, sleep seemed to be the best alternative. Although Nikki and David were sleepy, Angela wasn't, and as she lay in bed she became acutely aware of all the sounds the house made. She had never realized how noisy it was, particularly on a windy, rainy night. From deep in the basement she heard the oil burner kick on. There was even an intermittent, very low-pitched whine from wind coming down the master bedroom flue.

A sudden series of thumps made Angela jump, and she sat upright.

"What's that?" Angela whispered nervously. She gave David a shove.

"What's what?" David asked, only half awake.

Angela told him to listen. The thumping occurred again. "There," Angela cried. "That banging."

"That's the shutters hitting against the house," David said. "Goodness sake, calm down!"

Angela lay back against the pillow, but her eyes were wide open. She was even less sleepy than she was when she'd gotten into bed.

"I don't like what has been happening around here," Angela said.

David audibly groaned.

"Really," Angela said. "I can't believe so much has changed in so few days. I was worried this was going to happen."

"Are you talking specifically about finding Hodges' body?" David asked.

"I'm talking about everything," Angela said. "The change in the weather, Wadley's harassing me, Marjorie's death, Kelley's harassing you, and now a body in our basement."

"We're just being efficient," David said. "We're getting all the bad stuff out of the way at one time."

"I'm being serious, and . . ." Angela began to say, but she was interrupted by a scream from Nikki.

In a flash both David and Angela were out of bed and running down the central corridor. They dashed into Nikki's room. She was sitting in bed with a dazed look on her face. Rusty was next to her, equally confused.

It had been a nightmare about a ghoul in the basement. Angela sat on one side of Nikki's bed and David on the other. Together they comforted their daughter. Yet they didn't know quite what to say. The problem was that Nikki's nightmare had been a mixture of dream and reality.

David and Angela did their best to comfort Nikki. In the end they invited her to come sleep with them in their bed. Nikki agreed, and they all marched back to the master bedroom. Climbing into bed, they settled down. Unfortunately David ended up sleeping on the very edge because inviting Nikki also meant inviting Rusty.

14

THURSDAY, OCTOBER 21

THE WEATHER WAS NOT MUCH BETTER THE NEXT morning. The rain had stopped, but it was misting so heavily that it might as well have been raining. There was no break in the heavy cloud cover and it seemed even chillier than it had the day before.

While Nikki was doing her postural drainage the phone rang. David snatched it up. Considering the early morning hour, he was afraid the call was about John Tarlow. But it wasn't. It was the state's attorney's office requesting permission to send over an assistant to look at the crime scene.

"When would you like to come?" David asked.

"Would it be too inconvenient now?" the caller said. "We have someone in your immediate area."

"We'll be here for about an hour," David said.

"No problem," the caller replied.

True to their word, an assistant from the state's attorney's office arrived within fifteen minutes. She was a pleasant woman with fiery red hair. She was dressed conservatively in a dark blue suit.

"Sorry to bother you so early," the woman said. She introduced herself as Elaine Sullivan.

"No trouble at all," David said, holding the door open for her.

David led her down the cellar steps and turned on the floor lamp to illuminate the now empty tomb. She took out a camera and snapped a few pictures. Then she bent down and stuck a fingernail into the dirt of the tomb's floor. Angela came down the stairs and looked over David's shoulder.

"I understand that the town police were here last night," Elaine said.

"The town police and a district medical examiner," David said.

"I think I'll recommend that the state police crime-scene investigators be called," she said. "I hope it won't be a bother."

"I welcome the idea," Angela said. "I don't think the town police are all that accustomed to a homicide investigation."

Elaine nodded, diplomatically avoiding comment.

"Do we have to be here when the crime-scene people come?" David asked.

"That's up to you," Elaine said. "An investigator may want to talk with you at some point. But as far as the crime-scene people are concerned, they can just come in and do their thing."

"Will they come today?" Angela asked.

"They'll be here as soon as possible," Elaine said. "Probably this morning."

"I'll arrange for Alice to be here," Angela said. David nodded.

Shortly after the state's attorney's assistant had left, the Wilsons were off themselves. This was to be Nikki's first day back to school since she got out of the hospital. She was beside herself with excitement and had changed her clothes twice.

As they took her to school, Nikki couldn't talk about anything besides the body. When they dropped her off,

Angela suggested that she refrain from talking about the incident, but Angela knew her request was futile: Nikki had already told Caroline and Arni, and they'd undoubtedly passed the story on.

David put the car in gear, and they started for the hospital.

"I'm concerned about how my patient will be this morning," he said. "Even though I haven't gotten any calls I'm still worried."

"And I'm worried about facing Wadley," Angela said. "I don't know if Cantor has spoken to him or not, but either way it won't be pleasant."

With a kiss for luck, David and Angela headed for their respective days.

David went directly to check on John Tarlow. Stepping into the room he immediately noticed that John's breathing was labored. That was not a good sign. David pulled out his stethoscope and gave John's shoulder a shake. David wanted him to sit up. John barely responded.

Panic gripped David. It was as if his worst fears were coming to pass. Rapidly David examined his patient and immediately discovered that John was developing extensive pneumonia.

Leaving the room, David raced down to the nurses' station, barking orders that John should be transferred to the ICU immediately. The nurses were in the middle of their report; the day shift was taking over from the night shift.

"Can it wait until we finish report?" Janet Colburn asked.

"Hell, no!" David snapped. "I want him switched immediately. And I'd like to know why I haven't been called. Mr. Tarlow has developed bilateral pneumonia."

"He was sleeping comfortably the last time we took his temperature," the night nurse said. "We were supposed to call if his temperature went up or if his GI symptoms got worse. Neither of those things happened."

David grabbed the chart and flipped it open to the temperature graph. The temperature had edged up a little, but not the way David would have expected having heard the man's chest.

"Let's just get him to the ICU," David said. "Plus I want some stat blood work and a chest film."

With commendable efficiency John Tarlow was transferred into the ICU. While it was being done, David called the oncologist, Dr. Clark Mieslich, and the infectious disease specialist, Dr. Martin Hasselbaum, to ask them to come in immediately.

The lab responded quickly to lab work requested for the ICU, and David was soon looking at John's results. His white count, which had been low, was even lower, indicating that John's system was overwhelmed by the developing pneumonia. It was the kind of lack of response one might expect from a patient undergoing chemotherapy, but David knew that John hadn't been on chemo for months. Most ominous of all was the chest X ray: it confirmed extensive, bilateral pneumonia.

The consults arrived in short order to examine the patient and go over the chart. When they were finished they moved away from the bed. Dr. Mieslich confirmed that John was not on any chemotherapy and hadn't been for a long time.

"What do you make of the low white count?" David asked.

"I can't say," Dr. Mieslich admitted. "I suppose it is related to his leukemia. We'd have to do a bone marrow sample to find out, but I don't recommend it now. Not with the infection he's developing. Besides, it's academic. I'm afraid he's moribund."

This was the last thing David wanted to hear although he had begun to expect it. He couldn't believe he was about to lose a second patient in his brief Bartlet career.

David turned to Dr. Hasselbaum.

Dr. Hasselbaum was equally blunt and pessimistic. He thought that John was developing massive pneumonia with a particularly deadly type of bacteria and that, secondarily, he was suffering from shock. He pointed to the fact that John's blood pressure was low and that his kidneys were failing. "It doesn't look good. Mr. Tarlow seems to have very poor physiological defenses, undoubtedly due to his leukemia. If we treat, we'll have to treat massively. I have access to some experimental agents created to help combat this type of endotoxin shock. What do you think?"

"Let's do it," David said.

"These drugs are expensive," Dr. Hasselbaum said.

"A man's life hangs in the balance," David said.

An hour and fifteen minutes later, when John's treatment had been instituted and there was nothing else to be done, David hurried to his office. Once again, every seat in the waiting room was occupied. Some patients were standing in the hall. Everyone was upset, even the receptionist.

David took a deep breath and plunged into his appointments. In between patients he called the ICU repeatedly to check on John's status. Each time he was told there had been no change.

In addition to his regularly scheduled patients, a number of semi-emergencies added to the confusion by having to be squeezed in. David would have sent these cases to the emergency room if it hadn't been for Kelley's lecture. Two of these patients seemed like old friends: Mary Ann Schiller and Jonathan Eakins.

Although he was somewhat spooked by the way Marjorie Kleber's and now John Tarlow's cases had progressed, David felt compelled to hospitalize both Mary Ann and Jonathan. David just didn't feel comfortable treating them as outpatients. Mary Ann had an extremely severe case of sinusitis and Jonathan had a disturbing cardiac arrhythmia. Providing them with admitting orders, David sent them both over to the hospital.

Two other semi-emergency patients were night-shift nurses from the second floor. David had met them on several occasions when he'd been called into the hospital for emergencies. Both had the same complaints: flu-like syndromes consisting of general malaise, low-grade fever, and low white counts, as well as GI troubles including crampy pain, nausea, vomiting, and diarrhea. After examining them, David sent them home for bed rest and symptomatic therapy.

When he had a minute he asked his nurse, Susan, if a flu was going around the hospital.

"Not that I've heard," Susan said.

• • •

Angela's day was going better than expected. She'd not had any run-ins with Wadley. In fact, she hadn't seen him at all.

Midmorning she phoned the chief medical examiner, Dr. Walter Dunsmore, having gotten his number from the Burlington directory. Angela explained that she was a pathologist at the Bartlet Community Hospital. She went on to explain her interest in the Hodges case. She added that she had once considered a career in forensic pathology.

Dr. Dunsmore promptly invited her to come to Burlington someday to see their facility. "In fact, why don't you come up and assist at Hodges' autopsy?" he said. "I'd love to have you, but I have to warn you, like most forensic pathologists, I'm a frustrated teacher."

"When do you plan to do it?" Angela asked. She thought that if it could be put off until Saturday, she might be able to go.

"It's scheduled for late this morning," Dr. Dunsmore said. "But there's some flexibility. I'd be happy to do it this afternoon."

"That's very generous," Angela said. "Unfortunately, I'm not sure what my chief would say about my taking the time."

"I've known Ben Wadley for years," Dr. Dunsmore said. "I'll give him a call and clear it with him."

"I'm not sure that would be a good idea," Angela said.

"Nonsense!" Dr. Dunsmore said. "Leave it to me. I look forward to meeting you."

Angela was about to protest further when she realized that Dr. Dunsmore had hung up. She replaced the receiver. She had no idea what Wadley's reaction to Dr. Dunsmore's call would be, but she imagined she'd learn soon enough.

Angela heard even sooner than she expected. Hardly had she hung up than it rang again.

"I'm caught up here in the OR," Wadley said agreeably. "I just got a call from the chief medical examiner. He tells me he wants you to come up to assist with an autopsy."

"I just spoke with him. I wasn't sure how you'd feel about it." It was obvious to Angela from Wadley's cheerfulness that Cantor had not yet spoken with Wadley.

"I think it's a great idea," Wadley said. "My feeling is that whenever the medical examiner asks for a favor, we do it. It never hurts to stay on his good side. You never know when we'll need a favor in return. I encourage you to go."

"Thank you," Angela said. "I will." Hanging up she called David to let him know her plans. When he came on the line, David's voice sounded tense and weary.

"You sound terrible," Angela said. "What's wrong?"

"Don't ask," David said. "I'll have to tell you later. Right now I'm behind again and the natives are restless."

Angela quickly told him about the medical examiner's invitation and that she'd been cleared to go. David told her to enjoy herself and rang off.

Grabbing her coat, Angela left the hospital. Before setting out for Burlington, she headed home to change clothes. As she approached the house she was surprised to see a state police van parked in front of her house. Evidently the crime scene investigators were still there.

Alice Doherty met her at the door, concerned that something was wrong. Angela immediately put her at ease. She then asked about the state police people.

"They are still downstairs," Alice said. "They've been there for hours."

Angela went down to the basement to meet the technicians. There were three. They had the entire area around the back of the stairs blocked off with crime scene tape and brightly illuminated with floodlights. One man was using advanced techniques in an attempt to lift fingerprints from the stone. Another man was carefully sifting through the dirt that formed the floor of the tomb. The third was using a hand-held instrument called a luma-light, looking for fibers and latent prints.

The only man who introduced himself was the gentleman working on the fingerprints. His name was Quillan Reilly.

"Sorry we're taking so much time," Quillan said.

"It doesn't matter," Angela assured him.

Angela watched them work. They didn't talk much, each absorbed by his task. She was about to leave when Quillan asked her if the interior of the house had been repainted in the last eight months.

"I don't think so," Angela said. "We certainly haven't."

"Good," said Quillan. "Would you mind if we came back this evening to use some luminol on the walls upstairs?"

"What's luminol?" Angela asked.

"It's a chemical used to search for bloodstains," Quillan explained.

"The house has been cleaned," Angela said, taking mild offense that they thought any blood would still be detectable.

"It's still worth a shot," Quillan said.

"Well, if you think it might be helpful," Angela said. "We want to be cooperative."

"Thank you, ma'am," Quillan said.

"What happened to the evidence taken by the medical examiner?" Angela asked. "Do the local police have it?"

"No, ma'am," Quillan said. "We have it."

"Good," Angela said.

Ten minutes later, Angela was on her way. In Burlington, she found the medical examiner's office with ease.

"We're waiting for you," Dr. Dunsmore said as Angela was ushered into his modern and sparsely furnished office. He made her feel instantly at ease. He even asked her to call him Walt.

In minutes, Angela was dressed in a surgical scrub suit. As she donned a mask, a hood, and goggles, she felt a rush of excitement. The autopsy room had always been an arena of discovery for her.

"I think you'll find we are quite professional here," Walt said as they met outside the autopsy room. "It used to be that forensic pathology was somewhat of a joke outside of the major cities. That's not the case any longer."

Dennis Hodges was laid out on the autopsy table. X rays had been taken and were already on the X-ray view box. Walt introduced the diener to Angela, explaining that Peter would assist them in the procedure.

First they looked at the X rays. The penetrating fracture at the top of the forehead was certainly a mortal wound. There was also a linear fracture in the back of the head. In addition, there was a fracture of the left clavicle, the left ulna, and the left radius.

"There's no doubt it was a homicide," Walt said. "Looks like the poor old guy put up quite a fight."

"The local police chief suggested suicide," Angela said.

"He was joking, I hope," Walt said.

"I really don't know," Angela said. "He didn't impress me or my husband with his investigative skills. It's possible he's never handled a homicide."

"Probably not," Walt said. "Another problem is that some of the older local law enforcement people haven't had much formal training."

Angela described the pry bar that was found with the body. Using a ruler for determining the size of the penetrating fracture and then examining the wound itself they determined that the pry bar could have been the murder weapon.

Then they turned their attention to the bagged hands.

"I was delighted when I saw the paper bags," Walt said. "I've been trying to get my district MEs to use them on this kind of case for a long time."

Angela nodded, secretly pleased that she'd suggested it to Dr. Cornish the night before.

Walt carefully slipped the hands out of their covers and used a magnifying glass to examine under the nails.

"There is some foreign material under some of them," Walt said. He leaned back so Angela could take a look.

"Any idea what it is?" Angela asked.

"We'll have to wait for the microscopic," Walt said as he carefully removed the material and dropped it into specimen jars. Each was labeled according to which finger it came from.

The autopsy itself went quickly; it was as if Angela and Walt were an established team. There was plenty of pathology to make things interesting, and, as promised, Walt enjoyed his didactic role. Hodges had significant arteriosclerosis, a small cancer of the lung, and advanced cirrhosis of the liver.

"I'd guess he liked his bourbon," Walt said.

After the autopsy was completed, Angela thanked Walt for his hospitality and asked to be kept informed about the case. Walt encouraged her to call whenever she wanted.

On the way back to the hospital, Angela felt in a better mood than she had for days. Doing the autopsy had been a good diversion. She was glad that Wadley had let her go.

Pulling into the hospital parking lot, she couldn't find a space in the reserved area near the back entrance. She had to park way up in the upper lot instead. Without an umbrella, she was quite wet by the time she got inside.

Angela went directly to her office. No sooner had she hung up her coat than the connecting door to Wadley's office banged open. Angela jumped. Wadley loomed in the doorway. His square jaw was set, his eyes narrowed, and his customarily carefully combed silver hair was disheveled. He looked furious. Angela instinctively stepped back and eyed the door to the hall with the thought of fleeing.

Wadley stormed into the room, coming right up to Angela and crowding her against her desk.

"I'd like an explanation," he snarled. "Why did you go to Cantor of all people with this preposterous story, these wild, ridiculous, ungrounded accusations? Sexual harassment! My God, that's absurd."

Wadley paused and glared at Angela. She shrank back, not sure if she should say anything. She didn't want to provoke the man. She was afraid he might hit her.

"Why didn't you say something to me?" Wadley screamed.

Wadley paused in his tirade, suddenly aware that Angela's door to the hall was ajar. Outside, the secretaries' keyboards had gone silent. Wadley stomped to the door and slammed it shut.

"After all the time and effort I've lavished on you, this is the reward I get," he yelled. "I don't think I have to remind you that you are on probation around here. You'd better start walking a narrow path, otherwise you'll be looking for work with no recommendation from me."

Angela nodded, not knowing what else to do.

"Well, aren't you going to say anything?" Wadley's face was inches from Angela's. "Are you just going to stand there and nod your head?"

"I'm sorry that we've reached this point," she said.

"That's it?" Wadley yelled. "You've besmirched my reputation with baseless accusations and that's all you can say? This is slander, woman, and I'll tell you something: I might take you to court."

With that, Wadley spun on his heels, strode into his own office, and slammed the door.

Angela let out her breath unevenly as she fought back tears. She sank into her chair and shook her head. It was so unfair.

Susan poked her head into one of the examining rooms and told David that the ICU was on the line. Fearing the worst, David picked up the phone. The ICU nurse said that Mr. Tarlow had just gone into cardiac arrest and the resuscitation team was working on him at that very moment.

David slammed the phone down. He felt his heart leap in his chest, and he instantly broke out in a cold sweat. Leaving a distressed office nurse and receptionist, he dashed over to the ICU, but he was too late. By the time he arrived it was over. The ER physician in charge of the resuscitation team had already declared John Tarlow dead.

"Hey, there wasn't much point," the doctor said. "The man's lungs were full, his kidneys shot, and he had no blood pressure."

David nodded absently. He stared at his patient while the ICU nurses unhooked all the equipment and IV lines. As they continued to clean up, David went over to the main desk and sat down. He began to wonder if he were suited to be a doctor. He had trouble with this part of the job, and repetition seemed to make it more difficult, certainly not easier.

Tarlow's relatives came and, like the Kleber family, they were understanding and thankful. David accepted their kind words feeling like an impostor. He hadn't done anything for John. He didn't even know why he'd died. His history of leukemia wasn't a real explanation.

Even though he'd now been informed about the hospital autopsy policy, David asked the family if they would allow one. As far as David was concerned, there was no harm in trying. The family said they'd consider it.

Leaving the ICU area, David had enough presence of mind to check on Mary Ann Schiller and Jonathan Eakins. He wanted to be certain that they had been settled and their respective treatments started. He particularly wanted to be sure that the CMV cardiologist had visited Eakins.

Unfortunately, David discovered something that gave him pause. Mary Ann had been put in room 206: the room that John Tarlow had so recently vacated. David had half a mind to have Mary Ann moved, but he realized he was being irrationally superstitious. What would he have said to admitting: he never wanted one of his patients in room 206 again? That was clearly ridiculous.

David checked her IV. She was already getting her antibiotic. After promising he'd be back later, David went into Jonathan's room. He too was comfortable and relaxed. A cardiac monitor was in place. Jonathan said that the cardiologist was expected imminently.

When he returned to his office, Susan greeted David with word that Charles Kelley had called. "He wants to see you immediately," she said. "He stressed immediately."

"How many patients are we behind?" David asked.

"Plenty," Susan said. "So try not to be too long."

Feeling as if he were carrying the world on his shoulders, David dragged himself over to the CMV office. He wasn't exactly sure what Charles Kelley wanted to see him about, but he could guess.

"I don't know what to do, David," Charles Kelley said once David was sitting in his office. Kelley shook his head. David marveled at his role-playing ability. Now he was the wounded friend.

"I've tried to reason with you, but either you're stubborn or you just don't care about CMV. The very day after I talk to you about avoiding unnecessary consults outside of the CMV community, you do it again with another terminal patient. What am I going to do with you? Do you understand that the costs of medical care have to be considered? You know there's a crisis in this country?"

David nodded. That much was true.

"Then why is this so hard for you?" Kelley asked. He was sounding angrier. "And it's not only CMV that is upset this time. It's the hospital too. Helen Beaton called me moments ago complaining about the enormously expensive biotechnology drugs that you ordered for this sad, dying patient. Talk about heroics! The man was dying, even the consults said that. He'd had leukemia for years. Don't you understand? This is wasting money and resources."

Kelley had worked himself up to a fevered pitch. His face had become red. But then he paused and sighed. He shook his head again as if he didn't know what to do. "Helen Beaton also complained about your requesting an autopsy," he said in a tired voice. "Autopsies are not part of the contract with CMV, and you were informed of that fact just recently. David, you have to be reasonable. You have to help me or . . ." Kelley paused, letting the unfinished sentence hang in the air.

"Or what?" David said. He knew what Kelley meant, but he wanted him to say it.

"I like you, David," Kelley said. "But I need you to help me. I have people above me I have to answer to. I hope you can appreciate that."

David felt more depressed than ever as he stumbled back toward his office. Kelley's intrusion irritated him, yet in some ways Kelley had a point. Money and resources shouldn't be thrown away on terminal patients when they could be better spent elsewhere. But was that the issue here?

More confused and dejected than he could remember being, David opened the door to his office. He was confronted by a waiting room full of unhappy patients angrily glancing at their watches and noisily flipping through magazines.

Dinner at the Wilson home was a tense affair. No one spoke. Everyone was agitated. It was as if their Shangri-la had gone the way of the weather.

Even Nikki had had a bad day. She was upset about her new teacher, Mr. Hart. The kids had already nicknamed him Mr. Hate. When David and Angela arrived home that evening, she described him as a strict old fart. When Angela chided her about her language, Nikki admitted the description had been Arni's.

The biggest problem with the new teacher was that he had not allowed Nikki to judge her own level of appropriate exercise during gym and he'd not allowed Nikki to do any postural drainage. The lack of communication had led to a confrontation that had embarrassed Nikki.

After dinner David told everyone that it was time to cheer up. In an attempt to improve the atmosphere he offered to build a cozy fire. But when he descended to the basement, he suffered the shock of seeing yellow crime scene tape around his own basement stairs. It brought back the gruesome image of Hodges' body.

David gathered the wood quickly and dashed back upstairs. Normally he wasn't superstitious or easily spooked, but with the recent events he was becoming both.

After building the fire, David began to talk enthusiastically about the upcoming winter and the sports they would soon enjoy: skiing, skating, and sledding. Just when Angela and Nikki were getting in the spirit he'd hoped, headlight beams traversed the wall of the family room. David went to the window.

"It's a state police van," he said. "What on earth could they want?"

"I totally forgot," Angela said, getting to her feet. "When the crime scene people were here today they asked if they could come by when it was dark to look for bloodstains."

"Bloodstains? Hodges was killed eight months ago."

"They said it was worth a try," Angela explained.

The technicians were the same three men who had been there that morning. Angela was impressed with the length of their workday.

"We do a lot of traveling around the state," Quillan said.

Angela introduced Quillan to David. Quillan seemed to be in charge.

"How does this test work?" David asked.

"The luminol reacts with any residual iron from the blood," Quillan said. "When it does, it fluoresces."

"Interesting," David said, but he remained skeptical.

The technicians were eager to do their test and leave, so David and Angela stayed out of their way. They started in the mud room, setting up a camera on a tripod. Then they turned out all the lights.

They sprayed luminol on the walls using a spray bottle similar to those used for window cleaner. The bottle made a slight hiss with each spray.

"Here's a little," Quillan said in the darkness. David and Angela leaned into the room. Along the wall was a faint, spotty, eerie fluorescence.

"Not enough for a picture," one of the other technicians said.

They circled the room but didn't find any more positive areas. Then they moved the camera into the kitchen. Quillan asked if the lights could be turned off in the dining room and the hallway. The Wilsons readily complied.

The technicians continued about their business. David, Angela, and Nikki hovered at the doorway.

Suddenly portions of the wall near the mud room began to fluoresce.

"It's faint, but we got a lot here," Quillan said. "I'll keep spraying, you open the shutter on the camera."

"My God!" Angela whispered. "They're finding blood-stains all over my kitchen."

The Wilsons could see vague outlines of the men and hear them as they moved around the kitchen. They approached the table which had been left behind by Clara Hodges and which the Wilsons used when they ate in the kitchen. All at once the legs of the table began to glow in a ghostly fashion.

"My guess is this is the murder site," one of the technicians said. "Right here by the table."

The Wilsons heard the camera being moved, then the loud click of its shutter opening followed by sustained hissing from the spray bottle. Quillan explained that the bloodstains were so faint, the luminol had to be sprayed continuously.

After the crime-scene investigators had left, the Wilsons returned to the family room even more depressed than they had been earlier. There was no more talk of skiing or sledding on the hill behind the barn.

Angela sat on the hearth with her back to the fire and looked at David and Nikki, who had collectively collapsed on the couch. With her family arrayed in front of her, a powerful protective urge swept through Angela. She did not like what she had just learned: her kitchen had the remains of blood spatter from a brutal murder. This was the room that in many ways she regarded as the heart of their home and which she had thought she had cleaned. Now she knew that it had been desecrated by violence. In Angela's mind it was a direct threat to her family.

Suddenly Angela broke the gloomy silence. "Maybe we should move," she said.

"Wait one second," David said. "I know you're upset; we're all upset. But we're not going to allow ourselves to become hysterical."

"I'm hardly hysterical," Angela shot back.

"Suggesting that we have to move because of an unfortunate event which didn't involve us and which occurred almost a year ago is hardly rational," David said.

"It happened in this house," Angela said.

"This house happens to be mortgaged to the roof. We have both a first and second mortgage. We can't just walk away because of an emotional upset."

"Then I want the locks changed," Angela said. "A murderer has been in here."

"We haven't even been locking the doors," David said.

"We are from now on and I want the locks changed."

"Okay," David said. "We'll change the locks."

Traynor was in a rotten mood as he pulled up to the Iron Horse Inn. The weather seemed to fit his temperament: the rain had returned to tropical-like intensity. Even his umbrella proved uncooperative. When he couldn't get it open, he cursed and threw it into the back. He decided he'd simply have to make a run for the Inn's door.

Beaton, Caldwell, and Sherwood were already sitting in a booth when he arrived. Cantor got there just after him. As the two men sat down, Carleton Harris, the bartender, came by to take their drink orders.

"Thank you all for coming out in this inclement weather," Traynor said. "But I'm afraid that recent events mandated an emergency session."

"This isn't an official executive board meeting," Cantor complained. "Let's not be so formal."

Traynor frowned. Even in a crisis, Cantor persisted in irritating him.

"If I may continue," Traynor said, staring Cantor down.

"For chrissake, Harold," Cantor said, "get on with it."

"As you all know by now, Hodges' body turned up in rather unpleasant circumstances."

"The story has attracted media attention," Beaton said. "It made the front page of the *Boston Globe.*"

"I'm concerned about this publicity's potentially negative effect on the hospital," Traynor said. "The macabre aspects of Hodges' death may attract still more media. The last thing we want is a bunch of out-of-town reporters poking around. Thanks largely to Helen Beaton, we've been able to keep word of our ski-masked rapist out of the headlines. But big-city reporters are bound to stumble across that brewing scandal if they're in town. Between that and Hodges' unseemly demise, we could be in for a slew of bad press."

"I've heard from Burlington that Hodges' death is definitely being ruled a homicide," Cantor said.

"Of course it will be ruled a homicide," Traynor snapped. "What else could it be ruled? The man's body was entombed behind a wall of cinder blocks. The issue before us is not whether or not his death was a homicide. The issue is what can we do to lessen the impact on the hospital's reputation. I'm particularly anxious about how these events impact our relationship with CMV."

"I don't see how Hodges' death is the hospital's problem," Sherwood said. "It's not like we killed him."

"Hodges ran the hospital for twenty-plus years," Traynor said. "His name is intimately associated with Bartlet. Lots of people know he wasn't happy with the way we were running things."

"I think the less the hospital says the better," Sherwood said.

"I disagree," Beaton said. "I think that the hospital should issue a statement regretting his death and underlining the great debt owed him. The statement should include condolences to his family."

"I agree," Cantor said. "Ignoring his death would seem peculiar."

"I agree," Caldwell said.

Sherwood shrugged. "If everyone else feels that way, I'll go along."

"Has anyone spoken to Robertson?" Traynor asked.

"I have," Beaton said. "He doesn't have any suspects. Braggart that he is, he surely would have let on if he had."

"Hell, the way he felt about Hodges he could be a suspect himself," Sherwood said with a laugh.

"So could you," Cantor said to Sherwood.

"And so could you, Cantor," Sherwood said.

"This isn't a contest," Traynor said.

"If it were a contest, you'd be a leading contestant," Cantor said to Traynor. "It's common knowledge how you felt about Hodges after your sister committed suicide."

"Hold on," Caldwell said. "The point is that no one cares who did it."

"That might not be entirely true," Traynor said. "CMV might care. After all, this sordid affair still reflects poorly on both the hospital and the town."

"And that's why I think we should issue a statement," Beaton said.

"Would anyone like to make a motion for a vote?" Traynor said.

"Jesus, Harold," Cantor said. "There are only five of us here. We don't have to follow parliamentary procedure. Hell, we all agree."

"All right," Traynor said. "Does everybody concur that we should make a formal statement along the lines Beaton discussed?"

Everyone nodded.

Traynor looked at Beaton. "I think it should come from your office," he said.

"I'll be happy to do it," Beaton said.

15

FRIDAY, OCTOBER 22

IT HAD BEEN A TURBULENT NIGHT AT THE WILSON house. Just after two o'clock in the morning Nikki had begun screaming again and had to be awakened from yet another terrifying nightmare. The episode had upset everyone and had kept them all up for over an hour. David and Angela regretted having allowed Nikki to watch crime-scene technicians work, guessing they had contributed to her terror.

At least the day dawned bright and clear. After five days of continuous rain the sky was pale blue and cloudless. In place of the rain was a big chill. The temperature had plunged into the upper teens, leaving the ground blanketed with an exceptionally heavy hoarfrost.

There was little conversation as the Wilsons dressed and breakfasted. Everyone avoided making reference to the luminal test although Angela refused to sit at the kitchen table. She ate her cereal standing at the sink.

Before Angela and Nikki left, David asked Angela about lunch. Angela told him she'd meet him in the lobby at twelve-thirty.

On the way to school, Angela tried to encourage Nikki to give Mr. Hart more than one day's chance. "It's difficult for a teacher to take over someone else's class. Especially someone special like Marjorie."

"Why couldn't Daddy save her?" Nikki asked.

"He tried," Angela said. "But it just wasn't to be. Doctors can only do so much."

Pulling up to the front of the school, Nikki jumped out and was about to dash up the walk when Angela called her back.

"You forgot the letter," Angela said. She handed Nikki a letter Angela had written explaining Nikki's health problems and needs. "Remember, if Mr. Hart has any questions he should give either me or Dr. Pilsner a call."

Angela was relieved to find that Wadley wasn't around when she arrived at the lab. Quickly she immersed herself in her work, but no sooner had she started when one of the secretaries let her know that the chief medical examiner was on the phone.

"I have some interesting news," Walt said. "The material that we teased from beneath Dr. Hodges' fingernails was indeed skin."

"Congratulations," Angela said.

"I've already run a DNA screen," Walt said. "It is not Hodges' skin. I'd bet a thousand dollars it belongs to his assailant. It could prove to be critical evidence if a suspect is charged."

"Have you ever found evidence like this before?" Angela asked.

"Yes, I have," Walt said. "It's not rare in mortal struggles to find remnants of the attacker's skin under the victim's nails. But I have to admit that this case represents the longest interval from the time of the crime to the discovery of the body. If we can make an I.D. with a suspect it might be worth writing it up for one of the journals."

Angela thanked him for keeping her informed.

"I almost forgot," Walt added. "I found some black carbon particles embedded in the skin samples. It looks strange. It's as if the killer had scraped up against a hearth or a wood stove during the struggle. Anyway, I thought it was curious and that it might help the crime-scene investigators."

"I'm afraid it might only confuse them," Angela said. She explained about the luminol test the night before. "The blood spatter wasn't anywhere near a fireplace or the stove. Maybe the killer picked up the carbon earlier, someplace else?"

"I doubt it," Walt said. "There was no inflammation, just a few red blood cells. The carbon had to be picked up contemporaneous to the struggle."

"Maybe Hodges had carbon under his nails," Angela suggested.

"That's a good thought," Walt said. "The only trouble is the carbon is evenly distributed in the skin samples."

"It's a mystery," Angela said. "Especially since it doesn't jibe with what the crime-scene people found."

"It's the same with any mystery," Walt said. "To solve it you have to have all the facts. We're obviously missing some crucial piece of information."

After having been denied the opportunity to ride his bike for an entire week, David thoroughly enjoyed the trip from his home to the hospital. Taking a little extra time, he followed a route that was slightly longer than usual but much more scenic.

The exhilaration of the cold, crisp air and the views of the frost-filled meadows cleared David's mind. For a few minutes he was relieved of his anguish over his recent medical failures. Entering the hospital he felt better than he had for several days. The first patient he visited was Mary Ann Schiller.

Unfortunately Mary Ann was not bright and cheerful. David had to wake her up, and while he was examining her, she fell back asleep. Beginning to feel a little concerned, David woke her up again. He asked her how it felt when he tapped over her antral sinuses. With a sleep-slurred voice she said she thought there was less discomfort, but she wasn't sure.

David then listened to her chest with his stethoscope, and while he was concentrating on her breath sounds, she fell asleep again. David allowed her to fall back onto the pillows. He looked at her peaceful face; it was in sharp contrast to his state of mind. Her drowsiness was alarming him.

David went to the nurses' station to go over Mary Ann's chart. At first he felt a little better, seeing that the low-grade fever she had developed the day before had remained unchanged. But his apprehension grew when he read the nurses' notes and learned that GI symptoms had appeared during the night. She'd suffered from nausea, vomiting, and diarrhea.

David couldn't account for these symptoms. He wasn't sure how to proceed. Since her sinusitis seemed to be slightly better, he did not alter her antibiotics even though there was a slight chance the antibiotics were causing the GI problems. But what about the drowsiness? As a precaution, he canceled her PRN sleep order as he'd done with John Tarlow.

Going on to Jonathan Eakins' room, David's relatively buoyant spirits returned. Jonathan was in an expansive mood. He was feeling chipper and reported that his cardiac monitor had been beeping as regularly as a metronome without the slightest suggestion of irregularity.

Taking out his stethoscope, David listened to Jonathan's chest. He was pleased to hear that Jonathan's lungs were perfectly clear. David wasn't surprised with Jonathan's rapidly improved status. He had spent several hours going over the case with the cardiologist the previous afternoon. The cardiologist had been certain there would be no problems with the heart.

The rest of David's hospital patients were all doing as well as Jonathan. He was able to move from one to the other swiftly, even discharging a few. With his rounds finished, David headed to his office, happy to be early. After the experiences of the last few days, he'd made a vow to make every effort not to get behind again.

As the morning progressed, David remained acutely aware of the amount of time he spent with each patient. Knowing that his productivity was being monitored, he tried to keep each visit short. Although he didn't feel good about it, he was afraid he didn't have much choice. Kelley's implied threat of firing him had left him shaken. With their debt, the family could not afford for him to be out of work.

Having gotten an early start, David was able to keep ahead all morning. When two second-floor nurses called and asked to be seen as semi-emergencies, David was able to take them the moment they came in the door.

Both had flu-like symptoms identical to the two previous nurses. David treated them the same way: recommending bed rest and symptomatic therapy for their GI complaints.

With ample time to attend to other matters, David even had an opportunity to slip over to Dr. Pilsner's office. He told the pediatrician that he'd been seeing some flu already, and he asked him about Nikki's flu shot.

"She's already had it," Dr. Pilsner said. "I haven't seen any flu in my practice yet, but I don't wait to see it before I give the shots, especially to my cystic fibrosis patients."

David also asked Dr. Pilsner about his opinion regarding the use of prophylactic antibiotics for Nikki. Dr. Pilsner said he was not in favor of it. He thought it best to wait until Nikki's condition suggested she needed them.

David finished his morning patients before noon and even had time to dictate some letters before meeting Angela in the hospital lobby.

"With the weather as nice as it is, what do you say we go into town and have lunch at the diner?" David suggested. He thought some fresh air would be good for both of them.

"I was about to suggest the same thing," Angela said. "But let's get take-out. I want to stop by the police station and find out how they intend to proceed with the Hodges investigation."

"I don't think that's a good idea," David said.

"Why not?" Angela questioned.

"I'm not entirely sure," David admitted. "Intuition, I guess. And it's not like the town police have inspired much confidence. To tell you the truth, I didn't get the impression they were all that interested in investigating the case."

"That's why I want to go," Angela said. "I want to be sure they know that we're interested. Come on, humor me."

"If you insist," David said with reluctance.

They got tuna sandwiches to go and ate them on the steps of the gazebo. Although it had been well below freezing that morning, the bright sun had warmed the air to a balmy seventy degrees.

After finishing their meal they walked over to the police station. It was a plain, two-story brick structure standing on the town green directly across from the library.

The officer at the front desk was gracious. After a quick call he directed David and Angela down a creaky wooden corridor to Wayne Robertson's office. Robertson invited them in and hastily took newspapers and Dunkin' Donuts bags off two metal chairs. When David and Angela were seated, he leaned his expansive backside against his matching metal desk. He crossed his arms and smiled. Despite the lack of direct sunlight in the room, he was wearing his reflective aviator-style sunglasses.

"I'm glad you folks stopped in," he said once David and Angela were seated. He had a slight accent that had a vague similarity to a southern drawl. "I'm sorry we had to intrude the other night. I'd like to apologize for upsetting your evening."

"We appreciated your coming," David said.

"What can I do for you folks?" Robertson asked.

"We're here to offer our cooperation," Angela said.

"Well now, we appreciate that," Robertson said. He smiled widely, revealing square teeth. "We depend on the community. Without its support, we couldn't do our job."

"We want to see the Hodges murder case solved," Angela said. "We want to see the killer behind bars."

"Well, you're certainly not alone," Robertson said with his smile plastered on his face. "We want to see it solved as well."

"Living in a house where there's been a murder is very distressing," Angela said. "Particularly if the murderer is still on the streets. I'm sure you understand."

"Absolutely," Robertson said.

"So we'd like to know what we can do to help," Angela said.

"Well, let's see," Robertson said, showing signs of unease. He stammered, "Actually, there's not a whole bunch anybody can do."

"What exactly are the police doing?" Angela asked.

The smile faded from Robertson's face. "We're working on it," Robertson said vaguely.

"Which means what?" Angela persisted.

David started to stand up, concerned about the direction and tone of the conversation, but Angela wouldn't budge.

"Well, the usual," Robertson said.

"What's the usual?" Angela asked.

Robertson was clearly uncomfortable. "Well, to be truthful we're not doing much right now. But back when Hodges disappeared, we were working day and night."

"I'm a little surprised that there hasn't been a resurgence of interest now that there is a corpse," Angela said testily. "And the medical examiner has unquestionably ruled the case a homicide. We've got a killer walking around this town, and I want something done."

"Well, we certainly don't want to disappoint you folks," Robertson said with a touch of sarcasm. "What exactly would you like done so that we'll know in advance you'll be pleased?"

David started to say something, but Angela shushed him. "We want you to do what you normally do with a homicide," she said. "You have the murder weapon so test it for fingerprints, find out where it was purchased, that sort of thing. We shouldn't have to tell you how to carry out an investigation."

"The spoor is a little cold after eight months," Robertson said, "and frankly I don't take kindly to your coming in here telling me how to do my job. I don't go up to the hospital and tell you how to do yours. Besides, Hodges wasn't the most popular man in town, and we have to set priorities with our limited manpower. For your information we have a few more pressing matters just now, including a series of rapes."

"It's my opinion that the basics ought to be done on this case," Angela said.

"They were," Robertson said. "Eight months ago."

"And what did you learn?" Angela demanded.

"Lots of things," Robertson snapped. "We learned there was no break-in or robbery, which has now been confirmed. We learned there was a bit of a struggle ..."

" 'A bit of a struggle'?" Angela echoed. "Last night the state police crime-scene investigators proved that the killer chased the doctor through our house bashing him with a pry bar, spattering blood all over the walls. Dr. Hodges had multiple skull fractures, a fractured clavicle, and a broken arm." Angela turned to David, throwing her hands in the air. "I don't believe this!"

"Okay, okay," David said, trying to calm her. He had been afraid she'd make a scene like this. She had little tolerance for incompetence.

"The case needs a fresh look," Angela said, ignoring David. "I got a call today from the medical examiner confirming that the victim had skin from his attacker under his fingernails. That's the kind of struggle it was. Now all we need is a suspect. Forensics can do the rest."

"Thank you for this timely tip," Robertson said. "And thank you for being such a concerned citizen. Now if you'll excuse me, I have work to do."

Robertson stepped over to the door and held it open. David practically had to yank Angela from the office. It was all he could do to keep her from saying more on her way out.

"Did you catch any of that?" Robertson asked when one of his deputies appeared.

"Some of it," the deputy said.

"I hate these big-shot city people," Robertson said. "Just because they went to Harvard or someplace like that they think they know how to do everything."

Robertson stepped back inside his office and closed the door. Picking up the phone, he pressed one of the automatic dial buttons.

"Sorry to bother you," Robertson said deferentially, "but I think we might have a problem."

• • •

"Don't you dare paint me as a hysterical female," Angela said as she got into the car.

"Baiting the local chief of police like that certainly isn't rational," David said. "Remember, this is a small town. We shouldn't be making enemies."

"A person was brutally murdered, the body dumped in our basement, and the police don't seem too interested in finding out who did it. You're willing to let it rest at that?"

"As deplorable as Hodges' death was," David said, "it doesn't involve us. It's a problem that should be left up to the authorities."

"What?" Angela cried. "The man was beaten to death in our house, in our kitchen. We're involved whether you want to admit it or not, and I want to find out who did it. I don't like the idea of the murderer walking around this town, and I'm going to do something about it. The first thing is we should learn more about Dennis Hodges."

"I think you're being overly dramatic and unreasonable," David said.

"You've already made that clear," Angela said. "I just don't agree with you."

Angela seethed with anger, mostly at Robertson but partly at David. She wanted to tell him that he wasn't the paragon of rationality and agreeableness that he thought he was. But she held her tongue.

They reached the hospital parking lot. The only space available was far from the entrance. They got out and started walking.

"We already have plenty to worry about," David said. "It's not as if we don't have enough problems at the moment."

"Then maybe we should hire somebody to do the investigating for us," Angela said.

"You can't be serious," David said, coming to a halt. "We don't have the money to throw away on such nonsense."

"In case you haven't been listening to me," Angela said, "I don't think it's nonsense. I repeat: there's a murderer loose in this town. Someone who has been in our house. Maybe we've already met him. It gives me the creeps."

"Please, Angela," David said as he started walking again. "We're not dealing with a serial killer. I don't think it's so strange that the killer hasn't been found. Haven't you read stories about murders in small towns where no one would come forward even though it was common knowledge who the killer was? It's a kind of down-home justice where the people think the victim got what he deserved. Apparently Hodges wasn't uniformly admired."

They reached the hospital and entered. Just inside the door they paused.

"I'm not willing to chalk this up to down-home justice," Angela said. "I think the issue here is one of basic social responsibility. We're a society of laws."

"You're too much," David said. Despite his aggravation, he smiled. "Now you're ready to give me a lecture on social responsibility. You can be such an idealist sometimes, it blows my mind. But I do love you." He leaned over and gave her a peck on the cheek. "We'll talk more later. For now, calm down! You've got enough problems with Wadley to keep you occupied without adding this."

With a final wave David strode off toward the professional building. Angela watched him until he rounded the corner and disappeared from sight. She was touched by his sudden display of affection. Its unexpectedness mollified her for the moment.

But a few minutes later as she was sitting at her desk trying to concentrate, she replayed the conversation with Robertson in her mind and got furious all over again. She left her office to look for Paul Darnell. She found him where he always was: hunched over stacks of petri dishes filled with bacteria.

"Have you lived in Bartlet all your life?" Angela asked.

"All except four years of college, four of medical school, four of residency, and two in the navy."

"I'd say that makes you a local," Angela said.

"What makes me a local is the fact that Darnells have been living here for four generations."

Angela stepped into Paul's office and leaned against the desk. "I suppose you heard the gossip about the body found in my home," she said.

Paul nodded.

"It's really bothering me," Angela said. "Would you mind if I asked you a few questions?"

"Not at all," Paul said.

"Did you know Dennis Hodges?"

"Of course."

"What was he like?"

"He was a feisty old codger few people miss. He had a penchant for making enemies."

"How did he get to be hospital administrator?" Angela asked.

"By default," Paul said. "He took over the hospital at a time when no other doctors wanted the responsibility. Everybody thought that running the hospital was below their physician status. So Hodges had a free hand, and he built the place like a feudal estate, associating with a medical school for prestige and billing the place as a regional medical center. He even sank some of his own money into it in a crisis. But Hodges was the world's worst diplomat, and he didn't care one iota about other people's interests when they collided with the hospital's."

"Like when the hospital took over pathology and radiology?" Angela asked.

"Exactly," Paul said. "It was a good move for the hospital, but it created a lot of ill will. I had to take an enormous cut in my income. But my family wanted to stay in Bartlet so I adjusted. Other people fought it and eventually had to move away. Obviously Hodges made a lot of enemies."

"Dr. Cantor stayed as well," Angela remarked. ·

"Yes, but that was because he talked Hodges into a joint venture between himself and the hospital to create a world-class imaging center. Cantor wound up doing well financially, but he was the exception."

"I just had a conversation with Wayne Robertson," Angela said. "I got the distinct impression that he's dragging his feet about investigating who killed Hodges."

"I'm not surprised," Paul said. "There's not a lot of pressure to solve the case. Hodges' wife has moved back to Boston, and she and Hodges weren't getting along at the time of his death. They'd essentially lived apart these last few years. On top of that, Robertson could have done it himself. Robertson always had it in for Hodges. He even had an altercation with him the night Hodges disappeared."

"Why was there animosity between those two?" Angela asked.

"Robertson blamed his wife's death on Hodges," Douglas said.

"Was Hodges Robertson's wife's physician?" Angela asked.

"No, Hodges' practice was minuscule by then. He was running the hospital full time. But as director he allowed Dr. Werner Van Slyke to practice even though most everybody knew Van Slyke had a drinking problem. Actually Hodges left the issue of Van Slyke's privileges up to the medical staff. Van Slyke bungled Robertson's wife's appendicitis case while under the influence. Afterward, Robertson blamed Hodges. It wasn't rational, but hate usually isn't."

"I'm getting the feeling that finding out who killed Hodges won't be easy," Angela said.

"You don't know how right you are," Paul said. "There's a second chapter to the Hodges-Van Slyke affair. Hodges was friends with Traynor who is the present chairman of the hospital board. Traynor's sister was married to Van Slyke, and when Hodges finally denied Van Slyke privileges . . ."

"All right," Angela said, holding up her hand, "I'm getting the idea. You're overwhelming me. I had no idea the town was quite this byzantine."

"It's a small town," Paul said. "A lot of families have lived here a long time. It's practically incestuous. But the fact of the matter is there were a lot of people who didn't care for Hodges. So when he disappeared, not too many people were broken up about it."

"But that means Hodges' murderer is walking around," Angela said. "Presumably a man who is capable of extreme violence."

"You're probably right about that."

Angela shivered. "I don't like it," she said. "This man was in my home, maybe many times. He probably knows my house well."

Paul shrugged. "I understand how you feel," he said. "I'd probably feel the same way. But I don't know what you can do about it. If you want to learn more about Hodges, go talk to Barton Sherwood. As president of the bank he knows everyone. He knew Hodges particularly well since he's been on the hospital board forever and his father had been before that."

Angela went back to her office and again attempted to work, but she still couldn't concentrate. It was impossible to get Hodges out of her mind. Reaching for the phone, she called Barton Sherwood. She remembered how friendly he'd been when they bought the house.

"Dr. Wilson," Sherwood said when he came on the line. "How nice to hear from you. How are you folks making out in that beautiful house of yours?"

"Generally well," Angela said, "but that's what I'd like to chat with you about. If I were to run over to the bank, would you have a few moments to speak with me?"

"Absolutely," Sherwood said. "Any time."

"I'll be right over," Angela said.

After telling the secretaries that she'd be back shortly, Angela grabbed her coat and ran out to the car. Ten minutes later she was sitting in Sherwood's office. It seemed like just yesterday that she, David, and Nikki were there, arranging to buy their first house.

Angela came right to the point. She described how uncomfortable she felt about Hodges having been murdered in her house and about the murderer being on the loose. She told Sherwood she hoped he would be willing to help.

"Help?" Sherwood questioned. He was leaning back in his leather desk chair with both thumbs tucked into his vest pockets.

"The local police don't seem to care about solving the case," Angela said. "With your stature in the town a word from you would go a long way in getting them to do something."

Sherwood thumped forward in his chair. He was clearly flattered. "Thank you for your vote of confidence," he said, "but I truly don't think you have anything to worry about.

Hodges was not the victim of senseless, random violence or of a serial killer."

"How do you know?" Angela asked. "Do you know who killed him?"

"Heavens no," Sherwood said nervously. "I didn't mean to imply that. I meant . . . well, I thought . . . there's no reason for you and your family to feel at risk."

"Do a lot of people know who killed Hodges?" Angela asked, recalling David's theory of down-home justice.

"Oh, no. At least, I don't think so," Sherwood said. "It's just that Dr. Hodges was an unpopular man who'd hurt a number of people. Even I had trouble getting along with him." Sherwood laughed nervously, then went on to tell Angela about the spit of land that Hodges had owned, fenced, and refused to sell out of spite, keeping Sherwood from using his own two parcels.

"What you're trying to tell me is the reason no one cares who killed Hodges is because he was disliked."

"Essentially, yes," Sherwood admitted.

"In other words, what we have here is a conspiracy of silence."

"I wouldn't put it that way," Sherwood said. "It's a situation where people feel that justice has been served, so no one cares much whether someone is arrested or not."

"I care," Angela said. "The murder took place in my house. Besides, there's no place for vigilante justice in this day and age."

"Normally I would be the first to agree with you," Sherwood said. "I'm not trying to justify this affair on moral or legal grounds. But Hodges was different. What I think you should do is go talk with Dr. Cantor. He'll be able to give you an idea of the kind of animosity and turmoil that Hodges was capable of causing. Maybe then you'll understand and be less judgmental."

Angela drove back up the hill toward the hospital feeling confused about what she should do. She did not agree with Sherwood for one second, and the more she learned about the Hodges affair, the more she wanted to know. Yet she did not want to speak with Cantor, not after the conversation she'd had with him the day before.

Entering the hospital, Angela went directly to the section of the pathology lab where slides were stained and prepared. Her timing was perfect: slides that she'd been anticipating that morning had just been completed. Taking the tray, she hurried back to her office to get to work.

The moment she entered her office Wadley appeared at the connecting door. Like the day before, he was visibly distressed. "I just paged you," he said irritably. "Where the hell were you?"

"I had to make a quick trip to the bank," Angela said nervously. Her legs suddenly felt weak. She feared Wadley was about to lose control the way he had the day before.

"Restrict your visits to the bank to your lunch hour," he said. He hesitated for a moment, then stepped back into his office and slammed the door.

Angela breathed a sigh of relief.

Sherwood had not moved from his desk following Angela's departure. He was trying to decide what to do. He couldn't believe this woman was making such an issue about Hodges. He hoped he hadn't said something that he would regret.

After some deliberation, Sherwood picked up the phone. He'd come to the conclusion that it was best for him to do nothing other than pass on the information.

"Something has just happened that I thought you should know about," Sherwood said when the connection went through. "I just had a visit from the newest member of the hospital's professional staff and she's concerned about Dr. Hodges . . ."

David finished with his last office patient for the day, dictated a few letters, then hurried over to the hospital to make his late afternoon rounds. Fearing what he'd find, he left Mary Ann Schiller for last. As he'd intuitively suspected, she'd taken a turn for the worse.

Her low-grade fever had gradually climbed during the afternoon. Now it hovered a little over one hundred and one. The fever bothered David, especially since it had risen while she was on antibiotics, but there was something that bothered him more: her mental state.

That morning Mary Ann had been drowsy, but now as David tried to talk to her, he found her both drowsy and apathetic. It had been a distinct change. Not only was it hard to wake her and keep her awake, but when she was awake she didn't care about anything and paid little attention to his questions. She was also disoriented with respect to time and place although she still knew her name.

David rolled her on her side and listened to her chest. When he did so he panicked. He heard a chorus of rhonchi and rales. She was developing massive pneumonia. It was like John Tarlow all over again.

David raced back to the nurses' station where he ordered a stat blood count as well as a portable chest film. Going over Mary Ann's chart he found nothing abnormal. The nurses' notes for the day suggested that she had been doing fine.

The stat blood count came back showing very little cellular response to the developing pneumonia, a situation reminiscent of both Tarlow and Kleber. The portable chest film confirmed his fear: extensive pneumonia developing in both lungs.

At a loss, David called Dr. Mieslich, the oncologist, to confer by phone. After all the trouble with Kelley he was reluctant to ask for a formal consult even though that would have been far better.

Without having seen the patient, Dr. Mieslich could offer little help. He did confirm that the last time he had seen Mary Ann in his office there had been no evidence of her ovarian cancer. At the same time he told David that her cancer had been extensive prior to treatment and that he fully expected a recurrence.

While David was on the phone with the oncologist, a nurse appeared in front of the nurses' station and yelled that Mary Ann was convulsing.

David slammed down the phone and raced to the bedside. Mary Ann was indeed in the throes of a grand mal seizure. Her back was arched and her legs and arms were rhythmically thrashing against the bed. Fortunately, her IV had not become dislodged, and David was able to control the seizure quickly with intravenous medication. Nevertheless, in the wake of the seizure, Mary Ann remained comatose.

Returning to the nurses' station, David put in a stat call to the CMV neurologist, Dr. Alan Prichard. Since he was in the hospital making his own rounds, he called immediately. After David told him about the seizure along with a capsule history, Dr. Prichard told David to order either a CAT scan or an MRI, whichever machine was available. He said he'd be over to see the patient as soon as he could.

David sent Mary Ann to the Imaging Center for her MRI accompanied by a nurse in case she seized again. Then he called the oncologist back, explained what had happened, and asked for a formal consult. As he'd done with Kleber and Tarlow, he also called Dr. Hasselbaum, the infectious disease specialist.

David couldn't help but worry about Kelley's reaction to these non-CMV consults, but David felt he had little choice. He could not allow concern about Kelley to influence his decision making in light of the grand mal seizure. The gravity of Mary Ann's condition was apparent.

As soon as David was alerted that the MRI study was available, he dashed over to the Imaging Center. He met the neurologist in the viewing room as the first images were being processed. Along with Dr. Cantor they silently watched the cuts appear. When the study was complete David was shocked that there was no sign of a metastatic tumor. He would have sworn such a tumor was responsible for the seizure.

"At this point I cannot say why she had a seizure," Dr. Prichard said. "It could have been some micro emboli, but I'm only speculating."

The oncologist was equally surprised about the MRI result. "Maybe the lesion is too small for the MRI to pick up," he suggested.

"This machine has fantastic resolution," Dr. Cantor said. "If the tumor was too small for this baby to pick up, then the chances it could have caused a grand mal seizure are even smaller."

The infectious disease consult was the only one with anything specific to add, but his news wasn't good. He

confirmed David's diagnosis of extensive pneumonia. He
also demonstrated that the bacteria involved was a gram-
negative type organism similar but not identical to the
bacteria that had caused Kleber's and Tarlow's pneumonia.
Worse still, he suggested that Mary Ann was already in
septic shock.

From the Imaging Center David sent Mary Ann to the
ICU where he insisted on the most aggressive therapy available. He allowed the infectious disease consult to handle the
antibiotic regimen. The respiratory care he turned over to
an anesthesiologist. By then Mary Ann's breathing was so
labored she needed a respirator.

When everything that could be done for Mary Ann had
been done and after all the consults had departed, David
felt dazed. His group of oncology patients had become
far more emotionally draining than he'd originally feared.
Finally he left the ICU, and just to be reassured, he stopped
in again to see Jonathan. Thankfully Jonathan was doing
marvelously.

"I only have one complaint," Jonathan said. "This bed
has a mind of its own. Sometimes when I press the button
nothing happens. Neither the head nor the foot rises."

"I'll take care of it," David assured him.

Thankful for a problem that had an easy solution, David
went back to the nurses' station and mentioned the problem
to the evening head nurse, Dora Maxfield.

"Not his too," Dora said. "Some of these old beds break
down a little too often. But thanks for telling us. I'll have
maintenance take care of it right away."

David left the hospital and got on his bike. The temperature had dropped as soon as the sun had dipped below the
horizon, but he felt the cold was somehow therapeutic.

Arriving home David found a bedlam of activity. Nikki
had both Caroline and Arni over, and they were racing
around the downstairs with Rusty in hot pursuit. David
joined the melee, enjoying being pummeled and trampled
by three active children. The laughter alone was worth the
punishment. For a few minutes he forgot about the hospital.

When it was almost seven Angela asked David if he
would take Caroline and Arni home. David was happy to

do it, and Nikki came along. After the two children had been dropped off, David was glad for the moments alone with his daughter. First they talked about school and her new teacher. Then he asked her if she thought much about the body discovered in the basement.

"Some," Nikki said.

"How does it make you feel?" David asked.

"Like I don't want to ever go in the basement again."

"I can understand that," David said. "Last night when I was getting firewood I felt a little scared."

"You did?"

"Yup," David said. "But I have a little plan that might be fun and it might help. Are you interested?"

"Yeah!" Nikki said with enthusiasm. "What?"

"You can't tell anybody," David said.

"Okay," Nikki promised.

David outlined his plan as they continued home. "What do you say?" he asked once he had finished.

"I think it's cool," Nikki said.

"Remember, it's a secret," David said.

"Cross my heart."

As soon as David got into the house, he called the ICU to check on Mary Ann. He had been distressed that the floor nurses had missed the worsening condition of his two patients who had died. At the same time he recognized that his patients' vital signs had shown little change as their clinical states markedly deteriorated.

"There has been no alteration in Mrs. Schiller's status," the ICU nurse told him over the phone. She then gave him a lengthy review of Mrs. Schiller's vital signs, lab values, and even the settings on her respirator. The nurse's professionalism bolstered David's confidence that Mary Ann was receiving the best care possible.

Intentionally avoiding the kitchen table after the previous night's revelation, Angela served dinner in the dining room. It seemed huge with just three people and their skimpy dining-room furniture. But Angela tried to make it cozy with a fire in the fireplace and candles on the table. Nikki complained it was so dark she could hardly see her food.

After they had finished eating, Nikki excused herself
to watch her half-hour allotment of television. David and
Angela lingered at the table.

"Don't you want to ask me how my afternoon went?"
Angela asked.

"Of course," David said. "How was it?"

"Interesting," Angela said. She told him about her conversations with Paul Darnell and Barton Sherwood concerning Dennis Hodges. She conceded that David might have
been right when he suggested that some people in town
knew who did it.

"Thanks for giving me credit," David said, "but I'm not
happy about your asking questions about Hodges."

"Why not?" Angela asked.

"For a number of reasons," David said. "Mainly because
we both have other things to worry about. But beyond that,
did it occur to you that you might wind up questioning the
killer himself?"

Angela admitted she hadn't thought of that, but David
wasn't listening. He was staring into the fire.

"You seem distracted," she said. "What's wrong?"

"Another one of my patients is in the ICU fighting for
her life."

"I'm sorry," Angela said.

"It's another disaster," David said. His voice faltered as
he struggled with his emotions. "I'm trying to deal with it,
but it's hard. She's doing very poorly. Frankly, I'm worried
she'll die just like Kleber and Tarlow. Maybe I don't know
what I'm doing. Maybe I shouldn't even be a doctor."

Angela came around the table to put an arm around
David. "You are a wonderful doctor," she whispered. "You
have a real gift. Patients love you."

"They don't love me when they die," David said. "When
I sit in my office in the same spot where Dr. Portland killed
himself, I start thinking that now I know why he did it."

Angela shook David's shoulders. "I don't want to hear
any talk like that," she said. "Have you been speaking with
Kevin Yansen again?"

"Not about Portland," David said. "He seems to have lost
interest in the subject."

"Are you depressed?"

"Some," David admitted. "But it's not out of hand."

"Promise me you'll tell me if it gets out of hand?" Angela said.

"I promise," David said.

"What's this new patient's problem?" Angela asked. She sat down in the seat next to his.

"That's part of what's so upsetting," David said. "I don't really know. She came in with sinusitis which was improving with antibiotics. But then she began to develop pneumonia for some unknown reason. Actually, first she became drowsy. Then she became apathetic, and finally she had a seizure. I've had neurology, oncology, and infectious disease look at her. No one has any bright ideas."

"Then you shouldn't be so hard on yourself," Angela said.

"Except I'm responsible," David said. "I'm her doctor."

"I wish I could help," Angela said.

"Thank you," David said. He reached out and gave Angela's shoulder a squeeze. "I appreciate your concern because I know you mean it. Unfortunately, there's nothing you can do directly except understand why I can't get so worked up about Hodges' death."

"I can't just let it go," Angela said.

"But it could be dangerous," David said. "You don't know who you're up against. Whoever killed Hodges isn't likely to be thrilled by your poking around. Who knows what such a person might do? Look what he did to Hodges."

Angela looked into the fire, mesmerized for the moment by the white-hot coals that shimmered ominously in the intense heat. Potential danger to her family was her motivation for wanting Hodges' murder solved. She hadn't considered that her investigation itself could put them in greater jeopardy. Yet all she had to do was close her eyes and see the luminol glow in her kitchen or remember the horrid fractures on the X rays in the autopsy room to know that David had a point: a person capable of that kind of violence was not someone who should be provoked.

16

SATURDAY, OCTOBER 23

WORRIED ABOUT MARY ANN, DAVID WAS UP BEFORE the sun. He stole out of the house without waking Angela and Nikki and got on his bike. Just as the sun was inching above the eastern horizon, he crossed the Roaring River. It was as cold as it had been the previous morning. Another heavy frost blanketed the fields and covered the naked branches of the leafless trees with a vitreous sheen.

David's early-morning arrival surprised the ICU nurses. Mary Ann's condition had not changed dramatically although she had developed moderately severe diarrhea. David was amazed and grateful for how the nurses took such a development in stride. It was a tribute to their compassion and dedication.

Reviewing Mary Ann's case again from the beginning, David did not have any new ideas. He even called one of his past professors in Boston whom he knew to be a chronic early riser. After hearing about the case, the professor volunteered to come immediately. David was overwhelmed by the man's commitment and generosity.

While he waited for his professor to arrive, David made the rounds to see his other hospitalized patients. Everyone was doing fine. He thought about sending Jonathan Eakins home but decided to keep him another day just to be sure his cardiac status was truly stable.

Once his professor arrived some hours later, David presented Mary Ann as if he were back in his training program. The professor listened intently, examined Mary Ann with great care, then went over the chart in detail. But even he had no new insights. David saw him out to his car, thanking him profusely for having made the trip.

With nothing else to do at the hospital, David headed home. He avoided Saturday morning basketball since he was still smarting from the unpleasant confrontation with Kevin Yansen over their tennis match. In his precarious emotional state, David felt that he'd do well to avoid Kevin's unpleasant competitiveness for another week.

When he got home, Angela and Nikki were just finishing breakfast. David teased them that they'd missed half the day. While Angela tended to Nikki's respiratory treatment, David went down into the basement and removed the crime scene tape. Then he took some of the storm windows out to the yard via the steps leading outdoors.

He'd put the first-floor windows up by the time Nikki joined him.

"When are we going to . . ." Nikki began to ask.

David put his finger to his lips to shush Nikki while he pointed to the nearby kitchen window where Angela could be seen. "As soon as we clean up," he said.

David let Nikki help him carry each of the screens down into the basement. He could have done it more easily himself, but she liked to think she was helping. They leaned them up against the base of the stairs where the storm windows had originally been.

With that accomplished, David and Nikki announced to Angela that they were heading into town on a shopping mission. Then they rode off on their bikes. Angela enjoyed seeing them having so much fun, though she did feel excluded.

Left alone, Angela began to feel a little edgy. She noticed every creak the empty house made. She tried to immerse herself in the book she was reading, but before long she was up locking the doors and even the windows. Ending up in the kitchen, Angela could not suppress her imagination from coating the walls with blood.

"I can't live like this," Angela said aloud, realizing how paranoid she was becoming. "But what am I going to do?"

She stepped over to the kitchen table, the legs of which she had scrubbed with the strongest disinfectant Mr. Staley had in his hardware store. Her fingers brushed its surface. She wondered if luminol would still fluoresce now that she had cleaned it so thoroughly. She still didn't like the idea that Hodges' killer was free. Yet she took to heart David's warning that it was dangerous for her to be snooping around about the murder.

Walking over to the phone directory, she looked up "private investigators" but didn't find any entries. Then she looked up "detectives" and found a list. Most were security businesses, but there were several individuals listed as well. One—a Phil Calhoun—was in Rutland, which was only a short drive away.

Before she had time to reconsider, Angela dialed the number. A man with a husky, slow, and deliberate voice answered.

Angela hadn't given much thought to what she would say. She finally stammered that she wanted to investigate a murder.

"Sounds interesting," Calhoun said.

Angela tried to picture the man on the other end of the wire. Judging from the voice she imagined a powerfully built man with broad shoulders, dark hair, maybe even a mustache.

"Perhaps we could meet," Angela suggested.

"You want me to come there or do you want to come here?" Calhoun asked.

Angela thought for a moment. She didn't want David finding out what she was up to—not just yet.

"I'll come to you," she said.

"I'll be waiting," Calhoun said after he gave her directions.

Angela ran upstairs, changed clothes, then left a note saying "Gone shopping" for David and Nikki.

Calhoun's office was also his home. She had no trouble finding it. In the driveway she noticed his Ford pickup truck had a rifle rack in the back of the cab and a sticker on the back bumper that read: "This Vehicle Climbed Mount Washington."

Phil Calhoun invited her into his living room and offered her a seat on a threadbare sofa. He was far from her romantic image of a private investigator. Although he was a big man, he was overweight and considerably older than she'd guessed from his voice. She figured he was in his early sixties. His face was a little doughy, but his gray eyes were bright. He was wearing a wool black and white checkered hunting shirt. His cotton work pants were held up by black suspenders. On his head was a cap with the words "Roscoe Electric" emblazoned above the visor.

"Mind if I smoke?" Calhoun asked, holding up a box of Antonio y Cleopatra cigars.

"It's your house," Angela said.

"What's the story about this murder?" Calhoun asked as he leaned back in his chair.

Angela gave a capsule summary of the whole affair.

"Sounds interesting to me," Calhoun said. "I'll be delighted to take the case on an hourly basis. Now about me: I'm a retired state police officer and a widower. That's about it. Any questions?"

Angela studied Calhoun as he casually smoked. He was laconic like most New Englanders. He seemed forthright, a trait she appreciated. Beyond that, she had no way of judging the man's competence, although having been a state policeman seemed auspicious.

"Why did you leave the force?" Angela asked.

"Compulsory retirement," Calhoun said.

"Have you ever been involved in a murder case?" Angela asked.

"Not as a civilian," Calhoun said.

"What type of cases do you usually handle?" Angela asked.

"Marital problems, shoplifting, bartender embezzlement, that sort of thing."

"Do you think you could handle this case?" Angela asked.

"No question," Calhoun said. "I grew up in a small Vermont town similar to Bartlet. I'm familiar with the environment; hell, I even know some of the people who live there. I know the kinds of feuds that simmer for years and the mindset of the people involved. I'm the right man for the job because I can ask questions without sticking out like a sore thumb."

Angela drove back to Bartlet wondering if she'd done the right thing in hiring Phil Calhoun. She also wondered how and when she'd tell David.

Arriving at home Angela was distressed to find that Nikki was by herself. David had gone to the hospital to check on his patient. Angela asked Nikki if David had tried to get Alice to come over while he was away.

"Nope," Nikki said, unconcerned. "Daddy said he'd be back soon and that you'd probably show up before he did."

Angela decided she'd talk with David. Under the circumstances, she did not like Nikki being in the house by herself. She could hardly believe that David would leave Nikki alone, and the fact that he did eliminated any reservations Angela had about hiring Phil Calhoun.

Angela told Nikki that she wanted to keep the doors locked, and they went around to check them all. The only one that was open was the back door. As she prepared a quick snack for Nikki, she casually asked what she and her father had been doing that morning, but Nikki refused to say.

When David returned, Angela took him aside to discuss his leaving Nikki by herself. David was defensive at first but then agreed to avoid it in the future.

Soon David and Nikki were thick as thieves again, but Angela ignored them. Saturday afternoons were one of her favorite times. With little opportunity to cook during the week, she liked to spend a good portion of the day hovering over her recipe books and putting together a gourmet meal.

It was a therapeutic experience for her.

By midafternoon she had the menu planned. Leaving the kitchen, she opened the cellar door and started down. She was on her way to the freezer to get some veal bones to make a golden stock when she realized she'd not been back to the basement since the technicians had been there. Angela's steps slowed. She was a little nervous going down in the cellar by herself and toyed with the idea of asking David to accompany her. But she realized she was being silly. Besides, she didn't want to spook Nikki any more than she already was.

Angela continued the rest of the way down the stairs and headed toward the freezer against the far wall. As she walked she glanced in the direction of Hodges' former tomb and was relieved to see that David had stacked the window screens over the hole.

Angela was just reaching into the freezer when she heard a scraping sound behind her. She froze. She could have sworn the noise had come from behind the stairs. Angela allowed the freezer to close before she slowly turned around to face the dimly lit cellar.

With utter horror, Angela saw the screens begin to move. She blinked, then looked again, hoping that it had been her imagination. But then the screens fell over with a loud, echoing crash.

Angela tried to scream, but no sound came out of her mouth. She tried to move, but she couldn't. With great effort, she at last took a step, then another. But she was only halfway to the stairs when Hodges' partially skeletonized face emerged from the tomb. Then the man himself staggered out. He seemed disoriented until he saw Angela. Then he started toward her, his arms extended.

Angela's terror translated to motion. She ran for the stairs in earnest, but she was too late. Hodges cut her off and grabbed her arm.

Feeling the creature's hand on her wrist unlocked Angela's voice. She screamed, struggling to free herself. Then she saw another ghoul emerge from the tomb, a smaller but equally hideous fiend with the exact same face. Suddenly Angela realized that Hodges was laughing.

Angela could only stare, dumbfounded, as David pulled off a rubber mask. Nikki, the smaller ghoul, pulled an identical mask from her face. Both of them were laughing hysterically.

At first Angela was embarrassed, but her humiliation quickly turned to fury. There was nothing funny about this gag. She pushed David aside and stomped upstairs.

David and Nikki continued to laugh, but their laughter soon faltered as they began to understand how much they had frightened Angela.

"Do you think she's really mad?" Nikki asked.

"I'm afraid so," David said. "I think we'd better go up and talk with her."

Angela refused to even look at them as she busied herself in the kitchen.

"But we're sorry," David repeated for the third time.

"We both are, Mom," Nikki insisted. But then both Nikki and David had to suppress giggles.

"We never imagined you'd be fooled for a minute," David said, trying to control himself. "Honest! We thought you'd guess immediately; it was so corny."

"Yeah, Mom," Nikki said. "We thought you'd guess because next Sunday's Halloween. These are going to be our Halloween costumes. We even bought the same mask for you."

"Well, you can just throw it away," Angela said.

Nikki's face fell. Her eyes welled with tears.

Angela looked at her and her anger melted. "Now don't you get upset," she said. She drew Nikki to her. "I know I'm overreacting," she added, "but I was really scared. And I don't think it was funny."

Eager to get started on what was easily the most intriguing case he'd landed since he started his little side business to supplement his pension and social security, Phil Calhoun drove into Bartlet in the middle of the afternoon. He parked his pickup truck within the shade of the Bartlet library and walked across the green to the police station.

"Wayne around?" he asked the duty officer.

The duty officer merely pointed down the hall. He was reading a copy of the *Bartlet Sun*.

Calhoun walked down and knocked on Robertson's open door. Robertson looked up, smiled, and invited Phil to take a load off his feet.

Robertson tipped back in his chair and accepted an Antonio y Cleopatra from Calhoun.

"Working late on a Saturday," Calhoun said. "Must be a lot going on here in Bartlet."

"Goddamned paperwork," Robertson said. "It sucks. And it gets worse every year."

Calhoun nodded. "I read in the paper that old Doc Hodges turned up," he said.

"Yeah," Robertson said. "Caused a little stir, but it's already died down. Good riddance. The man was a pain in the ass."

"How so?" Calhoun asked.

Robertson's face became red as he aired yet again his litany against Dr. Dennis Hodges. He admitted that there had been numerous times he'd almost decked the man.

"I gather Hodges wasn't the most popular man in town," Calhoun said.

Robertson gave a short, caustic laugh.

"Much action on the case?" Calhoun asked casually, blowing smoke up toward the ceiling.

"Nah," Robertson said. "We spun our wheels a bit back when Hodges disappeared, but it was mostly going through the motions. Nobody cared much, not even his wife. Practically ex-wife. She'd just about moved back to Boston even before Hodges disappeared."

"What about now?" Calhoun asked. "The *Boston Globe* said the state police were investigating."

"They were just going through the motions, too," Robertson said. "The medical examiner called the state's attorney. State's attorney sent some junior assistant to check it out. This assistant called in the state police who then sent some crime-scene investigators to the site. But after that a state police lieutenant called me. I told him it wasn't worth his time and that we'd handle it. And as you know better than most people, the state police take their cue from us local guys on a case of this sort unless there's pressure from someplace like the state attorney's office or from some politician. Hell, the state police have more pressing cases to attend to. Same with us. Besides, it's been eight months. The trail's stone cold."

"What are you guys working on these days?" Calhoun asked.

"We've had a series of rapes and attacks up in the hospital parking lot," Robertson said.

"Any luck snagging the perpetrator?" Calhoun asked.

"Not yet," Robertson said.

After leaving the police station, Calhoun wandered down Main Street and stopped in the local bookstore. The proprietor, Jane Weincoop, had been a friend of Calhoun's wife. Calhoun's wife had been a big reader, especially the last year of her life when she'd been confined to bed.

Jane took Calhoun into her office, which was only a tiny desk stuck in the corner of the stock room. Calhoun said he was just passing through and after a bit of chitchat and catching up, he managed to steer the conversation to Dennis Hodges.

"The discovery of his body was certainly news in Bartlet," Jane admitted.

"I understand he wasn't a popular man," Calhoun said. "Who all had it in for him?"

Jane gave Calhoun a look. "Is this a professional or personal visit?" she asked with a wry smile.

"Just curiosity," Calhoun said with a wink. "But I'd still appreciate it if you'd keep my question to yourself."

Half an hour later Calhoun wandered back out into the fading afternoon sunlight clutching a list of over twenty people who had disliked Hodges. The list included the president of the bank, the owner of the Mobil station near the interstate, the town's retarded handyman, the chief of police whom Calhoun already knew about, a handful of merchants and store owners, and a half dozen doctors.

Calhoun was surprised by the length of the list but not unhappy. After all, the longer the list, the more billable hours he'd be logging in.

Continuing his trek up Main Street, Calhoun stopped into Harrison's Pharmacy. The pharmacist, Harley Strombell, was the brother of one of Calhoun's fellow troopers, Wendell Strombell.

Harley wasn't fooled any more than Jane had been about the nature of Calhoun's inquiries, but he promised to be discreet. He even added to Calhoun's list by offering his own name as well as those of Ned Banks, the owner of the New England Coat Hanger Company, Harold Traynor, and Helen Beaton, the new hospital administrator.

"Why did you dislike the man?" Calhoun asked.

"It was a personal thing," Harley said. "Hodges lacked even the rudimentary social graces." Harley explained that he'd had a small branch pharmacy up at the hospital until one day without explanation or warning, Hodges just kicked him out.

"I mean it was natural for the expanding hospital to have its own outpatient pharmacy," Harley said. "I understood that. But it was handled very badly, thanks to Dennis Hodges."

Calhoun left the pharmacy wondering how long his list would get before he could start whittling it down to serious suspects. He had close to twenty-five names and there were still a few more contacts in Bartlet he could check out before he considered the list complete.

Since most of the shops were closing for the night, Calhoun crossed the street and headed for the Iron Horse Inn. It was an establishment that held many pleasant memories for him. It had been his wife's favorite restaurant for special-occasion dinners, like celebrating anniversaries and birthdays.

Carleton Harris, the bartender, recognized Calhoun from across the room. By the time Calhoun got to the bar a glass of Wild Turkey neat was waiting for him. Carleton even drew half a mug's worth of draft beer for himself so they could clink glasses in a toast.

"Working on anything interesting these days?" Carleton asked after downing his spot of beer.

"I think so," Calhoun said. He leaned in toward the bar and Carleton instinctively did the same.

• • •

Angela didn't say a word to David and avoided eye contact as they got ready for bed. David guessed that Angela was still irritated about the basement prank with the Halloween masks. He disliked moodiness and wanted to clear the air.

"I'm getting the message you're still upset about Nikki and me scaring you," he said. "Can't we talk about it?"

"What makes you say I'm angry?" Angela asked innocently.

"Come on, Angela," David said. "You've been giving me the silent treatment ever since Nikki went to bed."

"I suppose I'm disappointed you'd do such a thing when you know how upset I am about that body. I would have thought you'd have been more sensitive."

"I said I was sorry," David said. "I still can't believe you just didn't laugh the second you saw us. It never occurred to me you'd get as frightened as you did. Besides, it wasn't just an idle prank. I did it for Nikki's benefit."

"What do you mean?" Angela asked skeptically.

"With the nightmares she's been having, I thought it would help to treat the subject with humor. It was a ruse to get her in the basement without being afraid. And it worked: she was so focused on surprising you, she didn't think about her fears."

"You could have at least warned me."

"I didn't think I had to. Like I said, I never thought you'd be fooled. And the conspiratorial nature of the activity is what got Nikki so involved."

Angela eyed her husband. She could tell he was remorseful as well as sincere. Suddenly she felt more embarrassed she'd fallen for the trick than angry. She put down her toothbrush and went over to David and gave him a hug. "I'm sorry I got so mad," she said. "I guess I'm stressed out. I love you."

"I love you, too," David echoed. "I should have told you what we were doing. You could have pretended not to know. I just didn't think. I've been so distracted lately. I feel so stressed out, too. Mary Ann Schiller is no better. She's going to die. I just know it."

"Come on now," Angela said. "You can never be sure."

"I don't know about that," David said. "Come on, let's get to bed." As they finished washing he told Angela about his professor's having driven all the way from Boston and that even he had nothing to add.

"Are you any more depressed?" Angela asked.

"About the same," David said. "I woke up at four-fifteen this morning and couldn't go back to sleep. I keep thinking there's something I'm missing with these patients; maybe they've picked up some unknown viral disease. But I feel as though my hands are tied. It's so frustrating to have to think about Kelley and CMV every time I order a test or a consult. It's gotten so bad that I even feel like I have to rush through my daily office schedule."

"You mean to see more patients?" Angela asked. They moved from the bathroom into the bedroom.

David nodded. "More pressure from CMV via Kelley," he said. "I hate to admit it, but what it means is that I have to avoid talking with patients and answering their questions. It's not hard because it's easy to bully patients, but I don't like it. I wonder if the patients realize they are being shortchanged. A lot of critical clues for making the right diagnosis come from the kind of spontaneous comments patients make when you spend a little time with them."

"I have a confession to make," Angela said suddenly.

"What are you talking about?" David asked as he got into bed.

"I also did something today I should have spoken to you about before I did it," Angela said.

"What?" he asked.

As Angela slipped under the covers, she told David about going to Rutland and hiring Phil Calhoun to investigate Hodges' murder.

David looked at her, then looked away. He didn't say anything. Angela knew he was angry.

"At least I took your suggestion that it was dangerous for me to investigate it," Angela said. "Now we have a professional doing it."

"What makes this man a professional?" David asked, looking back at Angela.

"He's a retired state policeman."

"I was hoping you were going to be reasonable about this Hodges affair," David said. "Hiring a private investigator is going a little overboard. It's throwing money away."

"It's not throwing money away if it is important to me," Angela said. "And it should be important to you if you expect me to continue living in this house."

David sighed, turned out his bedside light, and rolled away from Angela.

She knew she should have warned him about hiring the investigator. She too sighed as she reached for her light. Maybe she didn't go about it the right way, but she was still confident that hiring Calhoun had been a good idea.

Hardly had the lights been turned out than they heard several loud thumps followed by the sound of Rusty's barking.

Angela turned her light back on and got out of bed. David did the same. They grabbed their robes and stepped into the hall. David turned on the hall light. Rusty was at the top of the stairs, looking down toward the darkened first floor. He was growling ferociously.

"Did you check to see if the front door was locked?" Angela whispered.

"Yes," David said. He walked down the hall and patted Rusty's head. "What is it, big fellow?"

Rusty went down the stairs and began barking at the front door. David followed him. Angela stood at the top of the stairs.

David unlocked the front door.

"Be careful," Angela warned.

"Why don't you slip on one of those Halloween masks," David called up to Angela. "We'll give whoever it is a good scare."

"Stop joking," Angela said. "This isn't funny."

David stepped out onto the porch holding onto Rusty's collar. The dark sky was strewn with stars. A quarter moon provided enough light to see all the way down to the road, but there wasn't anything unusual to be seen.

"Come on, Rusty," David urged as he turned around. As he approached the door he saw a typed note nailed to the muntin. He pulled it off. It read: "Mind your own business. Forget Hodges."

Closing the door and locking it, David climbed the stairs and handed the note to Angela. She followed David into the bedroom.

"I'll take this to the police," Angela said.

"Hell, it could have come from the police," David replied. He climbed back into bed and turned out the light. Angela did the same. Rusty padded back down the hall to rejoin Nikki who'd evidently not stirred.

"Now I'm wide awake," David complained.

"So am I," Angela said.

The jangle of the telephone made them both jump. David answered it on the first ring. Angela turned on the light and watched her husband. His face fell as he listened. Then he hung up the phone.

"Mary Ann Schiller had another seizure and died," he said. "I told you it would happen." He raised a hand to his face and covered his eyes. Angela moved over and put her arms around him. She could tell he was crying silently.

"I wonder if this ever gets easier," he said. He wiped his eyes, then began to get dressed.

Angela accompanied him as far as the back door. After she saw him off, she locked the door behind him, then watched as the Volvo's taillights descended the driveway and disappeared.

Stepping from the mud room into the kitchen, Angela could still see the eerie glow of the luminol in her mind's eye. She shivered. She did not like being in the huge old house at night without David.

At the hospital, David met Mary Ann's husband, Donald, for the first time. Donald, his teenage son Matt, and Mary Ann's parents were in the patients' lounge across from the ICU quietly talking and consoling each other. As with the Kleber family and the Tarlow family, they were apprecia-tive of David's efforts. None of them had a bad word for him or a complaint.

"We had her for longer than Dr. Mieslich estimated," Donald said. His eyes were red and his hair was tousled as if he had been sleeping. "She even got to go back to her job at the library."

David commiserated with the family, telling them what they wanted to hear: she hadn't suffered. But David had to confess his confusion as to the cause of her seizures.

"You didn't expect seizures?" Donald asked.

"Not at all," David said. "Especially since her MRI was normal."

Everyone nodded as if they understood. Then, on the spur of the moment, David went against Kelley's orders and asked the family if they would permit an autopsy. He explained that it might answer a lot of questions.

"I don't know," Donald said. He looked over at his in-laws. They were equally indecisive.

"Why don't you think about it overnight?" David suggested. "We'll keep the body here."

Leaving the ICU, David felt despondent. He didn't go directly home. Instead, he wandered over to the dimly lit second-floor nurses' station. It was a quiet time of the night. Trying to keep his mind on other things, he glanced at Jonathan Eakins' chart. As he was perusing it, one of the night nurses told David that Mr. Eakins was awake, watching TV. David walked down and poked his head in.

"Everything okay?" David asked.

"What a committed doctor," Jonathan said with a smile. "You must live here."

"Is that ticker of yours staying nice and regular?" David asked.

"Like clockwork," Jonathan said. "When do I get to go home?"

"Probably today," David said. "I see they changed your bed."

"Sure did," Jonathan said. "They couldn't seem to fix the old one. Thanks for giving them a nudge. My complaints fell on deaf ears."

"No problem," David said. "See you tomorrow."

David left the hospital and got into his car. He started the engine but didn't put the car in gear. He'd had three unexpected deaths in one week: patients other doctors had been keeping alive and healthy. He couldn't help but question his competence. He wondered if he were meant to be a doctor. Maybe those three patients would still be alive if they'd had another physician.

He knew he couldn't sit in the hospital parking lot all night, so David finally put the car in gear and drove home. He was surprised to see a light on in the family room. By the time he'd parked and gotten out of the car, Angela was at the door. She was holding a medical journal.

"Are you all right?" she asked as she closed and locked the door behind David.

"I've been better," David said. "Why are you still up?" He removed his coat and motioned for Angela to precede him into the kitchen.

"There was no way I would sleep without you here," Angela said over her shoulder as she passed through the kitchen into the hall. "Not after that note was nailed to our door. And I've been thinking. If you have to go out in the middle of the night like this, I want to have a gun here."

David reached out and pulled Angela to a stop. "We'll have no guns in our house," he said. "You know the statistics as well as I do about guns in houses where there are children."

"Such statistics are not for physicians' families with a single, intelligent child," Angela countered. "Besides, I'll take responsibility for making sure Nikki is well acquainted with the gun and its potential."

David let go of his wife and headed for the stairs. "I don't have the energy or the emotional strength to argue with you."

"Good," Angela said as she caught up with him.

Upstairs, David decided to take another shower. When he came into the bedroom Angela was reading her pathology journal. She was as wide awake as he.

"Last night after dinner you said that you wished you could help me," David said. "Do you remember?"

"Of course I remember," Angela said.

"You might get your wish," David said. "An hour ago I asked the Schiller family if they would permit an autopsy. They said they'd think about it overnight and talk to me tomorrow."

"Unfortunately, it's not up to the family," Angela said. "The hospital doesn't do autopsies on CMV patients."

"But I have another idea," David said. "You could do it on your own."

Angela considered the suggestion. "Maybe I could," she said. "Tomorrow is Sunday and the lab is closed except for emergency chemistries."

"That was exactly my thought," David said.

"I could go to the hospital with you tomorrow and talk to the family," Angela said, warming to the idea.

"I'd appreciate it," David said. "If you could find some specific reason why she died, it would make me feel a whole lot better."

17

SUNDAY, OCTOBER 24

DAVID AND ANGELA WERE EXHAUSTED IN THE MORN-
ing, but Nikki was well rested. She'd slept through the night
without a nightmare and was eager to begin the day.

On Sundays the Wilsons got up early for church, followed by brunch at the Iron Horse Inn.

Attending church had been Angela's idea. Her motivation
wasn't religious, it was social. She thought it would be a
good way to join the Bartlet community. She'd settled on
the Methodist church on the town green. It was far and
away the most popular in town.

"Do we have to go?" David whined that morning. He was
sitting on the side of the bed. He was trying to dress with
clumsy fingers. He'd again awakened before dawn despite
having gone to sleep so late. He'd lain awake for several
hours. He'd just fallen back asleep when Nikki and Rusty
had come bounding into the room.

"Nikki will be disappointed if we don't go," Angela
called from the bathroom.

David finished dressing with resignation. A half hour later, the family climbed into the Volvo and drove into town. From past experience they knew to park in the Inn's parking lot and walk to the green. Parking near the church itself was always a disaster. The traffic on a Sunday was so bad it had to be supervised by one of the town's policemen.

That morning Wayne Robertson was on duty as traffic controller. A stainless-steel whistle protruded from his mouth.

"Isn't this handy," Angela said as soon as she spotted him. "You guys wait here."

Darting away before David could stop her, Angela went directly to the chief of police with the anonymous note in hand.

"Excuse me," Angela said. "I have something I'd like you to see. This was nailed to our door last night while we were in bed." She handed him the note, then rested her knuckles on her hips, her arms akimbo, waiting for his response.

Robertson allowed the whistle to drop from his mouth. It was attached by a cord around his neck. He glanced at the note, then handed it back. "I'd say it's a good suggestion. I recommend that you take the advice."

Angela chuckled. "I'm not asking your opinion as to the note's suggestion," she said. "I want you to find out who left it on our door."

"Well, now," he said slowly, scratching the back of his head, "it's not a lot to go on except for the fact that it was obviously typed on a nineteen fifty-two Smith Corona with a defective lowercase 'o.'"

For an instant, Angela began to reevaluate her estimation of Robertson's abilities. But then she realized he was making fun of her.

"I'm sure you'll do your best," Angela said with commensurate sarcasm, "but considering your attitude toward the Hodges murder case, I guess we can't expect miracles."

Honking horns and a few shouts from frustrated drivers forced Robertson's attention back to the traffic, which had quickly become a muddle. As he did his best to unsnarl the congestion, he said: "You and your little family are newcomers to Bartlet. Maybe you ought to think twice about interfering in matters that don't concern you. You'll only make trouble for yourself."

"So far I've only gotten trouble from you," Angela said. "And I understand that you happen to be one of the people who's not so sorry about Hodges' death. I understand you mistakenly blame him for your wife's death."

Robertson stopped directing traffic and turned to Angela. His chubby cheeks had become beet red. "What did you say?" he demanded.

Just then David slipped in between Angela and Robertson, forcing Angela away. He'd been eavesdropping on the conversation from a few feet away and he didn't like the direction it was taking.

Angela tried to repeat her statement, but David gave her arm a sharp tug. Through clenched teeth he whispered to her to shut up. When he got her far enough away he grabbed her shoulders. "What the hell has gotten into you?" he demanded. "You're taunting a man who's obviously got some kind of personality problem. I know you have a penchant for the dramatic but this is pushing it."

"He was ridiculing me," Angela complained.

"Stop it," David commanded. "You're sounding like a child."

"He's supposed to be protecting us," Angela snapped. "He's supposed to uphold the law. But he isn't any more interested in this threatening note than he is in finding out who murdered Hodges."

"Calm down!" David said. "You're making a scene."

Angela's eyes left David's and swept around the immediate area. A number of people had paused on their way into the church. They were all staring.

Self-consciously, Angela put the note away in her purse, smoothed her dress, and reached for Nikki's hand.

"Come on," she said. "Let's not be late for the service."

With Alice Doherty recruited to watch over Nikki and Caroline, David and Angela drove to the hospital. Nikki had met Caroline after the church service, and Caroline had accompanied them to the Iron Horse Inn for brunch.

At the hospital, David and Angela met Donald Schiller and his in-laws, the Josephsons, in the lobby. They sat on the benches to the right of the entrance to discuss the proposed autopsy.

"My husband has asked you for permission to do an autopsy," Angela said. "I'm here to tell you that I will be the one to do it if you agree. Since neither the hospital nor CMV will pay for this service, I'm offering to do it on my own time. It will be free. It also might provide some important information."

"That's very generous of you," Donald said. "We still weren't sure what to do this morning, but after talking to you, I think I feel okay about it." Donald looked at the Josephsons. They nodded. "I think Mary Ann would have wanted it too, if it could help other people."

"I think it might," Angela said.

David and Angela went down into the basement to retrieve Mary Ann's body from the morgue. They took it up to the lab and rolled it into the autopsy room. The room had not been used for autopsies for several years and had become a storeroom. They had to move boxes from the old stainless-steel autopsy table.

David had planned to assist, but it quickly became apparent to Angela that he was having a hard time dealing with the situation. He was not accustomed to autopsies, and this was the body of a patient he had been treating only the day before.

"Why don't you go see your patients?" Angela suggested when she was ready to begin.

"You sure you can manage?" David asked.

Angela nodded. "I'll page you when I'm done, and you can help me get her back downstairs."

"Thank you," David said. At the door he turned. "Remember, consider the possibility of an unknown viral disease. So be careful. And also, I want a full toxicological work-up."

"Why the toxicology?" Angela asked.

"I want to cover all the bases," David said. "Humor me, okay?"

"You've got it," Angela said agreeably. "Now get out of here!" She picked up a scalpel and waved for David to leave.

David let the autopsy room doors close behind him before he took off the hood, gown, and mask he'd donned for the postmortem. He was relieved to have been excused. David left the lab and climbed up to the patient floor.

He fully intended to discharge Jonathan Eakins, especially after he'd been told by the nursing staff that there'd been no abnormal heartbeats. But that was before he went into Jonathan's room to say hello. Instead of experiencing Jonathan's usual cheerfulness, David found the man depressed. Jonathan said he felt terrible.

Sensitized by recent events, David's mouth became instantly dry. He felt a rush of adrenaline shoot through his body. Afraid to hear the answer, he asked Jonathan what was wrong.

"Everything," Jonathan said. His face was slack and his eyes lusterless. A string of drool hung down from the corner of his mouth. "I started having cramps, then nausea and diarrhea. I've no appetite and I have to keep swallowing."

"What do you mean you have to keep swallowing?" David asked fearfully.

"My mouth keeps filling up with saliva," Jonathan said. "I have to swallow or spit it out."

David desperately tried to put these symptoms into some recognizable category. Salivation keyed off a memory from medical school. He remembered it was one of the symptoms of mercury poisoning.

"Did you eat anything strange last night?" David asked.

"No," Jonathan said.

"What about your IV?" David asked.

"That was removed yesterday on your orders," Jonathan said.

David was panicky. Except for the salivation, Jonathan's symptoms reminded him of the symptoms Marjorie, John, and Mary Ann had experienced prior to their rapid deterioration and deaths.

"What's wrong with me?" Jonathan asked, sensing David's anxiety. "This isn't something serious, is it?"

"I was hoping to send you home," David said, avoiding a direct answer. "But if you are feeling this bad, maybe we'd better keep you for a day or so."

"Whatever you say," Jonathan said. "But let's nip this in the bud; I've got a wedding anniversary coming up this weekend."

David hurried back to the nurses' station with his mind in an uproar. He kept telling himself that it couldn't happen again. It was impossible. The odds were too small.

David threw himself into a chair and took Jonathan's chart from the rack. He went over it carefully, re-reading everything, including all the nurses' notes. He noticed that Jonathan's temperature that morning had been one hundred degrees. Did that represent a fever? David didn't know; it was borderline.

Rushing back into Jonathan's room, David had him sit on the side of his bed so that he could listen to his chest. His lungs were perfectly clear.

Returning to the nurses' station David leaned his elbows on the counter and covered his face with his hands. He had to think. He didn't know what to do, yet he felt he had to do something.

Impulsively David reached for the phone. He already knew the response he could expect from Kelley and CMV, but he didn't care. He called Dr. Mieslich, the oncologist, and Dr. Hasselbaum, the infectious disease specialist, and asked them both to come in immediately. David told them he believed he had a patient who was in the very early stages of the same condition that had proved mortal three times in as many days.

While David was waiting for the consults to arrive, he ordered a barrage of tests. There was always the chance that Jonathan would wake up the next day feeling fine, but David didn't think he could risk his patient's going the route of Marjorie, John, and Mary Ann. His sixth sense was telling him that Jonathan was already locked in a mortal struggle, and lately David's intuition had not been wrong.

The infectious disease specialist was first to arrive. After a quick chat with David, he went in to see the patient. Dr. Mieslich came in next. He brought with him his records of Jonathan's treatment when he had been his patient. Dr. Mieslich and David went over the record page by page. By then Dr. Hasselbaum was finished examining Jonathan. He joined David and Dr. Mieslich at the nurses' station.

The three men had just begun to discuss the case when David became aware that the two doctors were looking over his shoulder. David turned to see Kelley looming above him.

"Dr. Wilson," Kelly said, "may I have a word with you in the patients' lounge?"

"I'm too busy right now," David said. He turned back to his consults.

"I'm afraid I must insist," Kelley said. He tapped David on the shoulder. David brushed his hand off. He did not like Kelley touching him.

"This will give me a chance to examine the patient," Dr. Mieslich said. He stood up and left the nurses' station.

"I'll use the time to write up my consult," Dr. Hasselbaum said. He took his pen from his jacket pocket and reached for Jonathan's chart.

"All right," David said, standing up. "Lead on, Mr. Kelley."

Kelley walked across the corridor and stepped into the patient lounge. After David entered the room Kelley closed the door.

"I presume you know Ms. Helen Beaton, the hospital president," Kelley said, "and Mr. Michael Caldwell, the medical director." He gestured toward both people, who were sitting on the couch.

"Yes, of course," David said. He remembered Caldwell from Angela's interviews, and he'd met Beaton at several hospital functions. David reached out and shook hands with each. Neither bothered to stand up.

Kelley sat down. David did likewise.

David anxiously glanced around at the faces arrayed around him. He expected trouble from Kelley, thinking this meeting had to do with the autopsy on Mary Ann Schiller. He guessed that was why the hospital people were there. He hoped this didn't spell trouble for Angela.

"I suppose I should be forthright," Kelley said. "You probably wonder how we've responded so quickly to your handling of Jonathan Eakins."

David was flabbergasted: how could these three be here to talk to him about Jonathan when he'd only just started investigating the man's symptoms?

"We were called by the nursing utilization coordinator," Kelley explained. "She had been alerted by the floor nurses according to previous instructions. Utilization control is vital. We feel the need to intervene. As I've told you before, you are using far too many consults, especially outside the CMV family."

"And far too many laboratory tests," Beaton said.

"Too many diagnostic tests as well," Caldwell said.

David stared at the three administrators in disbelief. Each returned his stare with impunity. They were a tribunal sitting in judgment. It was like the Inquisition. He was being tried for economic medical heresy, and not one of his inquisitors was a physician.

"We want to remind you that you are dealing with a patient who has been treated for metastatic prostate cancer," Kelley said.

"We're afraid you've already been too lavish and wasteful with your orders," Beaton said.

"You have a history of excessive use of resources on three previous patients who were clearly terminal," Caldwell said.

David struggled with his emotions. Since he'd already been questioning his competence as a result of the three successive deaths, he was vulnerable to the administrators' criticism. "My allegiance is to the patient," David said meekly. "Not to an organization or an institution."

"We can appreciate your philosophy," Beaton said. "But such a philosophy has led to the economic crisis in medical care. You must expand your horizons. We have an allegiance to the entire community of patients. Everything cannot be done to everybody. Judgment is needed in the rational use of limited resources."

"David, the fact of the matter is that your use of ancillary services far exceeds norms developed by your fellow physicians," Kelley told him.

There was a pause. David wasn't sure what to say. "My worry in these particular cases is that I'm seeing an unknown infectious disease. If that is the case, it would be disastrous not to diagnose it."

The three medical administrators looked at each other to see who would speak. Beaton shrugged and said: "That's out of my expertise; I'm the first to admit it."

"Mine too," Caldwell said.

"But we happen to have an independent infectious disease consult here at the moment," Kelley said. "Since CMV is already paying him, let's ask him his opinion."

Kelley went out and returned with both Dr. Martin Hasselbaum and Dr. Clark Mieslich. Introductions were made. Dr. Hasselbaum was asked if he thought that David's three deceased patients and Mr. Eakins might have been afflicted by an unknown infectious disease.

"I sincerely doubt it," Dr. Hasselbaum said. "There's no evidence whatsoever that they had an infectious disease. All three had pneumonia, but I feel the pneumonia was caused by generalized debility. In all three cases the agent was a recognized pathogen."

Kelley then asked both consults what form of treatment they thought should be given to Jonathan Eakins.

"Purely symptomatic," Dr. Mieslich said. He looked at Dr. Hasselbaum.

"That would be my recommendation as well," Dr. Hasselbaum said.

"You both have also seen the long list of diagnostic tests that have been ordered by Dr. Wilson," Kelley said. "Do you think any of these tests are crucial at this time?"

Dr. Mieslich and Dr. Hasselbaum exchanged glances. Dr. Hasselbaum was first to speak: "If it were my case I'd hold off and see what happened. The patient could be normal by morning."

"I agree," Dr. Mieslich said.

"Well then," Kelley said, "I think we all agree. What do you say, Dr. Wilson?"

The meeting broke up amid smiles, handshakes, and apparent amity. But David felt confused and humiliated, even depressed. He walked back to the nurses' station and canceled most of the orders he had written for Jonathan. Then he went in to see Jonathan himself.

"Thanks for having so many people come and examine me," Jonathan said.

"How do you feel?" David asked.

"I don't know," Jonathan said. "Maybe a little better."

When David got back to the autopsy room, Angela was just cleaning up. David's timing had been good. He helped return Mary Ann's body to the morgue. David noticed that Angela wasn't eager to talk about her findings. He practically had to grill her for answers.

"I didn't find much," Angela admitted.

"Nothing in the brain?" David asked.

"It was clean grossly," Angela said. "But we'll have to see what the microscopic shows."

"Any tumor?" David asked.

"I think there was a tiny bit in the abdomen," Angela said. "Again, I'll have to wait for the microscopic to be sure."

"So nothing jumped out at you as a cause of death?" David asked.

"She did have pneumonia," Angela said.

David nodded. He already knew that.

"I'm sorry I didn't find more," Angela said.

"I appreciate that you tried," David said.

As they drove home, Angela could tell that David was depressed. He'd only been answering questions in monosyllables.

"I suppose you're upset because I didn't find much on the autopsy," Angela said, pausing before she got out of the car.

David sighed. "That's just part of it," he said.

"David, you are a wonderful, talented doctor," Angela said. "Please stop being so hard on yourself."

David then told her about being hauled before the tribunal by Kelley. Angela was livid. "The nerve," she said. "Hospital administrators should not become involved in treatment."

"I don't know," David said with a sigh. "In some ways they're right. The cost of medical care is a problem. But it's so confusing when you get down to specifics with an individual patient. But the consults did side with the administrators."

At dinner, David discovered he wasn't hungry; he merely pushed his food around the plate. To make matters worse, Nikki complained that she didn't feel well.

By eight o'clock, Nikki started to sound congested and Angela took her upstairs for her respiratory therapy. When it was over, Angela found David sitting in the family room. The television was on but David wasn't watching; he was staring into the fire.

"It might be best to keep Nikki home from school tomorrow," Angela said. David didn't answer. Angela studied his face. For the moment she didn't know who she was more concerned about: Nikki or David.

18

MONDAY, OCTOBER 25

WHEN ANGELA FIRST OPENED HER EYES AT THE
sound of the alarm, she was disappointed not to find David
next to her. Getting up she pulled the drapes. The overcast
skies held the promise of showers.

Angela went down to look for David. She found him
sitting in the family room.

"Have you been up for long?" Angela asked, trying to
sound cheerful.

"Since four," David said. "But don't be alarmed. I think
I feel a bit better today." He gave Angela a half smile.

Although Angela was still concerned about David, she
was pleased with Nikki's respiratory status. Nikki woke
with no congestion. And she'd again made it through the
night with no nightmares. Even Angela had to admit that
David might have been right about the benefits of his silly
prank with the Halloween masks.

Unfortunately, Angela herself had had a nightmare. It
was a dream in which she came home from shopping,

carrying bags of groceries, only to find the kitchen drenched in blood. But it wasn't dried blood. It was fresh blood that was running down the walls and pooling on the floor.

After Nikki's respiratory treatment, Angela listened carefully to her chest. It was definitely clear. To Nikki's delight, Angela told her she could go to school.

Despite the possibility of rain, David insisted on riding his bike to work. Angela didn't try to talk him out of it. She felt it was encouraging that he was able to muster the enthusiasm for it.

After dropping Nikki off, Angela drove on to the lab, eager to get to work. Mondays were usually busy since there was a pile-up of laboratory work from the weekend. Breezing into her office, Angela had her coat on its hanger before she noticed Wadley. He'd been standing motionless near the connecting door.

"Good morning," Angela said, again trying to sound cheerful. She hung her coat up and turned to face her chief. It was immediately apparent he wasn't happy.

"It has been brought to my attention that you did an autopsy here in the lab," Wadley said angrily.

"It's true," Angela admitted. "But I did it on my own time."

"You might have done it on your own time, but it was done in my lab," Wadley said.

"It's true I used hospital facilities," Angela said. She didn't agree that it was Wadley's lab. It was a hospital facility. He was an employee just as she was.

"You were specifically told no autopsies," Wadley said.

"I was specifically told they were not paid for by CMV," Angela said.

Wadley's cold eyes bore into Angela. "Then allow me to clear up a misunderstanding," he said. "No autopsies are to be done in this department unless I approve them. I run the department, not you. Furthermore, I've ordered the techs not to process the slides, the cultures, or the toxicological samples."

With that, Wadley returned to his office and closed the connecting door with a slam.

As usual, after one of their increasingly frequent confrontations, Angela was upset. As soon as she had composed herself, she retrieved the tissue specimens, the cultures, and the toxicological samples she had taken from Mary Ann. She then carefully packed the cultures and the toxicological material and sent them to the department where she'd trained in Boston. She had enough friends there to get them processed. The tissue samples she kept, planning on doing the slides herself.

David made the rounds of his patients, purposefully leaving Jonathan for last. When he walked into his room he was shocked. The bed was empty.

Assuming he'd been transferred to another room for some ridiculous reason as John Tarlow had been, David went to the nurses' station to ask where he could find Jonathan. Janet Colburn told him that Mr. Eakins had been transferred to the ICU by the ER physician during the night.

David was dumbfounded.

"Mr. Eakins developed difficulty breathing and lapsed into a coma," Janet added.

"Why wasn't I called?" David demanded.

"We had a specific order not to call you," Janet said.

"Issued by whom?" David asked.

"By Michael Caldwell," Janet said. "The medical director of the hospital."

"That's absurd . . ." David shouted. "Why . . ."

"We were told that if you had any questions you should call Ms. Beaton," Janet said. "Don't blame us."

David was beside himself with fury. The medical director did not have the right to leave such an order. David had never heard of anything more absurd. It was bad enough that these administrators were second-guessing him. But to intercede in patient care so directly seemed a total violation.

But David understood his argument wasn't with the nurse. He left immediately to find his patient. He arrived to discover that Jonathan's condition was indeed critical. He was in a coma and on a respirator just as Mary Ann had so recently been. David listened to his chest. Jonathan was also developing pneumonia. Twisting the IV bottle around, David saw that he was getting continuous intravenous antibiotics.

David went to the central desk to study Jonathan's chart. He quickly realized that Jonathan's course had begun to mirror David's three deceased patients. Jonathan had developed problems of the GI system, the central nervous system, and the blood system.

David picked up the phone to call Helen Beaton when the ICU unit coordinator tapped him on the shoulder and handed him another phone. It was Charles Kelley.

"The nurses told me you'd come into the ICU," Kelley said. "I'd asked them to call me the moment you appeared. I wanted to inform you that the Eakins case has been transferred to another CMV physician."

"You can't do that," David said angrily.

"Hold on, Dr. Wilson," Kelley said. "CMV certainly can transfer a patient, and I have done so. I've also notified the family, and they are in full agreement."

"Why?" David demanded. Hearing that the family was also behind the change, his voice lost most of its sting.

"We feel that you are too emotionally involved," Kelley said. "We decided it was better for everyone if you were taken off. It will give you a chance to calm down. I know you've been under a lot of strain."

David didn't know what to think, much less say. He thought about pointing out that Jonathan's condition had gone downhill just as he'd feared, but he decided against it. Kelley wasn't likely to consider anything he had to say.

"Don't forget what we said yesterday," Kelley continued. "I know you'll understand our point of view if you give it some thought."

David was of two minds when he hung up. On the one hand he was still furious to have been unilaterally removed from the case. On the other, there was an element of truth in what Kelley had said. David had only to look at his trembling hands to recognize he was overly emotionally involved.

David stumbled out of the ICU. He didn't even look at Jonathan as he passed by. Out in the hall he checked his watch. It was still too early to go to his office. Instead, he went to medical records.

David pulled the charts on Marjorie, John, and Mary Ann. Sitting in the isolation of a dictation booth, he reviewed each chart, going over the respective hospital courses. He read all his entries, all the nurses' notes, and looked at all the laboratory values and the results of diagnostic tests.

David was still toying with the idea that an unknown infection was responsible, something that his patients may have contracted while in the hospital. Such an infection was called a nosocomial infection. David had read about such incidents at other hospitals. All his patients had had pneumonia but each case had been caused by a different strain of bacteria. The pneumonia had to have been the result of some underlying infection.

The only common element in all three cases was the history. Each patient had been treated for cancer with varying mixtures of surgery, chemotherapy, and radiotherapy. Of the three treatment modalities, only chemotherapy was common to all three patients.

David was well aware that one of the side effects of chemotherapy was a general lowering of a patient's resistance because of a depressed immune system. He wondered if that fact could have had something to do with the rapid downhill courses these patients experienced. Yet the oncologist, the expert in such matters, had given this common factor little import since in all three cases the chemotherapy had been completed long before the hospitalization. The immune systems of all three patients had long since returned to normal.

The pager on David's belt interrupted his thoughts. Looking at the LCD screen he recognized the number: it was the emergency room. Replacing the charts, David hurried downstairs.

The patient was Donald Anderson, another one of David's frequent visitors. Donald's diabetes was particularly hard to regulate. It was the main source of his frequent medical complaints. This visit was no exception. When David entered the examining stall he could immediately tell that Donald's blood sugar was out of control. Donald was semi-comatose.

David ordered a stat blood sugar and started an IV. While

he was waiting for the lab result, he spoke with Shirley Anderson, Donald's wife.

"He's been having trouble for a week," Shirley complained. "But you know how stubborn he is. He refused to come to see you."

"I think we'll have to admit him," David said. "It will take a few days to get him on a new regimen."

"I was hoping you would," Shirley said. "It's difficult when he gets like this with the kids and all."

When David got the results of the blood sugar he was surprised that Donald hadn't been even more obtunded than he was. As David walked back to talk with Donald, who was now lucid thanks to the IV, David did a double-take. Looking into one of the other examining stalls he saw a familiar face: it was Caroline Helmsford, Nikki's friend. Dr. Pilsner was at her side.

David slipped in alongside Caroline, opposite Dr. Pilsner. She looked up at David with pleading eyes. Covering the lower part of her face was a clear plastic mask providing oxygen. Her complexion was ashen with a slightly bluish cast. Her breathing was labored.

Dr. Pilsner was listening to her chest. He smiled at David when he saw him. When he finished auscultating, he took David aside.

"Poor thing is having a hard time," Dr. Pilsner said.

"What's wrong?" David asked.

"The usual," Dr. Pilsner replied. "She's congested and she's running a high fever."

"Will you admit her?" David asked.

"Absolutely," Dr. Pilsner said. "You know better than most that we can't take any chances with this kind of problem."

David nodded. He did know. He looked back at Caroline struggling to breathe. She looked so tiny on the big gurney and so vulnerable. The sight made him worry about Nikki. Given her cystic fibrosis, it could have been Nikki on the gurney, not Caroline.

"You've got a call from the chief medical examiner," one of the secretaries told Angela. Angela picked up the phone.

"Hope I'm not disturbing you," Walt said.

"Not at all," Angela answered.

"Got a couple of updates on the Hodges autopsy," Walt said. "Are you still interested?"

"Absolutely," Angela said.

"First of all, the man had significant alcohol in his ocular fluid," Walt said.

"I didn't know you could tell after so long," Angela said.

"If we can get ocular fluid it's easy," Walt said. "Alcohol is reasonably stable. We also got confirmation that the DNA of the skin under his nails was different from his. So it's undoubtedly the DNA of his killer."

"What about those carbon particles in the skin?" Angela asked. "Did you have any more thoughts about them?"

"To be honest, I haven't given it a lot of thought," Walt said. "But I did change my mind about it being contemporary with the struggle. I realized the particles were in the dermis, not the epidermis. It must have been some old injury, like having been stabbed with a pencil when he was in grammar school. I have such a deposit on my arm."

"I've got one in the palm of my right hand," Angela said.

"The reason I haven't done much on the case is because there's been no pressure from either the state's attorney or the state police. Unfortunately, I've been swamped with other cases where there's considerable pressure."

"I understand," Angela said. "But I'm still interested. So if there are any more developments, please let me know."

After hanging up Angela's thoughts remained on the Hodges affair, wondering what Phil Calhoun was doing. She'd heard nothing from him since she'd visited the man and had given him his retainer. And thinking about Hodges and Calhoun made her remember how vulnerable she'd felt when David had left in the night to go to the hospital.

Checking her watch, Angela realized it was time for her lunch break. She turned off her microscope, grabbed her coat, and went out to the car. She'd told David that she wanted to get a gun, and she'd meant it.

There were no sporting goods stores in Bartlet, but Staley's Hardware Store carried a line of firearms. When she explained what she wanted, Mr. Staley was instantly helpful. He asked her what her reasons were for wanting to purchase a gun. When she told him protection of her home, he talked her into a shotgun.

It took Angela less than fifteen minutes to make her selection. She bought a pump-action twelve-gauge shotgun. Mr. Staley was more than happy to show her how to load and unload the rifle. He was particularly careful to show her the safety. The firearm also came with a brochure, and Mr. Staley encouraged her to read it.

On the walk back to the car, Angela felt self-conscious about her package even though she'd insisted that Mr. Staley wrap it in manila paper; the object within was still quite recognizable. She'd never carried a gun before. In her other hand she had a bag containing a box of shells.

With definite relief Angela put the rifle in the trunk of the car. Heading around to the driver's side door she looked across the green at the police station and hesitated. Ever since the confrontation with Robertson the previous morning she'd felt guilty. She also knew David had been right; it was foolhardy for her to make an enemy of the chief of police despite the fact that he was such a dolt.

Letting go of the car door, Angela walked across the green and into the police station. Robertson agreed to see her after a ten-minute wait.

"I hope I'm not bothering you," Angela said.

"No bother," he said as she entered his office.

Angela sat down. "I don't want to take much of your time," Angela said.

"I'm a public servant," Robertson said brazenly.

"I've come to apologize for yesterday," Angela said.

"Oh?" Robertson said, clearly taken aback.

"My behavior was inappropriate," Angela said. "And I'm sorry. It's just that I've really been overwhelmed by the discovery of that dead body in my house."

"Well, it's nice of you to come in," Robertson said, clearly flustered. He hadn't expected this. "I'm sorry about

Hodges. We'll keep the case open and let you know if anything turns up."

"Something did turn up this morning," Angela said. She then told Robertson about the possibility of Hodges' killer having a deposit of carbon from a pencil on his arm.

"From a pencil?" Robertson asked.

"Yes," Angela said. She stood up and extended her right palm and pointed to a small, dark stain beneath the skin. "Something like this," she said. "I got it in the third grade."

"Oh, I see," Robertson said, nodding his head as a wry smile turned up the corners of his mouth. "Well, thank you for this tip."

"Just thought I'd pass it along," Angela said. "The medical examiner also said that the skin under Hodges' fingernails was definitely his killer's. He has a DNA fingerprint."

"Trouble is, super-sophisticated DNA malarkey is not much help without a suspect," Robertson said.

"There was a small town in England that solved a rape with a DNA fingerprint," Angela said. "All they did was do a DNA test on everybody in the town."

"Wow," Robertson said. "I can just imagine what the American Civil Liberties Union would say if I tried that here in Bartlet."

"I'm not suggesting you try," Angela said. "But I did want you to know about the DNA fingerprint."

"Thank you," Robertson said. "And thanks for coming by." He stood up when Angela got up to go.

He watched through his window as Angela got in her car.

As she drove off, Robertson picked up his phone and pressed one of the automatic dialers. "You're not going to believe this, but she's still at it. She's like a dog with a bone."

Angela felt a little better for having tried to clear things up with Robertson. At the same time she didn't delude herself into thinking that she'd changed anything. Intuitively she knew he still wasn't about to lift a finger to get Hodges' murder case solved.

At the hospital, all the parking slots reserved for the professional staff near the back entrance of the hospital were occupied. Angela had to zig-zag back and forth through the lot looking for a vacant spot. Finding nothing, she drove into the upper lot. She finally located a spot way up in the far corner. It took her almost five minutes to walk back to the hospital door.

"This isn't my day," Angela said aloud as she entered the building.

"But you won't even be able to see the parking garage from the town," Traynor said into the phone. His frustration was thinly masked. He was talking to Ned Banks, who had become one of the town's Selectmen the previous year.

"No, no, no," Traynor reiterated. "It's not going to look like a World War II bunker. Why don't you meet me sometime at the hospital and I'll show you the model. I promise you, it's rather attractive. And if Bartlet Community Hospital intends to be the referral hospital of the state, we need it."

Collette, Traynor's secretary, came into the room and placed a business card on the desk blotter in front of Traynor. At that moment Ned was carrying on about Bartlet losing its charm. Traynor picked up the card. It read: "Phil Calhoun, Private Investigation, Satisfaction Guaranteed."

Traynor covered the mouthpiece and whispered: "Who the hell is Phil Calhoun?"

Collette shrugged. "I've never seen him before, but he says he knows you. Anyway, he's waiting outside. I've got to run over to the post office."

Traynor waved goodbye to his secretary and then put down the business card. Meanwhile, Ned was still lamenting the recent changes in Bartlet, especially the condominium development near the interstate.

"Look, Ned, I've got to run," Traynor interrupted. "I really hope you give this hospital parking garage some thought. I know that Wiggins has been bad-mouthing it, but it's important for the hospital. And frankly, I need all the votes I can get."

Traynor hung up the phone with disgust. He had trouble

understanding the short-sightedness of most of the Selectmen. None of them seemed to appreciate the economic significance of the hospital, and that made his job as chairman
of the hospital board that much more difficult.

Traynor peered into the outer office to get a glimpse of
the PI he supposedly knew. Flipping through one of the
hospital quarterly reports was a big man in a black and
white checkered shirt. Traynor thought he looked vaguely
familiar, but he couldn't place him.

Traynor invited Calhoun inside. While they shook hands,
Traynor scoured his memory, but he still drew a blank. He
motioned toward a chair. The two men sat down.

It wasn't until Calhoun mentioned that he'd been a state
policeman that it came to Traynor. "I remember," he said.
"You used to be friends with Harley Strombell's brother."

Calhoun nodded and complimented Traynor on his
memory.

"Never forget a face," Traynor boasted.

"I wanted to ask you a few questions about Dr. Hodges,"
Calhoun said, getting to the point.

Traynor nervously fingered the gavel he used for hospital
board meetings. He didn't like answering questions about
Hodges, yet he was afraid not to. He didn't want to make
it an issue. He wished this whole Hodges mess would
go away.

"Is your interest personal or professional?" Traynor
asked.

"Combination," Calhoun said.

"Have you been retained?" Traynor asked.

"You might say so," Calhoun said.

"By whom?"

"I'm not at liberty to say," Calhoun said. "As a lawyer,
I'm sure you understand."

"If you expect me to be cooperative," Traynor said, "then
you'll have to be a bit more open yourself."

Calhoun took out his Antonio y Cleopatras and asked
if he could smoke. Traynor nodded. Calhoun offered one
to Traynor, but Traynor declined. Calhoun took his time
lighting up. He blew smoke up at the ceiling, and then
spoke: "The family is interested in finding out who was

responsible for the doctor's brutal murder."

"That's understandable," Traynor said. "Can I have your word that whatever I say remains discreet?"

"Absolutely," Calhoun said.

"Okay, what do you want to ask me?"

"I'm making a list of people who disliked Hodges," Calhoun said. "Do you have anyone to put on my list?"

"Half the town," Traynor said with a short laugh. "But I don't feel comfortable giving names."

"I understand you saw Hodges the night of his murder," Calhoun said.

"Hodges burst in on a meeting we were having at the hospital," Traynor said. "It was an unpleasant habit of his that he indulged all too frequently."

"I understand Hodges was angry," Calhoun said.

"Where did you hear that?" Traynor asked.

"I've been speaking to a number of people in town," Calhoun said.

"Hodges was angry all the time," Traynor said. "He was chronically unhappy with the way we manage the hospital. You see, Dr. Hodges had a proprietary feeling about the institution. He was also dated in his thinking. He was an old-school 'doc' who ran the hospital when it was a cost-plus situation. He had no feeling for the new environment of managed care and managed competition. He just didn't understand."

"I don't think I know too much about that, either," Calhoun admitted.

"You'd better learn," Traynor warned. "Because it's here. What kind of health plan are you under?"

"CMV," Calhoun said.

"There you go," Traynor said. "Managed care. You're already part of it and you don't even know it."

"I understand when Dr. Hodges burst into your hospital meeting he had some hospital charts with him."

"Parts of charts," Traynor corrected. "But I didn't get a look at them. I was planning on having lunch with him the following day to discuss whatever was on his mind. It undoubtedly concerned some of his former patients. He was always complaining about his former patients not getting

VIP treatment. Frankly, he was a pain in the ass."

"Did Dr. Hodges bother the new hospital administrator, Helen Beaton?" Calhoun asked.

"Oh, God, yes!" Traynor said. "Hodges would think nothing of barging into her office any time of the day. Helen Beaton was probably the person who suffered from Hodges' barrages the most. After all, she had his old position. And who knew how to do it better than himself?"

"I understand that you ran into Hodges a second time that night he burst in on your meeting," Calhoun said.

"Unfortunately," Traynor said. "At the inn. After most hospital meetings, we go to the inn. That night Hodges was there drinking as usual and as belligerent as usual."

"And he had unpleasant words with Robertson?" Calhoun asked.

"He sure did," Traynor said.

"And with Sherwood?" Calhoun said.

"Who have you been talking with?" Traynor asked.

"Just a handful of townsfolk," Calhoun said. "I understand Dr. Cantor said some unflattering things about Hodges too."

"I can't remember," Traynor said. "But Cantor hadn't liked Hodges for years."

"How come?" Calhoun asked.

"Hodges took over radiology and pathology for the hospital," Traynor said. "He wanted the hospital to accrue the windfall profits those departments generated from equipment the hospital owned."

"What about you?" Calhoun asked. "I've heard you weren't fond of Dr. Hodges either."

"I already told you," Traynor said. "He was a pain in the ass. It was hard enough trying to run the hospital without his continual interference."

"I heard it was something personal," Calhoun said. "Something about your sister."

"My, your sources are good," Traynor said.

"Just town gossip," Calhoun said. ·

"You're right," Traynor said. "It's no secret. My sister Sunny committed suicide after Hodges pulled her husband's hospital privileges."

"So you blamed Hodges?" Calhoun asked.

"More then than now," Traynor said. "Hell, Sunny's husband was a drunkard. Hodges should have taken away his privileges before he had a chance to cause real harm."

"One last question," Calhoun said. "Do you know who killed Dr. Hodges?"

Traynor laughed, then shook his head. "I haven't the slightest idea, and I don't care. The only thing I care about is the effect his death might have on the hospital."

Calhoun stood up and stubbed out his cigar in an ashtray on the corner of Traynor's desk.

"Do me a favor," Traynor said. "I've made it easy for you. I didn't have to tell you anything. All I ask is that you not make a big deal about this Hodges affair. If you find out who did it and plan to expose the individual, let me know so the hospital can make some plans with respect to publicity, especially if the killer has anything to do with the hospital. We're already dealing with a public relations problem on another matter. We don't need to be blindsided by something else."

"Sounds reasonable," Calhoun said.

After Traynor showed Calhoun out, he returned to his desk, looked up Clara Hodges' Boston number, and dialed.

"I wanted to ask you a question," he said after the usual pleasantries. "Are you familiar with a gentleman by the name of Phil Calhoun?"

"Not that I recall," Clara said. "Why do you ask?"

"He was just in my office," Traynor explained. "He's a private investigator. He was here to ask questions about Dennis. He implied that he'd been retained by the family."

"I certainly haven't hired any private investigator," Clara said. "And I cannot imagine anyone else in the family doing so either, especially without my knowing about it."

"I was afraid of that. If you hear anything more about this guy, please let me know."

"I certainly will," Clara said.

Traynor hung up the phone and sighed. He had the unpleasant feeling that more trouble was coming. Even beyond the grave, Hodges was a curse.

• • •

"You've got one more patient," Susan said as she handed David the chart. "I told her to come right in. She's one of the nurses from the second floor."

David took the chart and pushed into the examining room. The nurse was Beverly Hopkins. David knew her vaguely; she was on nights.

"What's the problem?" David asked with a smile.

Beverly was sitting on the examining table. She was a tall, slender woman with light brown hair. She was holding a kidney dish Susan had given her for nausea. Her face was pale.

"I'm sorry to bother you, Dr. Wilson," Beverly said. "I think it's the flu. I would have just stayed home in bed, but as you know, we're encouraged to come and see you if we're going to take time off."

"No problem," David said. "That's what I'm here for. What are your symptoms?"

The symptoms were similar to those of the other four nurses: general malaise, mild GI complaints, and low-grade fever. David agreed with Beverly's assessment. He sent her home for bed rest, telling her to drink plenty of fluids and take aspirin as needed.

After finishing up at the office, David headed over to the hospital to see his patients. As he walked, he began to mull over the fact that the only people he'd seen with the flu so far were nurses, and all five had been from the second floor.

David stopped in his tracks. He wondered if it were a coincidence that the nurses were all from the same floor, the same floor where all his mortally ill patients had been. Of course, ninety percent of the patients went to the second floor. But David thought it strange that no nurses from the OR or the emergency room were coming down with this flu.

David recommended walking, and as he did so his thoughts returned to the possibility that his patients had died from an infectious disease contracted in the hospital. The flu-like symptoms the nurses were experiencing could be related. Using a dialectic approach, David posed himself a question: what if the nurses who were generally healthy got a mild illness when exposed to the mysterious disease, but patients who'd had chemotherapy and, as a result, had mildly compromised immune systems, got a fulminating and fatal illness?

David thought his reasoning was valid, but when he tried to think of some known illness that fit this bill, he couldn't come up with any. The disease would have to affect the GI system, the central nervous system, and the blood, yet be difficult to diagnose even for an expert in the field like Dr. Martin Hasselbaum.

What about an environmental poison, David wondered. He remembered Jonathan's symptom of excessive salivation. The complaint had made David think of mercury. Even so, the idea of some poison being involved seemed farfetched. How would it be spread? If it were airborne, then many more people would have come down with symptoms than four patients and five nurses. But still, a poison was a possibility. David decided to reserve judgment until he received the toxicology results on Mary Ann.

Quickening his pace, David climbed to the second floor. What patients he had left were doing well. Even Donald didn't require much attention although David did adjust his insulin dosage again.

When he was finished with his rounds, David went down to the first floor to search the lab for Angela. He found her in the chemistry area trying to solve a problem with one of the multi-track analyzers.

"Are you finished already?" Angela asked, catching sight of David.

"For a change," David said.

"How's Eakins?" Angela asked.

"I'll tell you later," David said.

Angela looked at him closely. "Is everything all right?"

"Hardly," David said. "But I don't want to talk about it now."

Angela excused herself from the laboratory tech with whom she was working and took David aside.

"I had a little surprise when I got in here this morning," she said. "Wadley hit the ceiling about my doing the autopsy."

"I'm sorry," David said.

"It's not your fault," Angela said. "Wadley is just being an ass. His ego has been bruised. But the problem is, he's refused to allow any of the specimens to be processed."

"Damn," David said. "I really wanted the toxicology done."

"No need to worry," Angela said. "I sent the toxicology and cultures to Boston. I'm going to do the slides. In fact, I'll stay tonight to do them. Will you make dinner for you and Nikki?"

David told her he'd be happy to.

David was relieved to get out of the hospital. It was exhilarating to ride his bike through the crisp New England air. He felt disappointed the trip was over as he peddled up the driveway.

After sending Alice home, David enjoyed spending time with Nikki. The two of them worked out in the yard until darkness drove them inside. While Nikki did her homework, David made a simple meal of steak and salad.

After dinner David broke the news about Caroline.

"Is she real sick?" Nikki asked.

"She looked very uncomfortable when I saw her," David said.

"I want to go visit her tomorrow," Nikki said.

"I'm sure you do," David said. "But remember, you were a little congested yourself last night. I think we better wait until we know for sure what Caroline has. Okay?"

Nikki nodded, but she wasn't happy.

To be on the safe side, David insisted Nikki do her postural drainage even though she usually only did it in the morning unless she wasn't feeling well. Nikki didn't complain.

After Nikki went to bed, David began to peruse the infectious disease section of one of his medical textbooks. He wasn't looking for anything in particular. He thought there was a chance he might discover something along the lines of the infection he'd envisioned earlier in the day, but nothing jumped out at him.

Before he knew it, David was waking up with his heavy textbook of medicine open on his lap. Shades of medical school, he thought with a chuckle. It had been a while since he'd fallen asleep over one of his books. Checking the clock over the fireplace he was surprised to see it was after eleven. Angela still wasn't home.

Feeling mildly anxious, David called the hospital. The operator put him through to the lab.

"What's going on?" he asked when he heard Angela's voice.

"It's just taking me longer than I thought," Angela said. "The staining takes time. Makes me appreciate the techs who normally do it. I should have called you, but I'm almost finished. I'll be home within the hour."

"I'll be waiting," David said.

It was more than an hour by the time Angela was completely finished. She took a selection of slides and loaded them in a metal briefcase. She thought David might want to take a peek at them. Angela's own microscope was at home so he could easily have a look if he were interested.

She said goodnight to the night-shift techs, then headed out to the parking lot.

She didn't see her old Volvo in the reserved parking area. For a moment, she thought the car had been stolen, then she remembered she'd been forced to park in the far reaches of the upper lot.

Setting off at a brisk pace, Angela quickly slowed. Not only was she carrying a heavy briefcase, but she was exhausted. Halfway across the lot she had to transfer the briefcase to the other hand.

There were a few cars in the parking lot belonging to the night-shift personnel, but they soon fell behind as Angela trudged toward the path that led to the upper lot. Angela noticed that she was entirely alone. There were no other people; the evening shift had long since departed.

As Angela approached the path she began to feel uneasy. She was unaccustomed to being out at such an hour, and had certainly expected to see someone. Then she thought she heard something behind her. When she turned she saw nothing.

Continuing on, Angela started thinking about wild animals. She'd heard that black bears were occasionally spotted in the area. She wondered what she would do if she were suddenly confronted by a bear.

"You're being silly," she told herself. She pushed on. She had to get home; it was after midnight.

The lighting in the lower parking lot was more than adequate. But as Angela entered into the path leading up to the upper lot, she had to pause for a moment to allow her eyes to adjust to the darkness. There were no lights along the path, and dense evergreen trees on both sides formed a natural archway.

The barking of a dog in the distance made Angela jump. Nervously she moved deeper into the tunnel of trees, starting up a run of stairs constructed of railroad ties. She heard crackling noises in the forest and the rustling of the wind high in the pine trees. Feeling frightened, she recalled vividly the episode in the basement when David and Nikki had scared her, and the memory made her even more tense.

At the top of the stairs the path leveled and angled to the left. Up ahead Angela could see the light of the upper parking lot. There was only another fifty feet to go.

Angela had just about calmed herself when a man leaped out of the shadows. He came up on her so suddenly she didn't have a chance to flee. He was brandishing a club over his head; his face was covered by a dark ski mask.

Staggering back, Angela tripped on an exposed root and fell. The man flung himself at her. Angela screamed and rolled to the side. She could hear the thump of the club as it sliced into the soft ground where she had been only seconds before.

Angela scrambled to her feet. The man grabbed her with a gloved hand as he began to raise his club again. Angela swung her briefcase up into the man's crotch with all the strength she could muster. The man's grip on her arm released as he cried out in pain.

With the route back to the hospital blocked by the wheezing man, Angela ran for the upper lot. Empowered by terror Angela ran as she'd never run before, her flying feet crunching on the asphalt. She could hear the man behind her, but she didn't dare to look. She ran up to the Volvo with one thought in mind: the shotgun.

Dropping the briefcase to the pavement, Angela fumbled with her keys. Once she got the trunk open, she yanked the manila paper from the shotgun. Snatching up the bag of shells she hastily dumped them into the trunk. Picking up a single shell, she jammed it into the gun and pumped it into the firing chamber.

Angela whirled about, holding the gun at waist level, but no one was there. The lot was completely deserted. The man hadn't given chase. What she heard had been the echo of her own footfalls.

"Can't you do a little better than that?" Robertson asked. " 'Sorta tall.' Is that it? That's hardly a description. How are we supposed to find this guy if you women can't describe him better than that?"

"It was dark," Angela said. She was having a hard time keeping her emotions even. "And it happened so quickly. Besides, he was wearing a ski mask."

"What the hell were you doing out there in the trees after midnight anyway? Hell, all you nurses were warned."

"I'm not a nurse," Angela said. "I'm a doctor."

"Oh, boy!" Robertson said haughtily. "You think this rapist cared whether you were a nurse or a doctor?"

"The point I'm making is that I wasn't warned. The nurses may have been warned, but no one warned us doctors."

"Well, you should have known better," Robertson said.

"Are you trying to imply that this attack was somehow my fault?"

Robertson ignored her question. "What kind of club was he holding?" he asked.

"I have no idea," Angela said. "I told you it was dark."

Robertson shook his head and looked at his deputy. "You said Bill had just been up there in his cruiser?"

"That's right," the deputy said. "Not ten minutes before the incident he'd made a routine sweep of both parking lots."

"Christ, I don't know what to do," Robertson said. He looked down at Angela and shrugged his shoulders. "If you women would just be a little more cooperative, we wouldn't have this problem."

"May I use the phone?" Angela said.

Angela called David. When he answered she could tell he'd been asleep. She told him she'd be home in ten minutes.

"What time is it?" David asked. Then after a glance at the clock, he answered his own question. "Holy jeez, it's after one. What are you doing?"

"I'll tell you when I get home," Angela said.

After she'd hung up, Angela turned to Robertson. "May I leave now?" she asked testily.

"Of course," Robertson said. "But if you think of anything else, let us know. Would you like my deputy to drive you home?"

"I think I can manage," Angela said.

Ten minutes later, Angela was hugging David at their door. David had been alarmed not just by the late hour, but the sight of his wife coming from the car with a briefcase in one hand and a shotgun in the other. But he didn't ask about the gun. For the moment, he just hugged Angela. She was holding him tightly and wouldn't let go.

Angela finally released David, removed her soiled coat, and carried the briefcase and the shotgun into the family room. David followed, eyeing the shotgun. Angela sat on the couch, embraced her knees, and looked up at David.

"I'd like to stay calm," she said evenly. "Would you mind getting me a glass of wine?"

David complied immediately. As he handed her the glass he asked if she'd like something to eat. Angela shook her head before sipping the wine. She held the glass with both hands.

In a controlled voice Angela began to tell David about the attempted assault. But she didn't get far. Her emotions boiled over into tears. For five minutes she couldn't speak. David put his arms around her, telling her that it was his fault: he never should have let her work at the hospital so late at night.

Eventually, Angela regained her composure. She continued the story, choking back tears. When she got to the part about Robertson coming in to talk to her, her anger kicked in.

"I cannot believe that man," Angela sputtered. "He makes me so mad. He acted as if it were my fault."

"He's a jerk," David agreed.

Angela reached for the briefcase and handed it to David. She wiped the tears from her eyes. "All this effort and the slides didn't show much at all," she said. "There was no tumor in the brain. There was some perivascular inflammation, but it was nonspecific. A few neurons appeared damaged but it could have been a postmortem change."

"No sign of a systemic infectious disease?" David asked.

Angela shook her head. "I brought the slides home in case you wanted to look at them yourself," she said.

"I see you got a shotgun," David commented.

"It's loaded, too," Angela warned, "so be careful. And don't worry. I'll go over it with Nikki tomorrow."

A crash and the sound of breaking glass made them both sit bolt upright. Rusty started barking from Nikki's room, then he came bounding down the stairs. David picked up the shotgun.

"The safety is just above the trigger," Angela said.

With David leading, they made their way through to the darkened living room. David flipped on the light. Four panes of the bay window were smashed, along with their muntins. On the floor a few feet away from where they were standing was a brick. Attached to it was a copy of the note they'd received the night before.

"I'm calling the police," Angela said. "This is too much."

While they waited for the police to arrive, David sat Angela down.

"Did you do anything today related to the Hodges affair?" David asked.

"No," Angela said defensively. "Well, I did get a call from the medical examiner."

"Did you talk about Hodges with anyone?" David asked.

"His name came up when I talked with Robertson," Angela said.

"Tonight?" David asked with surprise.

"This afternoon," Angela said. "I stopped in to the police station to talk with Robertson on my way back from buying the shotgun."

"Why?" David asked with dismay. "After what happened in front of the church yesterday, I'm surprised you had the nerve to see the man."

"I wanted to apologize," Angela said. "But it was a mistake. Robertson is not about to do anything concerning Hodges' murderer."

"Angela," David pleaded, "we have to stop messing with this Hodges stuff. It's not worth it. A note on the door is one thing; a brick through the window is something else entirely."

Headlight beams played against the wall as a police cruiser pulled up the driveway.

"At least it's not Robertson," Angela said when they could see the approaching officer.

The policeman introduced himself as Bill Morrison. From the outset, it was clear he wasn't terribly interested in investigating this latest incident at the Wilsons' home. He was only asking enough questions to fill out the requisite form.

When he was ready to leave, Angela asked him if he was planning on taking the brick.

"Hadn't planned on it," Bill said.

"What about fingerprints?" Angela asked.

Bill's eyes went from Angela to David and then back to Angela. His face registered surprise and confusion. "Fingerprints?" he asked.

"What's so surprising?" Angela asked. "It's possible at times to get fingerprints from things like stone and brick."

"Well, I don't know if we'd send something like this to the state police," he said.

"Just in case, let me get you a bag," Angela said. She disappeared into the kitchen. When she returned she had a plastic bag. Turning it inside out, she reached down and picked up the brick. She handed the bag to Bill.

"There," Angela said. "Now you people are prepared if you happen to decide you want to try to solve a crime."

Bill nodded and went out to his cruiser. Angela and David watched it disappear down the driveway.

"I'm losing confidence in the local police," David said.

"I've never had any," Angela said.

"If Robertson is the only person you spoke to about Hodges today, it makes me wonder who's responsible for this brick coming through our window."

"Do you think the police might have done it?" Angela asked.

"I don't know," David said. "I can't believe they'd go that far, but it makes me think they know more than they're willing to say. Officer Bill certainly wasn't excited about the incident."

"I'm beginning to think this town is not quite the utopia we thought it was," Angela said.

David went out to the barn and cut himself a piece of plywood to fit over the hole in the bay window. When he returned to the house, Angela was eating a bowl of cold cereal.

"Not much of a dinner," he said.

"I'm surprised I'm hungry at all," Angela said.

She accompanied him into the living room and watched him struggle to open the stepladder.

"Are you sure you should be doing this?" she asked.

He flashed her an exasperated look.

"You haven't told me about your day," Angela said as David climbed up the ladder. "What about Jonathan Eakins? How's he doing?"

"I don't know," David said. "I'm not his doctor anymore."

"Why not?" Angela asked.

"Kelley assigned another doctor."

"He can do that?"

"He did it," David said. He tried to align the piece of plywood, then get a nail out of his pocket. "I was furious at first. Now I'm resigned. The good part is that I don't have to feel responsible."

"But you will still feel responsible," Angela said. "I know you."

David had Angela hand him the hammer, and he tried

nailing the plywood in place. Instead, one of the other window panes fell out and shattered on the floor. The noise brought Rusty out of Nikki's room to bark at the head of the stairs.

"Damn it all," David said.

"Maybe we should think about leaving Bartlet," Angela said.

"We can't just pick up and go. We've got mortgages and contracts. We aren't free like we used to be."

"But nothing is turning out the way we expected. We both have problems at work. I got assaulted. And this Hodges thing is driving me crazy."

"You have to let the Hodges affair go," David said. "Please, Angela."

"I can't," Angela said with new tears. "I'm even having nightmares now: nightmares about blood in the kitchen. Every time I go in there I think about it, and I can't get it out of my head that the person responsible is walking around and could come here any time he chose. It's no way to live, feeling you have to have a gun in the house."

"We shouldn't have a gun," David snapped.

"I'm not staying here at night when you go off to the hospital," Angela said irritably. "Not without a gun."

"You'd better be sure Nikki understands she's not allowed to touch it," David said.

"I'll discuss the gun with her tomorrow," Angela said.

"Speaking of Nikki," David said, "I happened to see Caroline in the emergency room. She's in the hospital with a high fever and respiratory distress."

"Oh, heavens no," Angela said. "Does Nikki know?"

"I told her this evening," David said.

"Does she have something contagious?" Angela asked. "She and Nikki were together yesterday."

"I don't know yet," David said. "I told Nikki she can't visit until we know."

"Poor Caroline," Angela said. "She seemed fine yesterday. God, I hope Nikki doesn't come down with the same thing."

"So do I," David said. "Angela, we've got more important things to think about than this nonsense involving

Hodges' body. Please, let's let it go, for Nikki's sake if not our own."

"All right," Angela said reluctantly. "I'll try."

"Thank goodness," David said. Then he looked up at the broken window. "Now what am I going to do with this mess?"

"How about tape and a plastic bag?" Angela suggested.

David stared at her. "Why didn't I think of that?" he questioned.

19

TUESDAY, OCTOBER 26

NEITHER DAVID NOR ANGELA SLEPT WELL. BOTH were overwrought, but they responded differently. While Angela had trouble falling asleep, David woke well before dawn. He was appalled to see the time: four A.M. Sensing he would not fall back asleep, David got up and tiptoed out of the bedroom, careful not to disturb Angela.

On his way to the family room, he paused at the head of the stairs. He'd heard a noise from Nikki's room and was surprised to see his daughter appear.

"What are you doing awake?" David whispered.

"I just woke up," Nikki said. "I've been thinking about Caroline."

David went into his daughter's room to talk with her about her friend. David told her that he thought Caroline would be a lot better by now. He promised to check on her as soon as he got to the hospital. He said he'd call Nikki and let her know.

When Nikki coughed a deep, productive cough, David

suggested they do her postural drainage. It took them almost half an hour. When it was over, Nikki said she felt better.

Together they went down into the kitchen and made breakfast. David cooked bacon and eggs while Nikki prepared a batch of drop biscuits. With a fire in the fireplace the meal had a festive quality that felt like a good antidote for their troubled spirits.

David was on his bike by five-thirty and at the hospital before six. En route, he made a mental note to arrange for someone to fix the bay window.

Several of David's patients were still asleep and David didn't disturb them. He went over their charts, planning to see them later. When he peeked into Donald's room he found the man was wide awake.

"I feel terrible," Donald said. "I haven't slept all night."

"What's the problem?" David asked, feeling his pulse quicken.

To David's dismay, the complaints were disturbingly familiar: crampy abdominal pain along with nausea and diarrhea. In addition, just like Jonathan, he complained of having to swallow continually.

David tried to remain calm. He spoke with Donald for almost half an hour, asking detailed questions about each complaint and ascertaining the sequence in which the complaints had appeared.

Although Donald's complaints certainly reminded him of his other deceased patients, there was an aspect of Donald's history that was different: Donald had never had chemotherapy.

Donald had been initially diagnosed as having pancreatic cancer, but surgery had proved this not to be the case. He'd undergone a massive operation called a Whipple procedure which included the removal of his pancreas, parts of his stomach and intestines, and a good deal of lymphatic tissue. When pathology examined the tumor it had been determined to be benign.

Since he had had such extensive surgery on his digestive system, but had not had chemotherapy to compromise his immune system, David was hopeful that Donald's complaints were purely functional and not harbingers of whatever afflicted David's other unlucky patients.

After finishing his rounds, David called admitting to find out Caroline's room number. On his way he had to pass the ICU. Steeling himself against what he might learn, he went in to check on Jonathan Eakins.

"Jonathan Eakins died about three this morning," the busy head nurse said. "It was a very quick downhill course. Nothing we did seemed to help. It was a shame. A young man like that. It proves you never know when you're going to have to go."

David swallowed hard. He nodded, turned, and left the unit. Even though he'd known in his heart that Jonathan would die, the reality of it was hard to take. David still had a hard time absorbing the staggering fact: he had now lost four patients in a little over a week.

On a brighter note, David discovered that Caroline had responded well to her treatment of IV antibiotics and intensive respiratory therapy. Her fever was gone, her color was pink, and her blue eyes sparkled. She smiled broadly the instant David appeared.

"Nikki wants to come to visit you," David said.

"Cool," Caroline said. "When?"

"Probably this afternoon," David said.

"Could you please ask her to bring me my reading book and my spelling book," Caroline said.

David promised he would.

The first thing David did when he got to his office was call home. Nikki answered. David told her that Caroline was much better and that Nikki could visit her that day. He also relayed Caroline's request for her books. Then David asked Nikki to put her mother on the line.

"She's in the shower," Nikki said. "Should she call you back?"

"No, it's not necessary," David said. "But I want you to remind her of something. She brought a gun home yesterday. It's a shotgun, and it is leaning against the newel post at the bottom of the stairs. She's supposed to show it to you and warn you not to touch it. Will you remind her to do all that?"

"Yes, Dad," Nikki said.

David could picture his daughter rolling her eyes.

"I'm serious," he said. "Don't forget."

Hanging up the phone, David wondered about the gun. He didn't like it. Yet he wasn't about to force the issue at the moment. More than anything, he wanted Angela to give up her obsession with Hodges' murder. A brick through the front window was all the warning David needed.

David decided to take this early-morning opportunity to get through some of the never-ending reams of paperwork he was forced to process in connection with his practice. As he laid the first form on his desk, the phone rang. The caller was a patient named Sandra Hascher. She was a young woman with a history of melanoma that had spread to regional lymph nodes.

"I didn't expect to get you directly," Sandra said.

"I'm the only one here just now," David explained.

Sandra told him she'd been having trouble with an abscessed tooth. The tooth had been pulled, but the infection was worse. "I'm sorry to bother you with this," she continued, "but my temperature is one hundred and three. I would have gone to the emergency room, but the last time I took my son there I had to pay for it myself. CMV refused."

"I've heard the story before," David said. "Why don't you come right over. I'll see you immediately."

"Thanks, I'll be right there," Sandra said.

The abscess was impressive. The whole side of Sandra's face was distorted by the swelling. In addition, the lymph nodes beneath her jaw were almost golf-ball size. David checked her temperature. It was indeed one hundred and three.

"You've got to come into the hospital," David said.

"I can't," Sandra said. "I've got so much to do. And my ten-year-old is home with the chicken pox."

"You'll just have to make arrangements," David said. "There's no way I'm going to let you walk around with this time bomb."

David carefully explained the anatomy of the region to Sandra, emphasizing how close the infection was to her brain. "If the infection gets into your nervous system, we're in deep trouble," David said. "You need continuous antibiotics. This is no joke."

"All right," Sandra said. "You have me convinced."

David called admitting to warn them Sandra would be coming. Then he gave her a written set of orders and sent her on her way.

Angela felt terrible. She was exhausted. Several cups of coffee had not been enough to revive her. It had been almost three o'clock before she'd fallen asleep, and once she had, she'd not slept soundly. She'd had nightmares again, featuring Hodges' body, the ski-masked rapist, and the brick through the window.

When she finally did wake up she was surprised to discover that David had already left for work.

As Angela dressed, she regretted her promise to David to try to forget about Hodges. She didn't see how she could "just let Hodges go" as David suggested.

Angela wondered again about Phil Calhoun. She still had not heard a word from him. She figured that the least he could do was check in. Even if he hadn't discovered something significant, he could at least let her know what he'd accomplished to date.

Angela decided to give Phil Calhoun a call, but all she got was his answering machine. Deciding against leaving a message, she simply hung up.

Downstairs, Angela found Nikki in the family room busily reading from one of her schoolbooks.

"Okay," Angela said. "Upstairs for postural drainage."

"I already did it with Dad," Nikki said.

"Really?" Angela said. "How about breakfast?"

"We had that too," Nikki said.

"What time did you two get up?" Angela asked.

"Around four," Nikki said.

Angela wasn't happy about David's getting up so early. Having trouble sleeping was often a sign of depression. She also didn't like the idea of having Nikki up so early.

"How did Daddy seem this morning?" Angela asked as she joined Nikki in the family room.

"Fine," Nikki said. "He called while you were in the

shower. He said that Caroline was okay and that I can visit her this afternoon."

"That's wonderful news," Angela said.

"He also asked me to remind you about a gun," Nikki said. "He acted weird, like I wouldn't know what a gun is."

"He's worried," Angela said. "It's no joke. Guns are bad business when it comes to kids. A lot of kids are killed each year because of family-owned guns. But more often than not those cases involve handguns."

Angela walked out into the front hall and brought the shotgun back into the family room. She took the shell out of the chamber and showed Nikki how to tell there were no more inside.

Angela spent the next half hour going over the gun with Nikki, allowing Nikki to pump it, pull the trigger, and even load and unload it. When they were finished with the instruction, they went outside behind the barn and each fired a shell. Nikki said she didn't like firing it because it hurt her shoulder.

Returning to the house, Angela told Nikki that she wasn't to touch the gun. Nikki told her not to worry, she didn't want to have anything to do with it.

Since the weather was warm and sunny, Nikki wanted to ride her bike to school. Angela watched as she started off toward town. Angela was pleased she was doing so well; at least Bartlet was good for Nikki.

Shortly after Nikki left, Angela did the same. After parking in the reserved area, Angela couldn't resist the temptation to examine the spot where she'd been attacked. She retraced her steps into the stand of trees that separated the parking lots and found her own footprints in the muddy earth. With the help of the footprints she found the spot where she'd fallen. Then she discovered the deep cut left in the earth by the man's club.

The cleft was about four inches deep. Angela put her fingers in it and shuddered. She could still vividly recall the sight and sound of that club whizzing by her ear. She even could vaguely recall the glint of a flash of metal streaking by.

Suddenly, Angela realized something she hadn't focused on before: the man had not hesitated. If she had not rolled out of the way, she would have been struck. The man hadn't been trying to rape her, he'd wanted to hurt her, maybe kill her.

Angela thought back to the injuries to Hodges' skull she'd examined during the autopsy. Hodges had been hit with a metal rod. Her head could have looked just like Hodges'!

Against her better judgment, Angela put in a call to Robertson.

"I know what you're calling about," Robertson said irritably, "and you can just forget it. I ain't sending this brick up to the state police lab for fingerprints. They'd laugh me out of the goddamn state."

"I'm not calling about the brick," Angela said. Instead, she conveyed her idea that her assault had been attempted murder, not attempted rape.

When Angela was finished, Robertson was so quiet, she was afraid that he'd hung up. "Hello?" she asked at last.

"I'm still here," Robertson said. "I'm thinking."

There was another pause.

"Nah, I don't buy it," Robertson said finally. "This guy is a rapist, not a murderer. He's had opportunity to kill in the past, but he didn't. Hell, he didn't even hurt the ones he did rape."

Angela wondered if the rape victims didn't feel hurt, but she wasn't about to argue the issue with Robertson. She merely thanked him for his time and hung up.

"What a flake!" Angela said out loud. She was a fool to have thought Robertson would give any credence to her theory. Yet the more she thought about the attack, the more sure she became that rape hadn't been the goal. And if it had been an attempted murder, then it had to be related to her interest in Hodges' murder. Maybe the man was Hodges' murderer!

Angela shivered. If she was right, then she'd been stalked. The idea terrified her. Whatever she did, she'd have to be sure to make it seem as if she were giving up on the affair.

Angela wondered if she should tell David her latest suspicions. She was indecisive. On the one hand, she never wanted there to be any secrets between them. On the other, she knew he'd only use it as more reason for her to give up her probe of Hodges' murder. For the time being, Angela decided that she'd only tell Phil Calhoun—if and when he contacted her.

"I'll have a little more coffee," Traynor said as he pointed toward his cup with the handle of his gavel for the waitress's benefit. As was their habit, Traynor, Sherwood, Beaton, and Caldwell were having a breakfast meeting in advance of the monthly hospital executive board meeting scheduled for the following Monday night. They were seated at Traynor's favorite table at the Iron Horse Inn.

"I'm encouraged," Beaton said. "The preliminary figures for the second half of October are better than those of the first half. We're not out of the woods yet, but they are significantly better than September's."

"We get one crisis under control and then have to face another," Traynor said. "It's never-ending. What's the story about a doctor being assaulted last night?"

"It was just after midnight," Caldwell said. "It was the new female pathologist, Angela Wilson. She'd been working late."

"Where in the parking lot did it take place?" Traynor asked. He began his nervous habit of hitting his palm with his gavel.

"In the pathway between the lots," Caldwell said.

"Have lights been put in there?" Traynor asked.

Caldwell looked at Beaton.

"I don't know," Beaton admitted. "But we'll check as soon as we get back. You ordered lights to be put there, but whether it got done or not I'm not sure."

"They'd better be," Traynor said. He hit his palm particularly hard and the sound carried around the room. "I've had no luck lobbying the Selectmen about the parking garage. There's no way it can even get on the ballot now until spring."

"I checked with the *Bartlet Sun*," Beaton said. "They

have agreed to keep the rape attempt out of the paper."

"At least they're on our side," Traynor said.

"I think their loyalty is inspired by the ads we run," Beaton said.

"Any new business to be brought up at the board meeting?" Sherwood asked.

"There's a new battle fomenting in the clinical arena," Beaton said. "The radiologists and the neurologists are squaring off for a bloody fight over which group is officially designated to read MRIs of the skull."

"You've got to be kidding," Traynor said.

"Honest," Beaton said. "If we gave them weapons it would be a fight to the death. It involves dollars and ego, a tough combination."

"Damn doctors," Traynor said with disgust. "They can't work together on anything. They're a bunch of lone rangers, if you ask me."

"Which brings me to M.D. 91," Beaton said. "He's planning on suing the hospital over his privileges."

"Let him sue," Traynor said. "I'm even tired of the medical staff's insistence that we call these 'compromised physicians' by code numbers. Hell, 'compromised physician' is a euphemism in itself."

"That's all the new business," Beaton said.

Traynor looked around the table. "Anything else?"

"I had a curious visit yesterday afternoon," Sherwood said. "The caller was a PI by the name of Phil Calhoun."

"He came to see me too," Traynor said.

"He makes me nervous," Sherwood said. "He asked a lot of questions about Hodges."

"Likewise," Traynor said.

"The problem was that he already seemed to know a fair amount," Sherwood said. "I was reluctant to give him any information, but I didn't want to appear to be stonewalling either."

"My feelings exactly," Traynor said.

"He hasn't come to see me," Beaton said.

"Who do you think retained him?" Sherwood asked.

"I asked him," Traynor said. "He implied that the family had. I assumed he meant Clara, so I called her. She said she didn't know anything about Phil Calhoun. Next I called Wayne Robertson. Calhoun had already been to see him. Wayne thought that the most likely candidate is Angela Wilson, our new pathologist."

"That makes sense," Sherwood said. "She came to see me about Hodges. She was very upset about her body being discovered in her house."

"That's a curious coincidence," Beaton said. "She's certainly having her troubles: first finding a body in her house and then experiencing a rape attempt."

"Maybe the rape attempt will dampen her interest in Hodges," Traynor said. "It would be ironic for something positive to come out of something so potentially negative."

"What if Phil Calhoun figures out who killed Hodges?" Caldwell asked.

"That could be a problem," Traynor said. "But it's been over eight months. What are the odds? The trail must be pretty cool by now."

When the meeting broke up, Traynor walked Beaton out to her car. He asked her if she'd had a change of heart about their relationship.

"No," Beaton said. "Have you?"

"I can't divorce Jacqueline right now," Traynor said. "Not with my boy in college. But when he gets out . . ."

"Fine," Beaton said. "We'll talk about it then."

As Beaton drove up to the hospital, she shook her head in dismay. "Men!" she said irritably.

After seeing off his last patient for the day, David stepped across the hall into his private office. Nikki was sitting at his desk leafing through one of his medical journals. David liked the fact that she was interested in medicine. He hoped that if her interest persisted, she would have the opportunity to study medicine.

"Are you ready?" she asked.

"Let's go."

It took them only a few minutes to cover the short distance to the hospital and up a flight of stairs. When they stepped into Caroline's room, Caroline's face lit up with joy. She was especially pleased that Nikki had remembered to bring the books that she'd requested. Caroline was a superb student, just like Nikki.

"Look what I can do," Caroline said. She reached up and grabbed an overhead bar and pulled herself completely off the bed, angling her feet up into the air.

David clapped. It was a feat that took considerable strength, more than David would have guessed her slender arms had. Caroline was in a large orthopedic bed with an overhead frame. David assumed they'd put her in it for its entertainment value since the child was obviously enjoying it.

"I'm going to check on my patients," David said. He shook a finger at Nikki. "I won't be long, and no terrorizing the nurses, promise?"

"Promise," Nikki said, then she giggled with Caroline.

David headed straight for Donald Anderson's room. He wasn't worried about Donald's status because he'd called to check on him throughout the day. The reports had always been the same: the blood sugars were all normal and the GI complaints had decreased.

"How are you, Donald?" David asked as he arrived at the bedside.

Donald was on his back. His bed was raised so that he was reclining at a forty-five-degree angle. When David spoke he slowly rolled his head to the side, but he didn't answer.

"How are you?" David said, raising his voice.

Donald mumbled something David couldn't understand. David tried again to talk with him, but quickly realized that the man was disoriented.

David examined him carefully. He listened intently to his lungs, but there were no adventitious sounds, indicating that his lungs were clear. Walking out to the nurses' station he ordered a stat blood sugar.

While the blood sugar was being processed, David saw his other patients. Everyone else was doing well, including Sandra. Although she'd been on antibiotics for less than twelve hours, she insisted the pain in her jaw was better. When David examined her, his impression was that the abscess was the same size, but the symptomatic improvement was encouraging. He did not change her treatment. Two other patients were doing so well he told them they could go home the following day.

As he was finishing his entry in the chart of his last patient, the floor secretary slipped the result of Donald's blood sugar under David's nose. It was normal. David picked up the scrap of paper and studied it. He didn't want it to be normal. He wanted it to explain the change in Donald's mental status.

David slowly walked back to Donald's room, puzzling over his condition. The only explanation that David could think of was that Donald's blood sugar had had a wild swing either up or down and had then corrected itself. The problem with that line of reasoning was that the patient's sensorium usually returned to normal simultaneous with the blood sugar.

David was still mulling over the possibilities when he reentered Donald's room. When he first saw Donald, David stared in utter disbelief. Donald's face was dusky blue and his head was thrust back in hyper-extension. Dark blood oozed from a half-open mouth. His body was only partially covered; the bedcovers were in total disarray.

David's initial shock quickly turned into motion. He alerted the nurses that there had been an arrest and started cardiopulmonary resuscitation. The resuscitation team arrived and followed their familiar routine. Even Donald's surgeon, Dr. Albert Hillson, came in. He'd been making rounds when he'd heard the commotion.

The resuscitation attempt was soon called off. It was apparent that Donald had suffered a seizure and respiratory arrest somewhere between fifteen and twenty minutes prior to David finding him. With that amount of time having passed with no oxygen getting to the brain, there was no hope. David declared Donald dead at five-fifteen.

David was devastated at having lost yet another patient, but he forced himself not to show it. Dr. Hillson was saddened but expansive. He said that it had been a tribute to good medical care that Donald had lived as long as he had. When Shirley Anderson came in with her two young boys, she voiced the same sentiment.

"Thank you for being so kind to him," Shirley said to David as she blotted her eyes. "You had become his favorite doctor."

After David had done all he could, he headed toward Caroline's room to get Nikki. He felt numb. It had all happened so quickly.

"At least you know why this patient died," Angela said after David had described what had happened to Donald Anderson. They were sitting in the family room. Dinner was long since over; Nikki was up in her room doing her homework.

"But I don't," David complained. "It all happened so fast."

"Now, wait a minute," Angela said. "With the other patients I could understand your confusion. But not with this one. Donald Anderson had had most of his abdominal organs rearranged if not removed. He was in and out of your office and the hospital. You can't possibly blame yourself for his death."

"I don't know what to think anymore," David said. "It's true; he was always teetering on the edge with his frequent infections and his brittle diabetes. But why a seizure?"

"His blood sugar was wandering all over the map," Angela said. "What about a stroke? I mean the possibilities are legion."

The phone startled them both. David reached for it by reflex. He was afraid it was the hospital with more bad news. When the caller asked for Angela, he was relieved.

Angela immediately recognized the voice: it was Phil Calhoun.

"Sorry I haven't been in touch," Calhoun said. "I've been busy, but now I'd like to have a chat."

"When?" Angela asked.

"Well, I'm sitting here in the Iron Horse Inn," Calhoun said. "It's only a stone's throw away. Why don't I come over?"

Angela covered the phone with her hand. "It's the private investigator, Phil Calhoun," she said. "He wants to come over."

"I thought you were letting the Hodges affair go," David said.

"I have," Angela said. "I haven't spoken to anyone."

"Then what about Phil Calhoun?" David asked.

"I haven't spoken to him either," Angela said. "Not since Saturday. But I've already paid him. I think we should at least hear what he's learned."

David sighed with resignation. "Whatever," he said.

A quarter of an hour later when Phil Calhoun came through their door, David wondered what could have possessed Angela to describe him as professional. To David he appeared anything but professional, with a red baseball cap on backwards and a flannel shirt. The sorrels on his feet didn't even have laces.

"Pleasure," Calhoun said when he shook hands with David.

They sat in the living room on the shabby old furniture that they'd brought from Boston. The huge room had a cheap dance-hall feel with such meager, pitiful furnishing. The plastic bag taped to the window didn't help.

"Nice house," Calhoun said as he looked around.

"We're still in the process of furnishing it," Angela said. She asked if she could get Calhoun something to drink. He said he'd appreciate a beer if she didn't mind.

While Angela was off getting the beer, David continued to eye their visitor. Calhoun was older than David had expected. A shock of gray hair bristled from beneath the red cap, which Calhoun made no attempt to remove.

"Mind if I smoke?" Calhoun asked as he brandished his Antonio y Cleopatras.

"I'm sorry, but we do," Angela said, coming back into the room and handing Calhoun his beer. "Our daughter has respiratory problems."

"No problem," Calhoun said agreeably. "I wanted to give you folks an update on my investigations. It's proceeding well, although not without effort. Dr. Dennis Hodges was not the most popular man in town. In fact, half the population seems to have hated him for one reason or another."

"We're already aware of that," David said. "I hope that you have more specific details to add to justify your hourly wage."

"David, please!" Angela said. She was surprised at David's rudeness.

"It's my opinion," Calhoun continued, ignoring David's comment, "that Dr. Hodges either didn't care what other people thought of him or he was socially handicapped. As a purebred New Englander, it was probably a combination of the two." Calhoun chuckled, then took a drink of his beer.

"I've made up a list of potential suspects," Calhoun continued, "but I haven't interviewed them all yet. But it's getting interesting. Something strange is going on here. I can feel it in my bones."

"Who have you spoken with?" David asked. There was still a rudeness to his voice that bothered Angela, but she didn't say anything.

"Just a couple so far," Calhoun said. He let out a belch. He made no attempt to excuse himself or even cover his mouth. David glanced at Angela. Angela pretended not to have noticed.

"I've talked to a few of the higher-ups with the hospital," Calhoun continued. "The chairman of the board, Traynor, and the vice chairman, Sherwood. Both had reasons to hold a grudge against Hodges."

"I hope you plan to speak with Dr. Cantor," Angela said. "I'd heard he really had it out for Hodges."

"Cantor's on the list," Calhoun assured her. "But I wanted to start at the top and work down. Sherwood's grudge involved a piece of land. Traynor's beef was far more personal."

Calhoun went on to explain the Traynor-Hodges-Van Slyke triangle, concluding with the suicide of Sunny Traynor, Traynor's sister.

"What a terrible story," Angela said.

"It's like a TV melodrama," Calhoun agreed. "But you'd think that if Traynor felt compelled to do anything about Hodges, he would have done it back then, not now. Besides, Hodges had hand-picked Traynor to take over the hospital board well after the suicide. I doubt he'd have done that if he and Traynor were still at odds. And Van Slyke's child, Werner, works for the hospital today."

"Werner Van Slyke is related to Traynor?" David questioned with surprise. "Now that smacks of nepotism."

"Could be," Calhoun said. "But Werner Van Slyke, Junior, had a long-term friendly relationship with Hodges. He'd taken care of this house for Hodges for years. His position at the hospital is probably more a result of Hodges' doing than Traynor's. At any rate, I don't suspect Traynor of murder."

"How can you be sure?" Angela questioned.

"Can't be sure of anything except Hodges' murder," Calhoun said. "After that we can only deal in probabilities."

"This is all very interesting," David said; "but have you come up with a suspect or at least narrowed the list down?"

"No, not yet," Calhoun said.

"How much have we spent to get to this dubious crossroad?" David asked.

"David!" Angela snapped. "I think you're being unfair. I think Mr. Calhoun has learned a lot in a short period of time. I think the important question now is whether he believes the case is solvable."

"I'll buy that," David said. "What's your professional assessment, Mr. Calhoun?"

"I think I need a cigar," Calhoun said. "Would you folks mind if we were to sit outside?"

A few minutes later they assembled on the terrace. Calhoun was utterly content with his smoke and another beer.

"I think the case is definitely solvable," he said. His broad, doughy face intermittently lit up as he puffed on his cigar. "You have to know something about small New England towns: they are more the same than they are different. I know these people and I understand the dynamics. The characters are generally the same from town to town, only the names are different. Anybody's business is everybody else's. In other words I'm sure that some people know who the killer is. The problem is getting somebody to talk. My hunch is that the hospital is involved on some level, and no one wants it to get hurt. And there's a chance it could get hurt because Hodges made the hospital his life's work."

"How have you gotten your information so far?" Angela asked. "I thought New Englanders were closed-mouthed, reluctant to talk."

"Generally true," Calhoun said. "But some of the best people for town gossip happen to be friends of mine: the bookstore owner, the pharmacist, the bartender, and the librarian. They've been my sources so far. Now, I just have to start eliminating suspects. But before I begin I have to ask you a question: Do you want me to continue?"

"No," David said.

"Wait a minute," Angela said. "You've told us that the case is definitely solvable. How long do you think it will take?"

"Not too long," Calhoun said.

"That's too vague," David said.

Calhoun lifted his cap and scratched his scalp. "I'd say within a week," he said.

"That's a lot of money," David said.

"I think it's worth it," Angela said.

"Angela!" David pleaded. "You told me you were going to drop this Hodges affair."

"I will," Angela said. "I'll let Mr. Calhoun do everything. I won't talk to a soul."

"Good Lord," David said dejectedly as he rolled his eyes in exasperation.

"Come on, David," Angela said. "If you expect me to live in this house then you have to support me in this."

David hesitated, then thought of a compromise. "Okay," he said. "I'll make a deal. One week, then it's over no matter what."

"All right," Angela said. "It's a deal." Then she turned to Calhoun. "Now that we have a time constraint, what's the next move?"

"First I'll continue interviewing my list of suspects," Calhoun said. "At the same time there are two other major goals. One is to reconstruct Dr. Hodges' last day, assuming he was killed on the day he disappeared. To do this I want to interview Hodges' secretary-nurse who'd worked for him for thirty-five years. The second goal is to get copies of the medical papers that were found with Hodges."

"They're in the custody of the state police," Angela said. "Having been on the force, can't you get copies easily?"

"Unfortunately, no," Calhoun said. "The state police tend to be inordinately guarded when it comes to evidence in their custody. I know because I used to work for a while in the crime-scene division up in Burlington. It makes for a kind of 'catch-22.' The state police with the expertise and the evidence aren't motivated to expend a lot of time and effort on this kind of case because they take their cue from the local police. If the local police don't care, then the state police let it slide. One of the reasons the local police don't care is they don't have the evidence to go on."

"Another reason is that they might be somehow involved," Angela said. She then told Calhoun about the brick through the window, the threatening notes, and the police's response.

"Doesn't surprise me," Calhoun said. "Robertson's on my list. He couldn't stand Hodges."

"I knew that," Angela said. "I was told that Robertson blames his wife's death on Hodges."

"I don't give that story a lot of significance," Calhoun said. "Robertson's not that stupid. I think the sorry episode about his wife was just an excuse. I think Robertson's anger toward Hodges stemmed more from Hodges' behavior which we know was less than diplomatic. I'd bet my last dollar that Hodges knew Robertson for the blowhard he is and never gave him any respect. I sincerely doubt that Robertson killed Hodges, but when I was talking with him, he gave me a funny feeling. He knows something he wasn't telling me."

"The way the police have been dragging their feet they have to be involved," Angela said.

"Reminds me of a case when I was a state trooper," Calhoun said after another long pull on his cigar. "It was also a homicide in a small town. We were sure the whole town, including the local police, knew who'd done it, yet no one would come forward. We ended up dropping the case. It's unsolved to this day."

"What makes you think Hodges' case is any different?" David asked. "Couldn't the same thing happen here?"

"Not a chance," Calhoun said. "In the case I just told you about the dead person was a murderer and a thief himself. Hodges is different. There are a lot of people who hated him, but there's also a bunch who think he was one of the town heroes. Hell, this is the only referral hospital in New England outside of the big cities, and Hodges was personally responsible for building it up. A lot of people's livelihood is based on what Hodges created here. Don't worry, this case will be solved. No doubt about it."

"How will you manage to get copies of Hodges' papers if you can't do it yourself?" Angela asked.

"You have to do it," Calhoun said.

"Me?" Angela asked.

"That's not part of the deal," David said. "She has to stay out of this investigation. I don't want her talking to anyone. Not with bricks coming through our window."

"There will be no danger," Calhoun insisted.

"Why me?" Angela asked.

"Because you are both a physician and an employee of the hospital," Calhoun said. "If you show up at the crime-scene division up in Burlington with the appropriate identification and say that copies of the papers are needed to take care of patients, they'll make you copies in a flash. Judges' and doctors' requests are always honored. I know. As I said, I used to work there."

"I guess visiting the state police headquarters couldn't be very dangerous," Angela said. "It's not as if I'm participating in the investigation."

"I suppose it's okay," David said. "Provided there's no chance of getting into trouble with the police."

"No chance," Calhoun said. "The worst thing that could happen is they wouldn't give her the copies."

"When?" Angela asked.

"How about tomorrow?" Calhoun suggested.

"It will have to be on my lunch hour," Angela said.

"I'll come pick you up at noon in front of the hospital," Calhoun said. He stood up, thanking them for the beers.

Angela offered to walk Calhoun to his truck while David went back in the house.

"I hope I'm not causing trouble between you and your husband," Calhoun said as they approached his vehicle. "He didn't seem at all pleased about my investigation."

"It won't be a problem," Angela said. "But we'll have to stick to the one-week agreement."

"Should be plenty of time," Calhoun said.

"There is something else I wanted to tell you," Angela said. She explained her new theory on her assault.

"Hmmm," Calhoun said. "This is getting more interesting than I thought. You'd better be doubly sure to leave the sleuthing to me."

"I intend to," Angela said.

"I've been careful about not letting it be known that you've retained me," Calhoun said.

"I appreciate the discretion."

"Maybe tomorrow I should pick you up in the parking lot behind the library instead of in front of the hospital," Calhoun said. "No sense taking chances."

20

WEDNESDAY, OCTOBER 27

TO DAVID'S AND ANGELA'S DISMAY, NIKKI AWOKE with congestion and a deep, productive cough. Both were fearful that she might be coming down with the same illness that had briefly afflicted Caroline. David was particularly concerned because it had been his decision to allow Nikki to visit Caroline the previous afternoon.

Despite extra attention to Nikki's morning respiratory therapy, she failed to improve. To Nikki's keen disappointment, David and Angela decided she shouldn't go to school. They called Alice, who agreed to come over for the day.

Already tense from events at home, David was edgy as he started his rounds. With so many recent deaths, he was spooked to see his patients. But his worries were groundless. Everyone was doing fine. Even Sandra was much better.

"Your swelling is down," David told her as he tenderly palpated the side of her face.

"I can tell," Sandra said.

"And your fever is below one hundred," David said.

"I'm pleased," Sandra said. "Thank you. I won't even pressure you about when I can get out of here."

"Very clever," David said with a laugh. "The indirect approach is often far more effective than the direct. But I think we have to keep you until we're one hundred percent sure this infection is under control."

"Oh, all right," Sandra said, feigning irritation. "But if I have to stay, could you do me a favor?"

"Of course," David said.

"The electric controls of my bed stopped working," Sandra said. "I told the nurses, but they said there wasn't anything they could do about it."

"I'll do something," David promised. "It's a chronic problem around here, I'm afraid. I'll go out and ask about it right away. We want you to be as comfortable as possible."

Returning to the nurses' station, David found Janet Colburn and complained about the bed situation. "There's really nothing that can be done?" David asked.

"That's what maintenance told us when we reported it," Janet said. "I wasn't about to argue with the man. It's hard enough talking with him. And frankly, we don't have another bed to spare at the moment."

David couldn't believe that he'd have to go to see Van Slyke over another maintenance detail. But it seemed his choice was either to go ask why the bed couldn't be repaired, or go to Beaton directly. It was an absurd situation.

David found Van Slyke in his windowless office.

"I have a patient upstairs who was told her bed couldn't be repaired," David said irritably after a cursory knock. "What's the story?"

"The hospital bought the wrong kind of beds," Van Slyke said. "They're a maintenance nightmare."

"It can't be fixed?" David asked.

"It can be fixed, but it will break again," Van Slyke said.

"I want it fixed," David said.

"We'll do it when we get around to it," Van Slyke said. "Don't bother me. I have more important work to do."

"Why are you so rude?" David demanded.

"Look who's talking," Van Slyke said. "You came down here yelling at me, not vice versa. If you have a problem, go tell it to administration."

"I'll do that," David said. He turned around and climbed up the stairs intending to go directly to Helen Beaton. But when he got to the lobby he saw Dr. Pilsner coming into the hospital, heading for the main stairs.

"Bert," David called. "Can I speak to you a moment?"

Dr. Pilsner paused.

David approached him, described Nikki's congestion, and started to ask whether he thought Nikki should start some oral antibiotics. But David stopped in mid-sentence. He noticed that Dr. Pilsner was agitated; he was hardly listening to what David was saying.

"Is something wrong?" David asked.

"I'm sorry," Dr. Pilsner said. "I'm distracted. Caroline Helmsford took an unexpected turn for the worse during the night. I've been here almost continuously. I just went home to shower and change."

"What happened?" David asked.

"Come and see for yourself," Dr. Pilsner said. He started up the stairs. David had to jog to stay with him.

"She's in the ICU," Dr. Pilsner explained. "It started with a seizure of all things."

David's steps faltered. Then he had to sprint to catch back up to the quickly moving pediatrician. David didn't like the idea of Caroline having a seizure. It brought back disturbing memories of his own patients.

"Then pneumonia developed rapidly," Dr. Pilsner continued. "I've tried everything. Nothing seemed to make a difference."

They arrived at the ICU. Dr. Pilsner hesitated, leaning against the door. He sighed from exhaustion. "I'm afraid she's now in septic shock. We're having to maintain her blood pressure. It doesn't look good at all. I'm afraid I'm going to lose her."

They went into the unit. Caroline was in a coma. A tube issued from her mouth and was connected to a respirator. Her body was covered with wires and intravenous lines.

Monitors recorded her pulse and blood pressure. David shuddered as he looked down at the stricken child. In his mind's eye he saw Nikki in Caroline's place, and the image terrorized him.

The ICU nurse handling Caroline gave a capsule report. Nothing had improved since Dr. Pilsner had left an hour earlier. As soon as Dr. Pilsner had been fully briefed, he and David walked over to the central desk. David used the opportunity to discuss Nikki's condition with him. Dr. Pilsner listened and then agreed that oral antibiotics were indicated. He suggested the type and dosage.

Before leaving the unit David tried to bolster Dr. Pilsner with an encouraging word. David knew all too well how the pediatrician felt.

Before seeing his office patients, David called Angela to tell her about Nikki's antibiotics. Then he told her about Caroline. Angela was dumbstruck.

"You think she's going to die?" Angela asked.

"That's Dr. Pilsner's feeling," David said.

"Nikki was with her yesterday," Angela said.

"You don't have to remind me," David said. "But Caroline was much better. She was afebrile."

"Oh, God," Angela said. "It seems to be one thing after another. Can you get the antibiotics for Nikki and take them home over your lunch hour?"

"Okay," David said agreeably.

"I'll be heading up to Burlington as planned," Angela said.

"You're still going?" David asked.

"Of course," Angela said. "Calhoun called me to confirm. Apparently he's already spoken to the officer in charge of the crime-scene division up in Burlington."

"Have a good trip," David said. He hung up before he could say something he might regret. Angela's priorities irked him. While he was worrying himself sick about Caroline and Nikki, she was still obsessed with the Hodges affair.

"I appreciate your seeing me," Calhoun said as he took a chair in front of Helen Beaton's desk. "As I told your secretary, I only have a few questions."

"And I have a question for you," Beaton said.

"Who should go first?" Calhoun asked. Then he held up his pack of cigars. "May I smoke?"

"No, you may not smoke," Beaton said. "There's no smoking in this hospital. And I think I should ask my questions first. The answer might affect the duration of this interview."

"By all means," Calhoun said. "You first."

"Who hired you?" Beaton asked.

"That's an unfair question," Calhoun said.

"And why is that?"

"Because my clients have a right to privacy," Calhoun said. "Now it's my turn. I understand that Dr. Hodges was a frequent visitor to your office."

"If I may interrupt," Beaton said. "If your clients choose to withhold their identity, then I see no reason to cooperate with you."

"That's up to you," Calhoun said. "Of course there are those who might wonder why the president of a hospital would have a problem speaking about her immediate predecessor. They might even start thinking you know who killed Hodges."

"Thank you for coming in," Beaton said. She stood up and smiled. "You won't goad me into talking, not without my knowing just who's behind your efforts. My main concern is the hospital. Good day, Mr. Calhoun."

Calhoun got to his feet. "I have a feeling I'll be seeing you again," he said.

Calhoun left administration and descended to the basement. His next interviewee was Werner Van Slyke. Calhoun found him in the hospital shop replacing electrical motors in several hospital beds.

"Werner Van Slyke?" Calhoun questioned.

"Yeah," Van Slyke said in his monotone.

"Name's Calhoun. Mind if I have a chat with you?"

"What about?"

"Dr. Dennis Hodges," Calhoun said.

"If you don't mind my working," Van Slyke said. He turned his attention back to the motors.

"Are these beds a frequent problem?" Calhoun asked.

"Unfortunately," Van Slyke said.

"Since you're head of the department, why are you doing them yourself?" Calhoun asked.

"I want to make sure it's done right," Van Slyke said.

Calhoun retired to the workbench and sat on a stool. "Mind if I smoke?" he asked.

"Whatever," Van Slyke said.

"I thought the hospital was a smoke-free environment," Calhoun said as he took out a cigar. He offered one to Van Slyke. Van Slyke paused as if he were giving it considerable thought. Then he took one. Calhoun lit Van Slyke's before his own.

"I understand you knew Hodges pretty well," Calhoun said.

"He was like a father to me," Van Slyke said. He puffed his cigar contentedly. "More than my own father."

"No kidding," Calhoun said.

"If it hadn't been for Hodges, I never would have gone to college," Van Slyke said. "He'd given me a job to work around his house. I used to sleep over a lot and we'd talk. I had a lot of trouble with my own father."

"How so?" Calhoun asked. He was eager to keep Van Slyke talking.

"My father was a mean son-of-a-bitch," Van Slyke said. Then he coughed. "The bastard used to beat the hell out of me."

"How come?" Calhoun asked.

"He got drunk most every night," Van Slyke said. "He used to beat me and my mother couldn't do anything about it. In fact, she got beat herself."

"Did you and your mother talk?" Calhoun asked. "Kinda team up against your father?"

"Hell, no," Van Slyke said. "She always defended him, saying he didn't mean it after he'd kicked the crap out of me. Hell, she even tried to convince me that he loved me and that was why he was hitting me."

"Doesn't make sense," Calhoun said.

"Sure as hell doesn't," Van Slyke said acidly. "What the hell are you asking all these questions for, anyway?"

"I'm interested in Hodges' death," Calhoun said.

"After all this time?" Van Slyke asked.

"Why not?" Calhoun said. "Wouldn't you like to find out who killed him?"

"What would I do if I found out?" Van Slyke said. "Kill the bastard?" Van Slyke laughed until he began coughing again.

"You don't smoke much, do you?" Calhoun asked.

Van Slyke shook his head after he'd finally controlled his coughing. His face had become red. He headed over to a nearby sink to take a drink of water. When he came back, his mood had changed.

"I think I've had enough of this chat," he said with derision. "I've got a hell of a lot of work to do. I shouldn't even be monkeying around with these beds."

"I'll leave then," Calhoun said as he slipped off the stool. "It's a rule I have: I never stay around where I'm not wanted. But would you mind if I returned some other time?"

"I'll think about it," Van Slyke said.

After leaving engineering Calhoun made his way around to the front of the hospital and walked over to the Imaging Center. He handed one of his cards to the receptionist and asked to speak with Dr. Cantor.

"Do you have an appointment?" the receptionist asked.

"No," Calhoun said. "But listen, tell him that I'm here to talk about Dr. Hodges."

"Dr. Dennis Hodges?" the receptionist asked with surprise.

"None other," Calhoun said. "And I'll just take a seat here in the waiting area."

Calhoun watched as the receptionist phoned in to the interior of the organization. Calhoun was just beginning to appreciate the architecture and lavish interior decor when a matronly woman appeared and asked him to follow her.

"What do you mean, you want to discuss Dennis Hodges?" Cantor demanded the moment Calhoun stepped through Cantor's office door.

"Exactly that," Calhoun said.

"What the hell for?" Cantor asked.

"Mind if I sit down?" Calhoun said.

Cantor motioned toward one of the chairs facing his desk. Calhoun had to move a pile of unopened medical journals to the floor. Once he was seated he went through the usual routine of asking to smoke.

"As long as you give me one," Cantor said. "I've given up smoking except for whatever I can mooch."

Once they'd both lit up, Calhoun told Cantor that he'd been retained to discover Hodges' killer.

"I don't think I want to talk about that bastard," Cantor said.

"Can I ask why?" Calhoun said.

"Why should I?" Cantor asked.

"Obviously, to bring his murderer to justice," Calhoun said.

"I think justice has already been served," Cantor said. "Whoever rid us of that pest should be given a medal."

"I've been told you had a low opinion of the man," Calhoun said.

"That's an understatement," Cantor said. "He was despicable."

"Could you elaborate?" Calhoun asked.

"He didn't care about other people," Cantor said.

"Do you mean people in general, or other doctors?" Calhoun asked.

"Mostly doctors, I guess," Cantor said. "He just didn't care. He had one priority and that was this hospital. But his concept of the institution didn't extend to the physicians who staff it. He took over radiology and pathology and put a bunch of us out to pasture. All of us wanted to throttle him."

"Could you give me names?" Calhoun asked.

"Sure, it's no secret," Cantor said. He then counted off on his fingers five doctors, including himself.

"And you are the only one of this group who's still around."

"I'm the only one still in radiology," Cantor said. "Thank God for my having the foresight to set up this imaging center. Paul Darnell's still here too. He's in pathology."

"Do you know who killed Hodges?" Calhoun said.

Cantor started to speak, but then stopped himself. "You know something," he said, "I just realized that I've been spouting off despite having prefaced this conversation by saying I didn't want to talk about Hodges."

"Same thing occurred to me," Calhoun said. "Guess you changed your mind. So how about it; do you know who killed Hodges?"

"If I knew I wouldn't tell you," Cantor said.

Calhoun suddenly drew out his pocket watch which was attached by a short chain to one of his belt loops. "My word," he said. He stood up. "I'm sorry, but I have to break off this chat. I didn't realize the time. I'm afraid I have another appointment."

Stubbing out his cigar on an ashtray in front of the surprised Cantor, Calhoun rushed from the room. He went immediately to his truck, then drove down to the library. He caught up to Angela as she was strolling along the sidewalk leading to the entrance.

"I'm sorry to be late," Calhoun said after he reached across and opened the passenger door for her. "I was having so much fun talking with Dr. Cantor I didn't realize the time."

"I was a few minutes late myself," Angela said. She climbed into the cab. It smelled of stale cigar smoke.

"I'm curious about Dr. Cantor," she said. "Did he say anything enlightening?"

"He's not the one who killed Hodges," Calhoun said. "But he interested me. Same with Beaton. There's something going on here, I can feel it."

Calhoun cracked the driver's side window. "Mind if I smoke?"

"I assumed that was the reason we were taking your truck," Angela said.

"Just thought I'd ask," Calhoun said.

"Are you sure this visit to the state police is going to go all right?" Angela asked. "The more I've thought about it, the more nervous it makes me. After all, I'll be misrepresenting myself to a degree. I mean, I work at the hospital, but I don't really need the papers to take care of patients. I'm a pathologist."

"No need to worry," Calhoun said. "You might not even have to say anything. I already explained the whole deal to the lieutenant. He didn't have a problem."

"I'm trusting you," Angela said.

"You won't be disappointed," Calhoun said. "But I have a question for you. Your husband's reaction last night is still bothering me. I don't want to cause any trouble between you and your husband. The problem is I'm having more fun on this case than on any since leaving the force. What if I lower my hourly rate. Will that help?"

"Thank you for your concern," Angela said, "but I'm sure David will be fine provided we stick to the one-week time frame."

Despite Calhoun's reassurances, Angela still felt nervous as she climbed out of the truck at state police headquarters in Burlington, but her concern was unnecessary. Calhoun's presence made the operation go far more smoothly than Angela could have hoped. Calhoun did all the talking. The policeman in charge of the evidence could not have been nicer or more accommodating.

"While you're at it," Calhoun said to the officer, "how about making two sets of copies."

"No problem," the officer said. He handled the originals with gloved hands.

Calhoun winked at Angela and whispered: "This way we'll both have a set."

Ten minutes later, Angela and Calhoun were back in the truck.

"That was a breeze," Angela said with relief. She slid the copies out of the envelope the officer had placed them in and began looking through them.

"I never say 'I told you so,'" Calhoun said with a smile. "I'd never say that. Nope. I'm not that kind of person."

Angela laughed. She'd come to enjoy Calhoun's humor.

"What are they?" Calhoun asked, looking over Angela's shoulder.

"They're copies of the admissions sheets on eight patients," Angela said.

"Anything unique about them?" Calhoun asked.

"Not that I can tell," Angela said with some disappointment. "There doesn't seem to be any common element. Different ages, different sexes, and different diagnoses. There's a fractured hip, pneumonia, sinusitis, chest pain, right lower quadrant abdominal pain, phlebitis, stroke, and kidney stone. I don't know what I expected, but this looks pretty ordinary."

Calhoun started the truck and pulled out into the traffic. "Don't make any snap decisions," he advised.

Angela slid the papers back into their envelope and gazed out at the surroundings. Almost immediately she recognized where they were.

"Wait a second," she said. "Stop a moment."

Calhoun pulled over to the side of the road.

"We're very close to the office of the chief medical examiner," Angela said. "What do you say we stop in? He did the autopsy on Hodges and a visit might generate a bit more interest on his part."

"Fine with me," Calhoun said. "I'd like to meet the man."

They did a U-turn in the middle of a busy street. The maneuver scared Angela, and she closed her eyes to the oncoming traffic. Calhoun told her to relax. A few minutes later they were in the medical examiner's building. They met Walter Dunsmore in a lunchroom. Angela introduced Calhoun.

"How about something to eat?" Walter suggested.

Both Angela and Calhoun got sandwiches out of a vending machine and joined Walt.

"Mr. Calhoun is helping investigate the Hodges murder," Angela explained. "We came up to Burlington to get copies of some evidence. While we were here I thought I'd stop in to see if there have been any new developments."

"No, I don't think so," Walt said as he tried to think. "Toxicology came back and was negative except for the alcohol level which I told you about. That's about it. As I said, nobody's making this case much of a priority."

"I understand," Angela said. "Anything more on that carbon under the skin?"

"Haven't had a chance to even think about it again," Walt admitted.

After they wolfed down their sandwiches Angela said she had to get back to Bartlet; she told Walt she was on her lunch hour. Walt encouraged her to come back any time.

The drive back to Bartlet seemed even faster than the drive to Burlington. Calhoun dropped Angela off behind the library so she could get her own car.

"I'll be in touch," Calhoun said. "And remember, stay out of it."

"Don't worry," Angela said. She waved as she got in behind the wheel. It was almost one-thirty.

Back in her office, Angela put the copies of Hodges' papers in the top drawer of her desk. She wanted to remember to take them home that evening. While she was donning her white lab coat Wadley opened the connecting door without bothering to knock.

"I've been looking for you for almost twenty minutes," he said irritably.

"I was out of the hospital," Angela said.

"That much was obvious," Wadley said. "I had you paged several times."

"I'm sorry," Angela said. "I used my lunch hour to run an errand."

"You've been gone longer than an hour," Wadley said.

"That might be," Angela said, "but I plan to stay later than scheduled, which I normally do anyway. Plus, I spoke to Dr. Darnell to cover in case there were any emergencies."

"I don't like my pathologists disappearing in the middle of the day," Wadley said.

"I was not gone long," Angela said. "I'm fully aware of my responsibilities and carry them out to the letter. I was not responsible for surgical specimens which would have been the only true emergency. Besides, my errand involved a visit to the chief medical examiner."

"You saw Walt Dunsmore?" Wadley asked.

"You can call him if you doubt me," Angela said. She could tell that Wadley was partially mollified. She was suddenly glad she'd made the spur-of-the-moment visit.

"I'm too busy to be checking on your whereabouts," Wadley said. "The point is that I'm concerned about your behavior of late. I should remind you that you are still on probationary status. I can assure you that you will be terminated if you prove to be unreliable."

With that, Wadley stepped back through the connecting door and slammed it shut.

For a moment Angela stared at the door. She detested this open hostility with Wadley. Still, she preferred it to the previous sexual harassment. She wondered if they would ever be able to develop a normal professional relationship.

After the last office patient had been seen, David reluctantly headed over to the hospital to make his afternoon rounds. He was beginning to dread the experience for fear of what he might face.

Before seeing his own patients David went to the ICU to check on Caroline. The child was doing poorly and was clearly moribund. David found Dr. Pilsner sitting at the ICU desk in a hopeless vigil. The man was despondent. David could relate all too well.

Leaving the ICU, David started seeing his own patients. Each time he went into another room he felt anxious, only to be relieved when he discovered the patient was doing well. But when he went into Sandra's room the anxiety remained. Sandra's mental status had deteriorated.

David was appalled. The change was dramatic to him even though the nurses weren't impressed. When David had visited her early that morning she'd been bright and aware. Now she was apathetic to her surroundings and was drooling. Her eyes had lost their luster. Her temperature, which had fallen, had now crept back up over one hundred degrees.

When David tried to talk to her, she was vague. The only specific complaint he could elicit was abdominal cramps, a symptom that reminded him of other patients he'd been trying to forget. David felt his pulse quicken. He didn't think he could tolerate losing another patient.

Back at the nurses' station, David pored over Sandra's chart. The only new fact was that she'd apparently lost her appetite as evidenced by an entry in the nurses' notes that recorded she'd not eaten her lunch. David checked all the IV fluids she'd had; they were all appropriate. Then he went over all the laboratory tests; they were all normal. He was desperate for some clue to explain the change in her mental status, but there were no clues in the chart. The only idea that came to his mind was the possibility of early meningitis, or inflammation of the coverings of her brain. It was the fear of her developing meningitis that had moved him to admit her in the first place.

David re-examined her, and although he could not elicit any signs of meningitis, he went ahead with the definitive test. He did a lumbar puncture to obtain cerebrospinal fluid. He knew immediately the fluid was normal because of its clarity, but he sent it to the lab for a stat reading to be certain. The result was normal. So was a stat blood sugar.

The only thing Sandra wasn't apathetic about was pain when David palpated her abscess. Consequently, David added another antibiotic to her regimen. Beyond that he had no ideas. He felt lost. All he could do was hope.

Climbing on his bike, David cycled home. He knew he was depressed. He got no enjoyment from the ride. He felt heartsick about Caroline and concerned about Sandra. But as soon as he arrived he realized he could not wallow in self-pity. Nikki was slightly worse than she'd been at lunchtime when he'd brought home her oral antibiotic. Her congestion had increased and her temperature had reached one hundred degrees.

David phoned the ICU and got Dr. Pilsner on the line. David apologized for disturbing him but felt obliged to let him know the oral antibiotic wasn't helping.

"Let's up it," Dr. Pilsner said in a tired voice. "And I think we'd better use a mucolytic agent and a bronchodilator with her respiratory therapy."

"Any change with Caroline?" David asked.

"No change," Dr. Pilsner answered.

Angela didn't get home until almost seven o'clock. After she checked on Nikki, who was doing better after a respiratory therapy session with David, she went to take a shower.

David followed her into the bathroom.

"Caroline is no better," David said as Angela stepped into the shower.

"I feel great compassion for the Helmsfords," Angela said. "They must be heartsick. I hope to heaven that Nikki doesn't come down with whatever Caroline got."

"I've got another patient—Sandra Hascher—who is scaring me the same way the others did."

Angela poked her head out of the shower. "What was her admitting diagnosis?"

"Abscessed tooth," David said. "It had responded nicely to antibiotics. Then this afternoon she suddenly had a mental status change."

"Disoriented?"

"Mostly just apathetic and vague," David said. "I know it doesn't sound like much, but to me it was dramatic."

"Meningitis?" Angela asked.

"That was the only thing I thought of," David said. "She hasn't had any headache or spiking fever. But I did a lumbar puncture just to be sure, and it was normal."

"What about a brain abscess?" Angela asked.

"Again, she's had little fever," David said. "But maybe I'll do an MRI tomorrow if she's not better. The problem is, she's reminding me of the other patients who died."

"I suppose you don't want to ask for any consults."

"Not unless I want to have her transferred to someone else," David said. "I might even get into trouble ordering the MRI."

"It's a lousy way to practice medicine," Angela said.

David didn't answer.

"The trip to Burlington went smoothly," Angela said.

"I'm glad," David replied without interest.

"The only trouble I had was when I got back. Wadley's being unreasonable. He even threatened to terminate me."

"No!" David said. He was aghast. "That would be a disaster."

"Don't worry," Angela said. "He's just blowing off steam. There's no way he could terminate me so soon after I complained about his sexual harassment. For that reason alone I'm glad I went to Cantor. The conversation officially established my complaint."

"That's not a lot of reassurance," David said. "I'd never even thought of the possibility of your being fired."

Later, when dinner was served, Nikki reported she wasn't hungry. Angela made her come to the table anyway, saying she could eat what she wanted. But during the dinner, Angela urged Nikki to eat more. David told Angela not to force her. Soon David and Angela exchanged words over the issue, causing Nikki to flee the table in tears.

David and Angela fumed, each blaming the other. For a while they didn't talk, preferring to turn on the TV and watch the news in silence. When it was time for Nikki to go to bed, Angela told David that she would see to Nikki's respiratory therapy while he cleaned up the kitchen.

David hardly had time to carry the soiled dishes into the kitchen when Angela returned.

"Nikki asked me a question I didn't know how to answer," Angela said. "She asked me if Caroline was coming home soon."

"What did you say?" David asked.

"I said I didn't know," Angela admitted. "With Nikki feeling as poorly as she is, I hate to tell her."

"Don't look at me," David said. "I don't want to tell her either. Let's wait until this bout of congestion is over."

"All right," Angela said. "I'll see what I can do." She left the kitchen and returned upstairs.

Around nine David called the hospital. He spoke at length with the head nurse who kept insisting that Sandra's condition had not changed, at least not dramatically. She did admit, however, that she'd not eaten her dinner.

After David had hung up the phone, Angela appeared from the kitchen.

"Would you like to look at the papers we got from Burlington today?" she asked.

"I'm not interested," David said.

"Thanks," Angela said. "You know this is important to me."

"I'm too preoccupied to worry about that stuff," David said.

"I have the time and energy to listen to your problems," Angela said. "You could at least extend the same courtesy to me."

"I hardly think the two issues are comparable," David said.

"How can you say that? You know how upset I am about this whole Hodges thing."

"I don't want to encourage you," David said. "I think I've been very clear about that."

"Oh, you're clear all right. What's important to you is important; what's important to me isn't."

"With everything else that's going on, I find it amazing that you are still fixated on Hodges. I think you have your priorities mixed up. While you're chasing off to Burlington, I'm here bringing antibiotics to our daughter while her friend is dying in the hospital."

"I can't believe you're saying this," Angela sputtered.

"And on top of it, you make light of Wadley threatening to fire you," David said. "All because it was so important to go to Burlington. I can tell you this: if you get fired it will be an unmitigated economic disaster. And that doesn't even account for the jeopardy you're putting us all in by pursuing this investigation."

"You think you are so rational," Angela yelled. "Well, you're fooling yourself. You think that problems are solved by denying them. I think you have your priorities mixed up by not supporting me when I need it most. And as for Nikki, maybe she wouldn't be sick if you hadn't allowed her to visit Caroline before we knew what the poor girl had."

"That's not fair," David yelled back. Then he restrained himself. He did think of himself as rational, and he prided himself on not losing his temper.

The problem was, the more controlled David became, the more emotional Angela got, and the more emotional Angela became, the more controlled David got. By eleven o'clock they were both exhausted and overwrought. By mutual agreement David slept in the guest room.

21

AT FIRST DAVID HAD NO IDEA WHERE HE WAS WHEN he opened his eyes in the dark. Fumbling with the unfamiliar bedside lamp, he finally managed to turn it on. He looked around in a daze at the unfamiliar furniture. It took him almost a minute to realize he was in the guest room. As soon as he did, the previous night's unpleasantness came back in a flash.

David picked up his wristwatch. It was quarter to five in the morning. He lay back on the pillow and shuddered through a wave of nausea. On the heels of the nausea came cramps followed by a bout of diarrhea.

Feeling horrid, David limped from the guest bath to the master bath in search of some over-the-counter diarrhea medication. When he finally found a bottle, he took a healthy dose. Then he searched for a thermometer and stuck it in his mouth.

While waiting for an accurate reading to register, David searched for aspirin. As he was doing so, he realized that he had to keep swallowing, just as some of his now dead patients had.

David stared at his reflection in the mirror as a new fear made itself known to him. What if he had caught the mysterious illness that had been killing his patients? My God, he thought, they had the same symptoms I'm manifesting now. With trembling fingers he took out the thermometer. It read one hundred degrees. He stuck out his tongue and examined it in the mirror. It was as pale as his face.

"Calm down!" he ordered himself harshly. He took two aspirins and washed them down with a glass of water. Almost immediately he got another cramp and had to hold onto the countertop until it had passed.

In a deliberately calm manner, he considered his symptoms. They were flu-like, similar to those of the five nurses he'd seen. There was no reason to jump to hysterical conclusions.

Having taken the diarrhea medication and the aspirin, David decided to take the same advice he'd given those nurses: he went back to bed. By the time the alarm in the master bedroom sounded, he was already feeling better.

He and Angela first eyed each other warily. Then they fell into each other's arms. They hugged each other for a full minute before David spoke.

"Truce?" he asked.

Angela nodded her agreement. "We're both stressed out."

"On top of that, I think I'm coming down with something," David said. He told her about the flu symptoms which had awakened him. "The only thing that's still bothering me is excessive salivation," he added.

"What do you mean by excessive salivation?" Angela asked.

"I have to keep swallowing," David said. "It's something like the feeling you get before vomiting, but not as bad. Anyway, it's better than it was."

"Have you seen Nikki?" Angela asked.

"Not yet," David said.

After they had washed they went down to Nikki's room. Rusty greeted them eagerly. Nikki was less enthusiastic.

She was a little more congested despite the oral antibiotics and the added effort at respiratory therapy.

While Angela made breakfast, David called Dr. Pilsner and told him about Nikki's status.

"I think I should see her right away," Dr. Pilsner said. "Why don't I meet you in the emergency room in half an hour?"

"We'll be there," David said. "And thank you. I appreciate your concern." He was about to hang up when he thought to inquire about Caroline.

"She died," Dr. Pilsner said. "The end came around three this morning. Her blood pressure could no longer be maintained. At least she didn't suffer, though that's not much consolation."

The news, though expected, hit David hard. With a heavy heart, he went into the kitchen and told Angela the news.

Angela looked as though she might burst into tears, but instead she lashed out. "I can't believe you let Nikki go in and visit her like you did," she said.

Stunned at the sharp rebuke, David came back. "At least I came home at lunch yesterday to be sure Nikki got her antibiotic." That said, he did feel guilty for having let Nikki spend time with Caroline.

David and Angela eyed each other, struggling with their irritation and fear.

"I'm sorry," Angela said finally. "I forgot about our truce. I'm just so worried."

"Dr. Pilsner wants to see Nikki in the ER right away," David said. "I think we better go."

They bundled Nikki up and went out to the car. David and Angela meticulously refrained from saying anything to provoke the other. They knew the other's weaknesses and vulnerabilities too well. Nikki didn't say anything either; she coughed most of the way.

Dr. Pilsner was waiting for them and immediately took Nikki into one of the examining stalls. David and Angela stood to the side while Dr. Pilsner examined Nikki. When he was finished he drew them aside.

"I want her in the hospital immediately," he said.

"Do you think she has pneumonia?" David asked.

"I'm not sure," Dr. Pilsner said. "But it's possible. I don't want to take any chances after what happened . . ." He didn't finish his sentence.

"I'll stay here with Nikki," Angela said to David. "You go do your rounds."

"All right," David said. "Page me if there's any problem." David was still feeling poorly himself; this latest development with Nikki only made him feel worse. He kissed his daughter goodbye, promising that he'd be by to see her all through the day. Nikki nodded. She'd been through this routine before.

David got several aspirins from an ER nurse, then headed upstairs.

"How is Mrs. Hascher?" David asked Janet Colburn as soon as he saw her. He sat down at the desk and pulled his patients' charts.

"Nothing much said at report," Janet said. "I don't think any of us have been in there yet this morning. We've been concentrating on getting the seven-thirty surgical cases down to the operating room."

David opened Sandra's chart hesitantly. First he looked at the temperature chart. There had been no spikes of fever. The last temperature taken was just over one hundred. Turning to the nurses' notes he read that Sandra had been sleeping each time a nurse had gone into her room.

David breathed a sigh of relief. So far so good. When he was finished with the charts he began seeing the patients. All were doing well except for Sandra.

When David entered her room he found her still asleep. Moving to the bedside, he glanced at the swelling on her jaw. It appeared unchanged. He gave her shoulder a gentle shake, calling her name softly. When she didn't respond, he shook her more vigorously and said her name more loudly.

Finally she stirred, lifting a trembling hand to her face. She could barely open her eyes. David shook her yet again. Her eyes opened a bit wider and she tried to speak, but all that came out was disconnected jabber. She was clearly disoriented.

Trying to remain calm, David drew some blood and sent it off for some stat lab work. Then he devoted himself to a careful examination, concentrating particularly on Sandra's lungs and the nervous system.

When David returned to the nurses' station a short time later he was handed Sandra's stat laboratory values. They were all normal, including the blood count. The white cells, which had been elevated from her abscessed tooth, had fallen with the antibiotics and were still low, ruling out infection as an explanation for her current clinical state. That said, the sound of her lungs suggested incipient pneumonia. David wondered again about a possible failure of her immune response.

Once again David was presented with the same trio of symptoms affecting the central nervous system, the GI system, and the blood or immune system. He was seeing a complex, but he had no idea what the underlying factor could be.

David agonized over what to do next. The life of a thirty-four-year-old woman hung in the balance. He was afraid to call any consults, partly because of Kelley and partly because the consults had not provided any help in the three similar cases. And calling in consults for Eakins had resulted in David's removal from the case. David was even reluctant to order further diagnostic or laboratory tests since nothing had proved to be of any value with the other patients. He was at a loss.

"We have a seizure in room 216," one of the nurses shouted from down the hall. David went running. Room 216 was Sandra's room.

Sandra was in the throes of a full-blown grand mal seizure. Her body was arched back as her limbs contracted rhythmically with such force that the whole bed was bouncing off the floor. David barked orders for a tranquilizer. In an instant it was slapped into his hand. He injected it into Sandra's IV. Within minutes the convulsions stopped, leaving Sandra's body spent and comatose.

David stared down at his patient's now peaceful face. He felt as if he was being mocked for his intellectual impotence. While he had been indecisively sitting at the desk puzzling over what to do, the seizure had taken over Sandra's body in a dramatic gesture.

David erupted in a whirlwind of activity. Anger replaced despair as he pulled out all the diagnostic stops. Once again he ordered everything: consults, lab tests, X rays, even an MRI of the skull. He was determined to figure out what was happening to Sandra Hascher.

Fearing a rapid downhill course, David also made immediate arrangements to transfer Sandra to the ICU. He wanted continuous monitoring of her vital signs. He did not want any more surprises.

The transfer occurred within half an hour. David helped push Sandra down the hall to the ICU. Once she was moved off the gurney, David started for the ICU desk to write new orders, but he stopped short of his goal. In a bed directly across from the central desk was Nikki.

David was stunned. He'd never expected to see Nikki in the ICU. Her presence there terrified him. What could it mean?

David felt a hand on his shoulder. He turned to see Dr. Pilsner. "I can see you're upset about your daughter being in here," he said. "Calm down. I just don't want to take any chances. There are some fabulously skilled nurses in here who are accustomed to taking care of patients with respiratory problems."

"Are you sure it's necessary?" David asked nervously. He knew how tough the ICU environment was on a patient's psyche.

"It's for her benefit," Dr. Pilsner said. "It's purely pre-cautionary. I'll be moving her out of here just as soon as I can."

"Okay," David said. But he was still anxious about this latest turn of events.

Before writing the new orders on Sandra, David went over to talk with Nikki. She was far less concerned about the ICU than David was. David was relieved to see her taking it so well.

Returning his attention to Sandra Hascher, David sat down at the ICU desk and began writing her orders. He was nearly through when the unit clerk tapped his arm.

"There's a Mr. Kelley out in the patient lounge to see you," he said.

David felt his stomach tighten. He knew why Kelley was there, but he wasn't eager to see him and didn't go immediately. He finished writing the orders first and gave them to the head nurse. Only then did he go out to meet Kelley.

"I'm disappointed," Kelley said as David approached. "The utilization coordinator called me a few minutes ago . . ."

"Just a minute!" David snapped, cutting off Kelley. "I've got a sick patient in the ICU and I don't have time to waste with you. So for now stay out of my way. I'll talk to you later. Understand?"

For a second David glared up into Kelley's face. Then he spun around and started out of the room.

"Just a minute, Dr. Wilson," Kelley called. "Not so fast."

David whirled around and stormed back. Without warning he reached out and grabbed Kelley by the tie and the front of his shirt and roughly pushed him back. Kelley collapsed into the club chair behind him. David shook a clenched fist in Kelley's face.

"I want you to get the hell out of here," David snarled. "If you don't, I don't take responsibility for the consequences. It's as simple as that."

Kelley swallowed, but he didn't move.

David spun on his heels and marched out of the lounge. Just as he was about out the door, Kelley called out to him, "I'll be talking with my superiors."

David turned back. "You do that," he said. Then he continued into the ICU. Returning to the desk, he paused. His heart was pounding. He wondered what he really would have done if Kelley had stood up to him.

"Dr. Wilson," the unit clerk called out. "I have Dr. Mieslich on the phone. He's returning your call."

"My husband teaches at the college," Madeline Gannon explained. "He gives courses in drama and literature."

Calhoun had been eyeing the many shelves of books that lined the Gannons' library walls.

"I'd like to meet him sometime," Calhoun said. "I read a lot of plays. It's been my hobby since retiring. Especially Shakespeare."

"What is it you wanted to talk to me about?" Madeline asked, diplomatically changing the subject. From Calhoun's appearance she doubted if Bernard would be terribly interested.

"I'm investigating Dr. Dennis Hodges' murder," Calhoun said. "As you know his body was recently found."

"That was distressing," Madeline said.

"I understand you worked for him for some time," Calhoun said.

"Over thirty years," Madeline said.

"Pleasant work?" Calhoun asked.

"It had its ups and downs," Madeline admitted. "He was a headstrong man who could be stubborn and cranky one minute and understanding and generous the next. I loved him and disliked him at the same time. But I was devastated by the news when they found his body. I'd secretly hoped he'd just had enough of everybody, and had gone to Florida. He used to talk about going to Florida every winter, particularly the last few."

"Do you know who killed him?" Calhoun asked. He glanced around for an ashtray but didn't see one.

"I haven't the slightest idea," Madeline said. "But with Dr. Hodges, there sure are a lot of candidates."

"Like who?" Calhoun asked.

"Well, let me take that back," Madeline said. "To be perfectly honest, I don't think that a single one of the people Dr. Hodges regularly infuriated would have actually done the man harm. In the same way Dr. Hodges would never had carried out any of the threats he voiced so frequently."

"Who did he threaten?" Calhoun asked.

Madeline laughed. "Just about everybody associated with the new administration at the hospital," she said. "Also the police chief, the head of the local bank, the Mobil station owner. The list goes on and on."

"Why was Hodges so angry with the new administration at the hospital?" Calhoun asked.

"Mostly on behalf of his patients," Madeline said. "Rather, his former patients. Dr. Hodges' practice fell off when he took over the directorship of the hospital, and then again when CMV came into the picture. He wasn't all that upset about it because he knew the hospital needed the HMO's business and he was ready to slow down. But then his former patients started coming back to him, complaining about their health care under CMV. They wanted him to be their doctor again, but it wasn't possible because their health care had to come through CMV."

"Sounds like Hodges should have been angry at CMV," Calhoun said. Before Madeline could respond, Calhoun asked if he could smoke. Madeline said no but offered to make him coffee. Calhoun accepted her offer, so they adjourned to the kitchen.

"Where was I?" Madeline asked while she put water on the stove to boil.

"I was suggesting Hodges should have been angry with CMV," Calhoun said.

"I remember," Madeline said. "He was angry with CMV, but he was also angry with the hospital because the hospital was agreeing to everything CMV proposed. And Dr. Hodges felt he carried some weight at the hospital."

"Was he angry about anything specific?" Calhoun asked.

"It was a bunch of things," Madeline said. "He was angry about the treatment, or the lack of it, in the emergency room. People couldn't go to the emergency room any more unless they paid cash up front. Other people couldn't get into the hospital when they thought they needed to. The day he disappeared he was really upset by the death of one of his former patients. In fact, several of his former patients had recently died. I remember it specifically because Dr. Hodges used to yell and scream that CMV physicians couldn't keep his patients alive. He felt they were incompetent and that the hospital was abetting their incompetence."

"Can you remember the name of the patient Hodges was upset about the day he disappeared?" Calhoun asked.

"Now you're expecting miracles," Madeline said as she poured the coffee. She handed a cup to Calhoun who helped himself to three heaping teaspoons of sugar and a dollop of cream.

"Wait a minute! I do remember," Madeline said suddenly. "It was Clark Davenport. No doubt in my mind."

Calhoun fished out his set of the copies he and Angela had obtained in Burlington. "Here it is," he said after leafing through. "Clark Davenport, fractured hip."

"Yup, he's the one," Madeline said. "The poor man fell off a ladder trying to get a kitten out of a tree."

"Look at these other names," Calhoun said. He handed the papers to Madeline. "Any of them mean anything to you?"

Madeline took the papers and shuffled through them. "I can remember each and every one," she said. "In fact, these are the patients I mentioned: the ones Dr. Hodges was irritated about. They had all died."

"Hmmm," Calhoun said as he took the papers back. "I knew they had to be related somehow."

"Dr. Hodges was also upset at the hospital people because of the attacks in the parking lot," Madeline added.

"Why was that?" Calhoun asked.

"He felt the hospital administration should have been doing a lot more than they were," Madeline said. "They were more concerned about keeping the incidents out of the news than they were about catching the rapist. Dr. Hodges was convinced that the rapist was part of the hospital community."

"Did he have anybody specific in mind?"

"He indicated that he did," Madeline said. "But he didn't tell me who."

"Do you think he might have told his wife?" Calhoun asked.

"It's possible," Madeline said.

"Do you think he ever said anything to the person he suspected?" Calhoun asked.

"I haven't the slightest idea," Madeline said. "But I do know that he planned to discuss the problem with Wayne Robertson even though he and Wayne did not get along. In fact, he'd planned to go see Robertson the day he disappeared."

"Did he go?" Calhoun asked.

"No," Madeline said. "That same day Dr. Hodges learned that Clark Davenport had died. Instead of seeing Robertson, Dr. Hodges had me make a lunch date for him with Dr. Barry Holster, the radiotherapist. The reason I remembered Clark Davenport's name was because I remember making the lunch arrangements."

"Why was Hodges so eager to see Dr. Holster?" Calhoun asked.

"Dr. Holster had recently finished treating Clark Davenport," Madeline said.

Calhoun put down his coffee cup and stood up. "You've been wonderfully cooperative and most gracious," he said. "I'm appreciative of both your coffee and your excellent memory."

Madeline Gannon blushed.

Angela had finished her work and was leafing through a laboratory journal just prior to her lunch break when the chief medical examiner called.

"I'm glad I caught you," Walt said.

"Why?" Angela asked.

"Something extraordinary has happened," Walt said. "And you are responsible."

"Tell me," Angela said.

"It's all because of your surprise visit yesterday," Walt said. "Would you be able to jump in your car and come up here?"

"When?"

"Right now," Walt said.

Angela was intrigued. "Can you give me an idea of what this is about?" she asked.

"I'd rather show you," he said. "It's really unique. I'll have to write this up or at least present it at the annual forensic dinner. I want you to be in on it right away. Consider it part of your education."

"I'd love to come," Angela said. "But I'm worried about Dr. Wadley. We've not been on the best of terms."

"Oh, forget Wadley," Walt said. "I'll give him a call. This is important."

"You're making it hard to refuse," Angela said.

"That's the whole idea," Walt said.

Angela grabbed her coat. On her way out she glanced into Wadley's office. He wasn't there. She asked the secretaries where he was. They told her that he'd gone to the Iron Horse Inn for lunch and wouldn't be back until two.

She asked Paul Darnell to cover for her again in case there was any type of emergency. She told him that she'd gotten a specific request from the chief medical examiner to come to see something extraordinary.

Before she left for Burlington, Angela dashed up to the ICU to check on Nikki. She was pleased to discover that her daughter was doing much better and was in fine spirits.

Angela made it to the chief medical examiner's office in record time. "Wow!" Walt said when she appeared at his office door. He glanced at his watch as he stood to greet her. "That was fast. What kind of a sports car do you drive?"

"I have to admit your call whetted my curiosity. I was eager to get here," Angela said. "And to tell you the truth, I haven't much time."

"We won't need much time," Walt said. He led her to a microscope set up on a workbench. "First, I want you to look at this," he said.

Angela adjusted the eyepieces and looked in. She saw a specimen of skin. Then she saw black dots in the dermis.

"Do you know what that is?" Walt asked.

"I think so," Angela said. "This must be the skin from under Hodges' nails."

"Precisely," Walt said. "See the carbon?"

"I do," Angela said.

"All right. Take a look at this."

Angela lifted her eyes from the microscope and accepted a photograph from Walt.

"This is a photomicrograph I obtained with a scanning electron microscope," Walt explained. "Notice that the dots don't look like carbon any longer."

Angela studied the photo. What Walt was saying was true.

"Now look at this," Walt said. He handed her a printout. "This is the output of an atomic spectrophotometer. What I did was elute the granules with an acid solvent and then analyze them. They aren't carbon."

"What are they?" Angela asked.

"They're a mixture of chromium, cobalt, cadmium, and mercury," Walt said triumphantly.

"That's wonderful, Walt," Angela said. She was completely baffled. "But what does it mean?"

"I was just as perplexed as you," Walt said. "I had no idea what it meant. I even started to think that the atomic spectrophotometer had gone on the fritz until I suddenly had an epiphany. It's part of a tattoo!"

"Are you sure?" Angela questioned.

"Absolutely," Walt said. "These pigments are used for tattooing."

Angela immediately shared Walt's excitement. With the power of forensics they'd made a discovery about the killer. He had a tattoo. She couldn't wait to tell David and Calhoun.

Returning to Bartlet, Angela ran into Paul Darnell. He'd been waiting for her.

"I got some bad news," Darnell said. "Wadley knows you left town and he's not happy about it."

"How could he know?" Angela asked. Darnell was the only person she'd told.

"I think he was spying on you," Darnell said. "That's the only explanation I can think of. He came in to see me fifteen minutes after you left."

"I thought he'd gone out for lunch," Angela said.

"That's what he told everybody," Darnell said. "Obviously he hadn't. He asked me directly if you had left Bartlet. I couldn't lie. I had to tell him."

"Did you tell him I went to see the chief medical examiner?" Angela asked.

"Yes," Darnell said.

"Then it should be fine," Angela said. "Thanks for letting me know."

"Good luck," Darnell said.

No sooner had Angela returned to her office than a secretary appeared to let her know that Dr. Wadley wanted to see her in his office. That was an ominous turn of events. Wadley had never used an intermediary before.

Angela found Wadley sitting at his desk. He stared at her with cold eyes.

"I was told you wanted to see me," she said.

"I did indeed," Wadley said. "I wanted to inform you that you are fired. I would appreciate it if you would pack up your belongings and leave. Your continued presence is bad for morale."

"I find this hard to believe," Angela said.

"Nonetheless, it is so," Wadley said coldly.

"If you're upset because I was gone at my lunch hour, you should know that I drove to Burlington to visit the chief medical examiner," Angela said. "He'd called to ask me to come as soon as I could."

"Dr. Walter Dunsmore does not run this department," Wadley said. "I do."

"Didn't he call you?" Angela asked. She felt desperate. "He told me he would call you. He was excited about something he'd discovered concerning the body found in my home." Angela quickly related the details, but Wadley was unmoved.

"I've only been gone for a little over an hour," Angela said.

"I'm not interested in excuses," Wadley said. "I warned you just yesterday about this very same thing. You chose to ignore my warnings. You've demonstrated yourself to be unreliable, disobedient, and ungrateful."

"Ungrateful!" Angela exploded. "Ungrateful for what? For your sniveling advances? For not wanting to rush off to Miami for a weekend of sun and fun with you? You can fire me, Dr. Wadley, but I'll tell you what I can do: I can sue you and the hospital for sexual harassment."

"You just try it, young lady," Wadley snapped. "You'll be laughed out of the courtroom."

Angela stormed out of Wadley's office. She was beside herself with rage. As she passed through the outer office, the secretaries quickly scattered in her wake.

Angela went to her office and gathered up her belongings. There wasn't much. All the equipment belonged to the hospital. Packing her things into a canvas tote bag, she walked out. She didn't talk to anyone for fear of losing her composure. She didn't want to give Wadley the satisfaction of making her cry.

She intended to go directly to David's office, but then she changed her mind. After her recent argument with David, she was afraid of his reaction to her losing her job. She didn't think she could handle a confrontation in the hospital. So instead she went directly to her car and drove aimlessly toward town.

Just as she was passing the library she put on the brakes and backed up. She'd spotted Calhoun's inimitable truck in the parking lot.

Angela parked her car. She wondered where Calhoun might be. She decided to check the library, recalling that Calhoun had mentioned he knew the librarian.

Angela found Calhoun reading in a quiet alcove overlooking the town green.

"Mr. Calhoun?" Angela whispered.

Calhoun looked up. "How convenient," he said with a smile. "I've got some news."

"I'm afraid I've got some news as well," Angela said. "How about meeting me up at the house."

"I'll look forward to it," Calhoun said.

As soon as Angela got home she put some water on to boil. While she was getting out cups and saucers, Calhoun's truck came up the drive. Angela called out that the door was unlocked when he knocked.

"Coffee or tea?" Angela asked when Calhoun came into the kitchen.

"Whatever you're having," Calhoun said.

Angela got out the teapot and busied herself getting the tea and the honey.

"You're off kinda early," Calhoun said.

Having reined in her emotions ever since she'd fled Wadley's office, Angela's response to Calhoun's innocent comment was overwhelming. She covered her face and sobbed. At a loss for what he had said or what to do, Calhoun stood helpless.

When Angela's tears reduced to intermittent choking sobs, Calhoun apologized. "I'm sorry," he said. "I don't know what I did, but I'm sorry."

Angela stepped over to him and put her arms around him and her head on his woolly shoulder. He hugged her back. When she'd finally stopped crying he told her that she better tell him what happened.

"I think I'll have some wine instead of tea," Angela said.

"I'll have a beer," Calhoun said.

Sitting at the kitchen table Angela told Calhoun about getting fired. She explained how dire the consequences could be for her family.

Calhoun turned out to be a good listener, and he had the intuitive sense of what to say. He made Angela feel better. They even discussed her concerns about Nikki.

When Angela had talked herself out, Calhoun told her that he'd made some progress in the investigation.

"Maybe you're not interested anymore," Calhoun said.

"I'm still interested," Angela assured him. She dried her eyes with a dish towel. "Tell me."

"First of all, I discovered how the eight patients whose admission summaries Hodges was carrying around are related," he said. "All of them were former patients of Hodges' who had been shifted to CMV and had subsequently died in the months preceding Hodges' murder. Apparently each death came as a surprise for Hodges. That's why he was so furious."

"Did he blame the hospital or CMV?" Angela asked.

"Good question," Calhoun said. "As far as I could find out from his secretary he blamed both, but his main beef was with the hospital. It makes sense: he still thought of the hospital as his baby. So he was more disappointed with its perceived faults."

"Does this help us find out who killed him?" Angela asked.

"Probably not," Calhoun admitted. "But it's another piece to the puzzle. I also discovered another one: Hodges believed he knew the identity of the parking lot rapist. What's more, he thought the perp was connected to the hospital."

"I see where you are going," Angela said. "If the rapist knew Hodges suspected him, then he might have killed

Hodges. In other words, the rapist and Hodges' murderer could be the same person."

"Exactly," Calhoun said. "The same person who tried to kill you the other night."

Angela shuddered. "Don't remind me," she said. Then she added: "I learned something specific about this person today, something that could make finding him a bit easier: he has a tattoo."

"How do you know that?" Calhoun asked.

Angela explained why she had gone to Burlington. She told Calhoun that Walter Dunsmore was absolutely convinced that Hodges had scraped off part of his killer's tattoo.

"Hell's bells," Calhoun said. "I love it."

When yet another nurse from the second floor called and asked to be seen for the flu, David was eager to see her. When she arrived, she was surprised that she didn't have to describe her symptoms; David described them for her. They were the same as his, only more pronounced. Her gastrointestinal problems had not responded well to the usual medications. Her temperature was one hundred and one.

"Have you had increased salivation?" David asked.

"I have," the nurse said, "and I've never had anything like it before."

"Nor have I," David said.

Seeing how uncomfortable this nurse was, David was thankful his own symptoms had waned during the day. He sent the nurse home for bed rest and told her to drink plenty of fluids and take whatever antipyretic medication she preferred.

After the last office patient had been seen, David started off to the hospital to see his patients. He'd been back and forth all day, checking on both Nikki and Sandra, so he expected no surprises.

When he entered the ICU, Nikki saw him immediately and beamed. She was doing remarkably well. She'd responded to the IV antibiotics and ministrations of the respiratory therapist. She hadn't even minded the hustle and bustle of the ICU. Still David was happy to learn that she was scheduled to be transferred out of the unit the following morning.

Sandra's condition was just the opposite, following a relentless downhill course. She'd never awakened from her coma. The consults had been no help. Hasselbaum said she didn't have an infectious disease. The oncologist merely shrugged and said there was nothing he could do. He insisted she'd had a good result from the treatment of her melanoma. It had been six years since the primary lesion on her thigh had been diagnosed, then removed along with a few malignant lymph nodes.

David sat at the desk in the ICU and leafed through Sandra's chart. The MRI of her skull had been normal: no tumor and certainly no brain abscess. David looked at the laboratory tests he'd ordered. Some were not back yet and wouldn't be for days. He'd ordered all body fluids to be cultured despite the infectious disease consult's findings. David had also ordered sophisticated searches of these same body fluids for viral remnants using state-of-the-art biotechnological techniques.

David had no idea what to do. The only possible alternative was to try to get Sandra transferred to one of the big teaching hospitals in Boston. But he knew CMV would take a dim view of such a proposition because of the expense, and David could not do it on his own.

While David was agonizing over Sandra, Charles Kelley came into the unit and approached the desk. His visit took David by surprise; the medical bureaucrats usually stayed clear of places like the ICU where they'd be forced to confront the critically ill. They much preferred to sit in their tidy offices and think of patients as abstractions.

"I hope I'm not disturbing you," Kelley said. His slick smile had returned.

"Lately you've disturbed me every time I've seen you," David said.

"Sorry," Kelley said condescendingly. "But I have a bit of news. As of this moment, your services here are no longer needed."

"So you think you can take Sandra Hascher away from me?" he said.

"Oh, yes," Kelley said with satisfaction. His smile broadened. "And all the other patients as well. You are fired. You're no longer employed by CMV."

David's mouth fell open. He was aghast. With bewilderment he watched as Kelley gave him a wave as if he were waving to a child, then turned around and left the unit. David leaped up from his chair and stumbled after Kelley.

"What about all the patients I'm scheduled to see?" David called out.

Kelley was already on his way down the hall. "They're CMV's concern, not yours," he answered without looking back.

"Is this decision final?" David called. "Or is it temporary, pending a hearing?"

"It's final, my friend." With that, he was gone.

David was in a daze. He couldn't believe he'd been fired. He stumbled into the patient lounge and collapsed into the same chair that he'd pushed Kelley into that morning.

David shook his head in disbelief. His first real job had only lasted four months. He began to consider the awful ramifications his firing would have on his family, and he began to tremble. He wondered how he would tell Angela. It was horribly ironic that only the night before he'd warned her about putting her job in jeopardy. Now here he was the one to get fired.

From where he was sitting, David suddenly spotted Angela entering the ICU. For a moment, David didn't move. He was afraid to face her but he knew he had to. He got up from the chair and followed Angela into the unit. She was standing alongside Nikki's bed. David slipped in along the opposite side.

Angela acknowledged David's arrival with a nod but continued her conversation with Nikki. David and Angela avoided each other's eyes.

"Will I be able to see Caroline when I leave the ICU?" Nikki asked.

David and Angela looked at each other briefly. It was clear neither knew what to say.

"Is she gone?" Nikki asked.

"She's gone," Angela said.

"She's already been discharged," Nikki cried. Her eyes began to fill with tears. She'd been looking forward to seeing her as soon as she got into a regular room.

"Maybe Arni will want to come in and visit," David suggested.

Nikki's disappointment made her moody and disagreeable. David and Angela knew that the ICU was taking its toll. They were afraid to tell her the truth about Caroline.

After David and Angela did what they could for Nikki's spirits, they left the ICU. They were chary with each other as they exited the hospital. Their conversation focused on Nikki and how pleased they were her clinical course was so smooth. Both of them were certain her emotional state would improve as soon as she was transferred out of the unit.

On the route home, Angela drove slowly to keep David in sight as he pedaled his bicycle. They arrived home at the same time. It wasn't until they were seated in the family room, ostensibly to watch the evening news, that David nervously cleared his throat.

"I'm afraid I have some rather bad news," he said. "I'm embarrassed to tell you I was fired this afternoon." David saw the shock registered in Angela's face. He averted his eyes. "I'm sorry. I know it'll be difficult for us. I don't know what to say. Maybe I'm not cut out to be a doctor."

"David," Angela said, reaching out and grabbing his arm. "I was fired, too."

David looked at Angela. "You were?" he asked.

She nodded.

He reached out and pulled her close. When they leaned back to look at each other again, they didn't know whether to laugh or cry.

"What a mess," David said at last.

"What a coincidence," Angela added.

They each shared the sorry details of their last acts at Bartlet. In the process, Angela also filled David in on Walt's latest discovery and her impromptu meeting with Calhoun.

"He thinks the tattoo will help find the murderer," Angela said.

"That's nice," David said. He still didn't share Angela's enthusiasm for the case, especially with the new turmoil in their lives.

"Calhoun had some intriguing news as well," Angela said. She explained Calhoun's theory that the hospital rapist and Hodges' killer were one and the same.

"Interesting idea," David said. But his thoughts were already elsewhere. He was wondering what he and Angela would do to support themselves in the immediate future.

"And remember those admission summaries Hodges was waving around? Calhoun figured out how they're related," Angela said. "They'd all died, and apparently all the deaths came as a surprise to Hodges."

"What do you mean a surprise?" David asked, suddenly becoming interested.

"I guess he didn't expect them to die," Angela said. "He had treated them before they transferred to CMV. Calhoun was told that Hodges blamed both CMV and the hospital for their deaths."

"Do you have any of the histories on these patients?" David asked.

"Just their admission diagnoses," Angela said. "Why?"

"Having patients die unexpectedly is something I can relate to," David said.

There was a pause in the conversation while David and Angela marveled at the day's events.

"What are we going to do?" Angela asked finally.

"I don't know," David said. "I'm sure we'll have to move, but what happens to the mortgages? I wonder if we'll have to declare bankruptcy. We'll have to talk to a lawyer. There's also the question of whether we'll want to sue our respective employers."

"There's no question in my mind," Angela said. "I'll sue for sexual harassment if not wrongful dismissal. There's no way I'll let that slime Wadley get off scot free."

"I don't know if suing is our style," David said. "Maybe we should just get on with our lives. I don't want to get bogged down in a legal morass."

"Let's not decide now," Angela said.

Later they called the ICU. Nikki was continuing to do well. She was still without a fever.

"We might have lost our jobs," David said, "but as long as Nikki is okay we'll manage."

22

FRIDAY, OCTOBER 29

ONCE AGAIN NEITHER DAVID NOR ANGELA SLEPT well. As was becoming his habit, David woke well before dawn. Although he was exhausted, he didn't feel ill like he had the previous morning.

Without waking Angela he went down to the family room to ponder their financial situation. He began to make a list of things to do and people to call, ranking them according to priority. He firmly believed their current plight required calm, rational thinking.

Angela appeared at the doorway in her robe. In her hand was a tissue; she'd been crying. She asked David what he was doing. He explained but she wasn't impressed.

"What are we going to do?" she cried. New tears spilled from her eyes. "We've made such a mess of everything."

David tried to console her by showing her his lists, but she shoved them away, accusing David of being out of touch with his feelings.

"Your stupid lists aren't going to solve anything," she said.

"And I suppose your hysterical tears will," David shot back.

Fortunately, they didn't let their argument go any further. They both knew they were overwrought. They also knew they each had their own way of dealing with a crisis.

"So what are we going to do?" Angela asked again.

"First, let's go to the hospital and check on Nikki," David said.

"Fine," Angela said. "It will give me a chance to talk with Helen Beaton."

"It will be futile," David warned. "Are you sure you want to expend the emotional effort?"

"I want to be sure she's aware of my complaint about sexual harassment," Angela said.

They had a quick breakfast before starting out. It felt strange for both of them to be going to the hospital yet not to work. They parked and went directly to the ICU.

Nikki was fine and antsy to get out of the unit. Although she'd found the bustle engrossing during the day, the night shift wasn't so pleasant. She'd gotten little sleep.

When Dr. Pilsner arrived he confirmed that Nikki was going to a regular room as soon as the floor sent someone to transport her.

"When do you think she'll be coming home?" Angela asked.

"As well as she's doing, she'll be home in just a few days," Dr. Pilsner said. "I want to make certain she doesn't suffer a relapse."

While David stayed with Nikki, Angela headed for Helen Beaton's office.

"Would you call Caroline and have her get my schoolbooks?" Nikki asked David.

"I'll take care of it," David promised. He was purposefully evasive. He was still reluctant to tell his daughter about Caroline's death.

David couldn't help but notice that Sandra's bed in the ICU was now occupied by an elderly man. It was half an hour before David mustered the courage to go to the unit clerk and ask about her.

"Sandra Hascher died this morning about three," the clerk said. He spoke as if he were giving a weather report; as accustomed to death as he was, he was unmoved.

David wasn't so unmoved. He'd been fond of Sandra, and his heart went out to her family, particularly her motherless children. Now he'd lost six patients in two weeks. He wondered if that was a record at Bartlet Community Hospital. Maybe CMV had been wise to fire him.

Promising Nikki that he and her mother would be back to see her later after she'd been moved to a regular room, David walked over to administration to wait for Angela.

Hardly had David sat down when Angela came storming out of the hospital president's office. She was livid. Her dark eyes shone with intensity, and her lips were clamped shut. She walked past David without slowing. He had to run to catch up with her.

"I suppose I shouldn't ask how it went," David said as they pushed through the doors to the parking lot.

"It was terrible," Angela said. "She's upholding Wadley's decision. When I explained to her that sexual harassment was at the bottom of the whole affair, she denied that any sexual harassment had taken place."

"How could she deny it when you'd spoken with Dr. Cantor?" David asked.

"She said that she asked Dr. Wadley," Angela said. "And Dr. Wadley said there had been no sexual harassment. In fact, he claimed it had been the other way around. He told Beaton that if there had been any impropriety it was that I'd tried to seduce him!"

"A familiar ploy of the sexual harasser," David said. "Blame the victim." He shook his head. "What a sleazebag!"

"Beaton said she believed him," Angela said. "She told me he was a man of impeccable integrity. Then she accused me of having made up the story to try to get back at him for spurning my advances."

When they arrived home they collapsed into chairs in the family room. They didn't know what to do. They were too depressed and confused to do anything.

The sound of tires crunching on gravel in their driveway broke the heavy silence. It was Calhoun's truck. Calhoun pulled up to the back door. Angela let him in.

"I brought you some fresh doughnuts to celebrate the first day of your vacation," Calhoun said. He passed by Angela and dumped his parcel on the kitchen table. "With a little coffee we'll be in business."

David appeared at the doorway.

"Uh oh," Calhoun said. He looked from David to Angela.

"It's okay," said David. "I'm on 'vacation' too."

"No kidding!" Calhoun said. "Lucky I brought a dozen doughnuts."

Calhoun's presence was like an elixir. The coffee helped as well. David and Angela even found themselves laughing at some of Calhoun's stories from his days as a state policeman. They were in high spirits until Calhoun suggested they get down to work.

"Now," he said, rubbing his hands with anticipation. "The problem has been reduced to finding someone with a damaged tattoo who didn't like Hodges. That shouldn't be so hard to accomplish in a small town."

"There's a catch," David said. "Since we are unemployed, I don't think we can afford to employ you."

"Don't say that," Calhoun whined. "Just when this whole thing is getting interesting."

"We're sorry," David said. "Not only will we soon be broke, but we'll obviously be leaving Bartlet. So among other things, we'll be leaving this whole Hodges mess behind."

"Hold on a second," Calhoun said. "Let's not be too rash here. I've got an idea. I'll work for nothing. How's that? It's a matter of honor and reputation. Besides, we might be catching ourselves a rapist in the process."

"That's very generous of you . . ." David said. He started to say more but Calhoun interrupted him.

"I've already begun the next phase of inquiry," he said. "I found out from Carleton, the bartender, that several of the town's policemen, including Robertson, have tattoos. So I went over and had a casual chat with Robertson. He was more than happy to show me his. He's rather proud of it. It's on his chest: a bald eagle holding a banner that reads 'In

God We Trust.' Unfortunately—or fortunately, depending on your perspective—the tattoo was in fine shape. But I used the opportunity to ask Robertson about Hodges' last day. Robertson confirmed what Madeline Gannon had said about Hodges' planning on seeing him, then canceling. So I think we're onto something. Clara Hodges may be the key. They were estranged at the time of the doc's death, but they still spoke frequently. I get the feeling living apart greatly improved their relationship. Anyway, I called Clara this morning. She's expecting us." He looked at Angela.

"I thought she'd moved to Boston," David said.

"She did," Calhoun said. "I thought Angela and I, er, now all three of us, could drive down."

"I still think Angela and I should drop this whole business, considering what's happened. If you want to continue, that's your business."

"Maybe we shouldn't be too rash," Angela said. "What if Clara Hodges can shed some light on the history of those patients who died? You were interested in that aspect of the case last night."

"Well, that's true," David admitted. He was curious to know how many similarities there were between Hodges' patients and his own. But he wasn't curious enough to visit Clara Hodges. Not after being fired.

"Let's do it, David," Angela said. "Let's go. I feel as if this town has conspired against us, and it bothers me. Let's fight back."

"Angela, you're beginning to sound a little out of control," David said.

Angela put her coffee cup down and grabbed David by the arm. "Excuse us," she said to Calhoun. Angela pulled David into the family room.

"I'm not out of control," she began once they were beyond Calhoun's earshot. "I just like the idea of doing something positive, of having a cause. This town has pushed us around the same way it's pushed Hodges' death under the carpet. I want to know what's behind it all. Then we can leave here with our heads held high."

"This is your hysterical side talking," David said.

"Whatever you want to call it is okay with me," Angela

said. "Let's give it one more final go. Calhoun thinks this visit to Clara Hodges might do the trick. Let's try it."

David hesitated. His rational side argued against it, but Angela's pleas were hard to resist. Underneath his veneer of calm and reason, David was just as angry as Angela.

"All right," he said. "Let's go. But we'll stop and see Nikki first."

"Gladly," Angela said. She put out her hand. David half-heartedly slapped it. Then when he put out his own, Angela hit it with surprising force.

David's next surprise was that they had to take Calhoun's truck so Calhoun could smoke. But with Calhoun driving, they were able to pull right up to the front door of the hospital. Calhoun waited while David and Angela ran inside.

Nikki was much happier now that she was out of the ICU. Her only complaint was that she'd been transferred to one of the old hospital beds and, as usual, the controls didn't work. The foot would rise but not the head.

"Did you tell the nurses?" David asked.

"Yeah," Nikki said. "But they haven't told me when it will be fixed. I can't watch the TV with my head flat."

"Is this a frequent problem?" Angela asked.

"Unfortunately," David said. He told her what Van Slyke had said about the hospital purchasing the wrong kind of beds. "They probably saved a few dollars buying the cheap ones. But any money saved has been lost in maintenance costs. It's that old expression: penny-wise and pound-foolish."

David left Angela with Nikki while he sought out Janet Colburn. When he found her he asked if Van Slyke had been alerted about Nikki's bed.

"He has, but you know Van Slyke," Janet said.

Back in Nikki's room, David assured her that if her bed wasn't fixed by that evening, he'd do it himself. Angela had already informed her that she and David were on their way to Boston but would be back that afternoon. They'd come see her as soon as they were back.

Returning to the front of the hospital, Angela and David piled into Calhoun's truck. Soon they were on their way south on the interstate. David found the trip uncomfortable

for more reasons than the truck's poor suspension. Even
though Calhoun cracked his window, cigar smoke swirled
around inside the cab. By the time they got to Clara Hodges'
Back Bay address in Boston, David's eyes were watering.

Clara Hodges struck David as having been a good match
for Dennis Hodges. She was a big-boned, solid woman with
piercing, deep-set eyes and an intimidating scowl.

She invited them into her parlor decorated with heavy
Victorian furnishing. Only a meager amount of daylight
penetrated the thick velvet drapes. Despite being midday
the chandelier and all the table lamps were turned on.

Angela introduced herself and David as the purchasers
of Clara's home in Bartlet.

"Hope you like it better than I did," Clara said. "It was
too big and drafty, especially for only two people."

She offered tea which David took with relish. Not only
were his eyes burning from the secondhand smoke in the
truck, but his throat was parched.

"I can't say I'm pleased about this visit," Clara said
once her tea was poured. "I'm upset this ugly business has
surfaced. I'd just about adjusted to Dennis' disappearance
when I learned that he'd been murdered."

"I'm sure you share our interest in bringing his killer to
justice," Calhoun said.

"It wouldn't matter much now," Clara said. "Besides,
we'd all be dragged through some awful trial. I preferred
it the way it was, just not knowing."

"Do you have any suspicions about who killed your
husband?" Calhoun asked.

"I'm afraid there are a lot of candidates," Clara said.
"You have to understand two things about Dennis. First off,
he was bullheaded, which made him hard to get along with.
Not that he didn't have a good side, too. The second thing
about Dennis was his obsession with the hospital. He was at
constant odds with the board and that woman administrator
they recruited from Boston.

"I suppose any one of a dozen people could have gotten
angry enough to do him in. Yet I just can't imagine any
one of them actually beating him. Too messy for all those
doctors and bureaucrats, don't you think?"

"I understand that Dr. Hodges thought he knew the identity of the ski-masked rapist," Calhoun said. "Is that a fair statement?"

"That's certainly what he implied," Clara said.

"Did he ever mention any names?" Calhoun asked.

"The only thing he said was that the rapist was someone connected to the hospital," Clara said.

"An employee of the hospital?" Calhoun asked.

"He didn't elaborate," Clara said. "He was purposefully vague. That man lived to lord things over you. But he did say he wanted to speak to the person himself, thinking he could get him to stop."

"Lordy," Calhoun said. "That sounds like a dangerous thing to do. Do you think he did?"

"I don't know," Clara said. "He might have. But then he decided to go to that abominable Wayne Robertson with his suspicions. We got into a fearful quarrel over the issue. I didn't want him to go since I was sure he and Robertson would only squabble. Robertson always did have it in for him. I told him to tell Robertson his suspicions by phone or write him a letter, but Dennis wouldn't hear of it. He was so stubborn."

"Was that the day he disappeared?" Calhoun asked.

"That's right," Clara said. "But in the end Dennis didn't see Robertson—not because of my advice, mind you. He got all upset over one of his former patients dying. He said he was going to have lunch with Dr. Holster instead of seeing Robertson."

"Was this patient Clark Davenport?" Calhoun asked.

"Why yes," Clara said with surprise. "How did you know?"

"Why was Dr. Hodges so upset about Clark Davenport?" Calhoun asked, ignoring Clara's question. "Were they good friends?"

"They were acquaintances," Clara said. "Clark was more a patient, and Dennis had diagnosed Clark's cancer which Dr. Holster had successfully treated. After the treatment Dennis had felt confident that they'd caught the cancer early enough. But then Clark's employer switched to CMV and the next thing Dennis knew, Clark was dead."

"What did Clark die of?" David asked suddenly, speaking up for the first time. His voice had an urgent quality that Angela noticed immediately.

"You've got me there," Clara said. "I don't recall. I'm not sure I ever knew. But it wasn't his cancer. I remember Dennis saying that."

"Did your husband have any other medically similar patients who ended up dying unexpectedly?" David asked.

"What do you mean by medically similar?" Clara asked.

"People with cancer or other serious diseases," David said.

"Oh, yes," Clara said. "He had a number. And it was their deaths that upset him so. He became convinced that some of the CMV doctors were incompetent."

David asked Angela for copies of the admission sheets she and Calhoun had gotten from Burlington. As Angela was searching for them, Calhoun pulled out his set from one of his voluminous pockets.

David fumbled with the papers as he unfolded them. He handed them to Clara. "Look at these names," he said. "Do you recognize any?"

"I'll have to get my reading glasses," Clara said. She stood up and left the room.

"What are you so agitated about?" Angela whispered to David.

"Yeah, calm down, boy," Calhoun said. "You'll get our witness all upset and she'll start forgetting things."

"Something is beginning to dawn on me," David said. "And I don't like it one bit."

Before Angela could ask David to explain, Clara returned with her reading glasses. She picked up the papers and quickly glanced through them.

"I recognize all these people," Clara said. "I'd heard their names a hundred times, and I'd met most of them."

"I was told all of them died," Calhoun said. "Is that true?"

"That's right," Clara said. "Just like Clark Davenport. These are the people whose deaths had particularly upset Dennis. For a while I heard about them every day."

"Were their deaths all unexpected?" Calhoun asked.

"Yes and no," Clara said. "I mean it was unexpected for these people to die at the particular time they did. As you can see from these papers, most of the people were hospitalized for problems that usually aren't fatal. But they all had battled terminal illnesses like cancer, so in that sense their deaths weren't totally unexpected."

David reached out and took the papers back. He glanced through them quickly, then looked up at Clara. "Let me be sure I understand," he said. "These admission summary sheets are the admissions during which these people died."

"I believe so," Clara said. "It's been a while, but Dennis carried on so. It's hard to forget."

"And each of these patients had a serious underlying illness," David said. "Like this one admitted for sinusitis."

Clara took the sheet and looked at the name. "She had breast cancer," Clara said. "She was in my church group."

David took the sheet of paper back from Clara and rolled it up with the others. Then he stood up and walked over to the window. Pulling back the drapes, he stared out over the Charles River, ignoring the others. He seemed quite distracted.

Angela was mildly embarrassed at David's poor manners, but it was apparent that Clara didn't mind. She simply poured them all more tea.

"I want to ask a few more questions about the rapist," Calhoun said. "Did Dr. Hodges ever allude to his age or height or details such as whether or not he had a tattoo?"

"A tattoo?" Clara questioned. A fleeting smile flashed across her face before her frown returned. "No, he never mentioned a tattoo."

With a swiftness that took everyone by surprise, David returned from the window. "We have to leave," he said. "We have to go immediately."

He rushed for the door and pulled it open.

"David?" Angela called, astonished at his behavior. "What's the matter?"

"We've got to get back to Bartlet immediately," he said. His urgency had grown to near panic. "Come on!" he yelled.

Angela and Calhoun gave a hurried goodbye to Clara Hodges before running after David. By the time Angela and Calhoun got out to the truck, David was already behind the wheel.

"Give me the keys," he ordered.

Calhoun shrugged and handed them to David. David started the truck and gunned the engine. "Get in," he shouted.

Angela got in first, followed by Calhoun. Before the door was closed behind them, David hit the gas.

For the first portion of the trip no one spoke. David concentrated on driving. Angela and Calhoun were still shocked by the sudden, awkward departure. They were also intimidated by the rapidity with which they were overtaking other motorists.

"I think we'd better slow down," Angela said as David passed a long row of cars.

"This truck has never gone this fast," Calhoun said.

"David, what has come over you?" Angela asked. "You're acting bizarre."

"I had a flash of insight while we were talking to Clara Hodges," he said. "It concerns Hodges' patients with potentially terminal illnesses dying unexpectedly."

"Well?" Angela asked. "What about them?"

"I think some disturbed individual at Bartlet Community Hospital has taken it upon himself to deliver some sort of misguided euthanasia."

"What's euthanasia?" Calhoun asked.

"It translates to 'good death,' " Angela said. "It means to help someone who has a terminal illness to die. The idea is to save them from suffering."

"Hearing about Hodges' patients made me realize that all six of my recent deaths had battled terminal illnesses," David said. "The same as his. I don't know why I didn't think about it before. How could I have been so dense? And the same is true with Caroline."

"Who's Caroline?" Calhoun asked.

"She was a friend of our daughter," Angela explained. "She had cystic fibrosis which is a potentially terminal illness. She died yesterday." Angela's eyes went wide. "Oh, no! Nikki!" she cried.

"Now you know why I panicked," David said. "We have to get back there as soon as we can."

"What's going on?" Calhoun said. "I'm missing something here. Why are you two so agitated?"

"Nikki is in the hospital," Angela said anxiously.

"I know," Calhoun said. "Before we went to Boston I took you there so you could visit her."

"She has cystic fibrosis just like Caroline had," Angela said.

"Uh oh," Calhoun said. "I'm getting the picture. You're worried about your daughter being targeted by this euthanasia fiend."

"You got it," David said.

"Would this be something like that 'Angel of Mercy' case on Long Island I read about?" Calhoun asked. "It was a number of years ago. It involved a nurse who was knocking people off with some sort of drug."

"Something like that," David said. "But that case involved a muscle relaxant. The people stopped breathing. It was pretty straightforward. With my patients I have no idea how they're being killed. I can't think of any drug or poison or infectious agent that would cause the symptoms these patients had."

"I can understand why you'd be worried about your daughter," Calhoun said. "But don't you think you're being a bit hasty with this theory?"

"It answers a lot of questions," David said. "It even makes me think of Dr. Portland."

"Why?" Angela asked. She was still uncomfortable any time his name came up.

"Didn't Kevin tell us that Dr. Portland said he wasn't going to take all the blame for his patient deaths and that there was something wrong with the hospital?"

Angela nodded.

"He must have had his suspicions," David said. "Too bad he succumbed to his depression."

"He committed suicide," Angela explained to Calhoun.

"Terrible waste," Calhoun said. "All that training."

"The question is," David said, "if someone is performing euthanasia in the hospital, who could it be? It would have to be someone with access to the patients and someone with a sophisticated knowledge of medicine."

"That would limit it to a doctor or a nurse," Angela said.

"Or a lab tech," David suggested.

"I think you people are jumping the gun," Calhoun said. "This isn't the way investigations are done. You don't come up with a theory and then go barreling off at ninety miles an hour like we're doing. Most theories fall apart when more facts are in. I think we should slow down."

"Not while my daughter is at risk," David said. He pushed the old truck harder.

"Do you think Hodges came to the same conclusion?" Angela asked.

"I think so," David said. "And if he did, maybe that's why he was killed."

"I still think it was the rapist," Calhoun said. "But whoever it turns out to be, this investigation is fascinating. Providing your daughter's okay, I haven't enjoyed myself this much in years."

When they finally reached the hospital, David pulled right up to the front door. He jumped out with Angela close at his heels. Together they charged up the main stairs and ran down the hall.

To their supreme relief, they discovered Nikki perfectly happy watching TV. David snatched her up in his arms and hugged her so tightly that she began to complain.

"You're coming home," David said. He held her away so he could examine her face, especially her eyes.

"When?" Nikki asked.

"Right now," Angela said. She started disconnecting the IV.

At that moment a nurse was passing in the hall. The commotion drew her attention. When she saw Angela detaching the IV, she protested.

"What's going on here?" she asked.

"My daughter is going home," David said.

"There are no orders for that," the nurse said.

"I'm giving the order right this minute," David said.

The nurse quickly ran out of the room. Angela started to

gather Nikki's clothes. David helped.

Soon Janet Colburn came back with several nurses in tow. "Dr. Wilson," Janet said, "what on earth are you doing?"

"I think it's rather apparent," David said as he packed Nikki's toys and books in a bag.

David and Angela had Nikki half dressed when Dr. Pilsner arrived. Janet had paged him. He urged them not to remove Nikki from the IV antibiotic or the hospital's talented respiratory therapist prematurely.

"I'm sorry, Dr. Pilsner," David said. "I'll have to explain later. It would take too long right now."

At that moment Helen Beaton arrived. She, too, had been called by the nurses. She was incensed. "If you take that child out of here against medical advice I'll get a court order," she sputtered.

"Just try," Angela said.

When they had Nikki fully dressed, they led her down the hall. The commotion had drawn a flock of gawking patients and staff.

Once outside they all climbed into the truck. Calhoun drove with Nikki and Angela in the cab. David had to sit in the truck bed.

The whole way home Nikki questioned her sudden discharge. She was happy to be out, but puzzled by her parents' odd behavior. But by the time she got in the house she was too excited to see Rusty to persist in her questioning. After she played with Rusty for a bit, David and Angela set her up in the family room and restarted her IV. They wanted to continue her antibiotics.

Calhoun stayed and participated as best he could. Following Nikki's request he brought wood upstairs from the basement and made a fire. But it wasn't his nature to stay silent. Before long he got into an argument with David over the motive for Hodges' murder. Calhoun strongly favored the rapist, whereas David favored the deranged "Angel of Mercy."

"Hell!" Calhoun exclaimed. "Your whole theory is based on pure supposition. Your daughter is fine, thank the Lord, so there's no proof there. At least with my theory there's

Hodges' ranting about knowing who the rapist was before a roomful of people the very day he got knocked off. How's that for cause and effect? And Clara thinks Hodges might have had the nerve to speak to the man. I'm so sure the rapist and the murderer are one and the same, I'll wager on it. What kind of odds will you give me?"

"I'm not a betting man," David said. "But I think I'm right. Hodges was beaten to death holding the names of his patients. That couldn't have been a coincidence."

"What if it is the same person?" Angela suggested. "What if the rapist is the same person behind the patient deaths and Hodges' murder?"

The idea shocked David and Calhoun into silence.

"It's possible," David said at last. "It sounds sort of crazy, but at this point I'm prepared to believe almost anything."

"I suppose," Calhoun added. "Anyway, I'm going after the tattoo clue. That's the key."

"I'm going to medical records," David said. "And maybe I'll visit Dr. Holster. Hodges might have said something to him about his suspicions regarding his patients."

"Okay," Calhoun said agreeably. "I'll go do my thing, you go ahead and do yours. How's about if I come back later so we can compare notes?"

"Sounds good," David said. He looked over at Angela.

"It's fine by me," she said. "What about having dinner together?"

"I never turn down dinner invitations," Calhoun said.

"Then be here by seven," Angela said.

After Calhoun left, David got the shotgun and proceeded to load it with as many shells as it would hold. He leaned it against the newel post in the front hall.

"Have you changed your mind about the gun?" Angela asked.

"Let's just say I'm glad it's here," David said. "Have you talked to Nikki about it?"

"Absolutely," Angela said. "She even shot it. She said it hurt her shoulder."

"Don't let anyone in the house while I'm gone," David said. "And keep all the doors locked."

"Hey, I'm the one who wanted the doors locked," Angela said. "Remember?"

David took his bike. He didn't want to leave Angela without a car. He rode quickly, oblivious to the sights. His mind kept going over the idea of someone having killed his patients. It horrified and infuriated him. But as Calhoun said, he didn't have any proof.

When David arrived at the hospital, the day shift was being replaced by the evening shift. There was a lot of commotion and traffic. No one paid the slightest attention to David as he made his way to medical records.

Sitting down at a terminal, David set out Calhoun's copies of the pages that had been interred with Hodges. He'd held onto them since their visit to Clara Hodges. He called up each patient's name and read the history. All eight had had serious terminal illnesses as Clara Hodges had said.

Then David read through the notes written during each patient's hospital stay when they died. In all cases, the symptoms were similar to those experienced by David's patients: neurological symptoms, gastrointestinal symptoms, and symptoms dealing with the blood or immune system.

Next, David looked up the final causes of death. In each case except for one, death resulted from a combination of overwhelming pneumonia, sepsis, and shock. The exception was a death subsequent to a series of sustained seizures.

Putting Hodges' papers away, David began using the hospital computer to calculate yearly death rates as a percentage of admissions. The results flashed on the screen instantly. He quickly discovered that the death rate had changed two years before when it had gone from an average of 2.8% up to 6.7%. The last year the figures were available, the death rate was up to 8.1%.

David then narrowed the death rate to those patients who had a diagnosis of cancer, whether the cancer was attributed as the cause of death or not. Although these percentages were understandably higher than the overall death rate, they showed the same sudden increase.

David next used the computer to calculate the yearly diagnosis of cancer as a percentage of admissions. With these statistics he saw no sudden change. On average, they were nearly identical going back ten years.

The increased percentage of deaths seemed to back up David's theory of an angel of mercy at work. Euthanasia would explain the fact that the relative incidence of all cancers was remaining stable while the death rate for people with cancer was going up. The evidence was indirect, but it couldn't be ignored.

David was about to leave when he thought of using the computer to elicit additional information. He asked the computer to search through all the medical histories on all the admissions for the words "tattoo" or "dyschromia," the medical word for aberrant pigmentation.

He waited while the computer searched. David sat back and watched the screen. It took almost a minute, but finally a list blazed on the screen. David quickly deleted the cases with medical or metabolic causes of pigmentary change. In the end, he came up with a list of twenty people who had been treated at the hospital with a mention of a tattoo in their records.

Using the computer yet again to match name and employment, David discovered that five of the people listed worked in the hospital. They were, in alphabetical order, Clyde Devonshire, an RN who worked in the emergency room; Joe Forbs from security; Claudette Maurice from dietary; Werner Van Slyke from engineering/maintenance; and Peter Ullhof, a lab technician.

David was intrigued to see a couple of the other names and occupations listed: Carl Hobson, deputy policeman, and Steve Shegwick, a member of the security force at Bartlet College. The rest of the people worked in various stores or in construction.

David printed out a copy of this information. Then he went on his way.

David had assumed his visit to medical records had gone unnoticed, but he was wrong. Hortense Marshall, one of the health information professionals, had been alerted to some of David's activities by a security program she'd placed in the hospital computer.

From the moment she'd been alerted, she'd kept an eye on David. As soon as he'd departed from records, she placed a call to Helen Beaton.

"Dr. David Wilson was in medical records," Hortense said. "He's just left. But while he was here he called up information concerning hospital death rates."

"Did he talk with you?" Beaton asked.

"No," Hortense said. "He used one of our terminals. He didn't speak with anyone."

"How did you know he was accessing data on death rates?" Beaton asked.

"The computer alerted me," Hortense said. "After you advised me to report anyone requesting that kind of data, I had the computer programmed to signal me if someone tried to access the information on their own."

"Excellent work," Beaton said. "I like your initiative. You're to be commended. That kind of data is not for public consumption. We know our rates have gone up since we've become a tertiary care facility for CMV. They're sending us a high proportion of critically ill patients."

"I'm sure statistics of that ilk would not help our public relations," Hortense said.

"That's the concern," Beaton said.

"Should I have said anything to Dr. Wilson?" Hortense asked.

"No, you did fine," Beaton said. "Did he research anything else?"

"He was here for quite a while," Hortense said. "But I have no idea what else he was looking up."

"The reason I ask," Beaton said, "is because Dr. Wilson has been suspended from CMV."

"That I wasn't aware of," Hortense said.

"It just happened yesterday," Beaton said. "Would you let me know if he comes back?"

"Most certainly," Hortense said.

"Excuse me," Calhoun said. "Is your name Carl Hobson?" He'd approached one of Bartlet's uniformed patrolmen as he came out of the diner on Main Street.

"Sure is," the policeman answered.

"Mine's Phil Calhoun," Calhoun said.

"I've seen you around the station," Carl said. "You're friends with the chief."

"Yup," Calhoun said. "Wayne and I go back a ways. I used to be a state policeman, but I got retired."

"Good for you," Carl said. "Now it's nothing but fishing and hunting."

"I suppose," Calhoun said. "Mind if I ask you a personal question?"

"Hell, no," Carl said with curiosity.

"Carleton over at the Iron Horse told me you had a tattoo," Calhoun said. "I've been thinking about getting one myself so I've been looking around and asking questions. Many people in town have 'em?"

"There's a few," Carl said.

"When did you get yours?" Calhoun asked.

"Way the hell back in high school," Carl said with an embarrassed laugh. "Five of us drove over to Portsmouth, New Hampshire, one Friday night when we were seniors. There's a bunch of tattoo parlors over there. We were all blitzed."

"Did it hurt?" Calhoun asked.

"Hell, I don't remember," Carl said. "Like I said, we were all drunk."

"All five of you guys still in town?" Calhoun asked.

"Just four of us," Carl said. "There's me, Steve Shegwick, Clyde Devonshire, and Mort Abrams."

"Did everybody get tattooed in the same spot?" Calhoun asked.

"Nope," Carl said. "Most of us got 'em on our biceps, but some chose their forearms. Clyde Devonshire was the exception. He got tattooed on his chest above each nipple."

"Who got tattooed on his forearm?" Calhoun asked.

"I'm not sure," Carl admitted. "It's been a while. Maybe Shegwick and Jay Kaufman. Kaufman's the guy who moved away. He went to college someplace in New Jersey."

"Where's yours?" Calhoun asked.

"I'll show you," Carl said. He unbuttoned his shirt and

pulled up the sleeve. On the outer aspect of his upper arm was a howling wolf with the word "lobo" below it.

By the time David returned home from his visit to medical records, Nikki had begun to feel worse. At first she only complained of stomach cramps, but by early evening she was suffering from nausea and increased salivation—the same symptoms David had experienced during the night. They were also the symptoms reported by the six night-shift nurses and, even scarier, by his six patients who had died.

By six-thirty Nikki was lethargic after several bouts of diarrhea, and David was sick with worry. He was terrified that they'd not gotten her out of the hospital quickly enough: whatever had killed his patients had already been given to her.

David did not share his fears with Angela. It was bad enough that she was concerned about Nikki's ostensible symptoms without adding the burden of a potential link to all those patients who died. So David kept his worries to himself, but he agonized over the possibility of an infectious disease of some kind. He comforted himself with the thought that his illness and the nurses' had been self-limiting, suggesting a low exposure to an airborne agent. David's great hope was that if such an agent was to blame, Nikki had only gotten a low dose as well.

Calhoun arrived at exactly seven. He was clutching a sheet of paper and carrying a paper bag.

"I got nine more people with tattoos," he said.

"I got twenty," David said. He tried to sound upbeat, but he couldn't get Nikki out of his mind.

"Let's combine them," Calhoun said.

When they combined the lists and threw out the duplicates, they had a final list of twenty-five people.

"Dinner's ready," Angela said. Angela had cooked a feast to buoy their spirits and to keep herself busy. She'd had David set the table in the dining room.

"I've brought wine," Calhoun said. He opened his parcel and pulled out two bottles of Chianti.

Five minutes later they were sitting down to a fine meal of chicken with chèvre, one of Angela's favorite dishes.

"Where's Nikki?" Calhoun asked.

"She's not hungry," Angela said.

"She doing okay?" Calhoun asked.

"Her stomach's a bit upset," Angela said. "But considering what we put her through, it's to be expected. The main thing is that she has no fever and her lungs are perfectly clear."

David winced but didn't say anything.

"What do we do now that we have the list of people with tattoos?" she asked.

"We proceed in two ways," Calhoun said. "First we run a background computer check on each person. That's the easy part. Second, I start interviewing them. There are certain things we need to find out, like where each person's tattoo is located and whether they mind showing it off. The tattoo that got scratched by Hodges must be the worse for wear and tear, and it has to be located someplace where it could have been scratched in a struggle. If someone has a little heart on their butt, we're not going to be too interested."

"What do you think is the most promising location?" Angela asked. "On the forearm?"

"I'd say so," Calhoun said. "The forearm, and maybe the wrist. I suppose we shouldn't rule out the back of the hand although that's not a common place for professional tattoos. The tattoo we're dealing with has to have been done by a professional. Professionals are the only ones who use the heavy metal pigments."

"How do we run a background computer check?" Angela asked.

"All we need is the social security number and the birth date," Calhoun said. "We should be able to get those through the hospital." Calhoun looked at David. David nodded. "Once we have that information the rest is easy. It's staggering what information can be obtained from the hundreds of data banks that exist. Whole companies are set up in the information business. For a nominal fee you'd be surprised what you can find out."

"You mean these companies can tap into private data banks?" Angela asked.

"Absolutely," Calhoun said. "Most people don't realize it, but anybody with a computer and a modem can get an amazing amount of information on anybody."

"What kind of information would people be looking for?" Angela asked.

"Anything and everything," Calhoun said. "Financial history, criminal records, job history, consumer purchasing history, phone use, mail order stuff, personal ads. It's like a fishing trip. But interesting stuff turns up. It always does, even if you have a group of twenty-five people who are ostensibly the most normal people in a community. You'd be shocked. And with a group of twenty-five people with tattoos, it will be very interesting. They will not be, quote, 'normal,' believe me."

"Did you do this when you were a state policeman?" Angela asked.

"All the time," Calhoun said. "Whenever we had a bunch of suspects we'd run a background computer check, and we always got some dirt. And in this case if David is right and the killer is committing euthanasia, I can't imagine what we'd run across. He or she would have to be screwed up. We'd find other crusades, like saving animals from shelters and being arrested for having nine hundred dogs in their house. I guarantee we'll come across lots of screwy, weird stuff. We'll need to get hold of some computer jock to help us tap into the data banks."

"I have an old boyfriend at MIT," Angela said. "He's been in graduate school forever but I know he's a computer genius."

"Who's that?" David asked. He hadn't heard about this old boyfriend before.

"His name is Robert Scali," Angela said. To Calhoun she asked: "Do you think he would be able to help us?"

"So why have I never heard of this guy?" David asked.

"I haven't told you every little detail of my life," Angela said. "I dated him for a short time freshman year at Brown."

"But you've been in touch since then?"

"We've gotten together a couple of times over the last few years," Angela said.

"I can't believe I'm hearing this," David said.

"Oh, please, David," Angela said with exasperation. "You're being ridiculous."

"I think Mr. Scali would probably do fine," Calhoun said. "If not, as I said, I know some companies who will gladly help for a modest fee."

"At this point, we'd do well to avoid any fees," Angela said. With that, she started to clear the table.

"Any chance of getting a description of the tattoos from medical records?" Calhoun asked.

"I think so," David said. "Most physicians would probably note them in a physical examination. I certainly would describe them in any physical I'd do."

"It sure would help prioritize our list," Calhoun said. "I'd like to interview those with tattoos on their forearms and wrists first."

"What about the people who work for the hospital?" David asked.

"We'll start with those," Calhoun said. "Absolutely. Also I've been told Steve Shegwick has a tattoo on his forearm. I'd like to talk with him."

Angela came back and asked who wanted ice cream and coffee. David said he'd pass, but Calhoun was eager for both. David got up and went to check on Nikki.

Later when they were sitting around the table after the meal was complete, Angela expressed an interest in organizing the efforts for the following day.

"I'll start interviewing the tattooed hospital workers," Calhoun said. "I still think it's best for me to be the front man. We don't want any more bricks through your windows."

"I'll go back to medical records," David said. "I'll get the social security numbers and birth dates and see about getting descriptions of the tattoos."

"I'll stay with Nikki," Angela said. "Then when David's gotten the social security numbers and birth dates I'll take a run into Cambridge."

"What's the matter with sending them by fax?" David asked.

"We'll be asking for a favor," Angela said. "I can't just fire off a fax."

David shrugged.

"What about that Dr. Holster, the radiotherapist," Calhoun said. "Someone has to talk with him. I'd do it but I think one of you medical people would do a better job."

"Oh yeah," David said. "I forgot about him. I can see him tomorrow when I finish at medical records."

Calhoun scraped back his chair and stood up. He patted his broad, mildly protuberant abdomen. "Thank you for one of the best dinners I've had in a long, long time," he said. "I think it's time for me to drive me and my stomach home."

"When should we talk again?" Angela asked.

"As soon as we have something to talk about," Calhoun said. "And both of you should get some sleep. I can tell you need it."

23

SATURDAY, OCTOBER 30

ALTHOUGH NIKKI SUFFERED FROM ABDOMINAL cramps and diarrhea throughout the night, by morning she was better. She still wasn't back to one hundred percent, but she was clearly on the mend and had remained afebrile. David was vastly relieved. None of his hospital patients had showed this kind of improvement once their symptoms had started. He was confident that from here on Nikki's course would mirror his own and that of the nurses.

Angela woke up depressed about her job situation. She was surprised that David's spirits were so high. Now that Nikki was so much better, he confessed his darker fears to Angela.

"You should have told me," she said.

"It wouldn't have helped," David said.

"Sometimes you make me so angry," Angela said. But instead of pouting, she rushed to David and hugged him, telling him how much she loved him.

The phone interrupted their embrace. It was Dr. Pilsner. He wanted to find out how Nikki was doing. He also wanted to put in another plug for continuing her antibiotics and respiratory therapy.

"We'll do it as often as you tell us," Angela said. She was on the phone in the bedroom while David listened on the extension in the bathroom.

"Sometime soon we'll explain why we spirited her away," David said. "But for now, please accept our apology. Taking Nikki out of the hospital had nothing to do with the care you were providing."

"My only concern is Nikki," Dr. Pilsner said.

"You're welcome to stop by," Angela said. "And if you think that continued hospitalization is needed, we'll take her into Boston."

"For now, just keep me informed," Dr. Pilsner said curtly.

"He's irritated," David said after they'd hung up.

"I can't blame him," Angela said. "People must think we're nuts."

Both David and Angela aided Nikki in her respiratory therapy, taking turns thumping her back as she lay in the required positions. "Can I go to school on Monday?" she asked once they were done.

"It's possible," Angela said. "But I don't want you to get your hopes up."

"I don't want to get too far behind," Nikki said. "Can Caroline come over and bring my schoolbooks?"

Angela glanced at David who was petting Rusty on Nikki's bed. He returned Angela's gaze, and a wordless communication flashed between them. Both understood that they could no longer mislead Nikki no matter how much they hated to tell her the sad truth.

"There's something we have to tell you about Caroline," Angela said gently. "We're all terribly sorry, but Caroline passed away."

"You mean she died?" Nikki asked.

"I'm afraid so," Angela said.

"Oh," Nikki said simply.

Angela looked back at David. David shrugged. He

couldn't think of what else to add. He knew that Nikki's nonchalance was a defense, similar to her response to Marjorie's death. David felt anger tighten in his throat as he recognized that both deaths could have been the work of the same misguided individual.

It took even less time than it had with Marjorie for Nikki's facade to crumble. Angela and David did what they could to console her, and her anguish tormented them. Both of them knew it was a devastating blow for her; not only had Caroline been her friend, but throughout her short life Nikki had been fighting the same disease from which Caroline had suffered.

"Am I going to die too?" Nikki sobbed.

"No," Angela said. "You're doing wonderfully. Caroline had a high fever. You have no fever at all."

Once they had calmed Nikki's fears, David set out for the hospital on his bike. Once he arrived, he went to medical records and immediately set about matching social security numbers and birth dates to the list of names he and Calhoun had compiled.

With that out of the way, David began to call up each medical record to sift through for descriptions of the tattoos. He hadn't gotten far when someone tapped him on the shoulder. He turned around to face Helen Beaton. Behind her was Joe Forbs from security.

"Would you mind telling me what you are doing?" Beaton asked.

"I'm just using the computer," David stammered. He hadn't expected to run into anyone from administration, particularly not on a Saturday morning.

"It's my understanding that you are no longer employed by CMV," Beaton said.

"That's true," David said. "But . . ."

"Your hospital privileges are awarded in conjunction with your employment by CMV," Beaton said. "Since that's no longer the case, your privileges must be reviewed by the credentials committee. Until that time you have no right to computer access.

"Would you please escort Dr. Wilson out of the hospital?" Beaton said to Joe.

Joe Forbs stepped forward and motioned for David to get up.

David knew it was pointless to protest. He calmly gathered up his papers, hoping Beaton wouldn't strip him of these documents. Luckily, Forbs simply escorted him to the door.

Now David could add "bodily thrown out of a hospital" to his brief and ignominious career record. Undaunted, he proceeded to the radiotherapy unit which was housed in its own ultra-modern building which had been designed by the same architect who had designed the Imaging Center.

The radiotherapy unit used Saturday mornings to see long-term follow-up patients. David had to wait half an hour before Dr. Holster could squeeze him in.

Dr. Holster was about ten years older than David, but he appeared even older than that. His hair was totally gray, almost white. Although he was busy that morning, he was hospitable and offered David a cup of coffee.

"So, what can I do for you, Dr. Wilson?" Dr. Holster said.

"You can call me David, for starters," David said. "Beyond that I was hoping to ask you some questions about Dr. Hodges."

"That's a rather strange request," Dr. Holster said. He shrugged. "But I guess I don't mind. Why are you interested?"

"It's a long story," David admitted. "But to make it short, I've had some patients whose hospital courses resembled some of Dr. Hodges' patients'. A few of these patients were ones you treated."

"Ask away," Dr. Holster said.

"Before I do," David said, "I'd also like to request this conversation be confidential."

"Now you're really piquing my curiosity," Dr. Holster said. He nodded. "Confidential it will be."

"I understand that Dr. Hodges visited you the day he disappeared," David said.

"We had lunch, to be precise," Dr. Holster said.

"I know that Dr. Hodges wanted to see you concerning a patient by the name of Clark Davenport."

"That's correct," Dr. Holster said. "We had a long discussion about the case. Unfortunately, Mr. Davenport had
just died. I'd treated him for prostate cancer with what we
thought was great success only four or five months prior to
his demise. Both Dr. Hodges and myself were surprised and
saddened by his passing."

"Did Dr. Hodges ever mention exactly what Mr. Davenport died of?" David asked.

"Not that I recall," Dr. Holster said. "I just assumed
it was a recurrence of his prostate cancer. Why do you
ask?"

"Mr. Davenport died in septic shock after a series of
grand mal seizures," David said. "I don't think it was
related to his cancer."

"I don't know if you can say that," Dr. Holster said. "It
sounds like he developed brain metastases."

"His MRI was normal," David said. "Of course, there
was no autopsy so we don't know for sure."

"There could have been multiple tumors too small for
the MRI to pick up," Dr. Holster said.

"Did Dr. Hodges mention that there was anything about
Mr. Davenport's hospital course that he thought was out of
the ordinary or unexpected?" David asked.

"Only his death," Dr. Holster said.

"Did anything else come up during your lunch?"

"Not really. Not that I can recall," Dr. Holster said.
"When we were done eating I asked Dennis if he'd like
to come back to the radiotherapy center and see the new
machine he'd been responsible for us having received."

"What machine is that?" David asked.

"Our linear accelerator," Dr. Holster said. He beamed
like a proud parent. "We have one of the best machines
made. Dennis had never seen it although he'd intended to
come by on numerous occasions. So we stopped in and I
showed it to him. He was truly impressed. Come on, I'll
show you."

Dr. Holster was out the door before David could respond
one way or the other. He caught up with Dr. Holster halfway down a windowless hallway. David wasn't much in the
mood to see a radiotherapy machine, but to be polite he felt

he had little choice. They reached the treatment room and approached a piece of high-tech equipment.

"Here she is," Dr. Holster said proudly as he gave the stainless-steel machine an affectionate pat. The accelerator looked like an X-ray machine with an attached table. "If it hadn't been for Dr. Hodges' commitment to the hospital we never would have gotten this beauty. We'd be still using the old one."

David gazed at the impressive apparatus. "What was wrong with the old one?" he asked.

"Nothing was wrong with it," Dr. Holster said. "It was just yesterday's technology: a cobalt-60 unit. A cobalt machine cannot be aimed as accurately as the linear accelerator. It's a physics problem having to do with the size of the cobalt source which is about four inches in length. As a result, the gamma rays come out in every direction and are difficult to collimate."

"I see," David said, although he wasn't quite sure he did. Physics had never been his forte.

"This linear accelerator is far superior," Dr. Holster said. "It has a very small aperture from which the rays originate. And it can be programmed to have higher energy. Also, the cobalt machine requires the source to be changed every five years or so since the half-life of cobalt-60 is about six years."

David struggled to suppress a yawn. This encounter with Dr. Holster was beginning to remind him of medical school.

"We still have the cobalt machine," Dr. Holster said. "It's in the hospital basement. The hospital has been in the process of selling it to either Paraguay or Uruguay, I can't remember which. That's what most hospitals do when they upgrade to a linear accelerator like this one: sell the old machine to a developing country. The machines are still good. In fact, the old machines have the benefit of rarely breaking down since the source is always putting out gamma rays, twenty-four hours a day, rain or shine."

"I think I've already taken too much of your time," David said. He hoped to extricate himself from this meeting before Holster went on for another half hour.

"Dr. Hodges was quite interested when I gave him the

tour," Dr. Holster said. "When I mentioned the fact that the old machines have this one benefit over the new ones, his face lit up. He even wanted to see the old machine. How about you? Want to run over there?"

"I think I'll pass," David said. He wondered how Helen Beaton and Joe Forbs would react if he returned to the hospital so soon after being shown the door.

A few minutes later David was on his bike crossing over the Roaring River on his way home. His morning had not been as productive as he would have liked, but at least he'd gotten the social security numbers and birth dates.

As he pedaled, his thoughts returned to what he had learned about Hodges' lunch with Dr. Holster. He wished that Hodges had shared whatever suspicions he'd been harboring with the radiotherapist. Then David recalled Dr. Holster's description of Hodges' face lighting up when he learned of the old cobalt machine's virtue of rarely breaking down. David wondered if Hodges had really been interested or if it was a case of Holster projecting his own enthusiasm on his captive audience. David figured it was probably the latter. Holster had probably come away with the impression that even David had been utterly riveted as far as the tour of the linear accelerator was concerned.

After sleeping late Calhoun didn't get back to Bartlet until midmorning. As he drove into town he decided to attack the list of hospital workers with tattoos alphabetically. That put Clyde Devonshire first.

Calhoun stopped off at the diner on Main Street for a large coffee to go, plus a look at the phone book. Armed with the five addresses, he set off for Clyde's.

Devonshire lived above a convenience store. Calhoun made his way up the stairs to the man's door and rang the bell. When there was no answer, he rang again.

Giving up after a third try, Calhoun went downstairs and wandered into the convenience store where he bought himself a fresh pack of Antonio y Cleopatra cigars.

"I'm looking for Clyde Devonshire," he told the clerk.

"He went out early," the clerk said. "He probably went

to work; he works lots of weekends. He's a nurse at the hospital."

"What time does he usually return?" Calhoun asked.

"He gets back about three-thirty or four unless he does an evening shift."

On his way out, Calhoun slipped back up the stairs and rang Devonshire's bell yet again. When there was still no response, he tried the door. It opened in.

"Hello!" Calhoun called out.

One of the benefits of not being on the police force any longer was that he didn't have to concern himself with the niceties of legal searches and probable cause. With no compunction whatsoever, he stepped over the threshold and closed the door behind him.

The apartment was cheaply furnished but neat. Calhoun found himself in the living room. On the coffee table he discovered a stack of newspaper clippings on Jack Kevorkian, the notorious "suicide" doctor in Michigan. There were other editorials and articles about assisted suicide.

Calhoun smiled as he remembered telling David and Angela that some strange things would pop up about their tattooed group. Calhoun thought that assisted suicide and euthanasia shared some areas of commonality and that David might like to have a chat with Clyde Devonshire.

Calhoun pushed open the bedroom door. This room, too, was neat. Going over to the bureau he scanned the articles on top, looking for photographs. There were none. Opening the closet Calhoun found himself staring at a collection of bondage paraphernalia, mostly items in black leather with stainless steel rivets and chains. On a shelf were stacks of accompanying magazines and videotapes.

As Calhoun closed the door, he wondered what the background computer search would uncover on this weirdo.

Moving through the rest of the apartment, Calhoun continued to search for photos. He was hoping to find one with Clyde displaying his tattoos. There were a number of photos attached to the refrigerator door with tiny magnets, but nobody in the pictures had any visible tattoos. Calhoun didn't even know which of the people photographed was Clyde.

Calhoun was about to return to the living room and go through the desk that he'd seen when he heard a door slam below, followed by footfalls on the stairs.

For an instant, Calhoun was afraid of being caught trespassing. He considered making a run for it, but then, instead of trying to flee, he went to the front door and pulled it open, startling the person who was about to open it from the other side.

"Clyde Devonshire?" Calhoun asked sharply.

"Yeah," Clyde said. "What the hell is going on?"

"My name is Phil Calhoun," Calhoun said. He extended a business card toward Clyde. "I've been waiting for you. Come on in."

Clyde shifted the parcel he was carrying to take the card.

"You're an investigator?" Clyde asked.

"That's right," Calhoun said. "I was a state policeman until the governor decided I was too old. So I've taken up investigating. I've been sitting here waiting for you to get home so I could ask you some questions."

"Well, you scared the crap out of me," Clyde admitted. He put a hand to his chest and sighed with relief. "I'm not used to coming home and finding people in my apartment."

"Sorry," Calhoun said. "I suppose I should have waited on the stairs."

"That wouldn't have been comfortable," Clyde said. "Sit down. Can I offer you anything?"

Clyde dumped his parcel on the couch, then headed into the kitchen. "I've got coffee, pop, or . . ."

"Have any beer?" Calhoun asked.

"Sure," Clyde called.

While Clyde got beer from the refrigerator, Calhoun took a peek inside the brown bag Clyde had come in with. Inside were videos similar in theme to those Calhoun had discovered in the closet.

Clyde came back into the living room carrying two beers. He could tell Calhoun had looked into his parcel. Putting the beers onto the coffee table, Clyde picked up the bag and carefully closed the top.

"Entertainment," Clyde explained.

"I noticed," Calhoun said.

"Are you straight?" Clyde asked.

"I'm not much of anything anymore," Calhoun said. He eyed his host. Clyde was around thirty. He was of medium height and had brown hair. He looked like he would have made a good offensive end in high-school football.

"What kind of questions did you want to ask me?" Clyde said. He handed a beer to Calhoun.

"Did you know Dr. Hodges?" Calhoun asked.

Clyde gave a short, scornful laugh. "Why on earth would you be investigating that detestable figure out of ancient history?"

"Sounds like you didn't think much of him."

"He was a tight-assed bastard," Clyde said. "He had an old-fashioned concept of the role of the nurse. He thought we were lowly life forms who were supposed to do all the dirty work and not question doctors' orders. You know, be seen but not heard. Hodges would have seemed outdated to Clara Barton."

"Who was Clara Barton?" Calhoun asked.

"She was a battlefield nurse in the Civil War," Clyde said. "She also organized the Red Cross."

"Do you know who killed Dr. Hodges?" Calhoun asked.

"It wasn't me, if that's what you're thinking," Clyde said. "But if you find out, let me know. I'd love to buy the man a beer."

"Do you have a tattoo?" Calhoun asked.

"I sure do," Clyde said. "I have a number of them."

"Where?" Calhoun asked.

"You want to see them?" Clyde asked.

"Yes," Calhoun said.

Grinning from ear to ear, Clyde undid his cuffs and took off his shirt. He stood up and assumed several poses as if he were a bodybuilder. Then he laughed. He had a chain tattooed around each wrist, a dragon on his right upper arm, and a pair of crossed swords on his pectorals above each nipple.

"I got these swords in New Hampshire while I was in high school," he said. "The rest I got in San Diego."

"Let me see the tattoos on your wrists," Calhoun said.

"Oh, no," Clyde said as he slipped his shirt back on. "I don't want to show you everything the first time. You won't come back."

"Do you ski?" Calhoun asked.

"Occasionally," Clyde said. Then he added, "You sure do jump all over the map with your questions."

"Do you own a ski mask?" Calhoun asked.

"Everybody who skis in New England has a ski mask," Clyde said. "Unless they're masochists."

Calhoun stood up. "Thanks for the beer," he said. "I've got to be on my way."

"Too bad," Clyde said. "I was just starting to enjoy myself."

Calhoun descended the stairs, went outside, and climbed into his truck. He was glad to get out of Clyde Devonshire's apartment. The man was definitely unusual, maybe even bizarre. The question was, could he have killed Hodges? Somehow, Calhoun didn't think so. Clyde might be weird, but he seemed forthright. Yet the chains tattooed on each wrist bothered Calhoun, especially since he'd not had a chance to examine them closely. And he wondered about the man's interest in Kevorkian. Was it idle curiosity or the interest of a sort of kindred spirit? For now, Clyde would remain a suspect. Calhoun was eager to see what the background computer check would bring up on him.

Calhoun checked his list. The next name was Joe Forbs. The address was near the college, not too far from the Gannons'.

At Forbs' house, a thin, nervous woman with gray-streaked hair opened the door a crack when Calhoun knocked. Calhoun introduced himself and produced his card. The woman wasn't impressed. She was more New England–like than Clyde Devonshire: tight-lipped and not too friendly.

"Mrs. Forbs?" Calhoun asked.

The woman nodded.

"Is Joe at home?"

"No," Mrs. Forbs said. "You'll have to come back later."

"What time?"

"I don't know. It's a different time each day."

"Did you know Dr. Dennis Hodges?" Calhoun asked.

"No," Mrs. Forbs said.

"Can you tell me where Mr. Forbs is tattooed?"

"You'll have to come back," Mrs. Forbs said.

"Does he ski?" Calhoun persisted.

"I'm sorry," Mrs. Forbs said. She shut the door. Calhoun heard a series of locks secured. He had the distinct impression Mrs. Forbs thought he was a bill collector.

Climbing back into the truck, Calhoun sighed. He was now only one for two. But he wasn't discouraged. It was time to move on to the next name on the list: Claudette Maurice.

"Uh oh," Calhoun said as he pulled up across the street from Claudette Maurice's house. It was a tiny home that looked like a dollhouse. What bothered Calhoun was that the shutters on the windows in the front were closed.

Calhoun went up to the front door and knocked several times since there was no bell. There was no response. Lifting the door to the mailbox, he saw it was almost full.

Stepping away from the house, Calhoun went to the nearest neighbor. He got his answer quickly. Claudette Maurice was on vacation. She'd gone to Hawaii.

Calhoun returned to the truck. Now he was only one for three. He looked at the next name: Werner Van Slyke.

Calhoun debated skipping Van Slyke since he'd talked to him already, but he decided to see the man anyway. On the first visit he'd not known about Van Slyke's tattoo.

Van Slyke resided in the southeastern part of the town. He lived on a quiet lane where the buildings were set far back from the street. Calhoun pulled to a stop behind a row of cars parked across the street from Van Slyke's home.

Surprisingly, Van Slyke's house was run-down and badly in need of paint. It didn't look like a house occupied by the head of a maintenance department. Dilapidated shutters hung at odd angles from their windows. The place gave Calhoun the creeps.

Calhoun lit himself an Antonio y Cleopatra and eyed the house. He took a few sips from his coffee which was now cold. There were no signs of life in and around the building and no vehicle in the driveway. Calhoun doubted anyone was home.

Figuring he'd take a look around the way he had at Clyde Devonshire's, Calhoun climbed out of the truck and walked across the street. The closer he got to the building, the worse its condition appeared. There was even some dry rot under the eaves.

The doorbell did not function. Calhoun pressed it several times but heard nothing. He knocked twice, but there was no response. Leaving the front stoop, Calhoun circled the house.

Set way back from the house was a barn that had been converted into a garage. Calhoun ignored the barn and continued around the house, trying to see into the windows. It wasn't easy since the windows were filthy. In the back of the house there were a pair of hatch doors secured with an old, rusted padlock. Calhoun guessed they covered stairs to the basement.

Returning to the front of the house, Calhoun went back up the stoop. Pausing at the door he looked around to make sure no one was watching. He then tried the door. It was unlocked.

To be absolutely certain no one was home, Calhoun knocked again as loudly as his knuckles would bear. Satisfied, he reached again for the doorknob. To his shock, the door opened on its own. Calhoun looked up. Van Slyke was eyeing him suspiciously.

"What on earth do you want?" Van Slyke asked.

Calhoun had to remove the cigar that he'd tucked between his teeth. "Sorry to bother you," he said. "I just happened to be in the area, and I thought I'd stop by. Remember, I said I'd come back. I have a few more questions. What do you say? Is it an inconvenient time?"

"I suppose now's all right," Van Slyke said after a pause. "But I don't have too much time."

"I never overstay my welcome," Calhoun said.

• • •

Beaton had to knock several times on Traynor's outer office door before she heard his footsteps coming to unlock it.

"I'm surprised you're here," Beaton said.

Traynor locked the door after letting her in. "I've been spending so much time on hospital business, I have to come in here nights and weekends to do my own," he said.

"It was difficult to find you," Beaton said as she followed him into his private office.

"How'd you do it?" Traynor asked.

"I called your home," Beaton said. "I asked your wife, Jacqueline."

"Was she civil?" Traynor asked. He eased himself into his office chair. Piled on his desk were various deeds and contracts.

"Not particularly," Beaton admitted.

"I'm not surprised," Traynor said.

"I have to talk to you about that young couple we recruited last spring," Beaton said. "They've been a disaster. Both were fired from their positions yesterday. The husband was with CMV and she was in our pathology department."

"I remember her," Traynor said. "Wadley acted like a dog in heat around her at the Labor Day picnic."

"That's part of the problem," Beaton said. "Wadley fired her, but she came in yesterday and complained about sexual harassment, threatening to sue the hospital. She said she'd gone to Cantor well before being fired to register a complaint, a fact Cantor has confirmed."

"Did Wadley have cause to fire her?" Traynor asked.

"According to him, yes," Beaton said. "He'd documented that she'd repeatedly left town while on duty, even after he specifically warned her not to do so."

"Then there's nothing to worry about," Traynor said. "As long as he had reason to fire her, we'll be fine. I know the old judges that would hear the case. They'll end up giving her a lecture."

"It makes me nervous," Beaton said. "And the husband,

Dr. David Wilson, is up to something. Just this morning I had him escorted out of medical records. Yesterday afternoon he'd been in there accessing the hospital's computer for death rates."

"What on earth for?" Traynor asked.

"I have no idea," Beaton said.

"But you told me our death rates are okay," Traynor said. "So what difference does it make?"

"All hospitals feel that their death rates are confidential information," Beaton said. "The general public doesn't understand how they're figured. Death rates can be a public relations disaster, something that Bartlet Hospital certainly doesn't need."

"I'll agree with you there," Traynor said. "So we keep him out of medical records. It shouldn't be hard if CMV fired him. Why was he fired?"

"He was continually at the lower end of productivity," Beaton said, "and at the upper end of utilization, particularly hospitalization."

"We certainly won't miss him," Traynor said. "Sounds like I should send Kelley a bottle of scotch for doing us a favor."

"This family is worrying me," Beaton said. "Yesterday they came flying into the hospital to yank out their daughter, the one with cystic fibrosis. They took her out of the hospital against medical advice from their pediatrician."

"That does sound bizarre," Traynor said. "How's the child? I guess that's the important issue."

"She's fine," Beaton said. "I spoke to the pediatrician. She's doing perfectly well."

"Then what's the worry?" Traynor said.

Armed with the social security numbers and birth dates, Angela headed into Boston. She'd called Robert Scali that morning so he'd expect her. She didn't explain why she was coming. The reason would take too long to explain and besides, it would sound too bizarre.

She met Robert at one of the numerous small Indian restaurants in Central Square in Cambridge. As Angela entered, Robert got up from one of the tables.

Angela kissed him on the cheek, then got down to business. She told him what she wanted and handed Robert her list. He eyed the sheet.

"So you want background checks on these people?" he said. He leaned across the table. "I was hoping that you had more personal reasons for calling so suddenly. I thought you wanted to see me."

Angela immediately felt uncomfortable. When they'd gotten together before, Robert had never intimated anything about rekindling their old flame.

Angela decided it was best to be direct. She assured Robert that she was happily married. She told him that she'd come purely because she needed his help.

If Robert was disheartened, it didn't show. He reached across the table and squeezed her hand. "I'm glad to see you no matter what the reason," he said. "I'll be happy to help. What is it you specifically want?"

Angela explained to Robert that she'd been told that a good deal of information could be obtained about a person through computer searches using just the social security number and the birth date.

Robert laughed in the deep, husky manner that Angela remembered so vividly. "You have no idea how much is available," he said. "I could get Bill Clinton's Visa card transactions for the last month if I were truly motivated."

"I want to find out everything I can about these people," Angela said, tapping the list.

"Can you be more specific?" Robert said.

"Not really," Angela said. "I want everything you can get. A friend of mine has described this process as a fishing trip."

"Who's this friend?" Robert asked.

"Well, he's not exactly a friend," Angela said. "But I've come to think of him that way. His name is Phil Calhoun. He's a retired policeman who's become a private investigator. David and I hired him."

Angela went on to give Robert a thumbnail sketch of the events in Bartlet. She started with Hodges' body being discovered in their basement, then went on to describe the fascinating clue of the tattoo, and finished up with the theory that someone was killing patients in a form of misguided euthanasia.

"My God!" Robert said when Angela ended her tale. "You're shooting holes in my romantic image of the peaceful country life."

"It's been a nightmare," Angela admitted.

Robert picked up the list. "Twenty-five names will yield a lot of data," he said. "I hope you're prepared. Did you come in a U-Haul?"

"We're particularly interested in these five," Angela said. She pointed to the people who worked in the hospital and explained why.

"This sounds like fun," Robert said. "The quickest information to get will be financial since there are quite a few databases we can tap with ease. So we'll soon have information on credit cards, bank accounts, money transfers, and debt. From then on it gets more difficult."

"What would the next step be?" Angela asked.

"I suppose the easiest would be social security," Robert said. "But hacking into their data banks is a bit trickier. But it's not impossible, especially since I have a friend here at MIT who is conveniently working on database security for various government agencies."

"Do you think he'd help?" Angela asked.

"Peter Fong? Of course he'll help if I ask him. When do you want this stuff?"

"Yesterday," Angela said with a smile.

"That's one of the things I always liked about you," Robert said. "Always so eager. Come on, let's go see Peter Fong."

Peter's office was hidden away at the rear of the fourth floor of a cream-colored stuccoed building in the middle of the MIT campus.

It looked less like an office than an electronics laboratory. It was filled with computers, cathode ray tubes, liquid crystal displays, wires, tape machines, and other electronic paraphernalia Angela couldn't identify.

Peter Fong was an energetic Asian-American with eyes even darker than Robert's. It was immediately obvious to Angela that he and Robert were the best of friends.

Robert handed Peter the list and told him what they wanted. Peter scratched his head and pondered the request.

"I agree social security would be the best place to start," Peter said. "But an FBI database search would also be a good idea."

"Is that possible?" Angela asked. The world of computer information was new to her.

"No problem," Peter said. "I've got a colleague in Washington. Her name is Gloria Ramirez. I've been working with her on this database security project. She's on line with both organizations."

Peter used a word processor to type out what he wanted. Then he slipped it into his fax. "We usually communicate by fax but for this she'll respond by computer. With that amount of data it will be faster."

Within minutes, data was pouring directly into his hard disk drive. Peter pulled some of the material up onto his screen.

Angela looked over Peter's shoulder and scanned the screen. It was a portion of the social security record on Joe Forbs, indicating the recent jobs he'd held along with his payments into the social security pool. Angela was impressed. She was also dismayed at how easy it was to get such information.

Peter activated his laser printer. It began spewing forth page after page of data. Robert walked over and picked up a sheet. Angela joined him. It was the social security file on Werner Van Slyke.

"Interesting," Angela said. "He was in the navy. That's probably where he got his tattoo."

"A lot of the enlisted men think of a tattoo as a rite of passage," Robert said.

Angela was even more surprised later when the criminal records began coming in on another printer. Peter had to activate a second machine since the first was still busy with the social security material.

Angela hadn't expected much criminal information since Bartlet was such a small, quiet town. But like so much else about Bartlet, her assumption was wrong. The most significant item, as far as she was concerned, was the discovery that Clyde Devonshire had been arrested and convicted of rape six years earlier. The incident had taken place in Norfolk, Virginia, and he had served two years in the state penitentiary.

"Sounds like a charming fellow to have in a small town," Robert said sarcastically.

"He works in the ER at the hospital," Angela said. "I wonder if anyone knew of his record."

Robert went back to the other printer and rummaged through the data until he found Clyde Devonshire's information.

"He was in the navy too," Robert called over to Angela, who was transfixed by the criminal material still coming out. "In fact, the dates seem to indicate that he was in the navy when he was arrested for rape."

Angela stepped over to Robert to look over his shoulder.

"Look at this," Robert said as he pointed to the sequence of dates. "There are a number of gaps in the social security history after Mr. Devonshire got out of prison. I've seen records like this before. Such gaps suggest that he either did more time or was using aliases."

"Good Lord!" Angela said. "Phil Calhoun said we'd be surprised by what turned up. He certainly was right."

Half an hour later, Angela and Robert walked out of Peter's office with several boxes full of computer paper. They headed for Robert's office.

Robert's work space looked much the same as Peter's as far as equipment was concerned. The one significant difference was that Robert had a window overlooking the Charles River.

"Let's get you some financial information," Robert said as he sat down at one of his terminals. Before long, material started coming back across his screen as if a hole had been poked in a dam.

As Robert's printers snapped into operation, pages flew into the collection trays with surprising rapidity.

"I'm overwhelmed," Angela admitted. "I've never thought such reams of personal information could be obtained with such ease."

"For fun, let's see what we can get on you," Robert said. "What's your social security number?"

"No, thank you," Angela said. "Knowing the amount of debt I have, it would be too depressing."

"I'll try to get more material on your suspects tonight," Robert said. "Sometimes it's easier at night when there's less electronic traffic."

"Thank you so much," Angela said as she tried to pick up the two boxes of material.

"I think I'd better give you a hand with all that," Robert said.

Once the material was stored in the trunk, Angela gave Robert a long hug.

"Thanks again," she said. She gave him an extra squeeze. "It's been good to see you."

Robert waved as Angela drove away. She watched his figure recede in her rearview mirror. It had been nice to see him, except for the brief moment of discomfort when she'd first arrived. Now she was looking forward to showing David and Calhoun all this material.

"I'm home!" Angela shouted as she entered through the back door. Hearing no response, she went back for the second box of information herself. When she returned, the house was still silent. With a growing sense of unease, Angela passed through the kitchen and dining room on her way to the stairs. She was startled to find David reading in the family room.

"Why didn't you answer me?" Angela asked.

"You said you were home," David said. "I didn't feel that required a response."

"What's the matter?" Angela asked.

"Nothing at all," David said. "How was your day with your old boyfriend?"

"Oh, is that what this is about?" Angela said.

David shrugged. "It seems strange to me that you've kept quiet about this man from your past for the four years we lived in Boston."

"David!" Angela said with a touch of exasperation. She walked over and threw herself into David's lap, wrapping her arms around his neck. "I didn't mean to keep Robert secret. If I'd meant to keep him a secret, do you think I would have named him now? Don't you know I love you and no one else." She kissed him on the nose.

"Promise?" David asked.

"Promise," Angela said. "How's Nikki?"

"She's fine," David said. "She's napping. She's still terribly upset about Caroline. But physically she's doing great. How did you do?"

"You won't believe it," Angela said. "Come on!"

Angela dragged David into the kitchen and showed him the boxes. He took out a few pages to look at them. "You're right," he said. "I don't believe it. This will take us hours to go through."

"It's a good thing we're unemployed," Angela said. "At least we have plenty of time."

"I'm glad to hear your humor's back," David said.

They made dinner together. When Nikki woke up she joined in, though it was difficult for her to move around since she still had an IV running. Before they sat down to eat, David called Dr. Pilsner. Together they decided that Nikki's IV could be pulled and the antibiotics continued orally.

During dinner David and Angela talked about having to break the news about their employment status in Bartlet to their parents. Both were reluctant.

"I don't know what you're worried about," David questioned. "Your mother and father will probably cheer. They never wanted us to come up here anyway."

"That's the problem," Angela said. "It will drive me bananas when they start in with the 'I told you so' routine."

After dinner while Nikki watched television, David and Angela began the chore of going through the computer data. David was progressively amazed and appalled at the wealth of the material accessible to hackers.

"This will take us days," David complained.

"Maybe we should concentrate on those with connections to the hospital," Angela said. "There are only five."

"Good idea," David said.

Like Angela, David found the criminal information the most provocative. He was particularly taken by the news that Clyde Devonshire had not only served time for rape but had also been arrested in Michigan for loitering outside Jack Kevorkian's house. Assisted suicide and euthanasia shared some philosophical justifications. David wondered if Devonshire could be their "angel of mercy."

David was also amazed to learn that Peter Ullhof had been arrested six times outside Planned Parenthood centers and three times outside of abortion clinics, once for assault and battery of a doctor.

"This is interesting," Angela said. She was looking through the social security material. "All five of these people served in the military, including Claudette Maurice. That's a coincidence."

"Maybe that's why they all have tattoos," David said.

Angela nodded. She remembered Robert's comment about tattoos being a rite of passage.

After helping Nikki do her respiratory therapy, they put her to bed. Then they returned downstairs and brought the computer printouts into the family room. They began to sift through again, creating a separate pile for each of the five hospital workers.

"I expected Calhoun to have called by now," Angela said. "I was looking forward to getting his opinion on some of this information, particularly regarding Clyde Devonshire."

"Calhoun's an independent sort," David said. "He said he'd call when he had something to tell us."

"Well, I'm going to give him a call," Angela said. "We have something to tell him."

Angela only got Calhoun's answering machine. She didn't leave a message.

"One of the things that surprises me," David said when Angela was off the phone, "is how often these people have changed jobs." David was going over the social security data.

Angela moved next to him and looked over his shoulder. All at once she reached over and took a paper that David was about to put on Van Slyke's pile.

"Look at this," she said, pointing to an entry. "Van Slyke was in the navy for twenty-one months."

"So?" David questioned.

"Isn't that unusual?" Angela asked. "I thought the short-est stint in the navy was three years."

"I don't know," David said.

"Let's look at Devonshire's service record," Angela said. She leafed through Devonshire's pile until she found the appropriate page.

"He was in for four and a half years."

"My God!" David exclaimed. "Will you listen to this? Joe Forbs has declared personal bankruptcy three times. With that kind of history, how can he get a credit card? But he has. Each time he's gotten all new cards at another institution. Amazing."

By eleven o'clock, David was struggling to keep his eyes open. "I'm afraid I have to go to bed," he said. He tossed the papers he had in his hand onto the table.

"I was hoping you'd say that," Angela said. "I'm bushed too."

They went upstairs arm in arm, feeling satisfied they'd accomplished so much in one day. But they might not have slept so soundly had they any inkling of the firestorm their handiwork had ignited.

24

SUNDAY, OCTOBER 31

HALLOWEEN DAWNED CLEAR AND CRISP WITH FROST on the grimacing pumpkins perched on porches and window-sills. Nikki awoke feeling entirely normal physically, and with the festive atmosphere of the holiday, even her spirits were much improved. Angela had made it a point earlier in the week to stock candies and fruits for possible trick-or-treaters.

Angela had no interest in going to church. The idea of trying to fit into the Bartlet community had lost its appeal. David offered to take them to the Iron Horse Inn for break-fast even if they didn't go to church, but Angela preferred to stay at home.

After breakfast Nikki began to agitate to be allowed to go trick-or-treating herself. But Angela was not enthusiastic. She was concerned about letting Nikki out into the cold so soon after she'd gotten over her latest bout of congestion. As a compromise, she sent David into town to try to buy a pumpkin while she got Nikki to help her prepare the house for the children coming to their door.

Angela had Nikki fill a large glass salad bowl to the brim with miniature chocolate bars. Nikki carried it to the front hall and placed it on the table by the door.

Next, Angela had Nikki start making Halloween decorations out of colored construction paper. With Nikki happily occupied, Angela called Robert Scali in Cambridge.

"I'm glad you called," Robert said as soon as he heard Angela's voice. "I've gotten some more financial data like I promised."

"I appreciate your efforts," Angela said. "But I've another request. Can you get me military service records?"

"Now you're pushing it," Robert said. "It's much more difficult to hack into military data banks, as you might imagine. I suppose I could get some general information, but I doubt I could get anything classified unless Peter's colleague is on line with the Pentagon. But I doubt that very much."

"I understand," Angela said. "You've said exactly what I thought you'd say."

"Let's not give up immediately," Robert said. "Let me call Peter and ask. I'll call you back in a few minutes."

Angela hung up and went over to see how Nikki was doing. She'd cut out a big orange moon and now was in the process of cutting out a silhouetted witch on a broomstick. Angela was impressed: neither she nor David had any artistic talent.

David returned with an enormous pumpkin. Nikki was thrilled. Angela helped spread newspaper on the kitchen table. David and Nikki were soon absorbed in carving the pumpkin into a jack o' lantern. Angela helped until the phone rang. It was Robert calling back.

"Bad news," he said. "Gloria can't help with Pentagon stuff. But I was able to get some basic info. I'll send it up with this additional financial material. What's your fax number?"

"We don't have a fax," Angela said. She felt guilty, as if she and David had not joined the nineties.

"But you do have a modem with your computer?" Robert said.

"We don't even have a computer, except one for Nikki's video games," Angela admitted. "But I'll figure out a way to get the material. In the meantime, can you tell me why Van Slyke was in the navy for only twenty-one months?"

There was a pause. Angela could hear Robert shuffling through papers.

"Here it is," he said finally. "Van Slyke got a medical discharge."

"Does it say for what?" Angela asked.

"I'm afraid not," Robert said. "But there is some interesting stuff here. It says that Van Slyke went to submarine school in New London, Connecticut, then on to nuclear power school. He was a submariner."

"Why is that interesting?" Angela asked.

"Not everybody goes out on submarines," Robert said. "It says he was assigned to the U.S.S. *Kamehameha* out of Guam."

"What kind of job did Clyde Devonshire have in the navy?" Angela asked.

There was more shuffling of paper. "He was a navy corpsman," Robert said. Then he added: "My gosh, isn't this a coincidence."

"What?" Angela asked. It was frustrating not to have the papers herself.

"Devonshire got a medical discharge, too," Robert said. "Having done hard time for rape, I would have guessed it would have been something else."

"That sounds even more interesting to me than Van Slyke's going to submarine school," Angela said.

After thanking Robert again for all his efforts, Angela hung up. Returning to the kitchen where David and Nikki were putting the finishing touches on the jack o' lantern's grotesque face, Angela told David that Robert had more material for them that she wanted to get. She also told him what she'd just learned about Devonshire and Van Slyke.

"So they both had medical discharges," David said. It was obvious he was preoccupied.

"What do you think?" David asked Nikki as they both stepped back to admire their work.

"I think it's great," Nikki said. "Can we put a candle in it?"

"Absolutely," David said.

"David, did you hear me?" Angela asked.

"Of course I did," David said. He handed a candle to Nikki.

"I wish we could find the reasons for these medical discharges," Angela said.

"I bet I know how we could," David said. "Get someone in the VA system to pull it out of their data banks. They'd have to have it recorded."

"Good idea," Angela said. "Do you have any suggestions who we could ask?"

"I have a doctor friend at the VA in Boston," David said.

"Do you think he would mind doing us a favor?" Angela asked.

"It's a she," David said. David told Nikki that she should cut out a little depression inside the pumpkin to hold the candle. She hadn't been able to get the candle to stay upright.

"So who's your doctor friend?" Angela asked.

"She's an ophthalmologist," David said, still overseeing Nikki's efforts to stabilize the candle inside the pumpkin.

"I wasn't referring to her specialty," Angela said. "How do you know her?"

"We went to high school together," David said. "We dated senior year."

"And how long has she been in the Boston area?" Angela asked. "And what's her name?" Two could play at this jealousy game.

"Her name is Nicole Lungstrom," David said. "She came to Boston at the end of last year."

"I've never heard you mention her before," Angela said. "How did you know she came to town?"

"She called me at the hospital," David said. He gave Nikki a congratulatory pat when the candle was finally stabilized. Nikki ran to get matches. David turned his attention to Angela.

"So have you seen her since she's come to Boston?" Angela asked.

"We had lunch once," David said, "and that was it. I told her it was better that we not see each other because she had romantic hopes. We parted friends."

"Honest?" Angela asked.

"Honest," David said.

"You think that if you call out of the blue she'll help us?" Angela asked.

"To tell you the truth, I doubt it," David said. "If we want to take advantage of her employment status with the VA, then I think I should go down there. There's no way I can ask her to violate confidentiality rules over the telephone. Besides, I'd do better to explain the whole sordid story in person."

"When would you go?" Angela asked.

"Today," David said. "I'll call her first to make sure she's available. Then I'll go. I'll even stop at MIT and pick up that material you want from Robert. What do you say?"

Angela bit the inside of her lip as she pondered. She was surprised to feel such a pang of jealousy. Now she knew how David felt. She shook her head and sighed. "Call her," she said.

While Angela cleaned up the mess from the gutting of the pumpkin, David went into the family room and called Nicole Lungstrom. Angela could hear bits and pieces of the conversation even though she tried not to. It bothered her that David sounded so cheerful. A few minutes later he came back into the kitchen.

"It's all arranged," David said. "She's expecting me in a couple of hours. Conveniently, she's on call at the hospital."

"Is she blond?" Angela asked.

"Yeah, she is," David said.

"I was afraid of that," Angela said.

Nikki had the candle lit in the pumpkin, and David carried the jack o' lantern out onto the front porch. He let Nikki decide where she wanted it.

"It looks cool," Nikki said, once it was in place.

Returning inside the house, David asked Angela to call Robert Scali and tell him he would be stopping by. While

David went upstairs to get ready to drive to Boston, Angela gave Robert a call.

"That will be interesting," Robert said once Angela explained the reason for her call.

Angela didn't know how to respond. She simply thanked him again for his help and hung up. Then she tried to call Calhoun. Once more she got his answering machine.

David came down wearing his blue blazer and gray slacks. He looked quite handsome.

"Do you have to get so dressed up?" Angela asked.

"I'm going to the VA hospital," David said. "I'm not going in jeans and a sweatshirt."

"I tried to call Calhoun again," Angela said. "Still no answer. That man must have come in late and gone out early. He's really involved in this investigation."

"Did you leave a message?" David asked.

"No," Angela said.

"Why not?"

"I hate answering machines," Angela said. "Besides, he must know we want to hear from him."

"I think you should leave a message," David said.

"What should we do if we don't hear from him by tonight?" Angela asked. "Go to the police?"

"I don't know," David admitted. "The idea of going to Robertson for anything doesn't thrill me."

After Angela watched David pull down their drive, she put her full attention on Nikki. More than anything she wanted her daughter to enjoy the day.

Motivated more by curiosity than anything else, David went to meet Robert Scali first. Hoping the man would look like a nerdy academic, David was crestfallen to discover that Robert was a handsome man with a tanned face and an athletic bearing. To make matters worse, he seemed like a genuinely nice guy.

They shook hands. David could tell Robert was also sizing him up.

"I want to thank you for your help," David said.

"That's what friends are for," Robert said. He handed over another box full of information.

"There's something new on the financial side that I should mention," Robert said. "I discovered that Werner Van Slyke has opened several new bank accounts in the last year, apparently traveling to both Albany and here to Boston to do so. I hadn't gotten that information yesterday because I'd been more interested in credit card history and debt."

"That's strange," David said. "Is it a lot of money?"

"There's less than ten thousand in each account, probably to avoid the rule that banks have to report movements of more than ten thousand."

"That's still a lot of money for a man running a maintenance department at a community hospital," David said.

"This day and age, it probably means the fellow is running a little drug ring," Robert said. "But if he is, he shouldn't be banking the money. He's supposed to bury it in PVC pipe. That's the norm."

"I'd heard from a couple of my teenage patients that marijuana was easily available in the local high school," David said.

"There you go," Robert said. "Maybe on top of whatever else you and Angela solve, you can do your part to help make America drug-free."

David laughed and thanked Robert again for all his help.

"Let me know when you guys next come to town," Robert said. "There's a great restaurant here in Cambridge called Anago Bistro. It will be my treat."

"Will do," David said as he waved goodbye. On his way out to the car, David doubted he'd feel comfortable getting together.

After stowing the computer data in the trunk, David drove across the Charles River and out the Fenway. It took only twenty minutes to get to the VA hospital; Sunday midafternoon was a traffic low.

Walking into the hospital, David thought it was ironic how lives could intersect after years of separation. He'd dated Nicole Lungstrom for almost a year, starting in the last part of junior year of high school. But after graduation she'd gone off to the West Coast for college, medical school, and residency. At one point David had heard through friends that she'd married. When she'd called the previous year,

David had learned she'd been divorced.

David had Nicole paged and waited for her in the lobby. When she first appeared and they greeted each other, they were both uneasy. David quickly learned that there was a new man in Nicole's life. David was pleased, and he began to relax.

For privacy, Nicole took David into the doctors' lounge. Once they were seated he told her the whole story of his and Angela's disastrous sojourn in Bartlet. He then told her what he wanted.

"What do you think?" David asked. "Would you mind seeing what information is available?"

"Will this be just between us?" Nicole asked.

"My word of honor," David said. "Except for Angela, of course."

"I assumed that," Nicole said. She pondered the situation for a few minutes, then nodded. "Okay," she said. "If someone is killing patients then I think the ends justify the means, at least in this instance."

David handed Nicole the short list of people: Devonshire, Van Slyke, Forbs, Ullhof, and Maurice.

"I thought you were only interested in two," Nicole said.

"We know all five of these people were in the military," David said. "And all five have tattoos. We might as well be thorough."

Using the social security numbers and birth dates Nicole obtained the military ID numbers on each person. She then began calling up the records. There was an immediate surprise. Both Forbes and Ullhof had also been given medical discharges. Only Maurice had mustered out normally.

Both Forbs' and Ullhof's discharge diagnoses were pedestrian: Forbs was released because of chronic back problems while Ullhof had been discharged because of nonspecific, chronic prostatitis.

Van Slyke's and Devonshire's were not so innocuous. Van Slyke's was the most complicated. Nicole had to scroll through page after page of material. Van Slyke had been discharged with a psychiatric diagnosis of "schizo-affective disorder with mania and strong paranoid ideation under stress."

"Good Lord," David said. "I'm not sure I understand all that. Do you?"

"I'm an ophthalmologist," Nicole said. "But I gather the translation is that the guy is schizophrenic with a large component of mania."

David looked at Nicole and raised his eyebrows. "Sounds like you know more about this stuff than I do," he said. "I'm impressed."

"I was interested in psychiatry at one point," Nicole said. "This Van Slyke fellow sounds like the kind of person I'd stay away from. But for all his mental trouble, look at all the schooling he went through, even nuclear power school. I hear that's quite rigorous."

Nicole continued to scroll through the material.

"Wait," David said, leaning on her shoulder. He pointed to a passage that described an incident where Van Slyke had had a psychiatric break while on patrol on a nuclear submarine. At the time, he'd been working as a nuclear-trained machinist's mate for the engineering department.

David read aloud: " 'During the first half of the patrol the patient's mania was apparent and progressive. He exhibited elevated mood which led to poor judgment and feelings of hostility, belligerence, and ultimately to persistent paranoid thoughts of being ridiculed by the rest of the crew and being affected by computers and radiation. His paranoia reached a climax when he attacked the captain and had to be restrained.' "

"Good grief," Nicole said. "I hope I don't see him in the clinic."

"He's not quite as wacko as this makes him sound," David said. "I've even spoken to him on several occasions. He's not sociable or even friendly, but he does his job."

"I'd say he was a time bomb," Nicole said.

"Being paranoid about radiation while on a nuclear submarine isn't so crazy," David said. "If I ever had to be on a nuclear submarine, it would drive me up the wall knowing I was so close to a nuclear reactor."

"There's more history here," Nicole said. She read aloud: " 'Van Slyke has a history of being a loner type. He was raised by an aggressive, alcoholic father and a fearful and compliant mother. The mother's maiden name was Traynor.' "

"I'd heard that part of the story," David said. "Harold Traynor, the fellow's uncle, is the chairman of the board of trustees."

"Here's something else interesting," Nicole said. She again read aloud: "The patient has demonstrated the tendency to idealize certain authority figures but then turn against them with minor provocation, whether real or fancied. This behavior pattern has occurred prior to entering the service and while in the navy." Nicole looked up at David. "I certainly wouldn't want to be his boss."

Moving on to Devonshire, they found less material, but it was just as interesting and even more significant as far as David was concerned. Clyde Devonshire had been treated for sexually transmitted diseases on several occasions in San Diego. He'd also had a bout of hepatitis B. Finally he'd tested positive for HIV.

"This might be really important," David said, tapping the computer screen and making reference to the AIDS virus. "The fact that Clyde Devonshire has a potentially terminal illness himself could be the key."

"I hope I've helped," Nicole said.

"Could I get copies of these records?" David asked.

"That might take some time," Nicole said. "Medical records is closed on Sundays. I'll have to get a key to get access to a printer."

"I'll wait," David said. "But I'd like to use the phone first."

After much grumbling and a few tears, Nikki finally accepted the fact that it was not in her best interest to traipse around the neighborhood trick-or-treating. The day that had started out so clear had turned gray. A distinct threat of rain was in the offing. But Nikki still dressed up in her fearful costume and derived enormous fun from going to the door and scaring the handful of children who showed up.

Angela still hated Nikki's costume, but she held her tongue. She was not about to detract from Nikki's enjoyment.

While Nikki hovered by the door waiting for more trick-or-treaters, Angela tried Calhoun one more time. Again, she got his answering machine. When she called earlier that afternoon, she'd left a message as David suggested, but Calhoun had never called back. Angela began to worry. Looking out the window at the gathering gloom, she also began to worry about David. Although he'd called many hours ago to say he'd be a bit later than expected, she thought he should have been home by now.

Half an hour later, Nikki was willing to call it quits. It was growing dark and getting late for trick-or-treaters. No one had been by for some time.

Angela was thinking about starting dinner when the doorbell chimed. Nikki had already gone upstairs to take a bath, so Angela headed for the front door. As she passed the table in the front hall, she picked up the glass bowl with the chocolates. Through the side light window she caught a glimpse of a reptile-headed man.

Angela unlocked the door, opened it, and began to say something about how great a costume it was when she noticed that the man was not accompanied by a child.

Before Angela could react, the man lunged inside, grabbed Angela around the neck with his left arm, and enveloped her in a headlock. His gloved right hand slapped over her mouth, suppressing a scream. Angela dropped the bowl of chocolates to the marble foyer floor where it shattered into hundreds of pieces.

Angela vainly struggled with the man, desperately trying to pull free. But he was strong and held her tightly in a vise-like grip. The only noises she could make were muffled grunts.

"Shut up or I'll kill you," the man said in a raspy half whisper. He gave Angela's head a fearful shake; a sudden stab of pain shot down Angela's back. She stopped struggling.

The man glanced around the room. He strained to see down the hallway toward the kitchen.

"Where's your husband?" he demanded.

Angela couldn't respond. She was beginning to feel dizzy, as if she might black out.

"I'm going to let you go," the man snarled. "If you scream I'll shoot you. Understand?" He gave Angela's head another shake, bringing tears of pain.

As promised, the man let Angela go. She staggered back a step but caught herself. Her heart was racing. She knew that Nikki was upstairs in the bathtub. Rusty, unfortunately, was out in the barn. He'd been a nuisance with the trick-or-treaters.

Angela looked at her attacker. His reptile mask was grotesque. The scales appeared almost real. A red forked tongue hung limply from a mouth lined with jagged teeth. Angela tried to think. What should she do? What could she do? She noticed the man had a pistol in his hand.

"My husband is not at home," Angela managed to say at last. Her voice was hoarse. The headlock had compressed her throat.

"What about your sick kid?" the man demanded.

"She's out trick-or-treating with friends," Angela said.

"When will your husband be back?" the man asked.

Angela hesitated, not knowing what was best to say. The man grabbed her arm and gave it a tug. His thumbnail bit into her flesh. "I asked you a question," he snarled.

"Soon," Angela managed.

"Good," the man said. "We'll wait. Meanwhile, let's take a look around the house and make sure you're not lying to me."

"I wouldn't lie," Angela said as she felt herself propelled into the family room.

Nikki was not in the bathtub. She'd been out for some time. When the door chimes sounded, she'd rushed to finish dressing and put on her mask. She'd hoped to get downstairs before the kids had left. She wanted to see their costumes and surprise them with her own. She'd just gotten to the head of the stairs when the glass bowl shattered, stopping her in her tracks. Helplessly she'd watched from upstairs as her mother began to struggle with a man wearing a serpent mask.

After the initial shock, Nikki ran down the hall to the master bedroom and picked up the telephone. But there was no dial tone. The line was dead. Rushing back down the hall, she'd peeked over the edge of the stairs just in time to see her mother and the man disappear into the family room.

Advancing to the head of the stairs, Nikki looked down. The shotgun was leaning against the back of the newel post.

Nikki had to jump back out of sight when her mother and the reptile man reappeared from the family room. Nikki could hear their footsteps crunching the broken glass of the candy bowl. Then the footsteps stopped. Nikki could only hear muffled voices.

Nikki forced herself to peek over the edge of the stairs again. She saw her mother and the man reappear briefly from the living room before they vanished down the central corridor toward the kitchen.

Nikki inched forward and again peered down at the shotgun. It was still there. She started down the steps, but no matter how slowly she moved, each step creaked under the weight of her light, seventy-pound frame.

Nikki only got halfway down the stairs before she heard Angela and the man coming back along the corridor. Panicked, Nikki raced back up the stairs and partway down the upstairs corridor. She stopped, intending to return to the top of the stairs and then to descend to the foyer when it was safe. But to her horror her mother and the man started up the stairs.

Nikki ran the rest of the way down the corridor and dashed into the master bedroom. She ducked into one of the walk-in closets. In the back of the closet was a second door leading to a short hall connecting with the barn. Several store rooms ran off it. At the end of the hall was a narrow, spiral staircase that led down to the mud room.

Nikki raced down these stairs, then through the kitchen and along the first-floor corridor, finally reaching the foyer. She snatched up the shotgun. She checked to see if there was a shell in the magazine just as her mother had taught her. There was. She released the safety.

Nikki's elation quickly changed to confusion. Now that she had the shotgun in her hands, she didn't know what to do next. Her mother had explained that the gun sprayed pellets in a wide arc. It didn't have to be aimed too carefully; it would hit just about everything it was pointed at. The problem was her mom. Nikki didn't want to hit her.

Nikki had little time to ponder her dilemma. Almost immediately she heard the intruder marching her mother back along the upstairs corridor and down the main stairs. Nikki backed up toward the kitchen. She didn't know whether to hide or run outside to the neighbors'.

Before Nikki could decide, her mother appeared in the foyer, stumbling down the last few stairs. Apparently she'd been pushed. Right behind her was the reptile man. In full view of Nikki the man gave Angela another cruel shove that sent her flying through the archway into the living room. In his right hand was a pistol.

The man started after her mother. He was about twenty feet away from Nikki, who was holding the shotgun at her waist. She had her left hand around the barrel and her right hand around the stock. Her finger was on the trigger.

The intruder turned briefly to face Nikki as he walked, then did a double take. He started to raise his gun in her direction. Nikki closed her eyes and pulled the trigger.

The sound of the blast from the shotgun was horrendous in the narrow hallway. The recoil knocked Nikki over backward, yet she stubbornly held onto the shotgun. Regaining her balance enough to sit up, she used all her strength to cock the gun. Her ears were ringing so much, she couldn't hear the mechanical click the shotgun made as a fresh shell was rammed into position and the spent cartridge ejected.

Angela suddenly appeared out of the smoky haze, coming from the direction of the kitchen. Immediately following the blast she'd run from the living room into the kitchen, doubling around and back up the main corridor. She took the shotgun from Nikki who was only too glad to give it up.

From the family room they heard the sound of a door banging open, then stillness.

"Are you all right?" Angela whispered to Nikki.

"I think so," Nikki said.

Angela helped Nikki to her feet, then motioned for her to follow her. Slowly they advanced toward the foyer.

They inched past the archway leading into the living room, catching sight of the damage caused by Nikki's shotgun blast. A portion of the pellets were embedded in the side of the arch. The rest of the charge had carried away another four panes of glass from the living room's bay window, the same window damaged by the brick.

Next they rounded the base of the stairs, trying to avoid the shards of broken glass. As they approached the archway leading into the family room, they felt a draft of cold air. Angela kept the shotgun trained ahead. Edging along together, Angela and Nikki spotted the source of the draft: one of the French doors leading to the terrace hung open and was gently swinging back and forth with the evening breeze.

With Nikki clutching one of Angela's belt loops, they advanced toward the open door. They gazed out at the dark line of trees bordering their property. For a few moments they stood absolutely still, listening for any sounds. All they heard was the distant bark of a dog, followed by Rusty's rebuttal from out in the barn. No one was in sight.

Angela closed the door and locked it. Still gripping the gun in one hand, she bent down and hugged Nikki with all her might.

"You're a hero," she said. "Wait until I tell your father."

"I didn't know what to do," Nikki said. "I didn't mean to hit the window."

"The window doesn't matter," Angela said. "You did splendidly." Angela went over to the phone. She was surprised to find it was dead.

"The one in your bedroom's not working either," Nikki said.

Angela shuddered. The intruder had gone to the trouble of cutting their lines first. Had it not been for Nikki, Angela hated to think what might have happened.

"We have to make sure the man is not still here," Angela said. "Come on, let's search the house."

Together they went through the dining room into the kitchen. They checked the mud room and the two small storage rooms. Returning to the kitchen they walked down the central corridor back to the foyer.

While Angela was debating whether to check upstairs, the door chimes rang. Both she and Nikki jumped.

Looking out the side lights on either side of the door, Angela and Nikki saw a group of children dressed as witches and ghosts standing on their stoop.

David pulled into the driveway. He was surprised to see that every light in the house was on. Then he saw a group of teenagers leap from the porch, dash across the lawn, and disappear into the trees lining the property.

David stopped the car. He could see that his front door was plastered with raw eggs. The windows had been soaped, and the jack o' lantern smashed. He had half a mind to give chase to the kids but decided that the chances of finding them in the dark were pretty slim. "Damn kids," he said aloud. Then he noticed that more of the living-room bay window had been broken.

"Good gravy!" David exclaimed. "That's going way too far." He got out of the car and went up to his front door. The place was a mess. Tomatoes as well as eggs had been thrown against the front of the house.

Not until he discovered the broken glass and candy scattered across the floor of the foyer did David become truly worried. Struck by a sudden stab of fear for his family, David cried out for Angela and Nikki.

Almost immediately Angela and Nikki appeared at the top of the stairs. Angela was holding the shotgun. Nikki started to cry and ran down the stairs into David's arms.

"He had a gun," Nikki managed to tell David through choking sobs.

"Who had a gun?" David asked with growing alarm. "What's happened?"

Angela came part of the way down the stairs and sat down.

"We had a visitor," Angela said.

"Who?" David demanded.

"I don't know," Angela said. "He was wearing a Halloween mask. He had a handgun."

"My God!" David said. "I never should have left you alone here. I'm sorry."

"It's not your fault," Angela said. "But you are later than you said you'd be when you called."

"It took longer than expected to get copies of the medical records," David explained. "I did try to call on my way up, but the phone was constantly busy. When I checked with the operator, I was told it was out of order."

"I think it was deliberately cut," Angela said. "Probably by the intruder."

"Did you call the police?" David asked.

"How were we to call the police when we had no phone?" Angela snapped.

"I'm sorry," David said. "I'm not thinking."

"All we've done since the man bolted is huddle upstairs," Angela said. "We've been terrified he'd come back."

"Where's Rusty?" David asked.

"I put him in the barn earlier in the day because he got so hyper with all the trick-or-treaters coming to the door."

"I'll get my portable phone from the car and I'll get Rusty while I'm at it," David said. He gave Nikki's shoulder a final squeeze.

Outside, he saw the same group of teenagers scatter.

"You'd better stay the hell away from here," David yelled into the night.

Angela and Nikki were waiting for him in the kitchen when he returned with the phone and Rusty.

"There's a wolf pack of teenagers out there," David said. "They've made a mess of the front porch."

"I think it's because we haven't been answering the door," Angela said. "All the trick-or-treaters have been turned away empty-handed. I'm afraid with no treats we've gotten our share of tricks. Believe me, compared to what we were facing, they're nothing."

"Not quite nothing: they've broken a few more window panes in the bay window," David said.

"Nikki broke the window," Angela said. She reached out and hugged her daughter. "She's our hero." Then Angela told him exactly what had happened.

David could hardly believe the peril his family had been in. When he thought of what might have happened . . . He couldn't bear to entertain the awful possibilities. When another barrage of raw eggs splattered against the front door, David's anger welled. Running to the foyer, he threw open the door fully intending to catch a couple of kids. Angela restrained him. Nikki held on to Rusty.

"They're not important," Angela said. Tears welled in her eyes.

Seeing his wife start to break down, David closed the door. He had no confusion in regard to his priorities. He consoled Angela as best he could. He knew that running after the kids would accomplish nothing; he'd just be blowing off steam in an attempt to assuage his guilt.

He drew Nikki to him as well and sat them both down on the family room couch. As soon as Angela had calmed down, David used his portable phone to call the police. While they waited for them to arrive, David cursed himself for having left Angela and Nikki.

"It's just as much my fault," Angela said. "I should have anticipated we'd be in danger." Angela then conceded that the rape attempt had possibly been an attempt on her life. She said that she'd told Calhoun about it, and he tended to agree with her.

"Why didn't you tell me this?" David demanded.

"I should have," Angela admitted. "I'm sorry."

"If nothing else, we're learning that we shouldn't hold secrets from each other," David said. "What about Calhoun? Have you heard from him yet?"

"No," Angela said. "I even left a message as you suggested. What are we going to do?"

"I don't know," David said. He stood up. "In the meantime let's take a look at that bay window."

The police were in no hurry. It took them almost three-quarters of an hour to arrive. To David's and Angela's chagrin, Robertson himself came in full uniform. Angela was tempted to ask if it was his Halloween costume. He was accompanied by a deputy, Carl Hobson.

As Robertson came through the front door he glanced at the refuse on the porch and noticed the broken window. He was carrying a clipboard.

"You people having a minor problem?" he asked.

"Not minor," Angela said. "Major." She then described what had happened from the moment the man appeared to David's arrival.

Robertson obviously had little patience for Angela's story. He fidgeted impatiently as she explained all that had happened, rolling his eyes for his deputy's benefit.

"Now, you sure this was a real gun?" Robertson asked.

"Of course it was a real gun," Angela said with exasperation.

"Maybe it was just a toy gun, part of a costume. You sure this guy wasn't just trick-or-treating?" He winked at Hobson.

"Just one goddamn minute," David said, breaking into the conversation. "I don't like what I'm hearing here. I'm getting the distinct impression that you're not taking this seriously. This man had a gun. There was violence here. Hell, even part of the bay window has been blown out."

"Don't you yell at me," Robertson said. "Your good wife has already admitted that your darling daughter blew out the window, not the purported intruder. And let me tell you something else: there's an ordinance against discharging a shotgun within the town limits unless it's done at the range by the dump."

"Get the hell out of my house," David raged.

"I'll be happy to," Robertson said. He motioned for Hobson to precede him. At the door, Robertson paused. "Let me offer you people some advice. You're not a popular family in this town, and it could get a whole lot worse if you shoot at some innocent child coming by for candy. God help you if you actually hit some kid."

David rushed to the door and slammed it behind Robertson as soon as the oaf was out the door.

"Bastard!" David fumed. "Well, we no longer have any illusions about the local police. We can't expect any help from them."

Angela hugged herself and fought off a new batch of tears. "What a mess," she said, shaking her head. David stepped over and comforted her. He also had to calm Nikki who was shocked by the sharp exchange between her father and the chief of police.

"Do you think we should stay here tonight?"

"Where can we go at this hour?" David said. "I think we should stay. We can make sure we have no more visitors."

"I suppose you're right," Angela said with a sigh. "I know I'm not thinking straight. I've never been this upset."

"Are you hungry?" David asked.

Angela shrugged. "Not really," she said. "But I'd started getting dinner ready before all this happened."

"Well, I'm starved," David said. "I didn't eat lunch."

"Okay," Angela said. "Nikki and I will put something together."

David called the phone company and reported that their phone was out of order. When he mentioned he was a doctor they agreed to send a repairman as soon as possible. Next, David went out to the barn and found some additional outdoor lighting. When he was finished, the entire outside of the house was brilliantly illuminated.

The phone repairman arrived while they were eating. He quickly determined the problem was outside; the phone line had been cut where it entered the house. While the repairman worked, the Wilsons continued their dinner.

"I hate Halloween," the repairman said when he came to the door to announce that the phone was fixed. David thanked him for coming out on a Sunday night.

After dinner David tended to additional security measures. First he boarded up a portion of the bay window in the living room. Then he went around and made sure all the doors and windows were locked.

Although the visit by the police had been exasperating, it did have one beneficial effect. After the police had been there the pesky teenagers gave up their harassment campaign. Apparently seeing the cruiser had been enough to scare them off. By nine o'clock the Wilsons had gathered in Nikki's room for her respiratory therapy.

After Nikki went to sleep, David and Angela retired to the family room to go over the material David had brought back from Boston. As an additional security aid David encouraged Rusty to leave Nikki's room where he customarily slept and stay with them in the family room. David wanted to take advantage of the dog's sensitive hearing. David also kept the shotgun close at hand.

"You know what I think," Angela said as David opened the envelope that contained the medical records. "I think the man who came in here tonight is the same person who's behind the euthanasia and Hodges' murder. I'm convinced of it. It's the only thing that makes sense."

"I agree with you," David said. "And I think our best candidate is Clyde Devonshire. Read this."

David handed Devonshire's medical record to Angela. She quickly scanned it. "Oh my," she said as she came near to the end. "He's HIV positive."

David nodded. "It means he's got a potentially terminal illness himself. I think we have a serious suspect here, especially when you combine his HIV status with the other facts like his having been arrested outside of Jack Kevorkian's house. He obviously has a strong interest in assisted suicides. Who knows? That interest could extend to euthanasia. He's a trained nurse so he has the medical expertise and he worked in the hospital so he has access, and if that isn't enough, he has a history of rape. He might be the ski-masked rapist."

Angela nodded, but she was troubled. "The only problem with all this is that it's completely circumstantial," she said. Then she asked: "Would you know Clyde Devonshire by sight?"

"No," David admitted.

"I wonder if I'd be able to identify him by his height or the sound of his voice," Angela said. "I kind of doubt it. I'd never be absolutely sure."

"Well, let's move on," David said. "The next best candidate is Werner Van Slyke. Take a look at his history." David handed Van Slyke's record to Angela. It was considerably thicker than Devonshire's.

"Good grief," Angela said as she came to the end. "What you don't know about people."

"What do you think of him as a suspect?" David asked.

"It's an interesting psychiatric history," Angela agreed. "But I don't think he's the one. Schizo-affective disorder with mania and paranoia is not the same thing as an anti-social psychotic."

"But you don't have to be antisocial to have misguided ideas about euthanasia," David said.

"That's true," Angela said. "But just because someone is mentally ill doesn't mean they're criminal. If Van Slyke had an extensive criminal history or a history of violent behavior, that would be different. But since he doesn't, I don't think he rates too high as a suspect. Besides, he may know about nuclear submarines, but he doesn't have a sophisticated knowledge of medicine. How could he be killing a bunch of patients employing a method even you can't detect if he didn't have specialized health-related training?"

"I agree," David said. "But look at this material I got from Robert today."

David handed Angela the sheet of paper listing Van Slyke's various bank accounts in Albany and Boston.

"Where on earth is he getting this money?" Angela asked. "Do you think it has anything to do with our concerns?"

David shrugged. "That's a good question," he said. "Robert didn't think so. He suggested that Van Slyke was dealing drugs. We do know there's marijuana in town, so it's possible."

Angela nodded.

"If it's not drugs it would be ominous," David said.

"Why?" Angela asked.

"Let's suppose Van Slyke is the one killing these people," David said. "If he's not selling drugs, he could be getting paid for each death."

"What an awful idea," Angela said. "But if that were the case we'd be back to square one. We still wouldn't know who was behind it. Who would be paying him and why?"

"I'd still guess it's some misguided mercy killer," David said. "All the victims had potentially fatal illnesses."

"I think we're getting too speculative," Angela said. "We've got too much information and we're straining to put it all into the same theory. Most of this information probably isn't related."

"You're probably right," David said. "But I just had an idea. If we were to determine Van Slyke was the culprit, then his psychiatric problems could work in our favor."

"What do you mean?" Angela asked.

"Van Slyke had a psychotic break under the stress of a submarine patrol. I don't find that all that surprising. I might have had one, too. Anyway, when he had his psychotic break, he had paranoid symptoms and turned against his authority figures. His history indicates he'd done that before. If we confronted him I'm sure he'd get stressed out. Then we could evoke his paranoia toward whoever is paying him. All we'd have to say is that this, quote, 'authority figure' is planning on letting Van Slyke take the blame if anything goes wrong. And since we're talking with him, obviously things are going wrong."

Angela flashed David an expression of disbelief. "You amaze me sometimes," she said. "Especially since you think you are so rational. That's the most convoluted and ridiculous idea I've ever heard. Van Slyke's history documented mania with belligerence. And you're suggesting that you could safely evoke this individual's schizophrenic paranoia? That's absurd. He'd explode in violence, and it would be directed at everyone, particularly you."

"It was just an idea," David said defensively.

"Well, I'm not going to get myself worked up," Angela said. "This is all too speculative and theoretical."

"Okay," David said soothingly. "The next candidate is Peter Ullhof. Obviously he has medical training. The fact that he's been arrested in connection with the abortion issue suggests that he has some strong feelings about moral issues in medicine. But after that, there's not much."

"What about Joe Forbs?" Angela asked.

"The only thing that makes him suspicious is his inability to handle his personal finances," David said.

"And what about the last person? Claudette Maurice."

"She's clean," David said. "The only thing I'm curious about is where she has the tattoo."

"I'm exhausted," Angela said. She tossed the papers she had in her hands onto the coffee table. "Maybe after a good night's sleep, something will come to us."

25

MONDAY, NOVEMBER 1

NIKKI AWOKE IN THE MIDDLE OF THE NIGHT WITH another nightmare and ended up sleeping in the master bedroom. David and Angela both slept restlessly. Even Rusty seemed unable to sleep soundly, growling and barking on several occasions during the night. Each time David leaped out of bed and grabbed the shotgun. But each time it proved to be a false alarm.

The only bright spot the next morning was Nikki's health. Her lungs were completely clear. Nevertheless, the Wilsons didn't even consider sending her to school.

They tried phoning Calhoun again but got the answering machine with the same message. They discussed calling the police about the investigator but couldn't make up their minds. They admitted they didn't know Calhoun that well, that his behavior was eccentric, and that they were probably jumping to conclusions. They were also reluctant to call the local police considering the experiences they'd had with them, particularly the previous night.

"The one thing I do know," Angela said, "I don't want to spend another night in this house. Maybe we should pack everything up and leave this town to its own devices and secrets."

"If we're thinking of doing that, then I'd better call Sherwood," David said.

"Do it," Angela said. "I'm serious about not wanting to spend another night here."

David phoned the bank to make an appointment to see the president. The first opening available was that afternoon at three o'clock. Although David would have preferred an earlier time, he took what he could get.

"We really should speak to a lawyer," Angela said.

"You're right," David said. "Let's call Joe Cox."

Joe was a good friend of theirs. He was also one of the shrewdest lawyers in Boston. When Angela called his office, she was told that Joe was unavailable; he was in court and would be all day. Angela left a message that she'd call back.

"Where should we spend the night?" Angela asked, hanging up the phone.

"Our closest friends in town are the Yansens," David said. "And that's not saying much. I haven't socialized with Kevin since that ridiculous tennis game, and I don't want to call him now." David sighed. "I suppose I could call my parents."

"I was afraid to suggest it," Angela said.

David made the call to Amherst, New Hampshire, and asked his mother if they could come for a few days. He explained that they were having some difficulties with the house. David's mother was delighted. There'd be no problem at all. She said she was looking forward to their arrival.

Angela tried to call Calhoun again with no luck. She then suggested they drive to his place in Rutland; it wasn't that far away. David agreed, so all three Wilsons climbed into the Volvo and made the trip.

"There it is," Angela said as they approached Calhoun's home.

David pulled into the parking area in front of the car

port. They were immediately disappointed. They'd hoped to be reassured, but they weren't. It was obvious no one was home. There was two days' worth of newspapers piled on the front stoop.

On their way back to Bartlet they discussed the investigator and found themselves even more indecisive. Angela mentioned that after she'd hired him he'd not contacted her for days. Finally they decided they'd wait one more day. If they couldn't reach him in twenty-four hours they would go to the police.

When they got home, Angela began packing for a stay at David's parents'. Nikki helped. While they were busy with that, David got out the telephone book and looked up the addresses of the five tattooed hospital workers. Once he had them written down, he went upstairs and told Angela that he wanted to cruise by their homes just to check out their living situations.

"I don't want you going anywhere," Angela said sternly.

"Why not?" David asked. He was surprised at her response.

"For one thing, I don't want to be here by myself," she said. "Second, we now understand that this affair is dangerous. I don't want you snooping around the house of a potential killer."

"Okay," David said soothingly. "Your first reason is quite sufficient. You didn't have to give me two. I didn't think you'd be nervous to be left alone during this time of the morning. And as far as it being dangerous, these people would probably be at work now."

"Probably isn't good enough," Angela said. "Why don't you give us a hand packing the car?"

It was almost noon before they were ready. After they made sure all the doors to the house were locked, they climbed into the Volvo. Rusty hopped in beside Nikki.

David's mother, Jeannie Wilson, welcomed them warmly, and made them feel instantly at home. David's father, Albert, was off for a day's fishing trip and wouldn't be back until that evening.

After carrying everything into the house, Angela collapsed

on the quilted bed in the guest room. "I'm exhausted," she said. "I could fall asleep this second."

"Why don't you?" David said. "There's no need for both of us to go back to talk with Sherwood."

"You wouldn't mind?" Angela asked.

"Not in the least," David said. He pulled the edge of the quilt down and encouraged Angela to slide under it. As he closed the door he heard her advise him to drive carefully, but her voice was already thick with sleep.

David told his mother and Nikki that Angela was napping. He suggested that Nikki do the same, but she was already involved in making cookies with her grandmother. Explaining that he had an appointment in Bartlet, David went out to the car.

David arrived back in town with three-quarters of an hour to spare. He stopped alongside the road to pull out the list of tattooed hospital employees and their addresses. The closest one was Clyde Devonshire's. Feeling a bit guilty, David put the car in gear and headed for Clyde's. He rationalized his decision by telling himself that Angela's fears were unwarranted. Besides, he wasn't going to do anything; he just wanted to take a look.

David was surprised to find a convenience store at the address listed for Devonshire. He parked in front of the building, got out, and went into the store. While paying for a carton of orange juice he asked one of the two clerks if he knew Clyde Devonshire.

"Sure do," the man said. "He lives upstairs."

"Do you know him well?" David asked.

"So-so," the man said. "He comes in here a lot."

"I was told he had a tattoo," David said.

The man laughed. "Clyde's got a bunch of tattoos," he said.

"Where are they?" David asked, feeling slightly embarrassed.

"He has tattooed ropes around both wrists," the second clerk said. "It's like he was all tied up."

The first clerk laughed again, only harder.

David smiled. He didn't get the humor, but he wanted to be polite. At least he'd found out Clyde had tattoos where they could be damaged in a struggle.

"He's also got a tattoo on his upper arm," the first clerk said. "And more on his chest."

David thanked the clerks and left the store. He walked around the side of the building and spotted the door to the stairs. For a brief instant he thought about trying the door, but then he decided against it. He owed Angela that much.

Returning to his car, David climbed in behind the wheel and checked the time. He still had twenty minutes before his meeting with Sherwood: time for one more address. The next closest was Van Slyke's.

In just a few minutes David turned onto Van Slyke's lane. He slowed down to check the numbers on the mailboxes, looking for Van Slyke's. Suddenly, David jammed on the brakes. He'd come abreast of a green truck that looked a lot like Calhoun's.

Backing up, David parked the Volvo directly behind the truck. It had a sticker on the back bumper that read: "This Vehicle Climbed Mount Washington." It had to be Calhoun's.

David got out of his car and peered into the truck's cab. A moldy cup of coffee was sitting on the open glove compartment door. The ashtray was overflowing with cigar butts. David recognized the upholstery and the air freshener hanging from the rearview mirror. The truck was definitely Calhoun's.

David straightened up and looked across the street. There was no mailbox in front of the house, but from where he was standing, he could see the address painted on the riser of the porch stairs. It was 66 Apple Tree Lane, Van Slyke's address.

David crossed the street for a closer look. The house was badly in need of paint and repair. It was even hard to be sure what color it had originally been. It looked gray but there was a greenish cast to it suggesting it had once been pale olive.

There were no signs of life. It hardly looked like the house was lived in except for the indentation of tire tracks in the gravel of the driveway.

David hiked back to the garage and peered inside. It was empty.

David then returned to the front of the house. After checking to see that no one was observing him from the street, he tried the door. It was unlocked and it opened with a simple turn of the knob. He pushed it open slowly; the rusty hinges groaned.

Ready to flee at the slightest provocation, David peered inside. What furniture he could see was covered with dust and cobwebs. Taking a deep breath, David called out to determine if anybody was home.

If there was, no one answered. He strained to hear, but the house was silent.

Fighting an urge to flee, David forced himself to step over the threshold. The silence of the house enveloped him like a cloak. His heart was racing. He didn't want to be there, but he had to find out about Calhoun.

David called out again, but again no one answered. He was about to call out a third time when the door behind him slammed shut. David nearly passed out from fright. Experiencing an irrational fear that the door had somehow locked, he frantically reopened it. He propped it open with a dusty umbrella stand. He did not want to feel enclosed in the building.

After composing himself as best he could, David made a tour of the first floor. He moved quickly from one dirty room to the next until he got to the kitchen. There he stopped. On the table was an ashtray. In it was the butt of an Antonio y Cleopatra cigar. Just beyond the table was an open door leading down to the cellar.

David approached the doorway and looked down into utter darkness. Beside the doorway was a light switch. David tried it. An anemic glow filtered up the stairs.

Taking a deep breath, David started down. He stopped midway and let his eyes sweep around the cluttered basement. It was filled with old furniture, boxes, a steamer trunk, and a hodgepodge of tools and junk. David noticed that the floor was dirt just as it was in his house, although near the furnace there was a slab of concrete.

David continued down the stairs, then went over to the

concrete. Bending down, he examined it closely. The slab
was still dark with dampness. He put his hand on it to be
sure. David shuddered. He straightened up and ran for the
stairs. As far as he was concerned, he'd seen enough to go
to the police. Only he wasn't going to bother with the local
police. He planned to call the state police directly. Reaching
the top of the stairs, David stopped in his tracks. He heard
the sound of car tires in the gravel of the driveway. A car
had pulled in beside the house.

For a second David froze, not knowing what to do. He
had little time to decide; the next thing he knew, he heard
the car door open, then slam shut, then footsteps in the
gravel.

David panicked. He pulled the door to the cellar shut and
quickly descended the stairs. He was confident there'd be
another way out of the basement, some sort of back stairs
leading directly out.

At the rear of the basement were several doors. David
lost no time weaving his way to them. The first one had
an open hasp. As quietly as possible, he pulled it open.
Beyond was a root cellar illuminated by a single low-
watt bulb.

Hearing footsteps above, David quickly went to the second door. He gave the knob a tug, but the door wouldn't
budge. He exerted more strength. At last, it creaked open.
It moved stiffly, as if it hadn't been opened for years.

Beyond the door was what David had been looking for:
a flight of concrete steps leading up to angled hatch-like
doors. David closed the door to the basement behind him.
He was now in darkness save for a sliver of light coming
from between the two nearly horizontal doors above him.

David scrambled up the stairs and crouched just beneath
the doors. He stopped to listen. He heard nothing. He put
his hands on the doors and pushed. He was able to raise
the doors half an inch, but no more; they were padlocked
from outside.

Letting the doors down quietly, David tried to keep himself calm. His pulse was hammering in his temples. He
knew he was trapped. His only hope was that he'd go
undiscovered. But the next thing he heard was the door

to the cellar crashing open followed by heavy footfalls on the cellar steps.

David squatted in the darkness and held his breath.

The footfalls drew nearer, then the door to his hideaway was yanked open. David found himself staring into the frenzied face of Werner Van Slyke.

Van Slyke appeared to be in a worse panic than David. He looked and acted as if he'd just taken an overwhelming dose of speed. His eyelids were drawn back, causing his unblinking eyes to bulge from their sockets. His pupils were so dilated he seemed to have no irises. Drops of perspiration were beaded on his forehead. His whole body was trembling, particularly his arms. In his right hand he clutched a pistol which he pointed at David's face.

For a few moments neither of them moved. David frantically tried to think of a plausible reason for his presence, but he couldn't think of a thing. All he could think about was the dancing barrel of the gun pointed at him. With Van Slyke's trembling growing worse by the minute, David was afraid the gun might go off accidentally.

David realized that Van Slyke was in the grip of an acute anxiety attack, probably triggered by his discovery of David hiding in his home. Remembering the man's psychiatric history, David thought there was a good chance Van Slyke was psychotic that very moment.

David thought about mentioning Calhoun's truck as a way of explaining his presence, but he quickly decided against it. Who knew what had transpired between Van Slyke and the private investigator? Mention of Calhoun might only exacerbate Van Slyke's psychotic state.

David decided that the best thing for him to do was to try to befriend the man, to acknowledge that he had problems, to admit that he was under stress, to tell him that David understood that he was suffering, and to tell him that David was a doctor and wanted to help him.

Unfortunately, Van Slyke gave David little chance to act on his plan. Without a word, Van Slyke reached out, grabbed David by his jacket, and rudely yanked him from the stairwell into the cellar itself.

Overwhelmed by Van Slyke's strength, David sprawled

headfirst onto the dirt floor, crashing into a stack of card-board boxes.

"Get up!" Van Slyke screamed. His voice echoed in the cellar.

David warily got to his feet.

Van Slyke was shaking so hard he was practically convulsing.

"Get into the root cellar," he yelled.

"Calm down," David said, speaking for the first time. Trying to sound like a therapist, he told Van Slyke that he understood he was upset.

Van Slyke responded by indiscriminately firing the gun. Bullets whizzed by David's head and ricocheted around the basement until they embedded themselves in an overhead floor joist, the stairs, or one of the wooden doors.

David leaped into the root cellar and cowered against the far wall, terrified of what Van Slyke might do next. Now he was convinced that Van Slyke was acutely psychotic.

Van Slyke shut the heavy wooden door with such force, plaster rained down on top of David's head. David didn't move. He could hear Van Slyke moving around in the cellar. Then he heard the sound of the hasp of the root cellar door being closed over its staple and a padlock being applied. David heard the click as the lock was closed.

After a few minutes of silence, David stood up. He looked around his cell. The only light source was a single bare bulb hanging by a cord from the ceiling. The room was bounded by large granite foundation blocks. On one wall were bins filled with fruit that appeared mummified. On the other wall shelves lined with jars of preserves reached to the ceiling.

David moved to the door and put his ear to it. He heard nothing. Looking more closely at the door he saw fresh scratch marks across it. It was as if someone had been trying desperately to claw his way out.

David knew it was futile but he had to try: he leaned his shoulder against the door and pushed it. It didn't budge. Failing in that, David started to make a complete tour of the cell when the light went out, plunging him into absolute darkness.

• • •

Sherwood buzzed his secretary and asked what time the appointment was scheduled with David Wilson.

"Three o'clock," Sharon said.

"What time is it now?" he asked. He was looking at the pocket watch he'd fished out of his vest.

"It's three-fifteen," she said.

"That's what I thought. No sign of him?"

"No, sir."

"If he shows up, tell him he'll have to reschedule," Sherwood said. "And bring in the agenda for tonight's hospital executive board meeting."

Sherwood took his finger off the intercom button. It irritated him that David Wilson would be late for a meeting that he had called to request. To Sherwood it was a deliberate snub, since punctuality was a cardinal virtue in his value system.

Sherwood lifted his phone and dialed Harold Traynor. Before he put in time on the executive meeting material, Sherwood wanted to be sure that the meeting hadn't been canceled. One had been back in 1981 and Sherwood still hadn't gotten over it.

"Six P.M.," Traynor said. "On schedule. Want to walk up together? It's a nice evening, and we won't be having too many more of these until next summer."

"I'll meet you right outside the bank," Sherwood said. "Sounds like you're in a good mood."

"It's been a good day," Traynor said. "I've just heard this afternoon from my nemesis, Jeb Wiggins. He's caved in. He'll back the parking garage after all. We should have the approval of the Selectmen by the end of the month."

Sherwood smiled. This was good news indeed. "Should I put together the bond issue?" he asked.

"Absolutely," Traynor said. "We've got to move on this thing. I have a call in to the contractor right now to see if there's any chance of pouring concrete before winter sets in."

Sharon came into Sherwood's office and handed him the agenda for the meeting.

"There's more good news," Traynor said. "Beaton called

me this morning to tell me the hospital balance sheet looks a lot better than we thought it would. October wasn't nearly as bad as predicted."

"Nothing but good news this month," Sherwood said.

"Well, I wouldn't go that far," Traynor said. "Beaton also called me a little while ago to tell me that Van Slyke never showed up."

"He didn't phone?" Sherwood questioned.

"No," Traynor said. "Of course, he doesn't have a phone so that's not too surprising. I suppose I'll have to ride over there after the executive meeting. Trouble is, I hate to go in that house. It depresses me."

Just as unexpectedly as the overhead light had gone out, it went on again. In the distance David could hear Van Slyke's footfalls coming back down the cellar stairs accompanied by the intermittent clank of metal hitting metal. After that, David heard the clatter of things being dropped onto the dirt floor.

After another trip up and down David heard Van Slyke drop something particularly heavy. After a third trip there was the same dull thud that David could feel as much as hear. It sounded almost like a body hitting the hard-packed dirt, and David felt himself shudder.

Taking advantage of the light, David explored the root cellar for another way out, but as he suspected, there was none.

Suddenly David heard the lock on the root cellar door open and the hasp pull away from the staple. He braced himself as the door was yanked open.

David sucked in a breath of air at the sight of Van Slyke. He appeared even more agitated than he had earlier. His dark, unruly hair was no longer lying flat against his skull; it now stood straight out from his head as if he'd been jolted with a bolt of electricity. His pupils were still maximally dilated, and his face was now covered with perspiration. He'd removed his green work shirt and was now clad in a dirty tee shirt which he hadn't tucked into his trousers.

David immediately noticed how powerfully built Van Slyke was, and he quickly ruled out the possibility of trying to overpower the man. David also noticed that Van Slyke had a tattoo of an American flag held by a bald eagle on his right forearm. A thin scar about five inches long marred the design. David realized then that Van Slyke was probably Hodges' murderer.

"Out!" Van Slyke yelled along with a string of expletives. He waved his gun recklessly, sending a chill down David's spine. David was terrified Van Slyke would again start randomly firing.

David complied with Van Slyke's command and quickly stepped out of the root cellar. He edged sideways, keeping Van Slyke in his line of vision at all times. Van Slyke angrily motioned for him to continue on toward the furnace.

"Stop," Van Slyke commanded after David had moved some twenty feet. He pointed down toward the ground.

David looked down. Next to his feet were a pick and shovel. Nearby was the new slab of concrete.

"I want you to dig," Van Slyke yelled. "Right where you are standing."

Afraid of hesitating for a second, David bent down and lifted the pick. David considered using it as a weapon, but as if reading his mind, Van Slyke stepped back out of reach. He kept the gun raised, and although it was shaking, it was still pointing in David's direction. David didn't dare risk charging toward him.

David noticed bags of cement and sand on the floor and guessed it had been the noise of those bags hitting the floor that he had heard from the root cellar.

David swung the pick. To his surprise it dug a mere two inches into the densely packed earthen floor. David swung the pick several more times but only succeeded in loosening a small amount of dirt. He dropped the pick and picked up the shovel to move the dirt aside. There was no doubt in his mind what Van Slyke had in mind for him. He was having him dig his own grave. He wondered if Calhoun had been put through the same ordeal.

David knew his only hope was to get Van Slyke talking. "How much should I dig?" he asked as he traded the shovel for the pick.

"I want a big hole," Van Slyke said. "Like the hole of

a doughnut. I want the whole thing. I want my mother to give me the whole doughnut."

David swallowed. Psychiatry hadn't been his forte in medical school, yet even he recognized that what he was hearing was called clanging or "loosening of associations," a symptom of acute schizophrenia.

"Did your mother give you a lot of doughnuts?" David asked. He was at a loss for words, but he desperately wanted to keep Van Slyke talking.

Van Slyke looked at David as if he were surprised he was there. "My mother committed suicide," he said. "She killed herself." Van Slyke then shocked David by laughing wildly.

David mentally ticked off another schizophrenic symptom. He could remember that this symptom was euphemistically called "inappropriate affect." David recalled another major component of Van Slyke's illness: paranoia.

"Dig faster!" Van Slyke suddenly yelled as if he'd awakened from a mini-trance.

David dug more quickly, but he did not give up on his attempt to get Van Slyke talking. He asked Van Slyke how he was feeling. He asked what was on his mind. But he got no response to either question. It was as if Van Slyke had become totally preoccupied. Even his face had gone blank.

"Are you hearing voices?" David asked, trying another approach. He swung the pick several more times. When Van Slyke still didn't answer, David looked over at him. His expression had changed from a blank look to one of surprise. His eyes narrowed, then his trembling became more apparent.

David stopped digging and studied Van Slyke. The change in his expression was striking. "What are the voices saying?" David asked.

"Nothing!" Van Slyke shouted.

"Are these voices like the ones you heard in the navy?" David asked.

Van Slyke's shoulders sagged. He looked at David with more than surprise. He was shocked.

"How did you know about the navy?" he asked. "And

how did you know about the voices?"

David could detect paranoia in Van Slyke's voice and was encouraged. He was cracking the man's shell.

"I know a lot about you," David said. "I know what you have been doing. But I want to help you. I'm not like the others. That's why I'm here. I'm a doctor. I'm concerned about you."

Van Slyke didn't speak. He simply glared at David, and David continued.

"You look very upset," David said. "Are you upset about the patients?"

Van Slyke's breath went out of him as if he'd been punched. "What patients?" he demanded.

David swallowed again. His mouth was dry. He knew he was taking risks. He could hear Angela's warnings in the back of his mind. But he had no choice. He had to gamble.

"I'm talking about the patients that you've been helping to die," David said.

"They were going to die anyway," Van Slyke shouted.

David felt a shiver rush down his spine. So it had been Van Slyke.

"I didn't kill them," Van Slyke blurted out. "They killed them. They pushed the button, not me."

"What do you mean?" David asked.

"It was the radio waves," Van Slyke said.

David nodded and tried to smile compassionately despite his anxiety. It was clear to him he was now dealing with the hallucinations of a paranoid schizophrenic. "Are the radio waves telling you what to do?" David asked.

Van Slyke's expression changed again. Now he looked at David as if David were deranged. "Of course not," he said with scorn. But then the anger came back: "How did you know about the navy?"

"I told you, I know a lot about you," David said. "And I want to help you. That's why I'm here. But I can't help you until I know everything. I want to know who 'they' are. Do you mean the voices that you hear?"

"I thought you said you knew a lot about me," Van Slyke said.

"I do," David said. "But I don't know who is telling you to kill people or even how you are doing it. I think it's the voices that are telling you. Is that true?"

"Shut up and dig," Van Slyke said. With that, he aimed the gun just to David's left and pulled the trigger. The slug thumped into the root cellar door, which then creaked on its hinges.

David quickly resumed his digging. Van Slyke's mania terrified him. But after a few more shovelfuls, David took the risk of resuming talking. He wanted to regain his credibility by impressing Van Slyke with the amount of information he had.

"I know you are being paid for what you've been doing," David said. "I even know you've been putting money in banks in Albany and Boston. I just don't know who's been paying you. Who is it, Werner?"

Van Slyke responded by moaning. David looked up from his digging in time to see Van Slyke grimacing and holding his head with both hands. He was covering his ears as if shielding them from painful sounds.

"Are the voices getting louder?" David asked. Fearing that Van Slyke wouldn't hear him with his hands over his ears, David practically shouted his question.

Van Slyke nodded. His eyes began to dart wildly around the room as if he were looking for a way to escape. While Van Slyke was distracted David gripped the shovel, gauging the distance between himself and Van Slyke, wondering if he could hit him, and if he could, whether he could hit him hard enough to eliminate the threat of the gun.

But whatever chance there had been while Van Slyke had been momentarily preoccupied was soon gone. Van Slyke's panic lessened and his wandering eyes refocused on David.

"Who is it, who is speaking to you?" David asked, trying to keep up the pressure.

"It's the computers and the radiation, just like in the navy," Van Slyke yelled.

"But you're not in the navy," David said. "You are not on a submarine in the Pacific. You are in Bartlet, Vermont, in your own basement. There are no computers or radiation."

"How do you know so much?" Van Slyke demanded again. His fear was again changing to anger.

"I want to help you," David said. "I can tell you're upset and that you're suffering. You must feel guilt. I know you killed Dr. Hodges."

Van Slyke's mouth dropped open. David wondered if he had gone too far. He sensed that he had evoked a strong paranoia in Van Slyke. He only hoped Van Slyke's rage wouldn't be directed toward him as Angela feared. David knew he had to get the conversation back to whoever was paying Van Slyke. The question was how.

"Did they pay you to kill Dr. Hodges?" David asked.

Van Slyke laughed scornfully. "That shows how much you know," he said. "They didn't have anything to do with Hodges. I did it because Hodges had turned against me, saying I was attacking women in the hospital parking lot. But I wasn't. He said he would tell everybody I was doing it unless I left the hospital. But I showed him."

Van Slyke's face went blank again. Before David could ask him if he were hearing voices, Van Slyke shook his head. Then he behaved as if he were waking from a deep sleep. He rubbed his eyes, then stared at David as if surprised to find him standing before him with a shovel. But his confusion quickly changed to anger. Van Slyke raised his gun, aiming it directly at David's eyes.

"I told you to dig," he snarled.

David rushed to comply. Even then, he fully expected to be shot. When no shots followed, David agonized over what to do next. His current approach was not working. He was stressing Van Slyke, but not enough or perhaps not in the right ways.

"I've already talked to the person who is paying you," David said after a few minutes of frantic digging. "That's one of the reasons I know so much. He's told me everything, so it doesn't matter if you tell me anything or not."

"No!" Van Slyke shouted.

"Oh, yes," David said. "He also told me something you should know. He told me that if Phil Calhoun got suspicious, you'd have to take the blame for everything."

"How did you know about Phil Calhoun?" Van Slyke

demanded. He began to shake again.

"I told you I know what's happening," David said. "The whole affair is about to destruct. As soon as your sponsor finds out about Phil Calhoun, it will be over. And he doesn't care about you, Van Slyke. He thinks you are nothing. But I care. I know how you are suffering. Let me help you. Don't let this person use you as a dupe. You are nothing to him. He wants you to be hurt. They want you to suffer."

"Shut up!" Van Slyke screamed.

"The person who is using you has told lots of people about you, Van Slyke. Not just me. And they have all had a good laugh over the fact that Van Slyke will be blamed for everything."

"Shut up!" Van Slyke screamed a second time. He lunged at David and rammed the barrel of the gun against David's forehead.

David froze as he peered at the gun cross-eyed. He let go of the shovel and it fell to the floor.

"Get back in the root cellar," Van Slyke screamed. He kept the tip of the gun pressed against David's skin.

David was terrified the gun would go off at any second. Van Slyke was in a state of frenzied agitation that bordered on absolute panic.

Van Slyke backed David into the root cellar. Only then did he withdraw the gun. Before David could reiterate his desire to help Van Slyke, the heavy wood door was slammed in his face and relocked.

David could hear Van Slyke running through the basement, crashing into objects. He heard his heavy footfalls on the cellar steps. He heard the cellar door slam shut. Then the lights went out.

David stayed perfectly still, straining to hear. Very faintly he heard a distant car engine start, then quickly fade. Then there was only silence and the pounding of his own heart.

David stood motionless in the total darkness thinking about what he'd unleashed. Van Slyke had dashed out of the house in a state of acute manic psychosis. David had no idea where Van Slyke was headed or what he had in mind, but whatever it was it couldn't be good.

David felt tears well up in his eyes. He'd certainly man-

aged to evoke the man's psychotic paranoia, but the result
was not what he'd hoped. He'd wanted to befriend Van
Slyke and get him to talk about his problems. David also
wanted to free himself in the process. Instead David was
still imprisoned and he'd released a madman into the town.
David's only source of solace was that Angela and Nikki
were safely in Amherst.

Struggling to control his emotions, David tried to think
rationally about his predicament, wondering if there were
any chance of escape. But as he thought of the solid stone
walls encircling him he had an acute rush of claustro-
phobia.

Losing control, David began to sob as he vainly attacked
the stout wooden door to the cellar. He hurdled his shoulder against it multiple times, crying for someone to let
him out.

At length David managed to regain a modicum of self-
control. He stopped his self-destructive batterings against
the unyielding door. Then he stopped crying. He thought
about the blue Volvo and Calhoun's truck. They were his
only hope.

With fear and resignation, David sank to a sitting position
on the dirt floor to wait for Van Slyke's return.

26

MONDAY, NOVEMBER 1
LATER THAT DAY

ANGELA SLEPT MUCH LONGER THAN SHE'D PLANNED. When she awoke around four-thirty, she was surprised to hear that David had neither returned nor called. She felt a pang of concern, but dismissed it. But as the time crept toward five, her concern grew with each passing minute.

Angela finally picked up the phone and called Green Mountain National Bank. But she only got a recording that told her the bank's hours were nine to four-thirty. Frustrated, Angela hung up. She wondered why David hadn't called on his portable phone. It wasn't like him. He'd surely know she'd start worrying if he were late.

Next Angela called Bartlet Community Hospital. She asked to be connected to the front information desk, then inquired there about David. She was told that Dr. Wilson had not been seen all day.

Finally Angela tried their home in Bartlet. There wasn't any other place she could think to try. But after letting the phone ring ten times, she gave up.

Replacing the receiver for the third time, Angela wondered if David had decided to play sleuth after all. The possibility only made her more concerned.

Angela went to the kitchen and asked her mother-in-law if she would mind if she borrowed the car.

"Of course not," Jeannie answered. "Where are you going?"

"Back to Bartlet," Angela said. "I left some things in the house."

"I want to go too," Nikki said.

"I think you'd better stay here," Angela said.

"No," Nikki said. "I'm coming."

Angela forced herself to smile at Jeannie before going over to Nikki. She took her daughter by the arm and walked her into the next room.

"Nikki, I want you to stay here," Angela said.

"I'm scared to stay here by myself," Nikki said. She broke into tears.

Angela was stymied. She much preferred that Nikki stay with her grandmother, yet she didn't have time to argue with the child. Nor did she want to explain to her mother-in-law why Nikki would be better off staying. In the end, Angela gave in.

It was close to six by the time Angela and Nikki entered Bartlet. It was still light out, but night would follow soon. Some of the cars already had their headlights on.

Angela only had a sketchy plan of what to do, and it mostly involved hunting for the Volvo. The first location she wanted to search was the bank, and as she neared the institution she saw Barton Sherwood and Harold Traynor walking toward the town green. Angela pulled over to the curb and jumped out. She told Nikki to wait in the car.

"Excuse me," Angela said as she caught up with the two men.

Sherwood and Traynor turned.

"I'm sorry to bother you," Angela said. "I'm looking for my husband."

"I have no idea where your husband is," Sherwood said irritably. "He missed our appointment this afternoon. He didn't even phone."

"I'm sorry," Angela said.

Sherwood touched the brim of his cap, and he and Traynor moved off.

Angela dashed back to the car. Now she was convinced that something bad had happened.

"Where's Daddy?" Nikki questioned.

"I wish I knew," Angela said. She made a rapid U-turn in the middle of Main Street that sent the car's wheels screeching.

Nikki reached out and steadied herself against the dash. She'd sensed that her mother was upset, and now she was certain.

"Everything will be all right," Angela told Nikki.

Angela sped to their house, hoping to see the Volvo parked near the back door. Maybe David had gone there by now. But as she pulled into the driveway, she was immediately disappointed. There was no Volvo.

Angela jerked to a stop next to the house. A quick glance told her it was just as they had left it, but she wanted to be sure.

"Stay in the car," she told Nikki. "I'll just be a second."

Angela went inside and called for David, but there was no answer. Taking a quick run through the house, she checked to see if the master bed had been disturbed. It hadn't. On her way back down the stairs Angela spotted the shotgun. She snatched it up and checked the magazine. There were four shells in it.

With shotgun in hand, Angela went into the family room and took out the phone directory. She looked up the addresses of Devonshire, Forbs, Maurice, Van Slyke, and Ullhof and wrote them down. Carrying both the list and the shotgun, she returned to the car.

"Mom, you're driving crazy," Nikki said as Angela left a patch of rubber on the road.

Angela slowed a little. She told Nikki to relax. The problem was, Angela was more anxious than ever and Nikki could sense it.

The first address turned out to be a convenience store. Angela angled in to its parking area and pulled to a stop.

Nikki looked at the store and then back at her mother.

"What are we doing here?" she asked.

"I'm not sure," Angela said. "Keep an eye out for the Volvo."

"It's not here," Nikki said.

"I realize that, dear." She put the car in gear and headed for the next address. It was Forbs' residence. Angela slowed as they came to the house. The lights inside were on, but there was no Volvo.

Disappointed, Angela again gunned the engine and they sped away.

"You're still driving weird, Mom," Nikki said.

"I'm sorry," Angela said. She slowed down. As she did, she realized she was gripping the steering wheel so hard, her fingers had gone numb.

The next house was Maurice's. Angela slowed but immediately saw that it was closed up tight with no sign of life. Angela sped on.

A few minutes later, when she turned onto Van Slyke's street, Angela spotted the Volvo instantly. So did Nikki. It was a ray of hope. Angela pulled directly behind the car, turned off the ignition, and jumped out.

As she approached the car she saw Calhoun's truck in front of it. She looked in both vehicles. In Calhoun's truck she noticed a moldy cup of coffee. It appeared as if it had been there for several days.

Angela looked across the street at Van Slyke's house. There were no lights whatsoever, fanning Angela's growing alarm.

Running back to the car, Angela got the shotgun. Nikki started to get out, but Angela yelled at her to stay where she was. Angela's tone let Nikki know there was to be no arguing.

Carrying the shotgun, Angela ran across the street. As she climbed the porch steps, she wondered if she should go directly to the police. Something was seriously wrong, there was no doubt about it. But what help could she expect from the police? Besides, she worried that time might be a factor.

She tried ringing the doorbell, but it clearly didn't work. Failing that, she banged on the door. When there was no

response, she tried the door. It was unlocked. She pushed
it open and cautiously stepped inside.

Then, as loudly as she could, she yelled David's name.

David heard Angela's yell. He straightened up. He'd
been slouched against a bin filled with desiccated apples.
The sound had come from such a distance and had been
so faint that at first he questioned if it had been real. He
thought he might have been hallucinating. But then he heard
it again.

This time David knew it was real, and he knew it was
Angela. He leaped to his feet in the utter darkness and
screamed Angela's name. But the sound died in the confined, insulated space with its dirt floor. David moved
blindly ahead until he hit against the door. Then he tried
yelling again, but he could tell it would be in vain unless
Angela were in the basement.

Groping along the shelves, David seized a jar of preserves. He carried it over to the door and pounded the
wood with it. But the sound was hardly as loud as he'd
hoped.

Then David heard what he thought were Angela's footsteps somewhere above. Changing tactics, he hurled the jar
of preserves against the ceiling. He covered his head with
his hands and closed his eyes as the glass smashed against
the floorboards.

Groping back to the shelving, David tried to climb up on
it so he could pound directly on the ceiling with his fists.
But he'd only pounded once when the shelf he was standing
on gave way. The shelf and all its jars collapsed to the floor,
David along with it.

Angela felt frantic and discouraged. She'd rapidly toured
the first floor of the filthy house, turning on what lights she
could. Unfortunately she found no evidence of either David
or Calhoun, save for a cigar butt in the kitchen that possibly
could have been Calhoun's.

Angela was ready to start on the second floor when she
thought about Nikki. Concerned, Angela dashed out to the
car. Nikki was anxious, but she was okay. Angela said she'd

be just a bit longer. Nikki told her to hurry because she was scared sitting by herself.

Angela ran back into the house and started up the stairs. She carried the shotgun with both hands. When she reached the second floor, she stopped and listened. She thought she'd heard something, but if she had, she didn't hear it again. She continued on.

The upstairs of the house was even dirtier than the main floor. It had a peculiar musty smell, as if no one had been up there for years. Giant cobwebs hung from the ceiling. In the upstairs hall Angela yelled David's name several more times, but after each shout there was nothing but silence.

Angela was about to head back downstairs when she noticed something on a small console table at the head of the stairs. It was a rubber Halloween mask fashioned to look like a reptile. It was the mask the intruder had worn the previous evening!

Trembling, Angela started down the stairs. Halfway down she paused to listen. Once again she thought she'd heard something. It sounded like distant thumping.

Angela was determined to find the source of the sound. At the base of the stairs she paused again. She thought she heard pounding from the direction of the kitchen. She hurried into the room. The noise was definitely louder. Bending down she put her ear to the floor. Then she heard the knocking distinctly.

She yelled David's name. With her ear still pressed to the floor she could just barely hear David answer, calling her by name. Angela scrambled to the cellar stairs.

She found the light and headed down, still clutching the shotgun. She began to hear David's voice more clearly, but it was still muffled.

Once she was down in the basement, she yelled his name again. Tears sprang to her eyes when she heard his reply. Weaving her way through the clutter, Angela followed the sound of his voice. There were two doors. By this time David was pounding so hard Angela knew immediately which one he was behind. But there was a problem: the door was padlocked.

Angela shouted to David that she'd get him out. Leaning

the shotgun against the wall, she scanned the basement for an appropriate tool. Her eyes soon came to rest on the pick.

Swinging the tool in a short arc, she hit the lock several times but with no result. Trying a different approach, she inserted the end of the pick beneath the hasp and used it as a pry bar.

Pushing with all her might, Angela was able to snap the hasp and its mounting screws out of the door. She then pulled the door open.

David rushed out and embraced her.

"Thank God you came!" he said. "Van Slyke is the one behind all this. He's killed the patients and he killed Hodges. Right this minute he's in a psychotic panic and he's armed. We've got to get out of here."

"Let's go," Angela said. She snatched up the shotgun. Together they hurried to the stairs.

Before they started up, David put a hand on Angela's arm. He pointed toward the cement slab next to the hole he'd been digging. "I'm afraid Calhoun is under there," he said.

Angela gasped.

"Come on!" David said, giving her a nudge.

They started up the stairs.

"I haven't learned who is paying Van Slyke," David said as they climbed. "But it's clear that's what's been happening. I also haven't learned how Van Slyke has been able to kill the patients."

"Van Slyke is also the one who was at the house last night," Angela said. "I found the reptile mask upstairs."

As David and Angela reached the kitchen, headlight beams suddenly filled the room, playing across their horrified faces. Van Slyke had come back.

"Oh, God, no!" David whispered. "He's back."

"I've turned on a lot of lights," Angela said. "He'll know something's wrong."

Angela thrust the shotgun into David's hands. He gripped it with sweaty palms. They heard the car door close, then heavy footsteps in the gravel of the driveway.

David motioned for Angela to step back through the

cellar door. David followed and pulled the door partially closed behind him. He left it open a crack so he could see into the kitchen.

The footsteps came to the back door, then abruptly stopped.

For a few terrorizing minutes there was no sound whatsoever. David and Angela held their breath. They guessed Van Slyke was wondering about the lights.

Then, to their surprise, they heard the footsteps recede. They listened until they couldn't hear them anymore.

"Where did he go?" Angela whispered.

"I wish I knew," David said. "I don't like not knowing where he is. He knows this place too well. He could get at us from behind."

Angela turned and looked down the cellar steps. The idea that Van Slyke could suddenly jump out at them made her skin crawl.

For a few minutes they stayed put, straining to hear any noises. The house was eerily silent. Finally David pushed the door open. Stepping back into the kitchen warily, he motioned for Angela to follow.

"Maybe it wasn't Van Slyke," Angela whispered.

"It had to have been him," David whispered back.

"Let's get the hell out of here. I'm afraid if I'm in here too long Nikki will get out of the car."

"What!" David whispered. "Nikki's here?"

"I couldn't leave her at your mother's," Angela whispered. "She insisted on coming with me. I couldn't fight with her. And there was no time to explain the situation to your mother."

"Oh my God!" David whispered. "What if Van Slyke has seen her?"

"Do you think he might have?"

David motioned for Angela to follow him. They went to the door to the yard, opening it as quietly as they could. It was completely dark outside. Van Slyke's car was twenty feet away but the man was nowhere to be seen.

Now David motioned for Angela to stay where she was. He sprinted to Van Slyke's car, keeping the shotgun ready. He looked in the passenger side window, just in case Van

Slyke was hiding, but he wasn't there. David waved for Angela to join him.

"Let's skirt the gravel of the driveway," David said. "It's too noisy. We'll stick to the grass. Where did you park?"

"Right in back of you," Angela said.

David led with Angela right behind him. As they reached the street their worst fears were realized. In the light of a street lamp next to Calhoun's truck, they could see Van Slyke's silhouette in the driver's seat of David's mother's Cherokee. Nikki was next to him.

"Oh, no!" Angela said as she impulsively started forward.

David restrained her. They looked at each other in horror. "We have to do something," Angela said.

"We have to think," David said. He looked back at the Cherokee. He was so tense, he thought he might pass out.

"Do you think he has a gun?" Angela asked.

"I know he has a gun," David snapped.

"Maybe we should get help," Angela suggested.

"It would take too long," David said. "Besides, Robertson and his crew wouldn't have any idea how to handle a situation like this—if they even took us seriously. We'll have to handle this ourselves. We've got to get Nikki far enough away so that we can use the shotgun if we have to."

For a few harrowing moments they simply stared at the car.

"Let me have the keys," David said. "I'm worried he might have locked the doors."

"They're in the car," Angela said.

"Oh, no!" David exclaimed. "He could just drive off with Nikki."

"Oh, God," Angela whispered.

"This is getting worse and worse," David said. "But have you noticed: the whole time we've been standing here looking at the car, Van Slyke hasn't moved. Last time I saw him he was in constant manic motion, unable to hold still for a moment."

"I see what you mean," Angela said. "It looks almost as if they're having a conversation."

"If Van Slyke isn't watching, we could slip behind the

car," David said. "Then you could go to one side and I to the other. We'll open the front doors simultaneously. You pull Nikki free and I'll aim the shotgun at Van Slyke."

"Good Lord!" Angela groaned. "Don't you think that's taking a lot of chances?"

"Tell me a better idea," David said. "We have to get her out of there before he drives off with her."

"Okay," Angela said reluctantly.

After crossing the street a good distance back from the Cherokee, David and Angela approached the car from behind. They remained crouched down as they moved in hopes of remaining undetected. Eventually they arrived at the very rear of the vehicle and squatted in its shadow.

"I'll first slip alongside to see if the doors are locked," David whispered.

Angela nodded and took the shotgun.

David crawled along the driver's side of the car until he was even with the rear door. Rising slowly, he saw that none of the doors were locked.

"At least something is going our way," Angela whispered once he came back and told her the good news.

"Okay," David whispered. "Are you ready?"

Angela gripped David's arm. "Wait," she said. "The more I think about your plan, the less I like it. I don't think we should go up on separate sides. I think we should both go to her door. You open the door, I'll pull her out."

David thought for a moment, then agreed. The main idea was to get Nikki away from Van Slyke. With Angela's plan there was more chance they'd succeed. The problem then would be how to handle Van Slyke once Nikki was safe.

"Okay," David whispered. "When I give the signal we do it."

Angela nodded.

David took the shotgun from Angela and held it in his left hand. He moved around Angela so that he was at the right side of the car. Slowly he rounded the car and started crawling along its side, holding the gun up against his chest. When he came abreast of the rear door, he turned around to make sure Angela was right behind him. She was.

David prepared to spring forward by positioning his feet

directly under his torso. But before he could give the signal
to Angela, Nikki's door opened and Nikki leaned out and
looked back. She was startled to see David's face so close
to her own.

"What are you guys doing?" Nikki asked.

David leaped forward and pulled the door completely
open. Nikki lost her balance and tumbled from the car.
Angela sprang forward and grabbed her, dragging her onto
the grass. Nikki cried out in shock and pain.

David trained the gun on Van Slyke. He was fully prepared to pull the trigger if need be. But Van Slyke didn't
have a gun. He didn't try to flee. He didn't so much as
move. He merely looked at David; his expression was
completely blank.

David warily moved a little closer. Van Slyke remained
seated calmly, his hands in his lap. He did not seem to
be the agitated psychotic that he'd been less than an hour
earlier.

"What's happening?" Nikki cried. "Why did you pull me
so hard? You hurt my leg."

"I'm sorry," Angela said. "I was worried about you. The
man you've been sitting with is the same man who was i
our house last night wearing the reptile mask."

"He couldn't be," Nikki said, wiping her tears away. "
Van Slyke told me he was supposed to talk with me
you came back."

"What has he been talking about?" Angela asked

"He was telling me about when he was my age
said. "How wonderful it had been."

"Mr. Van Slyke's childhood wasn't wonderf
David said. David was still intently watching
who still hadn't moved. Keeping the shotgun ai
at Van Slyke's chest, David leaned into the c
look. Van Slyke continued to stare back at

"Are you okay?" David asked. He wa
what to do.

"I'm all right," Van Slyke said in a
"My father took me to the movies all t'
I wanted."

"Don't move," David commanded.

aimed at him, David stepped around the front of the car and opened the driver's side door. Van Slyke didn't budge, but he kept his eyes on David.

"Where's the gun?" David demanded.

"Gun run done fun," Van Slyke said.

David grabbed Van Slyke by the arm and pulled him out of the car. Angela yelled at David to be careful. She'd heard what Van Slyke had said. She told David that he was clanging; he was obviously still acutely psychotic.

David pushed Van Slyke around so that he was facing the car. Then he frisked him for any weapons. He didn't find the pistol.

"What did you do with the gun?" David demanded.

"I don't need it anymore," Van Slyke said.

David peered into Van Slyke's calm face. His pupils were no longer dilated. The transformation was remarkable.

"What's going on, Van Slyke?" David asked.

"On?" Van Slyke said. "On top. Put it on top."

"Van Slyke!" David shouted. "What's happened to you? Where have you been? What about the voices you hear? Are you still hearing voices?"

"You're wasting your time," Angela said. She and Nikki had come around the front of the car. "I'm telling you, he's acutely psychotic."

"No more voices," Van Slyke said. "I made them stop."

"I think we should call the police," Angela said. "And I don't mean the local bozos. I mean the state police. Is your cellular phone in the car?"

"How did you quiet the voices?" David asked Van Slyke.

"I took care of them," Van Slyke answered.

"What do you mean you took care of them?" David was afraid to learn what Van Slyke meant.

"They won't be able to use me as a dupe," Van Slyke said.

"Who do you mean by they?" David asked.

"The board," Van Slyke said. "The whole board."

"David!" Angela said impatiently. "What about the gun. I want to get Nikki away from here. He's talking nonsense."

"I'm not so sure," David said.

"Well, then, what does he mean by the board?" Angela asked.

"I'm afraid he means the hospital board," David said.

"Board sword ford cord," Van Slyke said. He smiled. It was the first time his expression had changed since they'd confronted him in the car.

"David, the man is not connected to reality," Angela said. "Why are you insisting on having a conversation with him?"

"Do you mean the hospital board?" David asked.

"Yes," Van Slyke said.

"Okay, everything is going to be all right," David said. But he was trying to calm himself more than anyone else.

"Did you shoot someone?" David asked.

Van Slyke laughed. "No, I didn't shoot anyone. All I did was put the source on the conference room table."

"What does he mean by 'source'?" Angela asked.

"I have no idea," David said.

"Source force course horse," Van Slyke said, still chuckling.

Feeling frustrated, David grabbed Van Slyke by the front of his shirt and shook him, asking him again what he'd done.

"I put the source and the force on the table right next to the model of the parking garage," Van Slyke said. "And I'm glad I did it. I'm not a dupe for anybody. The only problem is, I'm sure I burned myself."

"Where?" David asked.

"My hands," Van Slyke said. He held them up so David could look at them.

"Are they burned?" Angela asked.

"I don't think so," David said. "They're slightly red, but otherwise they look normal to me."

"He's not making any sense," Angela said. "Maybe he's hallucinating."

David nodded absently. His thoughts were suddenly somewhere else.

"I'm tired," Van Slyke said. "I want to go home and see my parents."

David waved him off. Van Slyke walked across the street and into his yard. Angela stared at David. She'd not expected him to let Van Slyke go. "What are you doing?" she asked. "Shouldn't we call the police?"

David nodded again. He stared after Van Slyke while his mind began pulling everything together: his patients, the symptoms, and the deaths.

"Van Slyke is a basket case," Angela said. "He's acting like he just had electroshock therapy."

"Get in the car," David said.

"What is it?" Angela asked. She didn't like the tone of David's voice.

"Just get in the car!" David shouted. "Hurry!" He climbed into the driver's seat of the Cherokee.

"What about Van Slyke?" Angela questioned.

"There's no time for Van Slyke," David said. "Besides, he isn't going anywhere. Come on, hurry!"

Angela put Nikki into the back seat and climbed in next to David. David already had the car started. Before Angela could close her door, David was backing up. Then he made a quick U-turn and accelerated up the street.

"What's happening now?" Nikki asked.

"Where are we going?" Angela asked.

"To the hospital," David said.

"You're driving as bad as Mom," Nikki told her father.

"Why the hospital?" Angela asked. She reached back and patted Nikki's knee to reassure her.

"It's suddenly beginning to make sense to me," David said. "And now I have this terrible premonition."

"What are you talking about?" Angela asked.

"I think I might know what Van Slyke was talking about when he referred to 'the source.' "

"I thought that was just schizophrenic babble," Angela said. "He was clanging. He said source, force, course, and horse. It was just gibberish."

"He may have been clanging," David said, "but I don't think he was talking nonsense when he said source. Not when he was talking about putting it on a conference table that had a model of a parking garage on it. That's too specific."

"Well, what do you think he was referring to?" Angela asked.

"I think it has to do with radiation," David said. "I think that's what Van Slyke was talking about when he said he'd burned his hands."

"Oh, come on. You're sounding as crazy as him," Angela said. "You have to remember Van Slyke's paranoia on the nuclear submarine had to do with radiation, so any similar talk probably has more to do with the return of his schizophrenia than anything else."

"I hope you're right," David said. "But it has me worried. Van Slyke's training in the navy involved nuclear propulsion. That's driving a ship with a nuclear reactor. And nuclear reactors mean radiation. He was trained as a nuclear technician, so he knows something about nuclear materials and what they're capable of doing."

"Well, what you are saying makes sense," Angela said. "But talking about a source and having one are two vastly different things. People can't just go out and get radioactive material. It's tightly controlled by the government. That's why there is a Nuclear Regulatory Commission."

"There's an old radiotherapy unit in the basement of the hospital," David said. "It's a cobalt-60 machine Traynor's hoping to sell to some South American country. It has a source."

"I don't like the sound of this," Angela admitted.

"I don't like it either," David said. "And think about the symptoms my patients had. Those symptoms could have been from radiation, especially if the patients had been subjected to overwhelming doses. It's a horrendous possibility, but it fits the facts. At the time radiation had never entered my mind."

"I never thought about radiation when I did Mary Ann Schiller's autopsy," Angela admitted. "But now that I think of it, that could have been it. Radiation isn't something you consider unless there is a history of exposure. The pathological changes you see are nonspecific."

"That's my point exactly," David said. "Even the nurses with flu-like symptoms could have been suffering from a low level of radiation. And even . . ."

"Oh, no!" Angela exclaimed, immediately catching David's line of thought.

David nodded. "That's right," he said. "Even Nikki."

"Even Nikki what?" Nikki asked from the back seat. She'd not been paying attention to the conversation until she'd heard her name.

Angela turned around. "We were just saying that you had flu-like symptoms just like the nurses," she said.

"And Daddy too," Nikki said.

"Me too," David agreed.

They pulled into the hospital parking lot and parked.

"What's the plan?" Angela asked.

"We need a Geiger counter," David said. "There has to be one in the Radiotherapy Center for their certification. I'll find a janitor to let us in. Why don't you and Nikki go to the lobby?"

David found Ronnie, one of the janitors he vaguely knew. Ronnie was only too happy to help one of the doctors, especially since it took him away from the job of mopping the basement's corridor. David neglected to mention that he'd been fired from CMV and his hospital privileges had been suspended.

With Ronnie in tow, David went up to the lobby and found Angela. Nikki had discovered a TV and was content for the moment. David told Nikki not to leave the lobby; she promised she wouldn't.

Angela and David went to the Radiotherapy Center. It only took them about fifteen minutes to find a Geiger counter.

Back in the main hospital building, they met up with Ronnie in the basement. It had taken him a few minutes to find the key to the old radiotherapy unit.

"No one goes in here very often," he explained as he let the Wilsons in.

The unit consisted of three rooms: an outer room that had served as a reception area, an inner office, and a treatment room.

David walked straight back to the treatment room. The room was empty save for the old radiotherapy unit. The machine looked like an X-ray unit with a table attached for the patient to lie on.

David put the Geiger counter on the table and turned

it on. The needle barely moved on the gauge. There was no reading above background even on its most sensitive scale.

"Where's the source lodged in this thing?" Angela asked.

"I'd guess it's where the treatment arm and this supporting column here meet," he said.

David lifted the Geiger counter and positioned it where he thought the source should reside. There was still no reading.

"The fact that there's no reading doesn't necessarily mean anything," Angela said. "I'm sure this thing is well shielded."

David nodded. He walked around to the back of the machine and tried the Geiger counter there. There was still no reading.

"Uh oh," Angela said. "David, come here and look at this."

David joined Angela by the treatment arm. She pointed to an access panel that was attached by four nob screws. Several of the screws had been loosened.

David grabbed a chair from the reception room. He put it just under the arm. Standing on the seat of the chair, David was able to reach the panel. He unscrewed all four nob screws, removed the panel, and handed it all to Ronnie.

Behind the panel he discovered a circular metal plate secured with eight lug bolts. David had Angela hand him the Geiger counter. He pushed it inside the housing and tried again for radiation. There was none.

David moved the Geiger counter aside and reached in and grasped one of the lug bolts. To his dismay, it was loose. He checked all eight. All eight were loose. He began removing them, handing them down to Angela one by one.

"Are you sure you should be doing this?" Angela asked. She was still concerned about radiation, despite the readings, as well as David's questionable handyman skills.

"We have to know for sure," David said as he removed the last bolt. He then lifted the heavy metal covering and handed it to Ronnie. David peered down a long cylindrical cavity that was about four and a half inches in diameter. It looked like the barrel of a huge gun. Without a flashlight, he could only see a short distance in.

"I'm sure I'm not supposed to be able to look into the treatment arm like this," David said. "There would have to be a plug to act as a brake to stop the source when it was being moved out to the treatment position."

Just to be one hundred percent certain, David stuck the Geiger counter into the muzzle of the treatment arm. There was no reading above background.

David stepped down from the chair. "The source is not in there," he said. "It's gone."

"What are we going to do?" Angela asked.

"What time is it?" David asked.

"Seven-fifteen," Ronnie said.

"Let's get lead aprons from radiology," David said. "Then we'll do what we can."

They left the old radiotherapy unit and headed straight for the Imaging Center. They didn't need Ronnie to open the Imaging Center since it was open for emergency X rays, but David asked him to come to help carry the lead aprons. Ronnie didn't know what was going on, but whatever it was he could tell something serious was involved. He was eager to be as helpful as possible.

The X-ray technician was suspicious of David's request for lead aprons, but he decided that since David wouldn't be taking them any farther than the hospital next door, it would be okay. Besides, he wasn't used to contradicting doctors. He gave David, Angela, and Ronnie nine lead aprons as well as one pair of lead gloves used for fluoroscopy. David still had the Geiger counter, as well.

Weighed down with their burden, the three made their way back to the hospital. They got strange looks from the staff and visitors they passed on their way to the second floor, but no one tried to stop them.

"All right," David said once they reached the door of the conference room. He was practically out of breath. "Put everything right here." He dropped the aprons he was carrying to the floor next to the closed conference room door. Angela and Ronnie did likewise.

David tried the Geiger counter again. Immediately the needle pegged to the right. "Jesus Christ!" David said. "We couldn't get any better evidence than that." David thanked Ronnie and sent him on his way. He then explained to Angela what he thought they should do. David pulled on the lead gloves and picked up three aprons. He carried one in his hands while he tossed the other two over his shoulder. Angela picked up four in her arms.

David opened the door and went into the conference room, with Angela close behind. Traynor, who'd been interrupted in mid-sentence, glared at David. Those in attendance—Sherwood, Beaton, Cantor, Caldwell, Arnsworth, and Robeson—all turned to stare at the source of this rude interruption. As the assembled members of the board began to murmur, Traynor banged his gavel, crying for order.

Scanning the cluttered conference table, David spotted the source instantly. It was a cylinder about a foot long whose diameter matched the size of the bore in the treatment arm he'd examined only minutes ago. Several Teflon rings were embedded in its circumference. On its top was a locking pin. The cylinder was standing upright next to a model of a parking garage just as Van Slyke had indicated.

David started for the cylinder, clutching a lead apron in both hands.

"Stop!" Traynor yelled.

Before David could get to the cylinder, Caldwell leaped to his feet and grabbed David around his chest.

"What the hell do you think you are doing?" Caldwell demanded.

"I'm trying to save all of you if it isn't too late," David said.

"Let him go," Angela cried.

"What are you talking about?" Traynor demanded.

David nodded toward the cylinder. "I'm afraid you have been having your meeting around a cobalt-60 source."

Cantor leaped to his feet; his chair tipped over backward. "I saw that thing," he cried. "I wondered what it was." Saying no more, he turned and fled from the room.

A stunned Caldwell relaxed his grip. David immediately lunged across the table and snatched up the brass cylinder in his lead gloves. Then he rolled the cylinder in one of his lead aprons. Next he wrapped that apron in another and that one in another still. He proceeded to do the same with the aprons Angela was carrying while she stepped out of the conference room to get the others. David was anxious to cover the cylinder with as many layers of lead as possible.

As David was wrapping the last load of the aprons around the bulky parcel, Angela got the Geiger counter.

"I don't believe you," Traynor said, breaking a shocked silence. But his voice lacked conviction. Cantor's sudden departure had unnerved him.

"This is not the time for debate," David said. "Everyone better get out of here," he added. "You've all been exposed to a serious amount of radiation. I advise you to call your doctors."

Traynor and the others exchanged nervous glances. Panic soon broke out as first a few and then the remaining board members, including Traynor, ran from the room.

David finished with the last apron and took the Geiger counter. Turning it on, he was dismayed to see that it still registered a significant amount of radiation.

"Let's get out of here," David said. "That's about all we can do."

Leaving the cylinder wrapped in aprons on the table, they went out of the conference room, closing the doors behind them. David tried the Geiger counter again. As he expected, the radiation had fallen off dramatically. "As long as no one goes in the conference room, no else will get hurt tonight," he said.

He and Angela headed toward the lobby to collect Nikki. Just before they arrived David stopped.

"Do you think Nikki will be okay for a few more minutes?" he asked.

"In front of a TV she'll be fine for a week," Angela said. "Why?"

"I think I know how the patients were irradiated," David said. He led Angela back toward the patients' rooms.

Half an hour later they collected Nikki and went out into the hospital parking lot. They took the Cherokee back to Van Slyke's so that David could get the Volvo.

"Do you think there's any chance he could hurt anybody tonight?" David asked. He motioned toward Van Slyke's house.

"No," Angela said.

"I don't think so either," David said. "And the last thing I want to do is go back in there. Let's go to my parents'. I'm exhausted."

David got out.

"I'll follow you," he said.

"Call your mother," Angela said. "I'm sure she's beside herself with worry."

David got in the Volvo and started it up. He looked at Calhoun's truck in front of him and sadly shook his head.

As soon as they got on the main road, David picked up his cellular phone. Before he called his mother he called the state police. When he got an emergency officer on the line he explained that he wanted to report a very serious problem that included murder and deadly radiation at the Bartlet Community Hospital . . .

EPILOGUE
FOUR MONTHS LATER

DAVID KNEW HE WAS LATE AS HE PULLED UP TO A modest house on Glenwood Avenue in Leonia, New Jersey. He jumped out of the car and ran up the front steps.

"Do you know what time it is?" Angela asked. She followed David into their bedroom. "You were supposed to be home at one and here it is two. If I could get here on time I think you could have too."

"I'm sorry," David said as he quickly changed his clothes. "I had a patient who needed extra time." He sighed. "At least now I have the freedom to spend more time with a patient when I think it's called for."

"That's all well and good," Angela said. "But we have an appointment. You even picked the time."

"Where's Nikki?" David asked.

"She's out on the sun porch," Angela said. "She went out there over an hour ago to watch the '60 Minutes' crew set up."

David slipped on a freshly laundered dress shirt and did up the buttons.

"I'm sorry," Angela said. "I suppose I'm anxious about this TV thing. Do you think we should go through with it?"

"I'm nervous, too," David said as he selected a tie. "So if you want to cancel, it's fine with me."

"Well, we've cleared it with our respective bosses," Angela said.

"And everyone has assured us that it won't hurt us," David said. "And we both feel the public ought to know."

Angela paused to think about it. "Okay," she said at last. "Let's do it."

David tied his tie, brushed his hair, and put on a jacket. Angela checked herself in the mirror. When they both felt they were ready, they descended the stairs and walked out onto the sun porch, blinking under the bright lights.

Although David and Angela were nervous, Ed Bradley quickly put them at ease. He began the interview casually, getting them to relax, knowing he would be editing heavily as usual. He began by asking them what they were currently doing.

"I'm taking a fellowship in forensic pathology," Angela said.

"I'm working with a large medical group at Columbia Presbyterian Medical Center," David said. "We're contracted out with several HMO organizations."

"Are you both enjoying your work?" Bradley asked.

"We are," David said.

"We're thankful we've been able to put our lives back in some sort of order," Angela said. "For a while it was touch and go."

"I understand you had a difficult experience in Bartlet, Vermont," Bradley said.

Both David and Angela chuckled nervously.

"It was a nightmare," Angela said.

"How did it start?" Bradley asked.

David and Angela looked at each other, unsure of who should begin.

"Why don't you start, David?" Bradley said.

"My part of it started when a number of my patients began to die unexpectedly," David said. "They were patients with histories of serious illnesses like cancer."

David looked at Angela.

"It started for me when I began to be sexually harassed by my immediate superior," Angela said. "Then we discovered the body of a homicide victim entombed under our cellar steps. His name was Dr. Dennis Hodges, and he'd been the administrator of the hospital for a number of years."

With his usual clever questioning, Ed Bradley pulled out the whole sordid story.

"Were these unexpected patient deaths instances of euthanasia?" he asked David.

"That's what we thought initially," David said. "But these people were actually being murdered not through some misguided gesture of mercy, but to improve the hospital's bottom line. Patients with potentially terminal illness often use hospital facilities intensively. That translates to high costs. So to eliminate those expenses, the patients themselves were eliminated."

"In other words, the motivation for the whole affair was economic," Bradley said.

"Exactly," David replied. "The hospital was losing money, and they had to do something to stem the red ink. This was their solution."

"Why was the hospital losing money?" Bradley asked.

"The hospital had been forced to capitate," David explained. "That means furnish hospitalization for the major HMO in the area for a fixed fee per subscriber per month. Unfortunately, the hospital had estimated utilization at too low a cost. The money coming in was much less than the money going out."

"Why did the hospital agree to capitate in the first place?" Bradley asked.

"As I said, it was forced," David said. "It had to do with the new competition in medicine. But it's not real competition. In this case the HMO dictated the terms. The hospital had to capitate if it wanted to compete for the HMO's business. It didn't have any choice."

Bradley nodded as he consulted his notes. Then he looked back at David and Angela. "The new and current administrator of the Bartlet Community Hospital says that the allegations you're making are, in his words, 'pure rubbish.' "

"We've heard that," David said.

"The same administrator went on to say that if any patients had been murdered, it would have been the work of a single deranged individual."

"We've heard that as well," David said.

"But you don't buy it?"

"No, we don't."

"How did the patients die?" Bradley asked.

"From full-body radiation," Angela said. "The patients received overwhelming doses of gamma rays from a cobalt-60 source."

"Is that the same material that is used so successfully for treating some tumors?" Bradley asked.

"In very carefully targeted areas with carefully controlled doses," Angela said. "David's patients were getting uncontrolled full-body exposure."

"How was this radiation administered?" Bradley asked.

"An orthopedic bed was fitted with a heavily lead-shielded box," Angela said. "It was mounted under the bed and contained the source. The box had a remotely controlled window that was operated by a garage door opener with radio waves. Whenever the port was open the patient was irradiated through the bed. So were some of the nurses tending to these patients."

"And both of you saw this bed?" Bradley asked.

David and Angela nodded.

"After we found the source and shielded it as best we could," David explained, "I tried to figure out how my patients had been irradiated. I remembered that many of my patients had been in hospital beds that malfunctioned. They'd wound up being transferred to an orthopedic bed. So after we left the conference room we went looking for a special orthopedic bed. We found it in the maintenance shop."

"And now you contend that this bed was destroyed," Bradley said.

"The bed was never seen again after that night," Angela said.

"How could that have happened?" Bradley asked.

"The people responsible for the bed's use got rid of it," David said.

"And you believe the hospital executive committee was responsible?" Bradley said.

"At least some of them," David said. "Certainly the chairman of the board, the administrator, and the chief of the medical staff. We believe the operation was the brainchild of the chief of the medical staff. He was the only person who had the background necessary to dream up such a diabolical yet effective scheme. If they hadn't used it so often, it never would have been discovered."

"Regrettably, none of these people can defend themselves," Ed Bradley said. "I understand that all of them died of severe radiation sickness despite some heroic measures to save them."

"Unfortunately," David admitted.

"If they were so sick how could they have destroyed the bed?" Bradley asked.

"Unless the dose of radiation is so great that it is immediately lethal, there is a variable latent period before the onset of symptoms. In this case, there would have been plenty of time to get rid of the bed."

"Is there any way to substantiate these allegations?" Bradley asked.

"We both saw the bed," David said.

"Anything else?" Bradley asked.

"We found the source," Angela said.

"You found the source," Bradley said. "That's true. But it was in the conference room and not near any patients."

"Werner Van Slyke essentially confessed to us both," David said.

"Werner Van Slyke is the man you believe was the worker bee behind this operation," Bradley said.

"That's correct," David said. "He'd had nuclear technician training in the navy, so he knew something about handling radioactive materials."

"This is the same Werner Van Slyke who is schizophrenic and is now hospitalized with severe radiation sickness," Bradley said. "He's also the same Werner Van Slyke who's been in a psychotic state since the night the hospital executive committee got irradiated, who refuses to talk with anyone, and who is expected to die."

"He's the one," David admitted.

"Needless to say, he's hardly the most reliable corroborating witness," Bradley said. "Do you have any other proof?"

"I treated a number of nurses with mild radiation sickness," David said. "They had all been around my patients."

"But you thought that they had the flu at the time," Bradley said. "And there is no way to prove that they didn't."

"That's true," David admitted.

Bradley turned to Angela. "I understand you autopsied one of your husband's patients?" he asked.

Angela nodded.

"Did you suspect radiation sickness after the autopsy?" Bradley asked. "And if you didn't, why not?"

"I didn't because she'd died too quickly to manifest many of the symptoms that would have suggested radiation," Angela said. "She'd received so much radiation that it affected her central nervous system on a molecular level. If she'd had less radiation she might have lived long enough to develop ulceration of her digestive tract. Then I might have added radiation to the differential diagnosis."

"What I'm hearing is that neither of you has any hard evidence," Bradley said.

"I suppose that's true," David said reluctantly.

"Why haven't either of you been called to testify?" Bradley asked.

"We know there have been some civil suits," Angela said. "But all of them were quickly settled out of court. There have been no criminal charges."

"With the kind of accusations you've made it's incredible there have been no criminal charges," Ed Bradley said. "Why do you think there haven't been any?"

Angela and David looked at each other. Finally David spoke: "Basically we think there are two reasons. First, we think that everybody is afraid of this affair. If it all came out, it would probably shut the hospital, and that would be disastrous for the community. The hospital pumps a lot of money into the town, it employs a lot of people, and it serves the people medically. Secondly, there's the fact that in this case, the guilty, in a sense, have been punished. Van Slyke took care of that when he put the cobalt-60 cylinder on the conference table."

"That might explain why there hasn't been any local response," Bradley said. "But what about at the state level? What about the state's attorney?"

"Nationally, this episode cuts to the quick of the direction of health-care reform," Angela said. "If this story were to get out, people might begin to reevaluate their thinking on the route we seem to be taking. Good business decisions don't always equate with good medical decisions. Patient care is bound to suffer when the powers that be are too focused on the bottom line. Our experience at Bartlet Community Hospital may be an extreme example of medical bureaucrats run amok. Yet it happened. It could happen again."

"Rumor has it that you could profit from this matter," Bradley said.

David and Angela again exchanged nervous glances.

"We have been offered a large amount of money for a made-for-TV movie," David admitted.

"Are you going to take it?" Bradley asked.

"We haven't decided," David said.

"Are you tempted?"

"Of course we're tempted," Angela said. "We are buried under a mountain of debt from our medical training, and we own a house that we have not been able to sell in Bartlet, Vermont. In addition to that, our daughter has a medical condition and might develop special needs."

Ed Bradley smiled at Nikki who immediately smiled back. "I hear you were a hero in this affair," he said.

"I shot the shotgun at a man who was fighting with my mom," Nikki said. "But I hit the window instead."

Bradley chuckled. "I will certainly keep my distance from your mother," he said.

Everyone laughed.

"I'm sure you two are aware," Bradley said, resuming a more serious tone, "that there are people who contend that you have dreamed up this whole story to make the TV money and to get back at the hospital and HMO for firing you."

"I'm sure that those who don't want the true story out will do what they can to discredit us. But they really shouldn't blame the messenger for the bad news," Angela said.

"What about the series of rapes in the hospital parking lot?" Bradley asked. "Was that part of this plot?"

"No, they weren't," Angela said. "At one point we thought they were. So did the private investigator who lost his life investigating this episode with us. But we were wrong. The one indictment that has come out of this unfortunate episode is for Clyde Devonshire, an emergency-room nurse. DNA testing has proved he was responsible for at least two of the rapes."

"Have you learned anything from this experience?" Bradley asked.

David and Angela said yes simultaneously. Angela spoke first: "I've learned that as health care is changed, doctors and patients better know all the rules of any supposed cost-cutting plan so they can make appropriate decisions. Patients are too vulnerable."

"I've learned," David said, "that it is dangerous to allow financial and business people and their bureaucrats to interfere in the doctor-patient relationship."

"Sounds to me as if you two doctors are against health-care reform," Bradley said.

"Quite the contrary," Angela said. "We think health-care reform is desperately needed."

"We think it's needed," David said. "But we're worried. We just don't want it to be a fatal cure like that old joke about the operation being a success but the patient dying. The old system favored over-utilization through economic incentives. For example, rewarding a surgeon according to how frequently he operated. The more appendixes or tonsils he removed, the more money he made. We don't want to see the pendulum swing in the opposite direction by using economic incentives to under-utilize. In many health plans, doctors are being rewarded with bonuses not to hospitalize or not to treat in some specific way."

"It should be the patient's needs that determine the level and type of treatment," Angela said.

"Exactly," David said.

"Cut," Bradley said.

The cameramen straightened up from their equipment and stretched.

"That was terrific," Bradley said. "That's plenty of material and the perfect place to stop. It was a great wrap. My job would be a lot easier if everyone I interviewed were as articulate as you folks."

"That's sweet of you to say," Angela said.

"Let me ask you guys if you think the entire executive committee was involved," Bradley said.

"Probably most of them," David said. "All had something to gain from the hospital if it thrived and a lot to lose if it shut down. The board members' involvement wasn't as altruistic as most people would like to think, particularly Dr. Cantor, the chief of staff. His Imaging Center would have folded if the hospital went under."

"Damn!" Bradley said after he'd skimmed his notes. "I forgot to ask about Sam Flemming and Tom Baringer." He called out to the cameramen he wanted to do a little more.

David and Angela were puzzled. These names were not familiar to them.

As soon as the cameramen gave him the cue that the tape was rolling, Ed Bradley turned to David and Angela and asked them about the two men. Both said they could not place the names.

"These were two people who died in Bartlet Community Hospital with the exact same symptom complex as David's patients," Bradley said. "They were patients of Dr. Portland."

"Then we wouldn't know anything about them," David said. "They would have expired before we started working at the hospital; Dr. Portland killed himself shortly before we moved to town."

"What I wanted to ask," Bradley said, "is whether you believe that these two people could have died from radiation sickness as you allege your patients did."

"I suppose if the symptoms were the same in type, degree, and time frame, then I would say yes," David said.

"That's interesting," Bradley said. "Neither one of these two people had terminal illnesses or any medical problem other than the acute problem they'd been admitted with. But both had taken out multimillion-dollar insurance policies with the hospital as the sole beneficiary."

"No wonder Dr. Portland was depressed," Angela said.

"Would either of you care to comment?" Ed Bradley asked.

"If they had been irradiated, then the motive was even more directly economic than it was in the other cases," David said. "And it would certainly make our case that much more convincing."

"If the bodies were exhumed," Bradley asked, "could it be determined unequivocally whether or not they had died of radiation?"

"I don't believe so," Angela said. "The best anyone could say would be that the remains were consistent with radiation exposure."

"One last question," Bradley said. "Are you happy now?"

"I don't think we've dared ask ourselves that question yet," David said. "We're certainly happier than we were several months ago, and we're glad we're working. We're also thankful that Nikki has been doing so well."

"After what we've been through it will take some time to put it all behind us," Angela said.

"I think we're happy," Nikki said, speaking up. "I'm going to have a brother. We're going to have a baby."

Bradley raised his eyebrows. "Is that true?" he asked.

"God willing," David said.

Angela just smiled.

Seizure
by Robin Cook

Biotechnology has become the buzzword in the
campaign of Senator Ashley Butler, a self-appointed
guardian of "traditional American values."
The conservative politician has come down
staunchly against stem cell research. But when he
develops Parkinson's disease, the senator must
make an unwilling pact with the very doctor whose
groundbreaking—yet untested—technology
he is trying to destroy.

"LEAVE IT TO DOCTOR-TURNED-NOVELIST
ROBIN COOK TO SCARE US ALL TO DEATH."
—LOS ANGELES TIMES

"ROBIN COOK KNOWS HOW TO MAKE THE PAGES FLY."
—KIRKUS REVIEWS

0-425-19794-8

Available wherever books are sold or at
www.penguin.com